A SUMMER IN THE COUNTRY

MARCIA WILLETT

St. Martin's Paperbacks

First published under the title *Forgotten Laughter* in Great Britain
by HEADLINE BOOK PUBLISHING
A division of Hodder Headline

A SUMMER IN THE COUNTRY

ISBN: 0-312-99715-9

Printed in the United States of America

St. Martin's Press hardcover edition / April 2003
St. Martin's Paperbacks edition / June 2004

St. Martin's Paperbacks are published by St. Martin's Press, 175 Fifth Avenue, New York, NY 10010.

10 9 8 7 6 5 4 3 2 1

ST. MARTIN'S PAPERBACKS TITLES
BY MARCIA WILLETT

A Week in Winter
A Summer in the Country

TO ANNE ELLISON

ACKNOWLEDGEMENTS

I would like to thank Bridget Rochard. My thanks also to the RNLI, and especially the crew of the SALCOMBE LIFEBOAT, for allowing Jemima to "live" in the crew's rest quarters.

PART ONE

CHAPTER 1

The man sitting opposite, talking on his mobile telephone, was lying to his wife. His shoulder was hunched towards the table, his eyes fixed on the flying countryside, his voice low. Strong, well-manicured fingers, one bearing the weight of a broad gold ring, beat a restless tattoo on the table top and, from time to time, his breast expanded in a huge, silent, irritated sigh.

"Haven't we done all this, darling?" A savage impatience echoed warningly beneath the politely posed question and the "darling" was almost an insult, as much a slap on the cheek as an endearment. "I told you, didn't I, that I probably wouldn't be able to get home tonight? . . . Actually, I'm not terribly interested in how long Jill thinks the meeting should last. She knows nothing about it . . . OK, so she knows that Lisa will be there too . . . We did agree, didn't we, that it's not very sensible of you to interrogate my colleagues' wives every time you have one of these, well, attacks? . . . I know it did but I told you the truth. She happens to be a member of the department and we're working on this project together. Nothing more . . . Of *course* it's difficult, but I can't ask them to sack her because she's young and attractive . . . Oh, for God's sake . . ."

His voice rose, impatience no longer reined in, and he glanced warily across the table, his expression sulky, irritable. Embarrassed to be caught watching him, Louise looked swiftly away, out of the window. In a field which sloped to a narrow gleam of water a young woman stood, her child in her arms, gazing up at the passing train. She waved, encouraging the child to wave too, and then took his hand and waved it for him, laughing, jogging him on her hip, whilst he sat staring impassively, his face upturned. Louise stared back, shocked by recognition into a brief second of immobility, before leaning to wave, almost violently, until they were out of sight. Breathing quickly, she sank back in her corner and tried to control the uprush of emotion which so suddenly possessed her.

Her fellow traveller had finished his conversation and was watching her curiously. Without looking directly at him she knew that he was assessing her, summing her up as a fisherman might weigh up the possibilities of a pool; she saw, too, the exact moment at which he decided that he would test the water.

"Friends of yours?"

It was an innocent enough lure, a pretty fly, bobbing lightly, charming, faintly diverting. She decided that she might swim a little way towards this welcome distraction from her confused reaction to the sight of the woman with her child.

"No, no. A reflex reaction, I suppose. If someone waves it seems natural to respond, wouldn't you say?"

"Well, I'm not certain about that." He shifted his position, stretching his legs diagonally towards the empty seat beside her. "It all depends on who's waving."

His smile, the brief quirk of the brows, suggested that if it were she—or presumably some other attractive young woman—he would be prepared to follow it up, and she hid her own reaction to his utter predictability.

"You have a point." She swam idly around the lure; appeared to reject it.

"I'm sorry to have burdened you with my . . . uh . . . private problems." He spoke quickly, indicating the mobile telephone which now lay between them on the table. "Rather bad form but . . ." he pursed his lips humorously, inviting her complicity, ". . . these suspicious wives . . ."

The fly trembled temptingly, encouraging further inspection.

"How do you know," she asked casually—but with a hint, just the least hint, of amused flirtatiousness—"that I am not just such another suspicious wife?"

He settled more comfortably, confidently, so that she could imagine the tilt of the hat over the eyes, whilst his hand held the rod light but firm. "Oh, you don't look the type at all. Much too pretty."

"You think so?"

A bite? Metaphorically, he prepared to wind in the line a little. "Oh, definitely. And confident too, I suspect. Only insecure women get jealous. And plain ones, of course."

"Is your wife plain?" She toyed lightly with the bait, appearing to invite disloyalty. "Or insecure?"

"Difficult age." He shrugged a little, exhibiting a touch of pathos. "Just the least bit unbalanced. It gets rather wearing after a bit."

"So it's all in her imagination?" She sounded almost disdainful, the bait proving, after all, to be unexciting; rather tasteless.

"Oh, I wouldn't say that." He set the lure dancing again, the roguish smile promising experience, pleasure. "What the eye doesn't see . . ." He shrugged.

"It sounded as if she's seen more than you suspected."

He laughed then, unexpectedly, infectiously, and she smiled at this genuine response, oddly drawn to him, despite herself.

"Touché," he admitted and smiled back at her . . . A pause as they stared at each other. The line tautened.

"It must be rather tricky . . .?" She let the question hang in the air for a moment. "Perhaps I have a suspicious husband."

"I can't say I'd be the least bit surprised." His voice was warm. "He'd be a fool if he weren't."

"So." She leaned forward, elbows on the table, pretending intimacy. "How do you manage?"

"Ah." His smile was very nearly complacent and she had

the sensation of being drawn gently but inexorably through deliciously warm water towards him. "It's my friend here, you see."

He lifted the mobile telephone and she stared at it, puzzled. He chuckled.

"I have it with me always. No odd phone calls to my home number that pretend to be wrong numbers when my wife answers. I can be reached wherever I am. I can text messages. Well, always assuming the other person has a mobile phone. Nothing shows up on the phone bill or hotel bills. Of course," a tiny wink, "I switch it off when I'm in . . . meetings."

"Text messages?"

"That's right. You can write what you like to the person you love. No need to speak. You can stay in touch that way. Then it can be erased in a second. No evidence lying about. Don't you have one?"

"No," she said slowly. "No, I'm a bit of a technophobe. Microwaves and videos unnerve me so no, I don't have a mobile phone."

He leaned closer, smiling again, as though he could imagine her tucked up safely in his creel. "Perhaps you should get one. I'd be very happy to advise you . . ."

She stared at him for a long moment until her attention was caught by something beyond the window.

"It's my station," she said.

"You're not getting off here?" He stared incredulously, line snapped, his prey slipping away, his reel whizzing helplessly. "Where are we? Totnes?"

"That's right." She slipped her bag on to her shoulder, picked up a coat. "I'm on holiday for a fortnight. Thanks for the tips."

"Wait." He was scribbling a number, tearing a sheet from his Filofax. "Just in case you get bored . . ."

She shook her head, laughing. "I shan't be bored. Enjoy your . . . meeting."

The compartment doors opened and shut behind her.

Presently, the train stopped; he watched her walking along the platform.

"Shit," he muttered. He dialled a number, his expression moody. "Hello, Lisa . . . Of course it's OK." He settled back into his corner as the train drew out, his expression brightening. "Poor darling, were you panicking? Everything's fine. Just leaving Totnes. No, a deadly trip. I've been working all the way down . . ."

BRIGID FOSTER was waiting in her old estate car, watching the station exit, one anxious eye on the taxi rank lest she should block the traffic. As soon as she saw Louise she jumped out so as to help with the luggage and to give her an affectionate hug.

"I couldn't find anywhere to park so I couldn't come to find you," she said as they pulled away. "Thank goodness the train was on time. People were glaring at me. Good trip?"

"Yes. Yes, thanks."

Louise sounded preoccupied, slightly *distrait,* and Brigid gave her a quick sideways glance. During the three years that Louise had been coming to stay in one of the Fosters' holiday cottages the two women had formed a friendship that had its roots embedded in a respect for each other's privacy. Brigid knew that Martin Parry spent a fortnight twice a year on golfing holidays with three of his oldest friends and, at those times, Louise travelled to Devon for her own holiday. She liked to walk and was fascinated by the flora and fauna of the West Country, and if it seemed odd that she should prefer to do it alone it was no one's business but her own. Brigid, the wife of a submariner in the Royal Navy, knew all about being alone and it was very clear that Louise enjoyed these periods of solitude. Brigid's own unusual upbringing—the only child of an Irish archaeologist who had lived and worked on Dartmoor—had reinforced an already eccentric genetic brew and she saw nothing odd in a requirement to spend hours alone in the empty, silent stretches of the moor.

"I do rather worry about her," Humphrey said from time to time, when his leave coincided with Louise's holidays. "You were brought up here and you know the moor like the back of your hand but Louise's an urban animal. It can be dangerous out there."

"Simply because she lives in London doesn't make her a townie," Brigid answered calmly. "She knows what she's doing."

During those early visits, Brigid had shown Louise her own personal moor, had told her of the dangers, alerted her to possible risks. When she'd seen that Louise was no novice she had left her alone, recognising that she, too, preferred her own company when communing with nature. Brigid enjoyed Louise's visits. Once or twice they'd share an occasional supper, drive into Ashburton to shop and have coffee in the Café Green Ginger, trek over to Salcombe to have tea with Brigid's half-sister, Jemima Spencer. Yet neither imposed on the other nor threatened the other's privacy. Even now, when she hadn't seen her for seven months, Brigid made no attempt to break the train of Louise's thoughts.

Struggling to keep the doors of her mind closed against the unexpected breach of memory, caused by the sight of the mother and child waving in the field above the railway track, Louise was grateful for Brigid's restraint. It was good to see her again: the fine blonde hair chopped off just above her collarbones and held back, today, with a faded cotton scarf; huge, violet-blue eyes framed in a fine web of tiny lines. The outsize sweatshirt was probably Humphrey's, her jeans showed the sharpness of her knees and elegant length of leg from hip to thigh. It was an austere face whose cool expression hid a capacity for kindness. Louise knew about the kindness—and about other things, too: her enormous pride in her two boys and her delight in her new grandchild. As the car headed out towards Dartington Louise relaxed a little.

"How's everyone?" she asked. "Humphrey? Your mother? Blot?"

Brigid shook her head, rolling her eyes. "Don't ask. Humphrey's being sent off to the Bahamas for six months, as the logistics support officer—at least that's what it sounded like. Mummie's decided that she's in the early stages of Alzheimer's and needs constant amusement to prevent plunges into depression. Blot's sulking because we've got a friend's dog staying while they're on holiday and his nose is out of joint."

Louise chuckled. "Sounds like fun."

"I'm glad you think so," said Brigid resignedly. "Otherwise nothing changes at Foxhole. Oh, but I ought to warn you that there have been two murders in Devon recently."

"Goodness!" Louise gazed at her in alarm.

"Nowhere near Foxhole or the moor," Brigid hastened to reassure her. "The most recent one was over near the north coast and the other was up beyond Exeter. They were both women who lived alone so the police think that the murders are probably connected. Anyway, the second one was some weeks ago now and at least forty miles away." She hesitated. It was necessary to put Louise on her guard yet she had no desire to frighten her unnecessarily. "Devon's a very big county, remember. It's not quite the same as having two murders in Chiswick."

"No, I quite see that. Horrid, though." Louise shook off her instinctively fearful reaction. "Don't worry. I don't intend to get paranoid about it."

"Good. Have you had some lunch?"

"Oh, yes. I had a sandwich on the train." Glancing out of the window again, Louise sighed pleasurably. "It's good to be back, Brigid. The countryside looks so fresh and bright and green."

"That's because it's been raining for three days." Brigid negotiated the bridge over the A38, then took the turning for Buckfast, following the back road behind the abbey. "Do you want to stop in Holne to do some shopping or will you wait until tomorrow? First night supper with me, of course, as usual. And I've stocked up with the ordinary basics for you."

"Oh, tomorrow, I think. I won't be able to concentrate on food today. But I did bring a bottle for supper."

She stopped abruptly as the car approached Hembury

woods and entered a green, lacy tunnel of dappling light: bright, plump cushions of moss and delicate white wood anemones grew amongst ancient roots; two magpies swooped suddenly together, arguing raspingly, and a wood pigeon clappered upwards, startled from his perch.

"Sounds good." Brigid sympathised with Louise's sudden silence; certain places, even after forty-eight years of familiarity, still had the power to reduce her to speechlessness. "The older I get the greater my dependence on alcohol becomes. It's the one thing Mummie and I have in common. She's even worse than I am. I'm quite certain that her Alzheimer's is simply too much to drink before bed. Since her stroke she's not supposed to drink much at all."

"How does she get hold of it?" Louise asked the question lightly, pretending that she assumed Brigid spoke in the same vein. She knew that the relationship between Brigid and her mother was a difficult one but had no wish to probe.

"Jemima," answered Brigid shortly—and fell silent.

As the car climbed out of Holne and on to open moorland, Louise wondered why Brigid and her mother lived together in such antagonism at Foxhole. Frummie made no secret of the fact that she hated the countryside and Louise wondered if the isolation of Foxhole was the reason why she had left Brigid's father almost forty years ago. She now lived in one of the two cottages that Brigid and Humphrey had created from the barns which stood across the courtyard from the old, low, delightful longhouse. It could only be financial necessity which had driven Frummie back to seek sanctuary at Foxhole, and a very slight stroke hadn't made her any easier to deal with, although she was able to remain relatively independent.

Louise felt a partisanship with the self-contained woman beside her but could think of nothing helpful to say. Hoping that Brigid would interpret her silence correctly, she stared out of the car window. Holne Moor stretched away to the west and she sat up straight, eager as any child, for her first glimpse of Venford Reservoir: a tiny, secret lake, sparkling in its circlet of pinewoods. She gazed delightedly at the beloved and familiar landmarks—Bench Tor and Combe-stone Tor, and beyond, to the distant hills, drowsing violet and indigo in the afternoon sunshine; then they were cross-ing Saddle Bridge over the O Brook and she was watching now for the old, twisted thorn which marked the track lead-ing down to Foxhole, a sturdy ancient stronghold on the slopes above the rushing, tumbling water of the West Dart.

CHAPTER 2

Leaving Louise to unpack, Brigid put the car away and stood
for a moment in the warm May sunshine watching the swallows. They nested each year in the open-fronted barn and
she welcomed them with delight, despite the mess they
made of the floor beneath the beams. As a child she'd been
fascinated by the babies which cheeped and jostled in their
nests and, later, sat in bewildered huddled rows along the
beams, returning to this place of safety after terrifying trial
flights. How quickly their confidence grew, along with their
competence, until the nests and the barn were finally abandoned and she would see them grouping and gathering ready
for their migratory flight. Then, one morning, the sky would
be empty, the swallows gone—until next spring. As she
stood in the cobbled yard, Brigid knew that this reaffirma-
tion, nature's quiet progressive cycle, had become vitally
important in her small childhood world. Her mother's sudden departure had smashed the safe, assured order of her existence and nothing could be quite the same afterwards.
She'd loved her father, with whom she'd explored the moor,
visiting hut circles, cairns, settlements, disused mines, but
her witty, vivid mother had been a source of entertainment,
of excitement. There had been a tension in her company, a
breathlessness, a desire to please, to perform well, feelings
which had not been evoked in her father's paper-piled, book-
strewn study.

"I don't care," she'd said defiantly to well-meaning school-friends. "I'd rather be with Daddy," but she'd begun to avoid the interest her situation aroused, the spurious comfort of the shocked, yet curious, parents. Divorce was not so common then, and she'd felt isolated, odd. She'd cultivated a self-protective skin of indifference, a cool, brittle assurance which, as she grew, developed its own kind of glamour and impressed her peers. Her mother had sent presents, unusual and carefully chosen gifts, which the young Brigid would unwrap privately, sitting on her bed; holding them, smelling them, trying to draw some essence which was her mother from their shapes. She'd stare at the writing in the cards and on envelopes, imagining her mother holding the pen, touching the card, licking a stamp, closing the flap. When she'd heard, at the age of twelve, that her mother had had a baby, another daughter, it was as though the shock annihilated all feeling. Numb, silent, she'd listened whilst her father talked.

"She's called Jemima," he'd said at last, wearily. "I'm so sorry, my darling. I'm to blame for this. I should never have brought her here in the first place. It was crazy. I was a novelty, I think, a challenge . . ."

She'd watched him whilst he'd tried to puzzle his way through and then had gone to make them both some tea.

"Jemima." She'd tried the name aloud in the silence of the big, square, stone-flagged kitchen. "Puddle-duck. Jemima Puddle-duck. A fat stupid duck with big flat feet and small eyes."

She'd begun to laugh, forcing herself on to greater flights of imagination, ridiculing, gasping with scornful delight, numbness thawing. Sensation had returned, stinging, warming into a burning, hot hatred. When, later again, she'd heard that her mother had left her second husband she'd asked only one question.

"Did she take Jemima with her?"

The answer was "yes." So Puddle-duck, the despised, fat-bodied, ridiculous duck of a child, with unhealthily white skin, tiny eyes and big flat feet, had, after all, been too precious to be left behind. Brigid had absolutely needed to be able to hate and despise them both and, when she read *The Pursuit of Love,* she found a new name for her mother: the Bolter.

"It's from Bolter and Puddle-duck," she'd say dismissively, tossing a Christmas card to one side, but, later, privately, she'd stare hungrily at the enclosed photograph: the small fair-haired child, rosy-skinned, wide-eyed, tiny feet with curling toes, and the woman who held her lightly on her knee, with her mouth down-turned in that strange, self-mocking smile and cool, amused stare. Placing the photo face down, Brigid would gaze at herself in the looking-glass. It was her father's face: bony, autocratic, interesting—but not pretty. Yet no one who saw Brigid smile quite forgot the experience; such warmth and promise blossoming so unexpectedly took the observer by surprise and lodged in the memory, but Brigid had not smiled at her reflection. She'd only stared searchingly, analytically, and turned away with misery plucking at her throat.

Humphrey had removed some of the hurt, restored a measure of self-worth. He'd fallen in love with her with a satisfying promptness, adored her unconditionally, eased the pain. Their two boys had brought her a deep, heart-shaking joy and they'd become very precious companions, a solace during the long, empty months whilst Humphrey was at sea. He and her father had dealt splendidly together and, when the older man died, he'd left her everything he possessed, including Foxhole.

"Nothing for me?" her mother had asked, with that down-turned smile. She'd arrived uninvited for the funeral, immaculate in black at the back of the church in Holne, Jemima beside her, and Brigid had been obliged to invite them both back to Foxhole with the other mourners. "Nothing at all?"

She'd looked about her, as if amused at the gathering, but the fourteen-year-old Jemima had smiled at her half-sister.

"Hello," she'd said. "We're sisters. Isn't it funny? I've always wanted to meet you."

"Have you?" Grieving for her father, shocked by the unexpected appearance of her mother, dealing with her father's friends, Brigid had had no energy for more than this lame response. Jemima's thick fair hair had spilled from beneath her black beret, her cheeks pink, periwinkle-blue eyes wide and bright. She'd been a little on the plump side but this was no ugly duckling.

Brigid had choked on a nauseous churning. "I've always called you 'Puddle-duck'."

The brief spiteful flash had brought no answering ugliness. Jemima's laughter had been unforced, a delightful sound in that sombre room, a ready chuckle which brought involuntary smiles to sad faces.

"Have you? Oh, how funny. Well, Frummie always says I waddle about . . ."

"Frummie?" sharply.

"Yes. Well, you see Daddy called her Freda and I called her Mummie and it ended up as Frummie."

Brigid had stared at her mother, who had just returned, empty-handed, from the table piled with sandwiches and snacks. *Frummie?* This essentially *adult* woman? Could it be remotely possible?

"I was just telling Brigid that everyone calls you Frummie now." Jemima had wanted her family to be happy together. "She didn't know."

Their mother had been unmoved by her elder daughter's level, speculative, deliberately ironic gaze. "Not *everyone*, darling," she'd said. "Brigid won't. She's strait-laced like her papa. Not into nicknames; much too silly."

"Yes, she is." Jemima had been determined that her newly met sister should be included. "She's always called me Puddle-duck. She said so."

"Has she indeed?"

At this amused query, which indicated her mother's uncannily perceptive but instant grasp of the real truth behind the nickname, colour had washed over Brigid's face, flooding into her hairline. Her mother had laughed cruelly.

"And what do you think of my ugly duckling, Brigid darling?"

She'd turned away, enjoying the joke, in search of a drink. Jemima had shrugged, puzzled, smiling anxiously, and Brigid, looking at her, had felt the first stirrings of the painfully confusing emotions which would henceforward inform her relationship with her half-sister.

Now, twenty-two years later, standing in the sunshine she knew that very little had changed. Dissatisfied, frustrated, she crossed the yard and went into the house.

LOUISE DROPPED her suitcase at the foot of the stairs and looked about her with satisfaction. Odd, how returning here was like a homecoming. Since Frummie's arrival, Louise was obliged to book the larger cottage, which had certain advantages. Brigid had sensibly avoided the "holiday cottage" layout when she'd designed the conversions of her barns and she'd kept one big living-kitchen room as the centre of the dwelling. Since holidays were generally family affairs it was intelligent to have this comfortable, bright, roomy area where the group could eat, relax, make plans. There was a small sitting room containing a wood-burning stove and the ubiquitous television—"No one can live without it these days," Brigid had said, "not even on holiday"—and a tiny utility room with a shower unit at one end. Upstairs were two bedrooms and the bathroom: the largest bedroom had a double bed in it, a hanging cupboard built into the thickness of the wall, and a chest of drawers. The other room contained two bunk beds and another hanging cupboard so that the cottage could sleep six. Louise always shut the door on the bunk beds—this was not a family holiday—and settled contentedly to solitude.

This afternoon, however, uneasiness nibbled at her pleasure. Clamping her mind shut against it, she went through the familiar rites which she performed at the start of each visit to Foxhole. Her instinct was to make the cottage her own, to stamp her personality upon it so that it was, for this brief period, "home." Filling the kettle and switching it on, she left it to boil whilst she unpacked a small bag. A few books and a pair of binoculars on the window seat, a pashmina shawl draped over the armchair by the window, her favourite mug beside the kettle, a pretty notebook, some pencils and a small paintbox at one end of the square pine table; these few personal possessions quenched the impersonal, waiting atmosphere and gave the room life. She opened the window, which looked out on to the moor, and breathed deeply. Peace lapped at the windowsill: the distant murmur of the river, the joyful song of a lark ascending . . . The image of the woman and her child, waving, laughing, appeared for a moment, superimposed upon the moorland scene, and Louise turned away abruptly.

Seizing the heavy suitcase she lugged it upstairs, carrying it into the biggest bedroom and laying it upon the bed. She snapped open the locks and began to take out clothes, a sponge bag, slippers. Soon the bedroom looked as alive as the kitchen with all the paraphernalia of daily life and, pushing the empty suitcase inside the cupboard, hanging her dressing gown behind the door, she went out again on to the small landing. This time, however, she did not shut the other door automatically but paused, head bent, as if listening to murmured fragments of conversation in the room beyond . . . *"Will Daddy like my new bed, Mummy?"* . . . *"Of course he will, but you mustn't keep getting out of it and coming downstairs."* . . . *"Only babies have cots, don't they?"* . . . *"Yes, but big girls stay in their beds until the morning."* . . . *"Even if they can't sleep?"* . . . *"Big girls try very hard to go to sleep."* . . . *"Perhaps I could sleep if we had one more story."* . . . *"Very well, then. But only one more . . ."*

Louise stirred, her face bleak, and, closing the bedroom door firmly, she went downstairs to make some tea.

"HULLOOO THERE? May I come in?" Frummie's musical hail was accompanied by a sharp rapping on the front door, left open to the hall, and Brigid sighed. Her mother, by these exaggerated obeisances to their privacy, made her feel guilty yet she knew that she couldn't have borne a casual "my home is your home" approach. Frummie managed to imply that this need was some kind of weakness, that other less neurotic people would be perfectly happy to have their family strolling in and out at will. At these moments the implication that Jemima would be quite different, generous and welcoming, inflamed Brigid's sense of inadequacy and on one occasion she'd snapped at Frummie, asking why, in that case, she didn't make her home with Jemima. "Darling Brigid," Frummie had murmured. "Don't be so . . . *constipated*. You're so touchy these days."

She'd fumbled with the sugar bowl, spilling some from the spoon, and Brigid, looking at the withered, liver-spotted hands, the averted face, had been stabbed with compassion and remorse.

"Come in," she called now—and bent to greet the black spaniel who preceded Frummie into the kitchen. He'd been sick earlier and she'd refused to let him go with her to Totnes lest he might repeat the performance all over Louise's luggage. "Hello, you," she murmured, bending to stroke the excited animal. "Have you been behaving yourself?"

"I thought I heard the car." Frummie stood in the doorway, watching the reunion. "He's been fine. Whining a bit but no further problem."

"It's only because of poor Oscar. He's got himself worked up. Thank goodness Thea and George will be home tomorrow. I had no idea Blot would be so jealous. I'm having some tea, Mummie. Would you like some?"

"Don't bother for me, I've just had one." Frummie perched at the table. A thin woman with the bones of a bird, she looked frail, breakable, until the gleam in her eyes warned of the indomitable spirit burning within its fragile cage. "So Louise's arrived. How is she?"

"Oh, just as she usually is." Pouring the tea, Brigid wondered if that were an accurate answer. Louise had *not* been quite as she usually was although she couldn't have said why. "She'll be over to supper later on."

"I was wondering . . ." Frummie shifted a little on her chair. "Would it stretch to three?"

"Three?" Brigid glanced at her quickly. "Why . . .? I thought Jemima was taking you out to supper."

"Something's cropped up," said Frummie, shrugging, pretending indifference. "Some old friend down in Salcombe on holiday. Going back tomorrow or something. *Rather* inconvenient. I haven't got much in, actually. I was going to shop to-morrow."

"An old friend?" Brigid was frankly sceptical. "Bit sudden, isn't it? I bet it's male."

"Probably. Does it matter? Of course I don't want to be a nuisance. If you've got some spare eggs I can make myself an omelette."

"Oh, don't be silly." Brigid sounded cross, caught as usual between guilt and self-preservation. She enjoyed supper with Louise; there was an ease, a metaphorical kicking off of shoes which would be impossible with Frummie present, and she'd been looking forward to it enormously. She wanted to talk about her new grandson, Josh, and show the latest photographs, marvelling at his beauty and making up for the fact that because the little family lived in Geneva she was denied a closer contact. She knew that doing this under the cynical eye of her mother wouldn't be the same at all but there was nothing for it but to give in as graciously as she could. "There's plenty for three. It's just a bit casual of Jemima."

"Nonsense. She's young, that's all. She has her own life to lead."

Brigid thought: So do I but you don't worry too much about that.

"Well then." Having achieved the object of her visit, Frummie prepared to leave. "I'll be over at about eight, shall I? So sweet of you, darling."

She trailed out stopping to pat Blot, who wagged along behind her as far as the front door and then returned to sniff around the kitchen, pausing hopefully at the back door.

"Yes, he's out there," said Brigid. "Having some peace and quiet. Oh, hell. Come on then. We might as well all go for a walk and get rid of our frustrations together."

She put down her mug and opened the back door into a lean-to conservatory. A large Newfoundland, who had been lying asleep, roused up and struggled anxiously to his feet as Blot came hurtling out.

"Leave," said Brigid, struggling into gumboots, taking

down a coat. "I said, *'Leave.'* Come on, Oscar. He'll be less of a problem once we get going. Promise."

She opened the outer door, waited for Oscar to manoeuvre his great bulk out into the sunshine, and strode away towards the river with the dogs close upon her heels.

CHAPTER 3

Later, carrying the promised bottle, Louise crossed the yard. The long low house with its ancient thatch had a fairy-tale quality, and the white doves, murmuring cosily from their dovecot, enhanced this charming image. Outside the long lean-to, which ran the length of the kitchen, a large black dog lay stretched in deep sleep. This must be the visitor to whom Blot had taken exception. There was no sign of the spaniel, and Louise tapped on the silvered wood of the oaken door and went inside. In the small hall, she paused. The kitchen, on the right, was at the southeast end of the building and it was here that they would have supper. However, Louise couldn't resist a glance through the rooms which led one from the other in true longhouse fashion. These rooms looking east, to the moor, and west, into the courtyard, had slate floors and rough, granite, whitewashed walls; both had wood-burning stoves, back-to-back, sharing a chimney. The further room was the sitting room. Here a wooden staircase led to the upper floor and a door led to the children's quarters in the single-storey barn which formed one side of the courtyard. Nowadays, the big playroom with two bedrooms and a bathroom were kept for the two boys and their own young families, whilst the other half of the barn was used as a garage, but in the early days Brigid and Humphrey had been grateful for the extra space.

"Longhouses are very romantic-looking," Brigid had said

when Louise had first come to stay, "but there isn't much privacy. The bedrooms lead from one into another and it was a nightmare with two small children going to the loo several times a night."

As she looked at the evening sunshine slanting on white uneven walls, at thick, warm rugs, and at the tall jars holding dried flowers—burning blue cornflowers, sulphurous rudbeckia, scarlet poppies—Louise was seized with a spasm of covetousness. She knew all about the damp, the bone-chilling cold, the inconvenience, yet she was suddenly consumed with envy. Another image overlaid Brigid's living room: an image of a small stone cottage and the memory of the warmth of an arm lying along her shoulders, a quick flexible voice in her ear. *"No married quarters to be had. This will do, won't it? I've taken it for six months . . ."*

Brigid came running lightly down the stairs and through the two rooms towards her.

"Sorry to keep you waiting. I got a bit muddy out with the boys and felt I simply must shower and change. Come into the kitchen . . ."

Louise followed her, surrendering up the bottle, still half dazed, even frightened, by the flash of memory but Brigid was keeping up a light continuum of talk which required no serious response.

"Mummie's coming to supper," she said, dealing competently with the bottle and standing it beside an already opened claret. "Sorry about that but it can't be helped. Jemima's stood her up."

Louise murmured politely, took her glass and tried to concentrate but, before an answer was really necessary, there was a sharp rap on the door and Frummie came in.

"Louise, my dear." She kissed the younger woman lightly on the cheek. "How are you? So nice to see you again. Did Brigid tell you? I've been chucked. I do hope that I shan't be *de trop*. You mustn't mind me. I enjoy a good gossip." She glanced around the kitchen. "You know, this wasn't a kitchen in my day. It was Diarmid's study. It was the only room in which he could incarcerate himself without interruption. I can't imagine why you have it as a kitchen, Brigid. It would make a very pleasant sitting room. Of course, a drawing room would be ostentatious in a place like this but to use the only private room as a kitchen is such a waste."

"I've told you a hundred times why," answered Brigid, placing a dish of salad on the table. "I'm a kitchen-dweller, it's where I spend most of my time, and I like this room best. Have a drink, Mummie, and stop prowling. You know it makes me nervous." She took a dish from the Aga. "It's chops in a prune sauce so I hope you like it. There's a salad and new potatoes."

"Egyptian, I expect," said Frummie immediately. "Much too early for English ones."

"They're Cornish, actually."

Brigid answered sharply but, as she took her place at the table, Louise saw that it was Frummie, rather than Brigid, who wore a tiny, triumphant smile, as if she had been the victor in some age-old contest.

"It all looks delicious," Louise said warmly. "I always look forward to my first supper here. Everything afterwards is an anticlimax."

"Brigid's a wonderful cook," agreed Frummie. "*Such* a homemaker, aren't you, darling? Not like me or Jemima."

"I had to be," said Brigid briefly, serving chops. "My father wasn't what you might call terribly domesticated."

"He certainly wasn't." Frummie shuddered slightly. "I couldn't believe that he lived here alone with no help whatever. Of course, it all seemed simply too romantic to begin with but I'm afraid the charm wore off rather quickly. You know, there wasn't even electricity in those days. Oh, the smell of those oil lamps. Although I must say their light was very flattering." She helped herself to potatoes. "I'm afraid I did rather escape back to London as often as possible. Fortunately, Brigid took after her father and loved the countryside."

"Yes, it *was* fortunate, wasn't it?"

Brigid's voice was cool, reasonable, but Louise felt the crackle of tension between them and began to talk of other

things: the collecting of the hired car, shopping, her plans
for her holiday.

"We'll pick the car up in the morning," Brigid suggested,
"and then you can stock up. I've got to go into Ashburton."

"You must go over to Salcombe and see Jemima's new
flat," said Frummie brightly. "Mustn't she, Brigid? Jem's father died last Christmas, Louise, and left Jem a tiny legacy.
She's renting the flat over the RNLI's museum. Right on the
waterfront. It's absolute heaven."

"It would have been more sensible to use it as a deposit
on her own place." Brigid refilled the glasses and pushed the
salad bowl towards Louise. "It's silly to waste it on rent
when she could be buying."

"Such a sensible girl," murmured Frummie sweetly.
"Darling Jem doesn't have your practical streak. She couldn't
afford anything like that gorgeous flat. You simply must see
it, Louise. There were hundreds of people after it. She was
so lucky to get it, wasn't she, Brigid?"

"Terribly lucky." Brigid sounded faintly bitter, although
she tried to smile. "But then Jemima always falls on her
feet."

"That's what comes of having big, flat, yellow, webbed
ones, perhaps?"

Louise, puzzled, looking up in surprise, caught Frummie's malicious glance and Brigid's painful flush. Once
more she found herself hurrying into speech, diverting the
conversation away to more general subjects, accepting another chop. Spooning some of the delicious sauce on to her
plate, she wished that Frummie was somewhere else, having
dinner as planned with Jemima. Her first evening at Foxhole
was being spoiled. It was an important time, those first hours
of holiday: winding down, settling in, getting back into the
feel of the leisured pace and peaceful atmosphere. It was not
the first time she'd experienced the antagonism between
Brigid and Frummie, but tonight there seemed a different
quality—a cruelty on Frummie's side and depth of anguish
on Brigid's that she had never noticed before.

She thought: You're imagining things. You've been

peculiar all day, ever since you waved to that woman . . ."

"You don't have children, Louise, do you?" Frummie was watching Brigid collecting the empty plates together. "Of course, you're still young . . ."

"No, no children. Martin doesn't want children." She stood up abruptly, helping Brigid, putting out plates for the lemon pie and taking a bowl of thick, yellow clotted cream. "This looks good. Poor Humphrey! How he must hate going away."

"Oh, I send him off with food parcels and he spends a lot of the time with Michael and Sarah now he's at the Ministry of Defence. It's nice to think of them all getting together. I think that he's very touched that they should want him around."

"Oh, most people would want Humphrey around," said Frummie. "He's such a dear."

There seemed to be the faintest of insinuations that Brigid was one of the few who didn't and Louise, once again, felt a need to defend her.

"Are Michael and Sarah married now?" she asked quickly. "I know they were talking about it."

"Oh, the young don't get married any more," said Frummie, without giving Brigid time to answer. "It's the mortgage that's the commitment these days, though I can't say that I blame them. We all got married far too young in my day. It was expected of us and we all rushed headlong into quite unsuitable marriages. I envy the modern young their freedom."

"I can't imagine why." Brigid helped herself to cream. "You didn't exactly let marriage tie you down."

"But at least I married them, darling. All four of them. I'm rather ashamed of that now."

"Ashamed?" Brigid paused, fork upraised.

"Oh, yes. So dreary and respectable and middle class. But I simply couldn't quite bring myself to live in sin with them. Well, not for *too* long, anyway. Now Jemima is *much* more sensible. She doesn't tie herself down—at least, not yet. Why did you get married, Louise? Not to have children, obviously . . ."

"Mummie, *please*," cried Brigid, exasperated and embarrassed in equal measure. "It's none of your business.

Let's finish this wine, shall we? More pudding, Louise?"

"It doesn't matter at all." Louise smiled at her, letting her see that she wasn't in any way upset. "Honestly. Anyway," she grinned at Frummie, "I expect it was because I'm dreary, respectable and middle class."

"You and me both." Brigid raised her glass gratefully to her, shrugging helplessly. "Sorry."

"Oh, for goodness' sake," grumbled Frummie, hunching in her chair like a sulky child, "it was a perfectly innocent question. Surely there's no need to be so touchy about it. I'll have some more pudding, Brigid. It's very good."

Recognising the twig of an olive branch when she saw one, Brigid took her mother's plate and cut a generous slice of lemon pie, passed the cream, and stood up to make some coffee. Louise relaxed a little and, hoping to lead the conversation on to safer ground, decided to introduce the topic of Brigid's elder son. Although she feared that this might lead on to a too maternal depth of discussion for her own peace of mind, she hoped that Frummie's presence would keep this in check—and it would please Brigid.

"How's Julian?" she asked. "Are they all settling happily in Geneva?"

Frummie, tucking into her second helping and undeceived by these tactics, snorted to herself and poured the last of the wine into her glass. She felt suddenly assailed by an overwhelming weariness, pushed aside her empty plate and began to nod pleasantly over her glass whilst the conversation drifted quietly in the background. Presently Brigid glanced at her mother, who was now frankly asleep, and grimaced apologetically at Louise.

"I've got some photographs of the baby," she said quietly, unaware of Louise's instinctive shrinking. "He's gorgeous. Shall I be a proud grandmother and show you while we have our coffee?"

WATCHING HER mother wavering uncertainly across the courtyard, waving in response to Louise's soft "Goodnight and thanks, it was great," Brigid went back inside and closed the door thankfully. Immediately an enormous relief, mushrooming inside her, caused her to lean for a moment against the heavy, ancient door. A stony sanctuary: that's what Foxhole had been from her earliest memory; a stronghold. If she could not feel safe here then she might go quite mad. Yet surely she had little enough to fear? It was odd that it was only when she was alone that she could be utterly at peace. She suspected that it was due to a sense of inadequacy, born out of the shock of her mother's departure, which informed her behaviour with other people, breeding an anxiety lest she should in some way fall short of their requirements so that they, too, might leave her. It was easier to be alone. She knew very well that it was this at which Frummie had been hinting earlier and it was true that a small part of her dreaded Humphrey's retirement. It wasn't that she didn't love him— he and the boys were the most important people in her universe—yet she'd spent so much time alone that she couldn't imagine how it would be when he was permanently at home. The boys had been seven and five, and already away at prep school, when she'd inherited Foxhole, and she and Humphrey had agreed that it was time to stop moving between naval ports and settle down. For over twenty years she'd lived here alone, except for the boys' holidays from school and Humphrey's leaves, and during that time she'd made her own life. The conversion of the barns had taken a few years to complete because Brigid had done a great deal of the painting and decorating, tiling and curtain-making, herself. After that, there was the house to be renovated and out of all this industry had grown a small soft-furnishing business. It was very small, just enough work to keep her happily occupied without causing anxiety, but brought enormous satisfaction along with the tiny income. That, and letting out the cottages, had brought her a kind of contentment. It was, however, a contentment which could be fractured only too easily—which was why she needed her stony sanctuary.

Brigid went back into the kitchen, through to the lean-to,

and let Blot into the kitchen. Pausing to look through the window, she saw that Oscar was still peacefully asleep on the cobbles and decided to leave him there.

"He's quite happy outside," Thea had assured her. "Try not to think of him as a dog, more as a Shetland pony or something like that. Of course, he'll want a cuddle now and again."

Brigid, nevertheless, felt anxious that Oscar might be pining for his people and had given him lots of cuddles whether he'd seemed to want them or not. He'd borne her affection with great patience and enormous courtesy and had lain down again afterwards with a sigh of relief. She'd grown terribly fond of him but dealing with Blot's jealousy had rather taken some of the pleasure out of Oscar's visit.

"You're spoiled rotten, that's the problem," she murmured, as he padded before her into the kitchen, tail wagging. "But then, whose fault is that?"

She placed his bowl, with the leftovers from supper, beside the Aga and began to tidy up. She was happy now. The dishwasher was taking most of the load—"Young people nowadays don't know they're born," Frummie had muttered waspishly—and she enjoyed restoring the kitchen to its normal state: squeezing behind the rectangular oak table so as to plump up the cushions on the settle which was built in against the wall, replacing the blue lustre jug full of yellow tulips in the centre of the table, putting the remains of the cream into the fridge. She kneeled for a moment on the window seat, opening the window which looked east, leaning to listen to the murmuring lullaby of the West Dart, looking up at the stars. The owl which lived in Combestone woods was flying up the valley, his thin quavering call echoing tremulously over stone and heather; far below him a vixen yelped once and was silent.

Leaning on her folded arms, Brigid was lulled, enfolded, in the mystery of the scene: the deep rural silence, the vast empty tracts of moorland, the singing of the spheres. She breathed deeply, gratefully, and then turned back to the warm, bright kitchen, refreshed and at peace.

• • •

STANDING AT her bedroom window, which looked across the O Brook to Combestone Tor, Louise was also listening to the owl. For once, however, she was not soothed by the peacefulness of the countryside: she felt restless, confused. Ever since she'd watched the man in the train, noting his body language, listening to his conversation, she'd been uneasy, her suspicions about Martin coalescing into a tangible fear; and then the unexpected sight of the woman in the field with her child had jolted her mind from its habitual guardedness, leaving it open to assault from the past. The past was buried and done with: finished, over. Yet those whispers, those images, had already undermined her hard-won contentment. It was these, she was sure, which had made her abnormally aware of the rifts and tensions between Brigid and Frummie. She'd sensed other emotions underlying Frummie's barbs and Brigid's anguish.

The vixen, down in the valley, yelped. It was a wild, disturbing cry that set the blood tingling, and Louise turned abruptly from the window, seized her dressing gown and went quickly into the bathroom.

FRUMMIE SHUT her front door behind her, checked the locks with an unsteady hand and headed for the drinks cupboard beside the fireplace in her living room. It was a big, delightful room which faced south and west but she still hadn't forgiven Brigid for giving her the smaller of the two cottages.

"We simply can't afford to, Mummie," Brigid had said, almost pleadingly. "We can't lose the income from the bigger one. You must understand that. It's cost an awful lot to get them converted and we can't just give away the bigger one. We're very happy for you to have this one, though. *Please* try to see our point of view."

"Oh, there's no need to make it *quite* so clear that beggars can't be choosers," She'd answered bitterly. "Don't worry.

I'm entitled to benefit from the government and I shall be able to pay you rent."

She'd enjoyed Brigid's flush of embarrassment; it had eased her own shame.

"I'm not bothered about rent," Brigid had said. "You know I'm not. It's just . . . Oh, forget it. I'm not going to argue with you. If you can manage here then I'm glad we have it so as to help you out. You must suit yourself. Come over to the house when you've looked round and made up your mind."

Frummie opened the door of the cupboard and reached for the whisky, her lips twisting in a grimace of remembrance. There had been no luxury of choice for her. Her fourth husband, who was considerably younger than she was, had left her for a woman half her age and she'd had nowhere to go. The lease was up on their flat, she'd had no income of her own, and she'd been utterly unable to meet the stares and knowing glances of her friends. Humiliation waited; little quarter would be given to one who had, in the past, been so ready to discourse wittily and cruelly upon the downfall of others. Flight to the country had been her only hope; a desperate need for sanctuary. She'd known just how generous Brigid was being but her own fierce pride must be supported, fed, upheld. Her acceptance had been ungracious but, after all, she'd lived in this damned hole—Foxhole was a good name for it—for eight long, mind-numbing years. She'd deserved something for her trouble. Of course, he'd left the lot to Brigid.

Frummie poured the whisky with a shaking hand, put the decanter back into the cupboard, and made her uncertain way upstairs. She undressed slowly, pausing for sips from the glass, and climbed into bed. Sitting for a while, cradling the glass, a pleasant drowsiness stealing over her, she nodded against the piled pillows. She, too, heard the owl's haunting call, the vixen's scream, and, with a shudder of horror, she drained the last drop from the glass and huddled down beneath her blankets.

CHAPTER 4

"You're going home today," Brigid told Oscar, giving him his morning biscuit and then watching whilst he ate it, lest Blot should snatch the pieces that fell to the ground before Oscar should be ready for them. He scrunched thoughtfully, in a leisurely manner, as if pondering on her words, and Brigid stroked his large black head. "It's not that I want to get rid of you," she assured him. "Get off, Blot. Eat your own biscuits and leave him alone. I'd be only too pleased to have you if it weren't for this neurotic fleabag. Go *away*, Blot. You're a very calming influence, Oscar. No wonder Thea is always so serene. You're a bit like Humphrey, actually. Large and solid and dependable. Finished? Sure? Good. I'm going to have some coffee, then."

She left Oscar sitting outside the lean-to door, gazing down with a kind of regal astonishment at Blot who was hoovering busily round his large paws for any spare crumbs, and went back to the kitchen. The room was full of sunshine and she made coffee with an unusually heartfelt sense of gratitude. She'd discovered very early on that a surprising amount of holidaymakers who rented the cottages seemed to hold her responsible for the weather.

"I'd no idea it rained so much," they'd say disconsolately. "I thought Devon was supposed to be a sunny place." Or, discontentedly, "Wish we'd gone abroad again, at least you get the weather there," as if rain and mist weren't weather but some kind of scourge especially reserved for Devonians. To Brigid, who'd spent many sleepless nights and anxious days wondering if the cottages were up to the necessary standard, these remarks seemed to strike to her heart as personal criticism.

"My dearest girl," Humphrey had said, putting his arms about her, "even *you* are not able to control the weather. Let them go back to the Mediterranean, or wherever, next year if they don't like it here. Things will settle down and we'll start getting regulars, people who really love the place, coming back year after year."

He'd been right, yet she still felt a huge sense of relief when the sun shone on the first day of each visitor's holiday. Not that she needed to worry about Louise. Louise had Brigid's own kind of passion for the place and accepted the rain as part of the package. She was almost a member of the family. A great many of Brigid's visitors had become friends; they sent Christmas cards and she'd watched their children grow, year by year, so that the couples who'd been the first to stay were now grandparents as she and Humphrey were. Most of them were seeking peace and quiet, enjoyed walking and exploring, and fitted in quite naturally, making few demands. With some of them a closer relationship had developed: a supper together, or a trip to the Church House Inn in Holne; a showing of photographs—a wedding or a christening—over a cream tea or a barbecue. It was only with Louise, however, that Brigid had really let down the barriers; only Louise who had pierced the guard of Brigid's privacy.

It had been hard to tell these annual visitors that one of the cottages would no longer be available. It meant that some of them were booking holidays earlier in the spring or later in the autumn but Louise had been one of the favoured few who had been privileged to retain her usual fortnight twice a year. Since she'd always booked late May and mid-September there were fewer contenders but, even if there had been more, Brigid would have still kept those weeks sacrosanct.

"One can't help having favourites," she'd said, almost defensively, "and I just have this feeling that it's more important for Louise than it is for lots of the others."

"I think you're right." Humphrey had smiled at her. "You don't have to try to convince me, you know."

"I know." She'd laughed at herself but had shaken her head, frustrated. "It's so difficult having to refuse people we've known for so long . . ." She hadn't added, "and all because of my wretched mother," but he'd understood.

"We didn't have any choice," he'd said gently. "We couldn't leave her in some depressing boarding house."

"*She* left *me*," Brigid had cried hotly, resentfully, before she could help herself, and had turned away so that he might not see her tears.

"But not alone and amongst strangers," he'd said, just as gently. "It's hell but if we hadn't taken her in you'd be riddled with guilt. It's a Catch 22 situation."

"I know." She'd blown her nose, smiling at him gratefully. "Sorry."

"What for? We both know what it's like to have a selfish parent. At least we had one good one each."

Breaking the dead heads from her geraniums, refilling the Aga kettle, pottering quietly, Brigid wondered why she should fear Humphrey's retirement so much. He was so kind, so stable, and he could always cheer her out of any depression or anxiety; she missed him, looked forward to his weekends at home and his leaves, so why feel so anxious? He'd had several shore jobs during his career but a shore job wasn't the same as having him at home all the time. Would he be hurt by her requirement for periods of solitude? How would they manage being permanently together who had been so much apart? Eighteen years ago the prospect of the holiday cottages providing income so that Humphrey could take early retirement had seemed wonderful but now, as the time drew closer, she'd been assailed by this terrible anxiety. Humphrey was looking forward to it; he liked meeting the visitors, chatting to them, getting to know them. Did she imagine that his friendliness might inevitably lead to a

breakdown of her carefully preserved privacy? Both conversions had been designed so that no window looked across
the courtyard to the longhouse. The visitors, in the main,
needed very little assistance but it was possible that
Humphrey's extrovert tendencies might change the balance—or maybe something worse . . .? Quickly she pushed
this unnamed terror aside.

"I'm an introvert," she said to Blot, "that's my problem."

He watched her with sad, loving eyes, tail gently thump-
ing, and she crouched to pat him. His curly black coat was
soft and warm and she tickled his nose with one of his long
ears. The telephone rang and she rose reluctantly.

"Lovely evening, darling. I did enjoy myself." Frummie
sounded as fresh as paint. "I was just wondering. If you're
taking Louise to pick up her car perhaps I could cadge a lift.
I need a few things from Ashburton and it seems silly to take
two cars."

"Of course you can." Brigid was convinced that since her
stroke, minor though it had been, Frummie shouldn't be
driving at all. "Half an hour OK?"

"Perfect. Oh, by the way, Jem will be over later for lunch
and we're going to the pub to make up for last night. We
wondered if you'd like to join us?"

Brigid was silent for a moment. Frummie usually preferred to keep her outings with Jemima very private and this
invitation was the olive branch complete with dove. "That's
nice of you," she said at last. "The thing is, Thea's coming to
fetch Oscar and I don't quite know when she'll be here. She
said 'sometime after lunch,' which isn't very helpful."

"Well, we shan't be late back. And, after all, it won't hurt
her to wait for a few minutes. Anyway, she probably won't
arrive until tea-time and then you'll have missed a nice
lunch. Now don't be stuffy, darling."

"No. OK. I'll see if I can catch Thea and suggest tea-time."

"You do that."

She hung up abruptly and Brigid replaced the receiver.
"Well," she said to Blot, "there's a turn-up for the books.
Let's hope it doesn't turn into a slanging match."

She glanced into the mirror and grimaced, wishing she'd washed her hair, and then shrugged philosophically and sat down at the table to write a shopping list.

ACROSS THE courtyard, Louise had already made her list and was now standing at the open door in the sunshine, a mug of tea cradled in her hands. She'd been glad to wake from a troubled sleep to the clear, radiant dawn. It had rained heavily in the night and, beyond the open window, she'd seen the doves circling and wheeling, their wings shiningly, dazzlingly white against the delicate purity of the clean-rinsed sky. She'd leaned out, bundling back her springing, curling dark hair, breathing in the fresh, cool air, needing to be part of this sparkling magic scene. Pulling on jeans and a sweatshirt, pausing only to swallow down a glassful of orange juice, she'd laced on her walking boots and had made her way down to the river. She'd been rewarded by the magnificent sight of the tumbling, racing water, thundering towards its clamorous meeting with the East Dart further down the valley. This morning it was as if it could hardly wait for its union, so eagerly and noisily did it roar in its rocky bed. The birdsong was rendered inaudible by its rushing and the overhanging branches of the willows were drowned in its tumultuous passing.

Louise, overawed by so much passion, presently left the river at Week Ford and followed the footpath to Saddle Bridge where the O Brook was making its more sedate way beside the rowan trees. Leaning on the stone bridge, she'd watched two stonechats flirting in a gorse bush whilst the sun rose higher, until hunger compelled her to walk back to Foxhole along the deserted road. A little later, sitting at the table eating brown toast and honey, she'd made a note of the stonechats and recorded one or two other things of interest—the gorse in flower and the hawthorn tree blossoming on the rocky river bank—before settling to the more mundane business of making a shopping list.

Now, standing in the sunshine, drinking her tea, she examined her feelings cautiously. She'd embarked on her holiday with a suspicion casting a shadow over her normally sunny anticipation. This suspicion—that Martin was having an affair—had grown out of intangible sensations, subtle changes which could not easily be defined. There was nothing so positive as the telephone call cut short, no notes found in pockets, no sudden late night meetings at the office. No, her suspicion was centred in Martin himself. There was a brightness about him, a kind of shiny expansiveness which manifested itself in bursts of generosity—oh, nothing so vulgar or obvious as presents; there was nothing *guilty* about his demeanour—rather as if his new-found joy could not be contained, must be expressed, even to her who was not the cause of it and might have every reason to resent it. Even here, however, nothing was clear-cut. Martin had always been a warmly generous, thoughtful companion. It was his awareness and quick compassion, after all, which had drawn her to him in the first place; his cheerful, positive approach which had caught her in its undertow and been impossible to resist.

She'd met his ex-partner, an attractive woman with a sour smile and cynicism in her eyes. "Don't be taken in," she'd advised. "Martin loves everyone. But everyone. And everyone loves Martin but you have to remain a challenge for him. He's the original Mr. Fixit and he needs his fix." Louise had mumbled some inadequate reply, embarrassed and confused, and they hadn't met again. Louise never mentioned this conversation to Martin: she'd needed his happiness, his scope for enjoyment, his army of acquaintances far too much. For three years she'd bobbed in his wake, involved with his friends, busy with the social life he loved, entertaining clients from the advertising agency when necessary. There had been no dissensions or quarrels, no deviation from the usual routines, yet this doubt had crept into her consciousness and she was unable to explain it. Impossible to confront Martin with such implausible suspicions, yet she'd become wary. It was the man on the train who had given her a clue, conducting his affair with the aid of his mobile telephone. Martin always carried his mobile with him, never left it about, refusing to let her borrow it when she'd had to travel suddenly to Scotland by train—"You'd never understand how it works, sweetie. There will be a phone on the train if you need it"—yet it never rang when he was with her. Text messages?

Louise sipped her tea thoughtfully. Odd, too, that whilst she'd been on the train, watching him, wondering, she'd seen the woman and the child, so that the memories, which she'd thought were so safely buried, had come sliding back through cracks in her consciousness made by suspicion and fear.

"Good morning. And what a lovely one." Frummie was hanging clothes on the rotary washing line in the corner of her small paved garden. "Did you sleep well?"

"It's wonderful, isn't it? Yes, quite well, thank you. It takes time to get used to the silence after London."

Frummie pulled a face. "It's a myth that the countryside is peaceful. It's full of sex and violence. Terrible."

Louise laughed, glad to be distracted. "So is the city."

"At least city-dwellers are honest about it. All that harvest home and roses round the door—Helen Allingham should have been drowned at birth."

She snapped the last peg in place and disappeared indoors. Louise was still trying to place Helen Allingham when Brigid appeared.

"Are you ready? Great. I'm bringing Blot with me but I'll just go and shut Oscar in the lean-to. Could you give Mummie a call? Thanks."

Louise rinsed her mug under the tap, picked up her bag and came out again into the sunshine. Frummie appeared, shrugging herself into a coat, and Brigid drove out on to the track and stopped so that they could climb into the car. Louise settled herself comfortably, looking forward to the drive across the moor, resolutely banishing darker thoughts and fears.

Later, sitting in the Café Green Ginger, having coffee with Brigid whilst Frummie finished her shopping, Louise asked casually, "Who's Helen Allingham?"

Brigid looked surprised, frowned a little. "Wasn't she the Victorian artist who painted those rather idealised studies of country cottages and small children? Very pretty but rather sentimental. Why?"

"Oh, nothing, really," said Louise. "I just wondered."

CHAPTER 5

In possession of her hired car, and with Brigid and Frummie on their way to their lunch with Jemima, Louise felt a sudden surge of independence. Alone, free to go where she chose, the holiday was now truly begun. It was not until she found herself on a quiet road, however, that she stopped the car and started to make it her own. She and Martin agreed that it was unnecessary to have two cars in London, that it was sensible to hire a small economical car whilst she was in Devon. Nevertheless she needed to feel at home in this small Citroën. Rootling in her big carpet bag, she put her road map on the passenger seat, filled the cassette holder with her favourite music and found her sunhat, dark specs and a small plastic pot which contained change for car-park machines. Later she'd put her walking boots, a light rucksack and a rug in the small boot but, just for now, the car had already assumed a more personal look.

Settling herself behind the wheel Louise paused, luxuriating in a moment's escapism. For a brief time nothing mattered but this holiday mood. The warm May day unrolled gently before her and she sat quietly, the sun pouring through the car window, deciding what she might do. Unlike Brigid, Louise was not a cat who liked to walk by herself—although she chose her close companions with care. However, she totally sympathised with Brigid's need to commune with nature and understood her disappointment in Humphrey's utter lack of observation: his unawareness of the minutiae, his indifference to the majesty and grandeur amongst which they lived. For choice, Louise would have preferred a companion who was empathic, who could rejoice over a butterfly sunning itself on a patch of bell heather or would pause at the summit of a hill to gaze with silent reverence at some new vista. During that first holiday, walking with Brigid, it had needed only a touch on the arm, a nod of the head, to transport them both into some delight caused by a new foal, leggy and uncertain, nuzzling its mother, a dipper bobbing on a rock in turbulent white water, a crow riding insouciantly on a sheep's back. Their pleasure was communicated silently and conversation was kept to a minimum. Such companions were very rare and if one could not find them then it was better to be alone. When it came to eating or shopping, however, Louise preferred to go to shops and hostelries where she was known. She liked to see a welcoming smile, to hear a friendly greeting: "Hul*lo*. Nice to see you back again. Well, doesn't time fly . . .?"

So where to go first? She wouldn't venture too far afield, not on the first day, especially as she had to go back to Foxhole first to unload her shopping and collect her walking boots; she'd stay on the moor. So where to go? Not to the Church House Inn at Holne; not with the family foregathering there. The Ring o' Bells at Chagford? Perhaps a little too far to be comfortably in time for lunch. The Roundhouse at Buckland? It was always fun to see the Perrymans: to share in the warmth of their boisterous family life, to be teased by Margaret—who worked with them—and have a chat with Mary in the gift shop. Yes, the Roundhouse would make a good starting point and, after lunch, she'd walk up to the Beacon so as to ravish herself with the glorious view and examine the broken tablets of stone which were graven with the Ten Commandments.

Her decision made, filled with a sense of anticipation, Louise switched on the engine and set off towards Foxhole. It was odd that, though it was less than twenty-four hours since she'd passed this way with Brigid, she now felt subtly different; driving in her own car, listening to her own music, she was no longer a visitor, a guest, but part of the landscape. She drove over Saddle Bridge, up the hill and turned the car on to the track which bumped unevenly down to the house.

As she parked beside her little cottage and climbed out of the car, a woman and a child came out of the courtyard. Louise stopped, still holding the car door, staring. The tall, sweet-faced mother looked like the woman she'd seen yesterday, but the child was older, too big to be carried, at least six years old. The little girl reached her first; big eyes gazing up at her, long red-gold hair, the colour of ripe corn with the sun on it.

"We've come to fetch our dog," she said trustfully, distressfully. "Only we can't get in. I can see him through the window. I'm Hermione."

Hermione? Louise stared down at her, stiff and unresponsive, still clutching the car door.

"Darling," her mother sounded apologetic, "just wait a moment. I'm so sorry," she said to Louise. "Only she's been missing him, you see. There was a message on the machine this morning but there's some kind of fault and it crackles terribly. I thought it was Brigid's voice saying something about picking Oscar up before lunch but I think I've got it quite wrong. I'm Thea Lampeter."

Louise took the outstretched hand unwillingly. Thea was much about her own age, a few years older, perhaps, with her daughter's red-gold colouring. Holding the warm, firm hand, staring into amber-brown eyes, Louise had the strangest experience that she was falling, tumbling through space whilst this tall, strong woman held her from harm. She clung to her madly, dimly aware that the child was talking again.

"But we can't leave him now that he's seen us," she was saying. "We simply *can't*. What are we going to do?"

"If necessary we'll wait until Brigid comes back." Thea sounded quite resigned, even contented with this plan. "We'll camp outside the window so that he can see us."

"He'll get upset," warned the child. "He'll bark and jump at the door."

"Of course he won't." Thea still smiled at Louise, whilst continuing to address her daughter. "He'd find it *much* too exhausting . . . Are you feeling better now?" She asked the question gently.

Louise nodded, withdrawing her hand reluctantly, but she would not look at the child.

"Yes, of course. I . . . haven't been too well lately. Just the odd attack of dizziness." She felt the requirement to excuse her behaviour but another glance into those far-seeing eyes caused her to stumble in her explanation. "It's just . . . I'm . . ."

"Are you staying with Brigid?"

"Yes. Well, in this cottage. You could . . ." she hesitated, "you could wait here if you like."

"Oh, could we?" The child was beside her again, face alight with eagerness. "Then Mummy could have some coffee and I could talk to Oscar through the window."

"Hermione," admonished Thea, "please stop bothering Mrs. . . . I'm so sorry, you didn't tell us your name."

"I'm Louise Parry. And of course you can have some coffee. I have to unpack my shopping and get sorted out, so it's not a problem."

She was talking at random, crossing the paved sitting-out area to the door, digging into her pocket for the key. Hermione had disappeared into the courtyard and could now be heard telling Oscar the new plans at the top of her voice.

"But Brigid could be some time." Thea was following her. "And you're on holiday. We can't monopolise you for too long."

"I wish *I* lived here." Hermione was back. "Isn't it a dear little house? Shall I take my juice out so that I can stay with Oscar? I think he likes to know I'm there."

"Darling," remonstrated Thea, "Mrs. Parry hasn't offered you any juice yet."

"There's some orange juice in the fridge," muttered Louise. "Could you manage while I fetch the shopping?"

"Of course. This is very kind of you . . ."

Louise went back out to the car and opened the hatch. She stood quite still, hidden from the house, and presently the child passed her, carefully carrying her glass of orange juice.

"I shall stay with Oscar," she said. "Mummy's making coffee. Thank you," she called back, as an afterthought.

"This is extraordinarily kind of you." In the big living room Thea was calmly making coffee. "I can't apologise enough. So silly of me to come rushing out without calling Brigid back or being intelligent. George had taken Amelia and Julia—my two older daughters—to see his mother. She's elderly and he likes to see her as soon as we get home. And, of course, Hermione couldn't wait to fetch Oscar."

"If it helps," said Louise, putting her provisions away, "Brigid's having lunch at the pub in Holne with her mother and sister. Perhaps I could drive down and get the key or something while you're having your coffee. No, honestly, it's no trouble at all. I'm sure Brigid will understand."

Half an hour later she was watching Oscar's ecstatic reunion with his family and waving them off down the track. Brigid had seemed quite resigned to Thea's unexpected arrival, perfectly happy to give her the key, grateful to Louise for coming to her friend's rescue. The estate car accelerated slowly away, Oscar watching from the back window, Hermione waving furiously, and presently Louise went back inside and stared unseeingly at the remains of the small, impromptu feast. It was too late now to worry about lunch, and, anyway, she wasn't hungry. She turned quickly, thinking she heard a footstep, a chuckle. Hermione . . .?

"Don't!" she warned herself savagely. "Just don't think about it."

Hastily she began to assemble a picnic: a ham sandwich, an apple, a chunk of cheese. She made up a small bottle of elderflower cordial and put it all into a small, light knapsack. A few minutes later she was quite ready. Shutting the door behind her, dropping the key into her pocket, she set off, walking briskly in the direction of Combestone Tor.

* * *

BRIGID PUT the car away and went to see if Louise might be at home. The cottage was closed up and there was no answer to her knock. She was feeling guilty that Louise had been obliged to rescue Thea but, luckily, the distraction had done nothing to spoil the amicable atmosphere of the lunch party. Jemima had been on good form and Frummie had been on her best behaviour. Now her mother had disappeared to sleep off the effects of overeating and Brigid went into her own kitchen, wondering if it might be a good idea to get on with some work. Blot was quartering the rooms, looking for Oscar, and she felt all the languid flattening of the spirits which comes after a period of mental and physical effort amongst people with whom one cannot truly relax.

Faintly dissatisfied with herself, Brigid wandered upstairs, Blot at her heels, passed through the dressing room and bedroom and went into her workroom. This room, directly above the kitchen, looked east and south and was dominated by the huge table on which she did her cutting out. A smaller table, holding her sewing machine, was placed beneath one of the windows and an old-fashioned rosewood sewing box, opening tier upon tier and holding cotton reels, spools of silk, pins and needles, stood on long wooden legs in a corner near the table. On the cream-washed walls hung large picture frames containing collages of photographs. Black-and-white snapshots and glossy colour prints, they were records of the family—her own and Humphrey's—and they invariably drew her attention, even after all these years of their company. She paused now to look at them: Michael beaming gap-toothed at the school photographer, and, sixteen years later, in cap and gown at his graduation ceremony. Humphrey, straight-backed, serious-faced, at the Passing Out Parade at Dartmouth, and five years later carrying Julian in his christening gown. How she'd loved those early years when the boys were small; their need of her, their unconditional love, had filled the empty ache of missing Humphrey and, as she'd read to them and cuddled them, she'd vowed that they should never feel unwanted or unloved. How hard it had been to send them off to school, how desperately she'd missed them: wandering from room to room, standing at the doors of their bedrooms, feeling a physical longing for cheerful voices raised in friendly argument, shoes kicked off upon the floor, scattered toys.

"I know it's difficult," Humphrey had said gently, "but it's only fair to them. We move about too much and they'll always be having to make new friends, struggling with different teachers. You have to let go sometime, my darling."

"But not yet," she'd wanted to cry. "They're still little"— but she'd known that it would have been even more unkind to wait until they were older when it would be more difficult for them to be accepted into the system. If she'd known that her father would die so soon after Julian had started at Mount House she might have insisted that they need not go away at all. By the time she'd moved back to Foxhole, he was already happy and settled at school with all his small naval friends and, knowing Michael would follow him there, she hadn't had the heart to uproot them again for her own selfish needs. Instead she'd made the most of exeats and half-terms and had maintained a close and loving relationship with her boys: the kind of relationship she'd longed for with her own parents. Where, she sometimes asked herself, had she fallen short as a child? What had she lacked? Her father had been kind if distant; affectionate but remote. As for her mother . . .

She bent closer to look at a tiny snapshot of Frummie, laughing and beautiful, in a ridiculous hat and impossible shoes. It was creased and worn from being carried about and shown: "That's my mother." "Gosh! Isn't she pretty? But hasn't she . . . you know . . . left . . .?" "She's still my mother."

Brigid turned away and stared at the material stretched out upon the table: curtains, yet to be made. Was it impossible to change? To step free from the limitations of genes and character? To be rid of resentment that surged from nowhere, disabling love? Each time she believed that she had conquered, imagined that her very real affection for her sister was, at last, stronger than her jealousy, some reminder—a bitter thought,

some hastily spoken words—would undermine her efforts, as
if some demonic serpent lay curled, latent within her, waiting
to strike. She occasionally surprised a look on Jemima's face:
a mixture of puzzlement, disappointment, sadness—and
something else. It was a look of hopeful humility; it expressed a kind of longing but also acceptance. It was this that
was really difficult to deal with; as if Jemima understood
Brigid's dislike and took her sister's valuation to herself.
Puddle-duck. It could so easily have been a happy, loving
nickname. Yet, for Brigid, the word still held those connota-
tions with which she'd invested it as an unhappy, angry
schoolgirl. It stood for all the pain she'd suffered in the rejection by her mother, and Jemima was the living symbol on
which her anger had centred. Puddle-duck. She'd made so
many overtures, poor Puddle-duck, so many loving gestures,
tried to forge a real friendship with the older half-sister she'd
been so pleased to find, yet in the last resort it had been impossible for Brigid to make that final, total acceptance.

She thought: What sort of person am I, for God's sake?

Jemima had been so much fun at lunch, warm and amusing, generously insisting that it was her treat, and Frummie
had been so responsive, so affectionate, so—Brigid's hands
clenched unconsciously—so *approving*. How rarely did her
elder daughter bask in such motherly love! No, *her* portion
was dealt out in sarcastic observations, malicious witticisms,
cool irony. Brigid smoothed the fabric, turned on the radio,
bent to stroke Blot, curled now on his mat by the window.
Work could absorb, calm, satisfy. She lifted the heavy scis-
sors and cut with accurate, skilful confidence.

It was much later, back in the kitchen for a cup of tea, that
she noticed the red winking light on the answerphone.
Thea's voice was apologetic: "So sorry, Brigid. What a twit I
am! Bless you for having him. He's obviously been well
looked after. Have you seen the little pressie on the dresser?
Speak soon. Bring Louise over for tea? Yes? Lots of love."
The next voice contained a kind of hurried, brittle cheerfulness. "It's Jenny. Hope you're OK, Brigid. I wondered if I
could pop over and see you? Would Tuesday be OK? Don't

bother to phone back if it is. I'm all over the place at the moment. See you then. Late morning. Great. 'Bye for now."

Brigid pressed the replay button and, as she listened for a second time, a new anxiety clutched at her gut. She glanced absently at the dresser and saw a package, neatly wrapped, and a card, but she was not thinking of Thea: Jenny's voice had set alarm bells ringing and her heart was filled with fear.

CHAPTER 6

When shall I see you again? Jemima Spencer did not ask the question. She knew it was against the rules. Watching him dress, she wondered if she loved him or whether she knew exactly what the word meant. It was used so casually, so indiscriminately, although it contained such huge possibilities. He was important to her; she liked him enormously and he was a good lover. Yet she knew that she would be perfectly happy once he'd gone; content to be alone. She felt inhibited by any other presence in her flat, not quite at ease, and had often stated that she was by nature a mistress.

Leaning on an elbow she admired his long straight legs and supple, tanned back, watched his desirable, pleasure-giving body being swallowed up by his neat, concealing clothes.

"I might be down again on Tuesday."

She rolled on to her back so that he might not see her face. "I've got someone coming over to supper on Tuesday." He liked her to be casual; it fanned the flames of possessiveness. "Can't put it off."

"Who is it?" sharply.

She smiled, a private little smile. "No one you know."

He stared down at her and she knew that he was torn with pursuing this conversation, yet cautious lest it opened him up to accusations: *What's it got to do with you? You're going home to your wife. Why should I sit around waiting . . .?"* and so on. He'd heard it all before, though not from Jemima. Still, it was wise not to push your luck . . . Eyes narrowed, his hands flicking his tie into a knot, his thoughts might have been scrolling over his face so clear were they to her.

"Not Tuesday, then?"

He stooped deliberately to kiss her, one last lingering caress, and she felt laughter bubbling up from deep inside. This often happened at moments when she should have been moved with desire or sadness; instead this sudden upward-swooping joy, a flash of delight at her separateness. He released her abruptly, irritated by his failure to persuade her, his face sulky.

"Not Tuesday." She swung her legs out of bed, her toes feeling for her espadrilles. "Give me a buzz."

"OK." He could play it cool too. He hesitated. "Well, then."

She led the way into the passage, shrugging into a cotton wrapper, deciding not to offer him coffee or a drink.

"Safe journey." She kissed the tip of her forefinger and put it against his cheek. "See you soon."

There was nothing to do but smile, accept it graciously, and leave.

Closing the door behind him, Jemima was chuckling to herself. She padded back along the passage and opened the door into the sitting room. It still gave her a thrill. Looking out across the harbour the room seemed to shimmer tremulously with a watery light; cool, bright reflections danced on the pale green walls. The smoothly pale, ash-wood floor gleamed between white rugs and an enormous sofa, striped cream and blue and green like a deckchair, was set at right angles to the glass doors which led on to the balcony.

"He's gone," she said. "So now we can relax."

There was no response from the huge, long-haired Persian cat who lay curled in a basket-weave chair. He slept peacefully, his round face serene. Jemima bent over him, smoothing his long fur, and he opened one eye before settling himself more comfortably.

"You are lazy, MagnifiCat," she told him severely. "You

are an idle animal. But then so am I. That's why we like each
other, I suppose."

She took an apple from the bowl on the low, glass-topped
table and, opening the sliding doors, stepped on to the balcony. The evening was cool and the rising tidewater was
stained crimson with the last sunset rays; small waves lapping round the ferry pier, rippling from beneath the bows of
a small dinghy being rowed steadily out to one of the
moored yachts. People were sitting outside with their drinks
at the Ferryboat Inn and tiny, friendly lights twinkled from
East Portlemouth across the harbour. Jemima took a deep
breath of sheer joy and bit into her apple. She knew that
Brigid disapproved of the rent she was paying, knew that it
would have been more sensible to have used her small
legacy to make a down payment on a small cottage or a flat,
but she could never have afforded a mortgage on anything
like this. Even to win her sister's approval she could not
have resisted this flat.

"I know she despises me," she said sadly to MagnifiCat,
who had come out to investigate, "but I couldn't turn down a
chance like this, even if I can only afford it for a few years.
That's one of the differences between us, I suppose. I grasp
the shadow instead of the substance and she is level-headed
and responsible."

MagnifiCat sat down and stared insolently at a seagull
riding on the mast of a dinghy which was moored alongside
the quay. The seagull stared back with cold yellow eyes and
the cat's tail twitched.

"Don't even think about it," advised Jemima. "I've told
you before, we don't do seagulls. He'd have you for breakfast. Or supper."

She flung her apple core in a high arc and, with a hoarse
shriek, the seagull rose up from his perch, catching the core
on the upward beat of his flight. Jemima watched, rubbing
her bare arms. Her thick fair hair, loose and untidy, curled
over her shoulders and down her back and she shivered
slightly as she watched the brilliant crimson light dying into
the black water.

"Time to eat," she said—but she didn't move. The scene kept her leaning on the rail, captivated, reluctant to go back inside, even though she could continue to watch it from the comfort of her sofa. It was barely three months since she'd moved in; before that she'd rented a flat in Gloucester and worked for Home From Home, a company who arranged holidays in privately owned accommodation. She'd transferred to Devon not long after Frummie had moved to Foxhole and now had half a dozen properties in her charge. These were properties owned by people who lived abroad or who had no intention of becoming involved in the letting. Unlike Brigid, who dealt with everything from the booking to the cleaning, these owners rarely visited these cottages and Jemima had to make certain that they were kept in order, were cleaned and restocked, and that the holidaymakers who booked them were given access and kept happy. She had built up a very small team of part-time helpers who might be available to clean and deal with the changeover at the weekends but very often these people—who were self-employed or on social security—were not totally reliable and Jemima would find herself scurrying from cottage to cottage, changing sheets, dusting and cleaning, dashing back to give over the keys to the first arrivals.

"You should get proper cleaners," Brigid had said, "not people who are on social security. You're encouraging a black market economy by paying people who won't declare it."

"You make them sound like drug-crazed layabouts," Jemima had answered. "These are good, respectable people who can barely make ends meet. It helps them out to earn an extra bit here and there."

"It's cheating," Brigid had answered inexorably. "You could get them into trouble if they're collecting benefit."

"Not all of them are," Jemima had protested. "It's just that their men aren't earning much—fishermen or small builders, that sort of thing. Why shouldn't they put a few extra pounds in their pockets?"

"If they needed it that much they'd be more reliable," her sister had replied and Jemima had been left with the usual sense of ineffectiveness, of inadequacy. This was the problem: Brigid was so straight, so sure; there was no mess and muddle in her life; her own letting cottages and her small soft-furnishing business were organised efficiently and successfully, as was her marriage. She'd been a good mother, dealing calmly with all the dramas of the boys' childhood and adolescence during Humphrey's long absences, and it was clear that he adored her.

Jemima stirred. She'd hoped that, now that she was living near Brigid for the first time in their lives, she'd at last achieve the loving relationship with her sister for which she'd always yearned. She'd missed her father terribly when her mother had left him and she'd always imagined that Brigid would be able to share those feelings. Instead she'd been met with a smooth, ungraspable barrier. Occasionally it would be tantalisingly lowered and she'd see the warmth and humour for which she longed but, just when she'd believed that they were moving closer, she'd found that the barrier had been re-erected. She could understand why Brigid found her irritating, foolish, weak, but she still hoped that one day she might be loved for herself.

The telephone buzzed and Jemima hurried back through the window and picked up her mobile.

"I just thought I'd tell you," he said, "that I shall be joining the A38 soon so it's my last chance to ask if you're still quite sure about Tuesday."

She smiled, happy and secure in the distance between them, able to comfort him.

"Quite sure," she said, teasingly, "unless, of course, you might be able to arrive a bit later. Stay the night, perhaps?" She rarely encouraged this but she was feeling a little sorrier for him now that she could remember those lovely straight legs but not the sulky expression. "I'm sure Louise won't stay late."

"Louise?" His voice was alert, more cheerful.

"Why yes." She pretended surprise. "She's staying with my sister. Who did you think it was?"

"How should I know?" he grumbled. He could allow jealousy at this distance, not fearing a scene on the telephone. "I *might* be able to stay . . ."

"Think about it," she said lightly. "Must go. 'Bye."

Good humour and confidence restored, she bent to sweep MagnifiCat into her arms, burying her face in his fur.

"Supper," she said. "You can share my sushi. What do you say to that?"

She put him down again, groaning at his weight, and he followed her on short stocky legs into the kitchen.

"IT'S RATHER nice here, Fred!" Margot Spelman stretched her sturdy legs out in the sunshine. "You were damned lucky, you know, to have a daughter with a bit of property."

"You've got your granny flat." Frummie set down the tea-tray. It was odd, now, to be called Fred; odd but nice. It made her feel young again, careless and happy—especially as poor old Margot was showing her age.

"Mmm." Margot raised a ravaged face to the warmth. "But one feels so terribly *de trop*. Harry's a darling, of course, but Barbara . . ." She shuddered artistically. "Daughters-in-law are hell, Fred. You should give thanks, fasting, that you have daughters."

"Rubbish." Frummie sat down in the deckchair opposite. "The simple truth of it is, my dear Margot, that you are a cow to your daughters-in-law. Ginny had the sense to cart David away to furthest Cornwall but I'm amazed that Barbara lets you anywhere near her dear little granny flat. I bet she never gets a wink of sleep wondering what you'll be up to next."

"And what about you?" Margot remained unruffled at such accusations. "I think Brigid's a saint to have you here after you went off and left her as a small child. To be honest, I'm surprised *anyone* would agree to have you living within ten miles of them but then I've known you for a very long time."

Frummie grinned maliciously. "First day at boarding school, wasn't it? Thirteen years old—well, I wasn't quite thirteen, you're older than I am—and who was the one blubbing?"

"Oh, shut up and pour the tea. So how's Jemima?"

"Doing very well. Living in the most perfect flat in Salcombe. Right on the waterfront."

"Goodness." Margot sat up, alert. "Don't tell me Richard left you some money."

Frummie hoisted a disdainful shoulder. "He didn't leave *me* anything. But he left a tiny bit to Jem."

"I have to say, Fred," Margot accepted her tea with a nod of thanks, "that you were the most god-awful picker of men. Whatever did you see in them? Of course, Diarmid was rather gorgeous in a kind of untidy, absent sort of way. That tall, lean, fair look. Terrific legs. Brigid is just like him."

"Diarmid was different." Frummie sipped dreamily, her sharp face softened by memories. "I'd never known anyone like him before. And I was young and impressionable."

"Impressionable?" Margot raised her eyebrows. "You? Well, I suppose that's one way of describing it. And Richard?"

"Well, Richard was fun. And I was tired of competing with Bronze Age circles and Neolithic man. I went up to London one day and somehow just never came back." Silence. "Oh, don't do that disapproving thing again," said Frummie irritably. "I didn't just consciously walk away without a backward glance, you know. It was just too impossible to come back. And as the days passed it became more impossible. I wrote to Diarmid and told him I couldn't face it and he agreed that it hadn't been easy, and that I must do what was right for me, but that he was keeping Brigid. What could I do? I could hardly come down and kidnap her."

"I can see his point." Margot glanced at her old friend, not unsympathetically. "At least he could give her security. Richard wasn't what you might call the reliable type, was he?"

"You don't run off with reliable types, do you?"

"*You* don't," observed Margot pointedly. "If I remember rightly, William—William *was* number three, wasn't he?—played in a jazz band?"

"Only occasionally," replied Frummie with dignity. "He was a stockbroker."

"Oh, honestly . . ."

"He was very clever with money—"

"As long as it was other people's. The truth of it is you shouldn't have been let out alone, Fred. For one so cynical you were an absolute pushover when it came to con men."

"Did you come all this way simply to be unpleasant?"

"No. I came all this way to see you. You haven't been too easy to track down lately and—"

"And now I'm rather conveniently placed between Salisbury and Cornwall," finished Frummie sweetly. "A useful stopping place, wouldn't you say?"

"Better than the Little Chef at Buckfast," agreed Margot, unruffled. "I hope you do as good a breakfast."

"Since when did you eat breakfast? A cigarette and cup of black coffee shouldn't be too challenging for me."

A car drove up the track and pulled in beside the other cottage. Louise climbed out, waved to Frummie and disappeared inside.

"Who's that?" Margot peered after her. "Pretty girl."

"She's one of Brigid's regulars. Comes twice a year while her husband plays golf."

"Really?" Margot sounded sceptical.

"Quite. My reaction exactly. But you never know. I suppose some husbands are faithful . . ."

"Name three," suggested Margot idly. "If you can. *You* could certainly name three who *weren't,* of course, but Diarmid was pretty loyal."

"Oh, don't start on that again," said Frummie wearily. "You're getting dull in your old age. What about supper at the pub this evening?"

"What pub?" Margot sounded interested.

"Ten minutes away. You can drive us."

"I think we'll stay here." Margot settled herself comfortably. "I've got a rather nice malt whisky with me. Darling Harry always makes sure I'm looked after. Poor Barbara suffers agonies of embarrassment taking the empties to the bottle bank. So tell me about Jemima. What's she up to?"

The two women bent closer over the teacups, heads together.

CHAPTER 7

Louise, coming back to collect some belongings from the car, thought that there was an almost sinister air about them as they huddled together.

She thought: You're imagining things again. Seeing shadows . . .

The card was behind the door: a big square of white, pushed into the corner when she'd thrust the door open earlier. She left it lying there and went to dump her bags in the living room, emptying flasks, putting uneaten fruit away, taking off her walking boots, before going back into the small hall. The envelope had been delivered by hand with just the name "Louise Parry" written on it; no address, no stamp. She stood staring down at it, every instinct alert and warning her against picking it up and opening it.

"Will Daddy be at my party?" "No, darling. He's a long way away. He's left a present for you, though." "I'd rather Daddy was here."

She opened her eyes and allowed her tightly clenched fingers to stretch, relax, to pick up the card. Putting it on the table she filled the kettle and switched it on, forcing her mind to other things: supper with Jemima tomorrow, a day at Bigbury and lunch on Burgh Island . . . but the formula was no longer working. Her defence mechanism was faulty and the past was pressing in; she held it away desperately. Singing to herself—learning the words of songs, of poetry, was another protection against memories—she made tea, fetched milk, opened the window. Putting the mug of tea at the end of the big, square table, she sat down and pulled her notebook and tiny paintbox towards her, intent on bringing her diary up to date. The distant music of the West Dart drifted up to her, mingling with the lazy cooing of the doves in the courtyard, but today this quiet peacefulness was full of danger. Her attention was caught by the bright white square, lying just beyond reach, and she picked up her mug hastily, concentrating on the things that she had seen on her walk: hawthorn blossom and cuckoopint in the springtime beauty of Hembury woods; house martins wheeling and circling above her head whilst she was having coffee at the Forge Café in Holne; a peacock butterfly warming itself on a mossy stone at Dean Ford. She wrote quickly, making the tiny sketches, painting in the delicate hues. The voices were quite quiet, barely audible, murmuring quietly together.

"Can I do painting like Mummy?" "I should stick with the crayons. Less messy." "I could be very careful." "Tell you what. Let's do this one together first and then we'll see . . ."

Louise rinsed her paintbrush carefully and laid it down. Her face bleak, mouth grimly compressed, she reached for the card. It was not just a card, it was too bulky, and with a sense of dread she slit the envelope and drew out its contents. A card first: a clever cartoon of a Newfoundland, ears pricked, staring through the window of what was clearly Brigid's lean-to, beyond which a car waited. All his anxiety and suspense informed the animal's tense posture, yet there was something comic about the scene.

"Thanks so much," Thea had written inside. "Do please come and have tea with us. Would you like to have a word with Brigid about it? We should love to see you again."

Louise stared at the cartoon, something familiar about the style focusing her attention. Presently she picked up the folded sheet of paper and opened it out. The title "Oscar" was printed carefully, though in an uneven hand, the letter S a great deal taller than the O. The dog-shape had been crayoned in black with a large pink tongue.

"This is Oscar saying thank you. Please come to tea. Love Hermione."

The writing sloped alarmingly, slipping off the page, and the name was drawn in alternate blue and red crayon. Hermione. Louise was still staring at it when she heard the knock at the door. It opened an inch or two.

"May I come in?" called Brigid.

Only a lifetime's habit of good manners made it possible for her to answer. She was still sitting at the table when Brigid came into the living room. Louise forced herself to smile at her, trying to summon the control needed to rise, offer tea.

"I see you found it." Brigid nodded towards the card. "She sent it to me and I dropped it in earlier. I'm going over to see them later in the week and she seems anxious that you should come too. Would you like to, d'you think?"

"It's . . ." Louise swallowed in a dry throat, ". . . it's very kind. There's no need at all."

"Oh, I don't think it's politeness. Thea's a darling but she's not conventional. I think she simply liked you. And Hermione—"

"The thing is," interrupted Louise, quickly, "trying to fit everything in. A fortnight isn't long."

"I quite understand that. And there's no reason at all why you should go . . ."

She fell silent and, through her own fear, Louise dimly noticed that Brigid was looking very drawn.

She thought: I can't deal with this.

"Well then." Brigid smiled awkwardly, made as if to go. She looked as if, in some way, she had been recently hurt.

"Have some tea." Louise heard her own voice with surprise and cursed herself. "I've only just made some and I'm old-fashioned enough to make it in a pot. Can't bear the mess of squashed teabags in the sink." She spoke randomly, getting up, taking a mug from the dresser, whilst all the time an echo inside her head was saying: I can't *do* this. I can't.

Brigid placed her hands about the mug, as if they were cold, and gazed into the tea. Louise sat down again and stared at her.

"Are you OK?" She spoke quite gently.

Brigid's eyes were wide and blank with fright. "Yes, of course. Just a few things on my mind." She smiled a quick, automatic smile. "So then. What about Thea?"

"Maybe. Later on. Shall we see how things ... you know ... pan out?"

"Yes. Right. You'd love the Old Station House. And the girls. You've met Hermione, of course, and Julia and Amelia are gorgeous. And there's Percy, of course. Thea's famous. She writes and illustrates children's books and there was the show on the television. Not that you'd know if you don't have children. It was an absolute cult a few years ago—T-shirts and mugs and toys ..."

"Toys?"

"Percy the Parrot. He was gorgeous. Unfortunately, my boys were too old for him but we always watched the programme. It was a huge success. Anyway, have a think about it and let me know. Thanks for the tea."

The front door closed. In the silence which was left behind her Louise trembled, clammy hands knotted together. It was as if a huge wall of black water stood above her; building, rising, towering, threatening to engulf her. She could hear it roaring and then realised that the noise was inside her head. Dizzily she stumbled towards the table and sank into her chair, dropping her forehead on her arms, but, even now, she could not cry.

BRIGID, BACK in her own home, roamed restlessly. Her usual sense of peace, of sanctuary, was destroyed by her fear. What was Jenny coming to tell her? She'd telephoned several times but Jenny's answerphone was permanently switched on and she'd been unable to make contact. What could be wrong? It was three years now since Brigid had agreed to let one of her cottages stand security for the new business which Jenny, her oldest, closest friend, was planning with her husband and a partner. The proposal was to set up a sailing school on the Fal, an industry in which Bryn—Jenny's husband—had already had some experience, whilst the partner was a quite famous young man who had sailed the Atlantic single-handed. The business plan was submitted and approved by the Bank, hopes were high, interest intense, everything positive. It was merely a matter of form and Brigid's lawyer had seen no real danger in underwriting the fifteen thousand pounds. The little cottage was worth much more and, anyway, Jenny had assured her that Bryn had plenty of other ways of raising the cash if it should come to it—but the Bank wanted something solid. It was such a perfect opportunity and Brigid would get an annual payment, not much to begin with, but a surety of their confidence.

Jenny had been so happy, glowing with the idea of the school, the opportunities ahead, the new joy in her relationship with Bryn after her disastrous divorce from her first husband, Peter.

"Only don't tell Humphrey," she'd begged. "Please don't. He and Peter are still good friends and I can't bear him knowing all the details. Peter, I mean. You don't have to, do you, Brigid? I mean, Foxhole's yours, isn't it?"

"Well, it is," Brigid had answered, unhappy at the idea of subterfuge, yet longing to help her friend. "But we've mortgaged the longhouse so as to renovate the barns, and the mortgage is in our joint names. It's not a very big one but it's there and Humphrey is the one who pays it."

"But the cottages are unencumbered?"

"Yes," she'd said slowly. "The cottages are still in my name."

"Well, one of them would be enough. It's not much. Bryn and I are putting some in and Iain's got a bit. It's just to get started. We need a building so that we can get dormitories in, and things like that, and some sailing dinghies. It's going to be great. Could you help us, Brigid? It's just on paper but the Banks are funny after the recession."

"I don't like not telling Humphrey."

"Dear old Brigid," Jenny had smiled at her affectionately, "you were always so strait-laced. Even at school you made me feel naughty just by looking at me."

Strange how certain words and phrases had the power to

hurt. *"Brigid won't. She's strait-laced like her papa. Not into nicknames; much too silly."*

"It's not that," she'd said quickly, defensively. "I just don't like secrets between husbands and wives. It's dangerous."

"Join the real world," Jenny had sighed. "Lucky you, that's all I can say. I don't think Peter ever told me the truth in fifteen years of marriage."

"Oh, Jenny." Brigid's heart had been wrung with compassion. It was true that she'd been badly deceived and ultimately humiliated.

"If she'd ever stopped talking and started listening she might have noticed a few things," Humphrey had said unsympathetically. "It's not all Peter's fault."

"Trust you men to stick together," Brigid had answered, hurt and upset for Jenny. "Did you know he's been having an affair with that Wren for years?"

"I'm not saying anything." Humphrey had smiled, not unkindly. "Need-to-know basis, that's my motto."

Afterwards, she'd been glad that Humphrey had been so guarded. She'd been able to say, with absolute truth, that she knew nothing of Peter's affairs, and her own friendship with Jenny had remained intact. This was why she'd reluctantly agreed to keep the arrangement secret from Humphrey. It was, she told herself, the same need-to-know basis. It would be difficult for Humphrey, whilst he and Peter still worked together, not to let some information slip—and so she'd had the whole scheme checked out and put up one of her cottages as security. For the first two years she'd had her payment from the business and had heard good reports. Could something have gone wrong? But why should it? Why should this be anything more than a friendly visit?

She thought: Because Jenny's voice was all wrong on the answerphone. It was brittle. Too quick. Too light. And why isn't she answering any of my calls?

She stood at the window, looking across the valley, washed with the creamy colour of the rowan blossom and the hawthorn, vivid with yellow gorse, to the stony heights of Yar Tor. Sheep were climbing the winding track amidst the new, bright green bracken, whilst ponies grazed peacefully nearby. The afternoon sun cast long shadows into the valley and a lark was singing somewhere out of sight. Brigid went through to the lean-to, kicked off her shoes and slipped into her gum-boots. Blot struggled up from his sleep on the sun-warmed slates, wagging his stumpy tail with delighted welcome, and followed her gladly out of the courtyard and across the field.

STANDING AT the window, Louise watched her go. She'd managed to dredge up a measure of control and was now us-ing all her experience to regain her habitual poise. She had done it before and she could do it again: concentration and willpower could force back the sagging wall which had been so painstakingly built against the onslaught of memory. Martin: she would think of Martin, whose infidelity seemed, at this moment, to be hardly more than a counter-irritant to other, more terrible possibilities. Martin . . .

She willed herself to contemplate the situation; deliber-ately conjuring up reactions: humiliation, jealousy, misery. The difficulty was that, at present, Martin seemed so far away. An unreality persisted, an indifference which, she knew, would vanish as soon as she saw him again. These holidays, the sanctuary of Foxhole, had always had the power to isolate her from her ordinary, daily life. Here she was apart, out of time. They exchanged postcards almost im-mediately, on arrival at their destinations, and each accepted that this should be the extent of their communication until the very end of the holiday when another exchange took place. She hadn't yet received the first postcard—there was no telephone in the cottage—and, quite suddenly, it oc-curred to her that he might not be with the others at all. Per-haps this time he was with the woman who had been the cause of his new, inexplicable joyfulness.

The shock of this thought had the desired effect and she found that she was considering the idea very seriously. Of course, she had the number of his mobile telephone but that meant he might be anywhere. For the first time she had not been given the names of the hotels—they usually managed two separate golf courses within their fortnight—nor any telephone numbers except for Martin's mobile. Much more sensible, he'd assured her, since she could contact him anywhere and at any time. If it were switched off, she must simply leave a message.

"Of course," she remembered the wink, *"I switch it off when I'm in . . . meetings."*

She thought: I am a gullible fool.

The knock upon the door caused her to jump, her heart thudding suddenly in her side.

"Oh, for God's sake," she said irritably, taking refuge in anger. "Pull yourself together!"

She went out into the hall and wrenched open the door. Frummie beamed at her.

"We're having a little drink," she said. "It's such a lovely evening and quite warm enough to be outside, so we thought: Why not? And we wondered if you'd like to join us. You haven't met Margot, have you? She's a very old friend. Such a dear old friend that we thought we might need you as a referee later on."

Her wicked old face was so lively, so bright with fun, that Louise smiled too.

"I'd like that very much," she said. "Can I bring something to contribute?"

"Certainly not. Margot always brings enough booze to render a regiment of paratroopers insensible. She's never forgotten the horror stories she heard about prohibition when she was a susceptible child. It's quite terrible the effect it had on her young mind. We've got some supper on the go, so no need to worry about that either."

"That's really kind." Louise's relief was genuine. "Thanks. I'll fetch a shawl and be right over."

CHAPTER 8

The moment Jenny stepped from her car, pausing to stare across at the house, Brigid knew that her fears were all realised. Watching from the sitting-room window, she was consumed with a terror which curdled her gut and caused her to tremble. Fear was present in Jenny's posture, in the nervousness of her hands and, when Brigid met her at the door, she saw that it was carved into the lines of her face. Compassion held her own emotions at bay and she put out her arms and hugged her old friend warmly.

"Oh, Brigid." Jenny was shivering like a sick dog. "God, it's good to see you."

Brigid held her very tightly for a moment longer. "Come on into the kitchen," she said. "We need some coffee."

Jenny went straight to the Aga. She took hold of the rail and pressed herself against the range as if she were drawing the heat from it into her rigid body. Brigid lifted the lid and slid the kettle on to the hotplate. Try as she would she could think of nothing to say that was not trite and, looking at Jenny's worn face, it seemed insulting to offer banalities. Her old friend was born to be a round, jolly, comforting person but she'd lost a great deal of weight, which didn't suit her, and her hair was dry and lifeless.

As she made the coffee Brigid was struck by the odd perception she had of time. It ticked slowly by, second by second, regular as . . . well, clockwork, yet this never seemed to apply whilst you were actually living it. Whole chunks of life seemed to vanish in moments whilst others dragged for aeons. It was surely only a matter of months since she and Jenny were young mothers with small children, following Peter and Humphrey around the naval ports of the country. New quarters, playschools, picnics on the beach, childish illnesses, weekend expeditions when Humphrey and Peter were at sea, the first of the children—Jenny's Alan—starting school . . . Life had been settled in the quiet round of children's lives, despite the upheavals. She and Jenny had spent a lifetime—or so it seemed—walking: behind pushchairs, with toddlers on reins, with dogs and children in woods . . .

"How we walked," she said suddenly. "Do you remember? Miles and miles. It's a wonder that our children weren't muscle-bound. Looking back, it's as if it lasted for ever, those times when the children were small, yet it passed so quickly. Five years? Seven? Out of nearly thirty years of marriage."

Jenny didn't answer and when she glanced at her, Brigid saw that there were tears in her eyes.

"We didn't know when we were well off," she muttered.

"Possibly." Brigid tried for a lighter note, anxious to comfort her a little. "But there were pretty desperate moments. I was just remembering when Alan started school and you were terrified that no one would play with him. You insisted on hanging about opposite the playground, trying not to be seen, just in case he was crying."

"I wore a floppy sunhat so as not to be recognised," Jenny didn't know whether she was laughing or crying, "but you wouldn't let me wait."

"I always was a bossy cow," said Brigid cheerfully. " . . . some coffee."

Almost reluctantly, Jenny left her position by the Aga and came to the table. She took her mug, refused sugar, sat in tense silence whilst the clock ticked loudly.

Brigid thought: These few minutes since she entered the house have seemed like hours.

"Shit!" Jenny said suddenly, explosively. "This is so

bloody stupid. Sorry, Brigid. Apart from anything else it's the humiliation of it all. Having to admit, to tell you . . . Bryn's left me."

"What?" To her lasting shame Brigid knew a tiny stab of relief amongst the surge of shock and horror for Jenny. "But why? When?"

"About a month ago."

"But why didn't you telephone? Oh, Jenny, this is awful. I thought things were going so well."

"I thought so too. Me and Iain, both. Bryn was handling all the business side. Money was coming in, lots of bookings. I was concentrating on the catering. Iain had a couple of young assistants helping him to begin with and then a girl joined last summer. They were taking a year out before going off to university. Well, the boys were. Joanna was having a gap year before starting some kind of work as a physical instructor or something . . ."

A long pause. Blot rose from a puddle of sunshine on the slate floor and came to sit beside Jenny. She bent to stroke him, taking refuge, briefly, in this distraction.

"And Bryn went off with Joanna?" Brigid hoped it might be easier for Jenny if she spoke the words for her.

Jenny raised her eyes. "She's twenty-two," she said bleakly. *"Twenty-two.* Bryn's forty. He's younger than me."

Bitterness, misery, a sense of failure—the words were weighty with these reactions and Brigid was unable to think of any suitable reply. Nothing, given the circumstances, was adequate.

"That's not all." Jenny sat up, suddenly making up her mind to what had to be said. "He'd been planning it, you see. He'd been salting money away, taking it out of the business. Iain and I had no idea, of course. They just disappeared one day. He was going off for some meeting, hoping to raise new interest with a possible investor, so we didn't realise for a few days. Joanna phoned in to say that she had some bug and then I had this postcard. It was posted in Portugal and just had 'Sorry' scribbled on it . . ." She swallowed. A shorter silence. "Then the letters had to be opened. The rent to the boatyard hadn't been paid for three months, the creditors were waiting too. When I spoke to the Bank they told me that the loan hadn't been paid for several months and now they're going to foreclose."

The terror was back, churning in Brigid's stomach, anxious thoughts flapping like bats in her mind.

"So . . . so what does that mean exactly?"

"The trouble is, I don't quite know." Jenny stared at her, something akin to anguish masked on her face. "They take everything first, you see. There's a hierarchy of creditors. The staff are most important—well, there's not too much to worry about there—then the Inland Revenue and the VAT people, then the Bank and the unsecured creditors. As far as you're concerned, it depends if there's anything left when it comes to the Bank's turn."

"And . . . is that a possibility?" Brigid hated minding when Jenny was so desperate.

"I simply don't know." She sounded wretched. "We put in fifteen thousand and they matched it. Iain and I have talked it over and we think there's bound to be a shortfall."

"Right."

Jenny watched her miserably. "Obviously we shall sell everything we've got. Well, we'll have to . . ."

"Oh, Jenny, whatever will you do? I am so sorry. I still can't quite believe it."

"Join the club," said Jenny grimly. "My mother is out of her mind. She never liked Bryn and now I can see that she thinks she'll have to bail me out. Not that she's got any money, poor old thing, apart from her annuity, but I can tell that she's screwing herself up to the point of offering me a home." She laughed, a high hysterical shriek. "We'd kill each other in a fortnight."

"But how are you actually managing?" asked Brigid anxiously. "Where are you living? You can always come here, you know that."

"Thanks, that's really . . . kind but Iain's got a big caravan, a kind of mobile home near St. Neots. He's told me to use it. It's a bit basic but quite OK. He's living with his brother in

Fowey. At the moment we're still trying to keep the business ticking over. If it's a going concern we might be able to sell it. It's not that it hasn't worked, you see. It's just been milked of all the profits and we've nothing left. Anyway, Iain's decided that if we lose it all he'll get a berth on a boat later in the summer. There's always someone who needs a hand, or some yacht to be delivered, but he doesn't want to commit himself until everything's been sorted."

"But can Bryn just disappear? Can't he be traced? It's . . . it's unbelievable."

"The point is that the creditors aren't prepared to hang about waiting. I think he's been planning for a long time. He took so little with him. Joanna's father lives on the Continent and I wonder if they've gone to him. Obviously, a search has been organised but, from what I can gather, it would be foolish to hold my breath."

"I'm so sorry," Brigid said again, helplessly.

"Well, I feel such a shit dropping you in it like this. It seemed so . . . good. And we were . . . so happy."

"You didn't suspect anything with this Joanna?"

"Gullible, aren't I?" It was very nearly a sneer. "First Peter all those years and now Bryn. The odd thing was, he didn't seem to like her at all. Whenever he spoke about her it was only to say something rude. In fact I was worried that there might be a personality clash. In a tiny setup like ours you have to be careful. Now I see it was a smokescreen. I should have suspected something. Looking back, I see that he talked about her often, her name was often cropping up, but there it was always something derogatory, never anything good. I suppose he needed to talk about her but had to put me off the scent." A pause . . . "I suppose you'll have to tell Humphrey?"

Briefly, Brigid heard Humphrey's voice. *"The trouble is, Jenny's on self-destruct."* Loyalty stirred. "What do Alan and Rebecca say?"

Jenny smiled bitterly. "My children are patronisingly long-suffering. They didn't like Bryn either. Alan said, 'Poor old Ma. One day you'll simply have to grow up.' "

Brigid bit her lip, feeling Jenny's humiliation. "And Rebecca?"

"She said, 'God, your timing is always so great, isn't it?' She's about to have the baby."

Brigid thought about Rebecca; as a baby, sitting on Jenny's lap, Jenny flush-faced, bending over her singing to her, rocking her. Oh, the love! The time invested; the tiny— and the not so tiny—sacrifices. She said hesitantly, "Perhaps you need to be a parent to truly understand."

Jenny shrugged. "It's not a problem. It's you I'm worrying about. I'd never have asked if I thought there'd be the least danger. Of course, I didn't allow for this. Will you tell Humphrey?"

"Not yet. Let's see what happens. It might not be necessary."

"Thanks. That's . . . really good of you. It's just I feel such a heap of shit and I can't bear it all round the Navy."

"I don't think Humphrey would gossip."

"Oh, I know he's not going to think I'm that important," sharply, "but it might just slip out. I don't want Peter to know."

That was the real truth, of course. Marrying Bryn, setting up the school, these things had been the equivalent of two fingers in the air to Peter, a restoration of confidence and self-esteem.

"You haven't drunk your coffee. I'll make some more."

"I can't stay." Jenny looked about for her bag, stood up. "I've got an appointment in Exeter and I ought to get on. It's just that I had to tell you face to face."

"Are you sure you need to go yet? Can't you have some lunch?"

"No. Really. I wish I could . . ."

Brigid followed her out, standing behind her as she paused to look about.

"I always feel so safe here," she said. "I always felt like that about this place, even when I was a kid. You . . . you wouldn't have to sell the cottage, would you?"

"I hope not." Brigid tried to keep her voice even. "It depends."

"It won't be that much. It can't be. Just a few thousand, perhaps."

"Let's wait and see. Look, stay in touch. You know that you're welcome any time you want to come. Don't get desperate."

They embraced and Jenny drove away, grim-faced.

Brigid watched her go. A few thousand—or much more? Supposing the cottage had to be sold?

The telephone was ringing. She ran inside and snatched up the receiver.

"Hello, my love." Humphrey's voice was warm. "Just got a few moments so I thought I'd ring to see how you are. I'm hoping to get home before the weekend for a few extra days, not absolutely definite yet but I thought I'd give you a warning shot across the bows. How're things? Anything exciting happened down there?"

Brigid, staring at Jenny's mug of cold coffee, fought off an overwhelming longing to tell him the whole story. She took a deep breath. "No," she said. "No, absolutely nothing at all."

It was only after she'd replaced the receiver that the full horror of the situation slowly became clear. It wasn't simply the possible financial risk or the threat to the cottage, which were bad enough; it was her deception that was slowly revealing itself as the true danger. The fact that she had said nothing about it to Humphrey, had gone ahead with a scheme of which she'd known he would disapprove: this was at the root of her fear. Humphrey had never been diminished by the knowledge that Brigid owned Foxhole whilst he'd brought no property into their relationship. He wasn't the sort of man whose pride suffered at this particular kind of imbalance. He knew how important the old house was to her, was glad that she could bring up her own children within its secure walls and had seemed utterly indifferent to the fact that the estate belonged to her. Yet he had been very ready to agree to a mortgage on the longhouse, so as to have the cash to renovate the barns, and it was at this point that Brigid felt he'd truly become a joint owner with her. The barns were only viable units because Humphrey was able to pay the mortgage and, as they made plans and the conversions took place, Foxhole gradually changed and grew slowly into a different home; hers and Humphrey's and their children's home. Only the cottages remained as her sole property and, in entering into the agreement with Jenny, she had behaved with a secrecy which, until now, had never been allowed to be a part of their marriage.

Because of their particular backgrounds, they had each required a sense of absolute security before they could really trust the other and now, as she washed up the mugs, Brigid felt a very real fear as she wondered how Humphrey would react to her deception. How could she begin to tell him, to explain the risk she had taken—and for Jenny, of all people? It had always been a sadness to her that her closest friend and Humphrey had never been able to find any common ground on which to build a friendship. Humphrey found her scattiness, her impulsiveness and her refusal to think things through, utterly irritating; Jenny found his calm good sense, his steadiness and his refusal to be bounced into sudden impulses utterly boring. Standing between them, Brigid had tried to reconcile one to the other. To Humphrey: "She was such a comfort to me when I went to school. She never teased me about Mummie going off and leaving us and she's terribly loyal." And to Jenny: "You have to remember that his mother died when he was quite young and his father remarried almost immediately. It was a terrible shock to Humphrey. He adored his mother and he couldn't adjust to his father's heartlessness. She wasn't a very strong woman and Humphrey had a very quiet upbringing. His father more or less abandoned him for this Swedish woman and he had to cope with things all on his own."

So she'd tried to weave a friendship, based on their individual love and affection for her, appealing to their generosity, and, because they *did* love her, Jenny and Humphrey tried their best. They'd achieved a tolerant, bantering affection which could break down and descend very quickly into irritation so that Brigid was never relaxed when they were all three together. Thinking of these things, she wondered how she could have been crazy enough to agree to Jenny's plan in the first place.

As she made herself a sandwich, Brigid remembered that the proposal had come at a time when Humphrey was at his least sympathetic; he didn't like Bryn and had felt that Jenny was making a mistake in marrying him. His allegiance had always been to Peter during those early years and, with Jenny trying to build a new life, Brigid had been in one of her "solidarity with Jenny" phases which he resented. Occasionally their failure to get on had edged into a more general battle of wills, when personalities merged into the old gender war.

"Bloody men," Jenny would say. "Who needs them?"

"If only women were more honest about what they want," Humphrey would mutter. "Talk about devious! Men don't have a chance!"

It was at this time that Brigid had been told about Peter's long-standing involvement with a Wren and her loyalty to Jenny was at its height. When Jenny had arrived, full of enthusiasm, happy, an exciting future before her, it had been impossible not to agree to what had seemed such a foolproof plan.

Eating her sandwich with a distinct lack of enthusiasm, Brigid could guess just how hurt Humphrey would be—hurt and angry—and now he was coming home unexpectedly. How would she manage to behave normally? What might follow? The tiny, never-to-be-voiced doubt echoed warningly, disabling happiness, weakening confidence, making her shiver. Swallowing with difficulty, her gut knotting with anxiety, she shunted the rest of her lunch into Blot's bowl and watched him chomp it enthusiastically. She was tempted to take him off for a long walk—her usual practice in moments of stress or fear—but there was work to be done and she resisted his hopeful look and wagging tail. Putting her plate into the sink, passing through the two long rooms, she climbed the stairs to her workroom, Blot trailing disappointedly in her wake.

CHAPTER 9

"I'm so pleased that it's a fine evening," said Jemima contentedly. "I do so like to show off my view and it's not quite the same with rain streaming down the windows."

"It's terrific." Leaning on the balcony, Louise was unable to hide her envy. "I'd never go to bed at all if I were you. I'd sleep on the sofa."

"I mean to." Jemima looked almost guilty, as if she had been caught out in some misdemeanour, "but I can never quite resist my bed. The sofa's not nearly so comfortable and I need my sleep."

"This would be the perfect place for an insomniac. It must be very pretty on summer nights when it's really dark, with all the riding lights on the boats and the windows lit up in those houses on the shore opposite."

"That's East Portlemouth." Jemima curled up in one of the wicker chairs. "I have a complex of cottages over there which I look after, a courtyard development, but it's a devil to get to it. Miles round by road, of course. I go over on the ferry and keep a moped at the little café. It's a great way for getting round the lanes. So how is the holiday going?"

"Great." Louise continued to gaze out over the harbour, watching the reflections. "I'm doing a lot of walking and, fortunately, the weather's being very kind."

"You're like Brigid. She loves walking. Perhaps that's why she stays so thin." Jemima sighed enviously. "She's so elegant, isn't she? And so attractive. Cheekbones like razors and legs yards long. I wish I were tall."

Louise sat down in the other chair and looked at her. "You're not very alike, are you? But you don't seem to do too badly."

Jemima smiled reflectively. "I suppose we all want to be what we aren't, don't we? Brigid's so clear-cut. There's nothing messy about her. She's all clean lines and cool looks."

"Your mother thinks she's too thin."

"Who was it said 'You can never be too rich or too thin'? Anyway, Frummie just likes to be difficult."

"I had noticed." MagnifiCat strolled out on to the balcony and Louise bent to stroke him. He arched his back as he wound about her ankles, purring approvingly. "There does seem to be a certain amount of . . . well, tension."

"Watch out," warned Jemima, as MagnifiCat prepared to launch himself upwards. "He weighs a ton. Sorry," as MagnifiCat landed in Louise's lap and she gasped at his heaviness, "but he's simply a tart. Quite shameless when it comes to seeking attention." She chuckled. "Perhaps I should be careful. Aren't owners supposed to grow to be like their pets?"

"He's extraordinarily beautiful," said Louise lightly, stroking him. "You certainly have that in common."

Jemima flushed brightly, muttered something unintelligible and returned quickly to the subject of her family. "Frummie's not too well since her stroke, and it can't be very easy for Brigid sometimes. It's a very unfortunate situation. At the time, when she was left on her own, I couldn't afford much in the way of accommodation and Frummie wanted to get right out of London pretty quickly. It was all a bit tricky. The problem is that she's not too easy to live with and she does like space to herself, which is reasonable enough, but it was really good of Brigid and Humphrey to let her have one of their cottages and I wish she could be a tad more graceful about it. It's not easy, though, is it, being someone's pensioner?"

Louise buried her face in MagnifiCat's fur. "Blessed are the peacemakers," she murmured, muffled.

"Sorry?" Jemima edged forward on her chair, picking up her mug.

"Nothing. I was being biblical. MagnifiCat's fault. Yes, I'd love some more coffee and then I ought to be going, I suppose."

"You'll have to." Jemima grinned mischievously. "I've got another visitor, after you."

"Oh?" Louise looked at her, eyebrows raised, MagnifiCat forgotten. "Have you indeed?"

"I have. It's not often I get a sleepover, I can tell you. His wife doesn't like it."

"Wife?"

Louise's tone was sharper, edgy, and it was Jemima's turn to raise her eyebrows. "I think they're on the verge of splitting up. He doesn't say much but I think he might leave her."

"For you?"

"Oh, no." Jemima shook her head. "No, he knows I'm purely mistress material. I don't do the live-in bit. I tried it once but it was hell. It was so suffocating and we never seemed to be on the same wavelength at the same time. I just can't seem to relax with someone else around." She paused. "You look rather shocked."

"It's not that," Louise said quickly. "It's none of my business. It's just you saying that about his wife. It sounded a bit heartless."

Jemima continued to perch on the edge of her chair. "I suppose it is a bit." She sounded defensive. "I like him a lot and he's not particularly happy at home." She shrugged. "If it wasn't me it would be someone else. I don't make demands or stir up trouble. Like I said, I don't want to take her place. We just have fun together."

Louise, her eyes fixed on Jemima's face, was seeing instead Martin's glossy expression of satisfaction, of excitement. She felt a sudden longing to confide; to share her suspicions. To begin with she'd wondered if it might be possible to open her heart to Brigid but it was clear that Brigid had a private worry of her own. She was preoccupied, distracted, and Louise hesitated to burden her. She closed her eyes for a moment, feeling confused, even frightened, and when she opened them again she saw that Jemima was frowning anxiously.

"Are you OK?" she asked.

"Sorry," said Louise at last. "Sorry, Jemima. It's just . . ." The words came at last and she seemed powerless to prevent them. "I think Martin is having an affair and it sounded so odd—hearing it from the other side, as it were."

"Oh hell," said Jemima softly. "I had no idea. Well, obviously. How would I? Look, this is probably quite different. Could you just be feeling a bit . . . well . . .?"

"Neurotic about it?" She remembered the man on the train—"*these suspicious wives . . .*" and grimaced. "Anything's possible, I suppose." She pulled herself together, smiling at Jemima, who sat miserably, her mug swinging from a finger. "You're right. I'm probably imagining things." An uneasy pause. "Tell me," she said slowly, "how do you make contact? Without his wife suspecting, I mean."

"Oh, that's simple. We text each other messages on our mobiles." Jemima still looked unhappy. "Honestly, Louise—"

"I know." Louise touched her lightly on the knee. "I'm being stupid. But I think perhaps I ought to be on my way, after all."

When she'd gone, Jemima stood on the balcony unaware, for once, of the prospect before her. Louise was right to go; the atmosphere had been spoiled, harmony jangled, intimacy destroyed. Her own pleasure at the thought of the night ahead was tinged with guilt, even shame. Supposing this was Louise's husband, about to arrive, how would she feel about him then? Would it still be simply a few hours of stolen fun? It was easy to ignore the unknown, faceless wife whilst she remained out of the frame, but supposing she were Louise; a woman she knew and liked? A dinghy pulled away from the slip, its outboard puttering, shivering the inky water in its wake into choppy wavelets. A door opened, spilling light out on to the street: a burst of laughter, then silence.

Two quick rings on the doorbell. Jemima hesitated, still holding on to the rail, and then went to open the door.

• • •

"I DON'T think that was in the book," said Margot as Frummie rewound the video. "Not the stripping off and plunging into the lake bit."

"Who's complaining?" asked Frummie. "If Jane Austen had thought of it I bet she'd have written it in. She just never thought of it, that's all."

"I don't know about that," argued Margot. "I'm rather against directors messing about with the text."

"I'd no idea you were such an expert on television productions, dear," said Frummie acidly. "Does it matter? Jane Austen's books are all about sex and money, the director's certainly picked that up. Anyway, if she'd seen Colin Firth I bet she'd have written the scene in specially for him."

"I enjoyed it very much," conceded Margot hastily, lest Frummie should get into a huff and withhold future viewing; even as a girl she'd been very tetchy if crossed. "I saw it on the television, of course, but I think I'll have to ask Harry to get me one of these video recorders. Is that it for this evening?"

"I think that's enough for one session." Frummie was enjoying her position of power. "Time for a nightcap."

Margot brightened. "Splendid idea." She got up with a grimace of pain and pottered stiffly along beside the bookshelf where Frummie kept her video library. "*What* a selection you've got. I've never seen half these."

"Pity you're not staying a little longer," observed Frummie carelessly. She was surprised at how much she was enjoying having her old friend—not to mention her supply of whisky—with her. "We could work through them."

Margot, bending sideways so as to read the titles, tried not to look too keen. "It would be rather fun, wouldn't it?" she murmured casually. "Oh, you've got *I, Claudius*. Now that was quite brilliant."

"A week's viewing all on its own," said Frummie absently, admiring her glass of amber liquid. "Well, it's up to you, of course . . ."

"I wonder if I might get away in the autumn for a few weeks?" Margot sounded doubtful.

Frummie's lip curled. "Don't bust a gut, dear," she advised with some asperity. "I'm sure your social diary's positively bursting at the seams and I doubt Barbara could spare you."

Margot hobbled back to the sofa and sat down gratefully. She took her glass and sipped thoughtfully, her eyes roaming about the room. It would be cosy here in the autumn with the wood-burner alight, a video at the ready and a good supply of alcohol. If she thought she might be free of her mother-in-law for a few weeks, there was little doubt that dear Barbara would be lavish with a few necessities to encourage the visit; anyway, darling Harry would see to that side of things.

"We could have some fun, couldn't we?" she asked suddenly. "I'd kick in with the housekeeping, of course, and Harry would be generous with the booze."

"Dear old boy," exclaimed Frummie, with unusual warmth. "Even as a child at prep school he had a ready grasp on the essentials of life. Do you remember his swapping his new geometry set for a term's supply of Mars bars? What acuity in so young a child! And starting up a still at Gordonstoun? What initiative! I remember him inviting me to lunch in his rooms at Oxford and we were still at it at five o'clock. What a time we had! No wonder he's done so well for himself."

"He's delighted to be in the Cabinet," agreed Margot complacently.

"He should be Prime Minister," declared Frummie generously, reaching almost absent-mindedly for the decanter. "At the very least. That's what we lack these days: leaders with vision and the courage to implement their ideas. Another drop?"

"Just a dribble. Thanks. Perhaps we should look at our diaries, Fred?"

"Perhaps we should. In the morning. We'll get something planned. What fun. Here's to a little autumn jollity."

They touched glasses, giggling a little.

"I'll drink to that," said Margot.

• • •

IT WAS raining when Brigid set off to fetch Humphrey from the station at Totnes. Soft, drifting cloud rolled in from the west, obliterating the craggy tors, filling the valleys, hanging like smoke above the river. Moisture clung, gossamer-like, to the weighty swags of hawthorn blossom and shimmered in tiny droplets on the short turf. The road gleamed black, winding across the moor, vanishing into the mist as it climbed towards Combestone Tor. On the verges bedraggled sheep grazed indifferently and, in Hangman's Pit, several heavy-headed ponies stood, blinking thoughtfully, huddled together in chill, clammy contemplation.

Brigid drove carefully but her thoughts had already hurried ahead to the meeting with Humphrey. With anxious fingers she pushed back her fine, fair hair, catching it behind her ears, frowning as she hunched into her fleece, feeling for the heater knob and turning it full on. She knew that, if she could behave quite easily and naturally with him, he would suspect nothing. Why should he? Humphrey was not devious; he was straightforward, open, cheerful. He could be impatient with anything which he considered affected and he was not impressed with flights of fancy or high drama. Kind, practical and down-to-earth, he could be uncomfortably outspoken and occasionally intolerant. Jenny was one of the few people who had always seemed to catch him on the raw but, even as she approached the station and pulled in, Brigid was still wondering if she might, cautiously and tactfully, be able to engender some sympathy for her old friend.

The minute she saw him, she knew that it was quite impossible. Strange that, even after all these years of separations and reunions, there should still be this shock of recognition as the solid, living reality of Humphrey collided with the private world she inhabited in his absence. He flung his grip on to the back seat, climbed quickly in beside her and leaned across to kiss her. The bustle of traffic, passengers hurrying to meet friends, a dog leaping in front of the car— all these things kept her busy; excellent reasons for being a little preoccupied, helping her over the first awkward moments. Frummie, Louise, the Navy and Blot carried her several more miles until at last she knew that he'd turned a little in his seat and was watching her. Instinctively she made as if to look out of her side window so that her straight hair flew forward, screening her face a little. The silence lengthened. At last she glanced at him, fearing in her guilt that he might have already guessed something was wrong, and surprised a puzzled, almost anxious expression on his face.

"Are you all right?" she asked quite involuntarily—and it was he who looked away with a quick reassurance and began to talk about trivial matters, as if to prevent further questions.

CHAPTER 10

Louise sat in her bedroom before the looking-glass, twisting her long dark hair into a rope, pinning it into a knot. As she plunged the long horseshoe-shaped pins into the curling mass of hair she stared critically at her face with its small, square chin and short straight nose. Her skin had lost its city pallor and had gained a rosy flush from the sun and wind; her eyes were only a little darker than the cinnamon-coloured silk shirt she wore over a black T-shirt. She'd decided on black velvet slacks, hoping that she'd struck the right smart but casual note, and wound a long silk scarf round her neck.

"Don't go all London on me," Brigid had begged. "Remember that I haven't been further east than Exeter for years."

"With your height and figure you'd look terrific in a sugar sack," she'd replied. "Are you absolutely sure that you want me to come to supper with Humphrey only home for a few days?"

"Quite certain." Brigid was looking rather strained. "He's asked me to ask you specially. You know he loves to see you and, anyway, we're hardly newlyweds. Mummie's coming too. Margot left this morning and she's feeling a bit flat. Humphrey was hoping to barbecue but it's turned too cold. See you about eight."

Louise glanced at her watch. Five to eight. She leaned on

her elbows, frowning a little. A card, posted the day before, had finally arrived from Martin: a cheerful, uninformative scrawl. It was the usual kind of postcard and message she received from him on these occasions but its lateness alerted her. Her senses were working overtime now, and she was thinking of reasons for its delay. She'd very nearly convinced herself that the card had been written in advance and posted by one of Martin's cronies. Perhaps he'd forgotten it—or perhaps he was waiting for Martin to arrive safely at his own destination. Embarrassing if he should have an accident miles away from the place in which he'd supposedly arrived quite safely.

"Oh, for heaven's sake!" She stood up abruptly, disgusted with her suspicions, slightly shocked at how devious her thoughts had become. Pushing her feet into black suede loafers, picking up a black shawl splashed with gold and scarlet flowers, she let herself out into a swirling mist. The lights from the longhouse shone out into the courtyard and she hurried towards them, passing into the hall with a call of greeting. Humphrey came out of the kitchen to meet her and hugged her warmly. He was a big man, strongly built, with a short, black beard, and, each time she saw him, she pictured him in some firelit medieval hall, eating ravenously and flinging the bones to large, lean wolfhounds who rose out of the shadows behind him.

"You're looking wonderful," he said, holding her at arms' length. "Nearly as good as Brigid's supper. Come on in and have a drink."

She followed him into the kitchen, smiled at Brigid and stooped to pat Blot and fondle his long, soft ears.

"I haven't brought anything," she said repentantly. "I was hoping to drive into Ashburton to buy some special chocolates but the mist was so thick I lost my nerve."

"Don't give it a thought." Brigid, busy at the Aga, shook her head, dismissing such a notion. "Have some wine and sit down. Don't give Blot any more Pringles, Humphrey, or he'll slobber on Louise."

"You wouldn't do that, would you, old chap?" Humphrey

passed Louise her glass and paused to fill Brigid's to the top. "Drink up, love," he said, "but don't stop the good work."

"I was telling him about Oscar," said Brigid, frying small pieces of bacon, "and how you had to come and get the key."

Louise sat down at the table, keeping Blot beside her. Good manners fought with a desperate desire to change the subject but she could think of nothing to say.

"So what did you think of our Thea?" asked Humphrey. "One of the nicer sorts of nutter, I think. Don't you?"

Louise smiled politely, vaguely, while Brigid said, "Honestly, darling, you are so rude," and Humphrey topped up his own glass.

"Quite potty," he insisted. "But fun. We were all dumbfounded when George married her. He was having an affair with another woman, you know, and then, all of a sudden, he ups and marries Thea."

"Really?" murmured Louise, busy with Blot.

"Poor Felicity," said Brigid, suddenly serious. "How awful all that was. Still, Thea's made George very happy."

"Felicity was terrifying," said Humphrey cheerfully. "An absolute harpy. Thea may be potty but she's terribly sweet with it. The little girls are delightful but Hermione particularly is just like her. I hear that you met Hermione too. She's a sweetie, isn't she?"

"That smells wonderful, Brigid," said Louise desperately. "I'm absolutely starving."

"Oh, good." Brigid transferred the pieces of crispy bacon on to plates containing slices of avocado sprinkled with tiny spinach leaves. "Do you think you could get Mummie, Humphrey? She's probably forgotten the time . . . Ah," as they heard a yodelling in the hall, "that's probably her."

"Good evening, everyone. Oh, good. I'm so glad you didn't wait for me, Brigid. Sorry I'm late."

"That'll do," said Humphrey good-naturedly, accepting her kiss, whilst Brigid floundered between excuse and apology. "No needling the cook or you'll be out on your ear."

She grinned at him wickedly. "Did you finish the crossword this morning?"

"Naturally. Bet you didn't get the 'Soviet privileged class' clue." .

She made a face like a naughty child and he roared with laughter, pulling out a chair for her, pouring some wine, whilst she quizzed him on the other clues. Louise, gasping with relief, gave Blot a final pat and sat up straight. As Brigid put a plate before her, she saw that the thin hand was trembling slightly and she glanced up at her quickly. The huge, violet eyes were darkly shadowed, the thin lips compressed. For a moment Louise forgot her own problems and touched the older woman lightly on the arm.

"That looks good," she said warmly. Brigid smiled quickly, almost nervously, and Louise felt a huge surge of affection for her. "Your sugar sack looks pretty good too."

Brigid's face relaxed and she chuckled, looking down at her linen overshirt and narrow moleskin jeans. "I really must do something about clothes. Perhaps we could go to Exeter and have a session. But you wouldn't want to waste time in a city, not when you're on your hols."

"I should love it," answered Louise firmly.

Humphrey gave a great shout of laughter, which almost drowned Frummie's malicious cackle, and Brigid rolled her eyes with humorous despair as she turned away to give Frummie her plate.

"Thank you, darling," she said sweetly. "What a clever child it is. *So* delicious. I've invited Margot to stay for a few weeks in the autumn and then I'll do a return match."

"But I shan't be here in the autumn," complained Humphrey. "I shall be stuck in the Bahamas."

"My heart bleeds for you," said Brigid sarcastically. "How you'll miss the rain and the storms. All that sea and sunshine. However will you manage?"

"With great difficulty," said Humphrey comfortably, "but I'll be home for Christmas."

Brigid thought: What a Christmas, if I have to tell him we owe thousands of pounds!

She sat down and stared at her plate, reached for her glass, caught Humphrey's eye. He raised his glass to her and she saw again that compassionate, anxious look. Was it possible—her gut twisted at the thought—that he'd heard some rumour about Jenny's disaster and, not knowing how she herself was implicated, was feeling sympathetic? She grinned at him, swallowing down fear, raising her glass in return.

"So what is it, exactly," asked Louise, picking up her fork, "that you'll be doing in the Bahamas?"

LATER, WHEN their guests had gone and they were washing up together, Brigid gathered up her courage.

"Is everything OK, darling?" she asked.

Humphrey turned from the sink and dried his hands on the towel.

"Oh, love," he said, "no, it isn't. I've been wondering how to break the news. I've had a letter from my father. You remember Agneta died last year? Well, he's coming back to England and he's asked if we can put him up for a few months. I simply didn't know how to tell you."

"NIGHTCAP?" ASKED Frummie invitingly, pausing by the gate. "Just a quick one?"

A cool breeze had sprung up, tweaking at the mist so that stars could be seen in the darkening sky, and carrying with it the music of the river, faint but insistent in the valley below. Frummie gave a tiny squawk as a bat swooped over her head and as Louise caught at her arm they both staggered, a little off balance. Humphrey had been very generous with the wine.

"That would be lovely." She was aware of Frummie's loneliness, her sense of isolation in these wild, empty spaces of the moor, and felt a tremor of empathy. Tonight, she had no desire to be alone either.

The living room was warm, mysterious; the scarlet flames flickering behind the glass door of the wood-burner sent long shadows dancing up the walls and gleamed on polished wood. Frummie switched on a lamp and the room settled abruptly into normality; no ghosts here. Louise sat down, still clasping her shawl about her, and, without thinking or asking permission, opened the door of the stove.

"Put a log on," Frummie advised. "Stir it up a bit."

"I love open fires," said Louise dreamily. "We don't have one in London. Martin says it's too much mess and it never seems worth it when I'm here. It's just too early or too late. It seems luxurious to light a fire in May."

"Oh, I can't be doing with all that nonsense." Frummie gave her a well-filled glass and sat opposite. "If it's cold, it's cold. Doesn't matter whether it's January or July. It's bone-chilling up here, dank and damp and miserable. You need fires to keep the houses habitable."

"You don't really like Dartmoor, do you?" asked Louise lightly.

Frummie leaned her head back against a cushion and crossed her pointed, bony knees.

"I hate the country," she said. "Hate it, simply."

Louise remained silent. To sympathise further might sound like inquisitiveness, so she sat, surprised by an unfamiliar sensation of peace. Frummie seemed quite content to let the silence continue and they stayed like this for a while, sipping occasionally, relaxing, watching the flames. Without looking at her, Louise was aware of an odd companionship with the older woman, a natural ease and comfort, which seemed to flow from some distant point in time past where women grouped together, working, sharing, supporting: laughter and tears, joys and tragedies, all these would have been contained, worked through, borne communally. Such problems as hers would have been understood; she would have received advice, comfort, nourishment . . .

Her head jerked and her eyes flew open. She'd been nearly asleep, lulled by the warmth without and within. Frummie remained quite still, lying almost horizontally in her chair, her glass—now half empty—supported on her chest; her eyes glinted, a liquid blue gleam in the firelight.

"Frummie." Louise still felt sleepy, her voice was slow and heavy. "How can you tell if someone's having an affair?"

Frummie displayed no undue surprise at this question. Her eyes swivelled towards her guest and the corners of her mouth turned down in its characteristic smile.

"You mean if your *husband*'s having an affair," she amended drily.

Louise frowned thoughtfully. She'd drunk a great deal of her whisky and she wasn't used to it. "No," she said, quite kindly. "No, I don't mean that. I'm not married to Martin."

"Not?" With an effort Frummie dragged herself into a less supine position. "*Not* married to him? But you said you married him because you were dreary, respectable and middle class."

Louise looked at her with undisguised admiration. "Fancy you remembering that."

"I'm not senile yet," she answered with a great deal of dignity. "So you're not married?"

Louise thought about it. "Not to Martin," she answered at last.

"Well!" Frummie raised her eyebrows—and her glass. "Here's looking at you, kid. So . . ." She seemed to lose her grip on the subject for a moment. "What was the question?"

"I think Martin's having an affair but I'm not sure."

Frummie frowned, concentrating. "What's made you suspicious?"

"He's all bright and shiny. Nothing gets him down. He's . . . he's ebullient." She said the word with care.

"Presents?" asked Frummie immediately—but Louise shook her head.

"Not presents. But he's very . . . solicitous." She was surprised at how many sibilants the word contained and she repeated it quietly to herself.

"Ah." Frummie looked like a knowing old bird, head on one side, eyes bright, nose sharp. "Does he mention anyone in particular?"

"No. At least, not like you mean. There's a woman in marketing but she drives him mad. He goes on about how inefficient and bossy she is. And she's a dyed blonde. Martin hates that."

Exhausted by such an effort, Louise rested her head against the back of the chair, her eyes closing.

"It'll be her." Frummie sounded quite confident.

Louise forced her eyes open. "No. He can't stand her. I told you."

"You'll see." Frummie sounded almost triumphant, pleased by such a ready solution to the problem. "You look tired, child. Bed-time?"

"But I'm so comfortable." Louise found that Frummie was standing beside her chair and she caught her hand with sudden desperation. "I don't want to be on my own."

"Oh, my dear," Frummie sounded infinitely sad, "which of us does? Margot's bed's still made up. Could you cope with her sheets?"

"Yes," said Louise, thankfully. "Oh yes, please."

She stumbled behind Frummie into the bedroom and, kicking off her shoes, collapsed into the bed.

Frummie pulled the quilt over her and stood for a moment, staring down at her.

"You have to have a strong head for malt whisky," she murmured kindly. "*Not* married. Well, well, well."

She wandered unsteadily from the room, visited the bathroom, sat for a moment on the side of her bed. The moon peered, not quite full, staring in at the window. She stared back belligerently, rocking a little.

"Bugger off!" she said distinctly and, turning her back, she pulled her blanket over her head and fell into instant slumber.

CHAPTER 11

"I've never even met him," said Brigid wretchedly, for the third or fourth time. Sleep seemed out of the question and, although they were now upstairs, she was sitting cross-legged on the bed whilst Humphrey lay stretched out, ankles crossed, his arms folded behind his head. "I know you've told me things but, let's face it, your stories about him have hardly endeared him to me."

Humphrey was silent. It would be specious, at this late stage, to attempt to gloss over the negative aspects of his father's character; nor would Brigid be taken in by such an attempt. He thought of one or two remarks but realised that each of them was open to criticism. The obvious retort was "It's OK for you. You'll be in the Bahamas." He could point out that they'd already taken her mother in for the rest of her life, whilst his father only asked for a few months' sanctuary, but he was waiting for Brigid to think of that one for herself. Meanwhile, Humphrey remained carefully silent.

Brigid looked at him. "And what about our autumn visitors? Do I tell them they can't come?"

"I was wondering," said Humphrey, his eyes fixed on the ceiling, "whether he could use the stable wing. If either of the boys comes home they'll have to muck in together."

"You're joking?" Brigid's voice was laced with panic. "I don't want him in the house with me. He'd have to use the kitchen, you know that. That's why we had to give Mummie the cottage. The wing isn't self-contained."

"That wasn't the only reason," said Humphrey gently, "was it? The thing is that Frummie is a . . . long-term proposition. Father's asking for three months with us before he moves into his other place."

Brigid thought: Three months with *me*. With *me*, not with you. You won't be here!

She drew up her knees, her long arms locked around them, and rocked herself, resting her head on her knees.

"I know what you're thinking," she said, her voice muffled. "You're thinking three months isn't much to ask since we've allowed my mother to have the other cottage with no strings attached. I know all that. It's simply that I don't know your father and . . . you won't be here."

Humphrey uncrossed his legs and pressed one of them against her thigh. It was a loving gesture, showing a kind of solidarity, an understanding. She wasn't accusing him even if she might be thinking it. Brigid was too fair-minded for that; she was just stating the case.

"It seems he has nowhere else to go," he said after a moment. "Well, he has one or two friends who could fit him in for short bursts but it would mean being shunted about like a parcel. He's a bit old for that sort of thing."

Brigid raised her head. "I'm surprised you should care after the way he behaved to your mother," she said protestingly.

Humphrey shifted a little. "Are you? You shouldn't be."

"Oh, I know all that," she cried. "I know it's the same with me and Mummie. It's just . . . too much." She feared that she might suddenly burst into tears and caught herself back from the edge of such self-indulgence. She longed to tell him about Jenny, to share her fears with him, but was even more afraid of his reaction. "Sorry," she muttered. "It's just a bit of a shock. The thought of having both of them here is . . . slightly overwhelming. But I can't have him with me in the house for three months, Humphrey. I simply can't."

"OK." He sounded quite calm. "That's perfectly reasonable. In that case, it'll have to be the cottage. Have you got any October bookings yet?"

She shook her head. "The Davisons aren't coming this year. He's had a slight stroke and they've cancelled. Louise's down for the middle of September and that's it, at the moment."

"Right. So I'll write and tell him that he can be here from the last week in September. He'll have to find somewhere else for the first two weeks. It seems he needs somewhere from early September until the end of November but I don't think it's too much to ask if he has to stay with one of his friends for a week or so to begin with. We might lose a bit of income for those three months but I expect we can live with that. Thank God he doesn't need a permanent home or my retirement plans would be right up the spout. We can't afford to lose another cottage."

Brigid's stomach contracted with terror. "I suppose we'd manage," she muttered. "You'll have your pension and your gratuity."

"We shall need it," he prophesied cheerfully. "I'm very expensive. Anyway, we want to make up for lost time, don't we? We're going to have lots of fun together."

He was trying to cheer her up, to help her to look beyond the temporary problem of his father, but his words struck her like blows. How could she possibly tell him that there might be no cottage or that the mortgage would have to be substantially increased to deal with Jenny's disaster?

"Of course we are." She struggled to sound convincing.

"Well, then. Come and give us a cuddle."

She crawled up the bed and surrendered herself to his warm embrace.

"I shall miss you," she mumbled—and realised that it was terribly true; that she couldn't bear the thought of six long months without his reassuring bulk and steady cheerfulness. Her arms tightened about him and he held her closely, entwining his legs with hers.

"Home for Christmas," he reminded her, longing to reassure her, angry to have to leave her in such a predicament but wise enough to know that railing at fate was pointless and exhausted one's mental resources. "What shall I bring you back from the Bahamas?"

She laughed, comforted by his presence, momentarily resigned, filled with a kind of desperate carelessness. "A coral necklace," she said. "Beautiful enough to drive all my friends wild with envy."

"Done!" he said—and bent to kiss her.

Towards dawn, Louise woke with a dry mouth and pounding head. She lay for some moments, frowning, until she remembered—somewhat fuzzily—the events of the preceding evening. Stiff with embarrassment she tried to remember exactly how much she had told Frummie, wondered how much the older woman would recall. They'd both had far too much to drink but she suspected that Frummie's capacity for alcohol was much greater than her own and could only trust that she'd have too much tact to mention Louise's indiscretions.

Groaning quietly she sat up, clutching her head, realising that she was still fully dressed. Slipping her feet into her shoes, picking up her shawl as she passed through the living room, she let herself out into the cool, fresh morning. The soft, clean air washed over her like water and the familiar distant sound of the river calmed her troubled spirit. In her own kitchen, she poured a tumbler of orange juice, gulped it back greedily and refilled the glass. Sipping more slowly now, she climbed the stairs and went into the bathroom to switch on the shower. She stripped, dropping her crumpled clothes in a pile, and stood, head bowed, beneath the hot jets of water, letting them stab and prickle on the back of her neck. Gradually, weariness, stiffness, the patina of sticky grubbiness were slowly washed away, gurgling with the water, down the plughole.

Dressed again in clean jeans and a warm, fleecy shirt, she stood at the living-room window, waiting for the kettle to boil and watching the sunrise. Rosy light, streaming from the east, touched the world alive; reaching with long bright fingers into valleys and combes; smoothing rough, stony tors with gold; caressing dark, massed woodland into fiery, leafy filigree. The doves whirled up, their wings dazzlingly white against the pure tender blue of the sky, swooping and wheeling in an aerial dance of delight.

The voice, behind her, seemed to drift in from the hall, plaintive, anxious. *"I've lost Percy, Mummy. Have you seen him anywhere?"*

Louise closed her eyes against the brightness of the doves' wings, against her own hot tears. Tired, confused, she felt quite weak with a sudden onslaught of despair.

"I'm sorry." Her voice shook. "So terribly sorry."

She turned, staring round the empty room, into the deserted hall beyond, and then with trembling hands switched on her radio and made some coffee.

She thought: I'm going mad. What shall I do?

Flight was the only solution: flight into busyness, planning, doing; escape through exhaustion so that there was no time to think about the past. Only it wasn't working any more; her carefully built defence mechanism was crumbling. Why? Why now?

She thought: It's because of Martin. The shock of it has unbalanced me. Concentrate on Martin. It can't be Carol. Frummie's wrong. He can't stand her. It can't be . . . she's so *obvious*. Everything he loathes.

Gradually, by sheer willpower, she drew away again from the abyss of that other, darker fear, and began to make some breakfast. Singing with the radio, talking to herself, she drove back the haunting echoes, back behind the wall which had contained them for so long.

"I KNOW it's early," said Jemima ruthlessly, "but you've got a long way to go. And I have my reputation to think about."

He stared up at her blinkingly, his face creased with puzzled, unwilling irritation. "What time is it?"

"Time you were gone. Coffee's ready."

"Can't you bring it in here?"

"No," she said—and went away.

He dropped back, face down in the pillow, but he was

already mentally alert, considering. He'd broken one of his rules but he couldn't bring himself to regret it and he was wondering how much further he might go. Not just one night—but two. He felt a clutch of self-preservation which he immediately combated with bravado. So what? He was down in the West Country on business for three days—nothing odd about that—and he'd carefully covered his tracks but it was still a great risk. He rolled over, stood up and, dragging his bathrobe round him, wandered out into the passage. The sitting room was swimming in bright watery light and he frowned against it as he tied the towelling belt around his narrow waist. The cat with the outlandish name was sitting in a basket chair staring at him with an inimical gaze.

"I don't like you either, Buster," he muttered. "Why don't you go catch a mouse? Be useful, why not?"

Jemima came in from the balcony and raised her eyebrows. "Not dressed yet? Well, have some coffee now you're here."

He tried to catch her as she passed but she eluded him so naturally that he wondered if she'd even noticed his attempt. He sat down, a slight dissatisfaction tingeing his sense of physical wellbeing.

"You seem to be in a hurry to get rid of me."

Jemima smiled, poured some coffee and realised quite suddenly that she was bored with him. She was possessed by a great need to be alone. It might have been that conversation with Louise which had spoiled her contentment in his company but, whatever it was, the magic was gone. It had coloured that first evening and she'd been edgy when he'd arrived, unable to respond quite so readily. He'd been suspicious, disappointed, and she'd felt guilty enough to agree to a second night, but now she was regretting it. The familiar requirement to be here, in her own place, in solitude, was pressing in and she could hardly bear to sit across the table watching him drink his coffee. She was visited with an urgent desire to snatch his cup from him, propel him out of the door and throw his belongings out after him. It was such a ridiculous notion that she chuckled and then choked on her coffee.

"What's so funny?"

His touchiness amused her even more and she was aware of that upthrust of joy, the reminder of wholeness: she was still free of any emotion which might bind her to him; she remained unaffected by his moods, uninvolved in his needs. He was not her responsibility and he had no power to render her happy or miserable. This being the case, she should leave him alone.

"Nothing, really." She answered his question, smiling at him. "An old joke. Not worth repeating. Do you want anything to eat? It's quite a way down to Truro, so you mustn't hang around or you'll be late for your meeting."

"I was wondering—no, nothing to eat, thanks—whether I might drop in on my way back, tonight."

"Tonight? Not possible." She shook her head, giving him what she hoped was a regretful smile. "Sorry. I'm busy."

"All night?" The light, casual query did not quite hide his annoyance—and something more than that.

"Maybe." She made herself look directly at him. "I thought you didn't do sleepovers?"

"I don't, not usually. You're special."

She thought: Rats! So what do I do now?

"Thanks," she said. "That's . . . nice. But it doesn't change the situation tonight."

He thought: There's something wrong. Is she backing off or playing hard to get? I don't want to lose her but staying two nights has given her a lever. Watch it!

"That's a pity," he said. "I might not be down for a while."

Jemima very nearly shrugged but stopped herself in time and he felt his irritation grow at her lack of response.

"Well, then." He pushed back his chair. "Better get dressed, I suppose."

She made no attempt to follow him, giving him no opportunity for any physical persuasion, and when he came back she was out on the balcony again. The cat gazed at him unblinkingly and he stared at it with dislike.

"All ready?" Jemima was watching him from the doorway and he forced a smile.

"All ready. Thanks for . . . everything."

"It was a pleasure." Was there mockery in her smile? He couldn't tell. "Drive carefully."

"I shall." She was already opening the door and he could only kiss her quickly, his bag knocking uncomfortably between them, before he was out on the stairs alone.

"That was mean of me." She scooped MagnifiCat into her arms and laid her cheek against his fur. "Oh, I know you don't like him but I was a bit of a cow, throwing him out like that. I'm such rubbish at relationships. I get it wrong: feel the right thing at an inappropriate moment, and vice versa, and then get panicky. Oh hell! Let's have some breakfast."

She carried MagnifiCat into the kitchen and dumped him in a chair where he spread comfortably, soft and boneless as an old cushion. Whilst she put bread in the toaster and reached for some of Brigid's home-made marmalade, she continued to wonder why none of her relationships ever quite gelled. So far and no further, seemed to be her motto. She thought of Brigid, her stable relationship with Humphrey and commitment to her children, and sighed sadly.

"It's not for me," she told MagnifiCat. "Anyway, I only get married men. Perhaps they can tell that I'm a natural-born mistress."

She wished that Louise's remarks had not made such an impression on her and wondered if Martin was actually having an affair or if Louise were simply imagining it. Either way, it had certainly affected the last two nights. She glanced at the diary hanging on the wall and her spirits rose: lunch in The Wardroom with Mandy and Ness, who owned the Cove's Quay Gallery.

"I'll bring you back a sardine," she said teasingly to MagnifiCat—and went away to dress.

FRUMMIE WOKE clear-headed and refreshed, and lay for a moment, gazing at the ceiling.

"*Not* married," she murmured. "Extraordinary."

She hopped out of bed, paused on the landing to see that the spare room bed was empty, and pattered downstairs.

"Coffee," she told herself, cheerfully. "Hot, black coffee. Oh, *poor* Louise. She'll be trying to remember exactly what she told me. You need a strong head for malt whisky," and, humming aloud, she switched on the radio for her morning fix of Terry Wogan.

CHAPTER 12

"I'll write to him then," said Humphrey, as they washed up together after breakfast. "If you're really sure. I'm sorry, love, I really am, but I think it's the right thing to do. Which is very easy for me to say when I shall be thousands of miles away."

"It's only difficult," said Brigid slowly, "because of knowing how you feel about him. It's like . . . being disloyal, if you see what I mean."

"I know exactly what you mean," he answered at once. "Don't you think I feel the same way about Frummie? It drives me mad when she comes in here and starts winding you up. I long to smack her hard and sometimes I can barely keep my temper."

"It's the unfairness of it," agreed Brigid. "*She* behaves very badly and *I* feel guilty if I react to it. Just because she's old . . ."

"It's not simply that, though, is it? It's because, when all's said and done, she is your mother and some genetic instinct keeps you tied to her. Even now, something deep inside you still longs for her approval."

Brigid stared at him, shocked. "Is it so obvious?"

Humphrey sighed. "Don't you see that it's because I feel exactly the same about the old man? I was furious with him when he remarried so quickly after Mother died. It was so heartless and it was clear as daylight that he'd been having an affair with Agneta for years. I shall never know if Mother knew. She was so loyal and gentle and devoted, and she was hardly buried before he was off. I know I wasn't a child, I was at Dartmouth, but even so, twenty-one's not very old. He couldn't wait to be shot of me. Yet I still feel I owe him something. It's like you and Frummie. We can't just wash our hands of them the way they washed theirs of us."

"I know." Brigid was saddened by the look on his face. "I wish I'd met your mother. Look, it'll be OK. I doubt he'll want to spend much time with me, anyway."

Humphrey gave a crack of laughter. "Frummie can deal with him," he said, as he dried his hands. "They were made for each other."

Brigid grinned unwillingly. "That would solve all our problems. Where is he actually moving to, when he leaves here?"

"Some village in the north, I think he said. The Scottish Borders. Perhaps he has friends there. Anyway, a nice, long way off. He can take Frummie with him and leave us in peace. Now, let's forget both of them and decide what we'll do today. Shall we go off somewhere and have lunch? Torcross? Dartmouth? Exeter?"

"Oh, yes," she said at once, hanging the damp cloth over the Aga rail. "Let's go off on our own for the day. I don't really mind where as long as we're together."

He smiled, reaching out for her, hugging her. "We'll take it as it comes. Let's head for the coast and see what happens. Blot can come along and we'll give him a walk at Start Point. It should be wonderful up on the cliffs today. How about that?"

"Great," she said, holding him tightly for a moment, refusing to think about anything but the few hours ahead. "Let's get organised and creep away before anyone sees us."

FRUMMIE WATCHED them go. Unlike Brigid she took no great pleasure in her own company and viewed the day ahead with a lowering of spirits. Anyway, she was missing Margot. What fun it had been, remembering times past, gossiping, shredding their mutual friends' reputations to pieces. Returning to her breakfast, Frummie reflected that there was nothing mealy-mouthed about Margot; no finer feelings hindered her outspoken views. In sixty years she'd barely changed. Of course, she was looking her age, poor dear—Frummie smiled her down-turned smile—and her legs were a terrible sight. Not that she'd ever had good legs. No, Frummie shook her head regretfully, even when Margot was a girl, her legs wouldn't have looked out of place supporting a piano and the varicose veins certainly added to the problem. Now if only she were wise enough to lower her hems *just* a little— well, several inches—and why not? *Perfectly* fashionable and attractive—it would be a great deal better for everyone. And it was a mistake to be *quite* so determined in maintaining the original colour of her hair. If you were naturally very dark it was probably more sensible to go gracefully grey. Of course—Frummie patted her own hair absent-mindedly—it was simply good luck to be born blonde so that one's hair gently faded into a kind of pretty, soft, fair colour but, in other cases, dyeing often did more harm than good, aesthetically speaking. It was certainly so in Margot's case. Her poor old face, surrounded by those unnaturally bright chestnut locks, looked so . . . well, "haggard" was the word which came to mind. The contrast was so cruel: all that lovely young-looking hair and those terrible lines round the eyes. "Craggy" was putting it kindly—and unfortunately make-up was no substitute for a smooth skin. Now if only dear old Margot could be persuaded not to *ladle* the foundation cream on—it positively congealed in those furrows which ploughed between her nose and chin; Polyfilla just wasn't in it—she'd look so much better. But she wouldn't listen. And as for that quite startling eye-shadow. Impossible to explain that her eyes were no longer that extraordinary green—if they ever had been. Actually, as far as she could remember, Margot's eyes had always had a brownish tinge, rather muddy-looking, in fact, rather like her skin, and darling old Nanny had often remarked that Margot's diet had a lot to answer for . . .

As for the chin . . . Frummie shuddered sympathetically as she refilled her coffee cup. Of course, bones were all a question of luck and there was no doubt that, as one grew older, saggy jowls didn't actually *help*—she smoothed her own sharp jawline reflectively—but it was sad that her dear old friend had such a bulldog look. One was reminded of darling Winston—though without question, it was much more acceptable in a man—but poor Margot's cheeks simply *swagged* about when she laughed, no two ways about it. And it would be much more sensible if she simply accepted the fact that she was as blind as a bat and wore her spectacles all the time, instead of pretending that she didn't need them except for driving and the television. Really, one got the *least* bit weary of reading the menus to her in pubs and watching her trying to focus on things only a few feet away. There were plenty of *very* attractive spectacles about these days and it was extremely unusual to reach the mid-seventies without needing them—she, Frummie, happened to be one of the lucky exceptions—but, really, why not face facts?

Frummie shook her head and began to clear the table. Funny old Margot, what an old chum she was; it would be good to have her to stay in the autumn. She glanced at her watch: a bit too early to put on a video, perhaps. Sighing a little, feeling rather at a loose end, she decided that she'd strip Margot's bed and wash the sheets. It was a gloriously sunny, warm day; a good drying day.

As she climbed the stairs, she thought about Louise again. "*Not* married," she murmured. "Well, well well."

Louise passed through the wicket gate and stood quite still, transfixed by an incredulous joy. The waters of the reservoir, polished and level as a metal shelf, mirrored the heavenly blue of the sky; dark reflections of tall pines striking across its surface, clear and sharp as paper cutouts. The soft, bright green needles of the larch shimmered, delicately luminous in the sunshine, whilst, somewhere out of sight, the cuckoo called. His evocative cry echoed in the woods and across the lake; speaking of other springs, of May mornings belonging to some distant past, and touching the melancholic, restless, plangent chords of undefined longing which vibrated in her heart.

The song ceased abruptly and with it her unearthly moment of ecstatic joy, although the restlessness remained. Concentrating carefully, determinedly, on the beauty of this magic place she set off around the reservoir. The path was well defined, gravelly, and running, for the most part, at the water's edge. To her left, beneath the pines, delicate white wood anemones flowered palely on the dense, fibrous, springy carpet of brown needles. It was warm, here, in the shelter of the trees, and presently she stopped at one of the benches, taking a Thermos from her rucksack. She sat staring out across the water, drinking her coffee, a resolution beginning to form at the back of her mind. It was important to make some kind of gesture, to be proactive, before she was engulfed by the rising tide of fear. Already it had breached the strong wall of her defences and now it lapped at the edges of her reason. Who knows what might happen if she simply allowed herself to be swamped, rendered helpless and floundering? This tide of fear, sucking and swallowing at the solid footholds of her security, was already uncovering her weaknesses, her terrors and her guilt.

It was anxiety about Martin which had fractured her confidence, allowing the first trickle of unease to seep into the locked, defended fortress of her mind. In addressing the fear of his infidelity, she might shore up the crumbling wall again. Sitting on the bench, the wood, rough and splintery beneath her fingers, her eyes on the water, which washed gently, demurely, against the tiny semi-circle of gritty beach, she hardened the resolve, steeling herself to it. The hot coffee was a stimulant, giving courage, and now she swung her rucksack on her back with a lighter heart and stepped out more courageously.

Back at the car park, she changed her walking boots for Timberlands, took off her fleece and climbed into the car. It was hot, almost airless, and she wound down the window whilst she fiddled for a tape. She needed something in keeping with this new decisive mood and chose her Alison Moyet tape, which she sang to, defiantly, until she reached Ashburton and parked again.

In the telephone box, she took out her BT chargecard and gave the operator the number of Martin's mobile telephone. He answered immediately, his voice slightly wary.

"It's me," she said, trying hard to sound as she usually did. "Surprise!"

"It is indeed, sweetie." His voice was warm now, quite in control. "I wondered if it could be, although I didn't recognise the number."

"Recognise . . .?"

"It comes up in the little box." He sounded amused. "You really will have to move into the twenty-first century one of these days, my sweet. What's the problem?"

"Problem? Why should there be a problem? Can't I telephone you without there being a problem?"

"Well, of course." He sounded very slightly nonplussed. "It's just that we don't usually—do we?—on our holidays. Not that I can telephone you, anyway, immured in the fastnesses of Dartmoor. Is everything OK?"

"Yes." She deliberately drew the word out, implying doubt. "It's just that . . . I'm missing you."

"Oh, sweetie," his laughter was forced, "that's nice."

"Is it?"

"How do you mean?" The least, the *very* least tinge of irritation coloured his question.

"I just wondered if it really *is* nice. To be missed, I mean. I was thinking that I might come home early."

"Early?" sharply. "How early?"

"I don't really know. A few days. How about you?"

"Me? Well, to be honest, Louise, it would be damned difficult. After all, it's not quite that simple, is it?"

His extravagant use of endearments was habitual and she noted both the sudden and unusual demotion from "sweetie" and also the annoyance which he was now making very little effort to mask but reminded herself that both could be perfectly reasonable, that there was nothing necessarily suspicious about his reaction.

"How are the boys?"

"The . . .? Oh, fine. Absolutely fine. But that's the point. I can't just chuck it in and go home, can I?"

"Can you only play golf in foursomes?"

"Sweetie, please. I'm not being unsympathetic but what is this all about?"

Quite suddenly she remembered the man in the train: the impatience echoing beneath his careful question; his endearment almost an insult.

"Oh, I'm just feeling a bit low. I know it's not the norm but there we are." She hesitated. "By the way, Martin, what's the name of the hotel? I might telephone again this evening."

A silence. When he spoke his voice was cool.

"I've told you a million times, sweetie, haven't I? Do what you've just done and telephone the mobile. It worked, didn't it? We don't want people chasing all over, looking for me. I might be in the bar, or in the dining room, or anywhere. The boys often like to go on somewhere else for a pint after dinner. I promise you, it's the safest thing to do."

"Oh, I was thinking of later than that. Much later."

"Not too late, I hope." His jocular tone was unconvincing. "I get pretty knackered with all the fresh air. We walk a fair few miles, most days, you know. Anyway, whatever time it is the answer's still the same. Use the mobile. It's cheaper than hotel rates and I imagine you're using your charge-card."

"Yes. Yes, I am. But where are you, Martin? I know you're touring some of the golf courses in the northwest, aren't you? What are they like?"

"Pretty good." His anxiety was palpable. "Look, I know it's not your scene, sweetie, is it, a blow-by-blow of the golf courses of the British Isles? Not really? So why this fit of the glooms, d'you think?"

"Oh, I don't know." She could understand how infuriating she must sound, noted his unsubtle change of direction. "It's just not working very well for me this time, for some reason. I'm not feeling too well, which doesn't help."

"In what way 'not well'?"

There was none of that caressing, loving anxiety which had so characterised their early relationship. It had been his chief attraction and oh! how she had needed that tender, caring awareness. Now the authentic note was missing; she was a tiresome appendage who could not, however, be brushed aside too lightly.

"Look, it doesn't matter. I'm OK, really." Her voice was much more cheerful, deliberately light. "Forget it. I'm being an idiot. Sorry, darling. I just wanted to hear your voice."

"That's very sweet of you." His relief, his gratitude at being let off the hook, blossomed into an unnatural excess of warmth. "Honestly, honey, I'm missing you too. Well, of course I am. But I can't simply walk out on the boys, can I?" He appealed to her now with confidence in her response, chuckling a little, luscious with thankfulness. "Now look, sweetie. Have a word with a pharmacist or something, if you're a bit off colour. Could you do that?"

"Oh, it's not that important. Just the wrong time of the month. You know?"

"Ah, I *see*." He was completely reassured. "Well, if you're certain . . .?"

"Quite certain. I suppose I'd better let you get back to whatever it is you're doing. I hope I haven't disturbed anything; put anyone off their stroke."

"Of course not. But if you're absolutely sure, perhaps I ought to be catching up with the boys."

"Positive. How's Alec's ankle?"

"Alec's . . .?"

"He sprained his ankle, didn't he? I thought there was some question as to whether it would hold up?"

"Oh, his *ankle*. Sorry. I lost my signal there for a moment. Thought you said his *uncle*. He's fine. Fine. The walking's doing it good. Well, sweetie . . ."

"Sure. Off you go. Enjoy. I might phone again sometime."

She hung up. It was odd that she'd almost enjoyed the

contest; that during the brief battle of wits she'd been able to ignore the gnawing, sick feeling in the pit of her stomach. She crossed the road and walked back to the car park, pausing, as she always did, to look at the books displayed in the window of the Dartmoor Bookshop. Usually there was nothing she enjoyed more than a browse amongst the tantalising selection of second-hand books, and a chat with Barbara or Anne, but now she felt unequal to any social intercourse, however friendly. She felt suddenly tired, depressed, and she needed time alone, to think, to sift her information, weigh shades of expression, consider his words. Yet in her heart she already knew the truth of it.

What would she do without Martin? How would she manage without him, standing, as he did, between her and the past? She simply mustn't think about it. Fear plucked in her throat, scraped along her veins, squeezed her heart. Trembling and confused she delved for her keys and unlocked the door. Getting into the car, she sat for a few moments. Where should she go? To whom should she turn? Brigid was her first thought: but Brigid was sharing precious time with Humphrey and it was impossible to imagine a scenario which included taking Humphrey into her confidence; anyway, it was clear that at present Brigid had her own problems.

Louise shook her head, resisting weak tears. She longed to rest, to stop the clamouring of memories in her head. In her mind's eye she saw a bright, airy room full of watery reflections; a cat asleep in a chair. She remembered an atmosphere of warm, comforting friendliness. Switching on the engine she drove out of the town, heading towards the coast.

CHAPTER 13

Jemima sat staring at the computer screen, checking dates, noting which cottages would need cleaning on Saturday morning. She hated changeover day: harrying recalcitrant holidaymakers, who had no desire to go home, so as to make all fresh and clean for those who were already on their way to the West Country. She'd compiled her list and was about to telephone—in order of reliability—the various members of her team of assistants when the doorbell buzzed.

"Rats!" she muttered, replacing the receiver, glancing at her watch. She left her little office and crossed the hall to the front door. Louise was standing outside. She looked tired and desperate, in a muted kind of way, as if she were holding herself under strict control.

"What a lovely surprise. Come on in." Jemima stood aside, smiling warmly but feeling anxious. Their last meeting had ended somewhat inconclusively. "I can't tell you what good timing this is."

"Is it?" Louise sounded relieved, although her smile was slipping a little, and she looked about her as though puzzled to find herself in Jemima's flat. "It was . . . I just thought . . . I was driving about, you see . . ."

"Oh, I know just what you mean." Jemima took charge, herding her towards the sitting room. "That feeling of being at a loose end and being quite incapable of deciding what you should do next."

"That's it." Louise looked at her, pleased with such ready understanding. "I just couldn't think straight and then I found myself here."

"Brilliant." Jemima scooped MagnifiCat from the sofa and almost pushed Louise down in his place. "I have a wonderful excuse now to stop and make some tea. Work is very dull sometimes, isn't it, and it's always great to have an excuse to stop. Sit there in the sun while I switch the kettle on."

She hurried away to the kitchen, almost afraid to leave her. There was a strange blankness in Louise's eyes which made Jemima feel nervous. Whilst the kettle began to boil, and in between preparing the tray, Jemima ran back to the door several times just to check up; but Louise was sitting quite still, staring at nothing. Her hand lay on MagnifiCat's back but she seemed utterly unaware of his presence. Jemima's own hand shook a little as she poured boiling water into the teapot. She had a horrid premonition that Louise's state of mind might be in some way related to their conversation about infidelity and she felt unqualified to deal with the possible result. She decided to keep the conversation casual if she could.

"So how's everyone at Foxhole?" She put the tray on the low glass table. "Is Humphrey still there?"

Louise frowned a little, almost as if she were wondering who Humphrey might be, and Jemima felt another frisson of anxiety.

"Yes. Yes, he's there." Louise took her cup. "Sorry. We all had dinner together last night, and drank rather a lot. It was very late by the time we got to bed and I was up at dawn. My head feels as if it's full of cotton wool."

"Oh, that's more or less standard for me," said Jemima cheerfully. "I'm a Bear of very little Brain. Dear old Humphrey has a generous hand with the wine, hasn't he? Brigid will miss him when he goes off to the Bahamas. It's a long way off and six months is a long time." And ten out of ten for banality, she jeered silently to herself. "Of course, she's used to it," she added desperately, when Louise made no attempt to respond.

There was a short silence.

"I telephoned Martin earlier." Louise seemed unaware that Jemima had spoken. "He didn't want to tell me where he's staying. Don't you think that's odd? Suspicious, I mean?"

Jemima stared at her. She thought: Help me, someone.

Louise sipped her tea, frowning again. "It's the little things," she murmured, after a moment, rather as though she were talking aloud to herself. "Tiny things give you away. It wasn't Alec's ankle that was sprained, you see. It was Steve's. It was a test question."

"Right." Jemima nodded, swallowed some tea, smiled anxiously.

"But he didn't pick it up. He'd forgotten." Louise shook her head. "Unlikely, don't you think, if he's playing golf with him every day?"

"Absolutely!" Jemima's response was so enthusiastic that Louise glanced at her, jolted momentarily from her preoccupation. "Pretty difficult to forget," sheer nerves moved Jemima to elaborate, "if they're together all the time."

"That's what I thought." Louise set her cup in its saucer and yawned suddenly. "Sorry." She pushed back the cloud of dark, curly hair and closed her eyes for a second. "I am just *so* tired. I can't think straight."

Jemima forgot her own fear at the sight of the strained, pinched face. "You look exhausted," she said gently. "Don't talk for a bit. Just relax in the sun."

"It's a bit rude." Louise tried to smile but the effort was too great and, for one appalling moment, Jemima thought that she was going to weep. Her face crumpled, her lips trembling, her brow furrowing as if in protest at some internal pain, but she was too tired for any emotional outburst and her face smoothed into a kind of weary indifference. "Sorry," she murmured again.

"Please." Jemima moved the tray away. "It's not a problem. You just need some rest. Sleep, if you can, while I make a few telephone calls and then we'll have another chat. You could stay for supper."

"Thanks. That's so . . . kind."

Her eyes were almost closed; her head rolled sideways.

Standing, the tray in her hands, Jemima looked down at her.

She thought: It's almost as if she's too unhappy to be able to care. It's like something's given way. Finding out that she's right about Martin, I suppose.

She edged quietly from the room, pulled the door so that it was not quite shut and, having dumped the tray in the kitchen, she hurried into her study, closing the door behind her. She dialled quickly, one ear straining towards the sitting room, but there was no reply from the telephone at Foxhole and she replaced the receiver without leaving a message. After a moment, she made the few calls necessary to her work and stood up. Going out quietly into the hall, creeping up to the door, she peered into the sitting room. Louise was soundly asleep; relaxed into the deep cushions, bathed in the late afternoon sunshine, MagnifiCat curled beside her. Jemima stood watching her for a few moments and then went into the kitchen and poured herself some more tea. She sipped at the hot liquid, her face thoughtful, and then, taking her cup with her, she went back to her study to try to telephone Brigid again.

FRUMMIE COULD hear the telephone ringing as she stood watching the doves. Sometimes, when she knew that Brigid had gone off in the car, she went into the courtyard to sit on the bench in the sunshine and look at the flowers in the big wooden tubs. Her own small patch of garden faced south too, but it was open to the hills and moorland and Frummie felt more at home here, flanked by stone walls. She preferred this enclosed, ordered space, the neat round cobbles, the bright flowers in terracotta pots and painted tubs. Up here, on the moor, summer arrived a little later than in the valleys and coastal villages but Brigid always managed some clever arrangement, some warm splash of colour, in this sheltered corner. In January and February, snowdrops and winter aconites grew in a container fixed to a wooden post over which ivy trailed, making a charming varicoloured backdrop to the white and yellow blooms; in March purpley-blue, wineglass-shaped crocuses blossomed in the terracotta crocus-pot whilst dwarf narcissi and puschkinias filled the painted tubs, and daffodils nodded in long troughs against the walls.

Now, in May, the tulips, tall and elegant in their stone bowls edged with pansies and hyacinthus, were almost over but, as she sat on the bench, listening to the cooing of the doves in the sunshine, Frummie inhaled the wallflowers' heady scent and was transported back forty years in time. Even then, before people had begun to do such clever things with tubs and containers, wallflowers had grown in the narrow border beneath the windows. There had been a bench too—not this elegant affair of wood and cast iron but a simple rough bench, brought from one of the stables and placed in the angle of the wall to catch the sunshine. It was here that she'd read the letter from Richard, inviting her back to London for some party or social gathering; a light-hearted, amusing letter but underpinned with a deeper emotion. The postman, bumping down the track in his van, pausing for a chat, could have had no idea that he'd delivered such a momentous package.

Her eyes closed, Frummie remembered that she'd offered him coffee, casually, easily, the letter rustling in the pocket of her tweed jacket, hiding any eagerness or impatience. He'd refused—he'd been running late, some problem or other—and she'd raised a hand to him as he'd turned the van and driven away. She'd even—she shook her head, amused now, at the remembrance—she'd even gone indoors to make some coffee and had carried it out here, to this same spot, before she'd opened the letter; as if this deliberate postponement might possibly convince herself of her indifference.

She'd read the letter, whilst the doves tittuped over the cobbles on thready feet, eyes bright, heads tilted, hoping for corn.

"Darling Fred . . ."

Strange, this stinging stab of vivid, agonising memory. No doubt the sun, the doves, the wallflowers, even the mug of coffee in her hand, had recreated that moment, first lived forty years before, and made it real. So real that her fingertips were surprised to find drill, not tweed, as they brushed against her thigh, and, when she opened her eyes, she half expected to see Diarmid, returning unexpectedly from the farmers' market in Buckfastleigh.

"I forgot my chequebook," he'd said cheerfully, self-deprecatingly, and she'd stared at him, shocked by the strength of her resentment at his intrusion.

"I didn't hear the car."

"I left it up the track. It's nearly out of petrol so I walked down." He'd been clearly surprised by the sharpness in her voice and he'd glanced at the letter, eyebrows raised. "Not bad news, I hope?"

"No." She'd looked down, folding the letter with carefully slow fingers. "Just the usual screed from Margot."

"Ah."

What was he waiting for? she'd wondered irritably—and had refused to look at him but raised her cup of coffee and sipped calmly.

"Hadn't you better get on?"

Now, forty years later, she flinched against the needling pang of remorse. Perhaps he would have liked some coffee, would have been happy to sit in the sun with her for a moment, watching the doves, breathing the scented air. Instead, he'd turned away and gone indoors whilst she'd sat quite still, waiting with a clenched impatience.

"See you later." He'd waved the chequebook, smiled and then gone away up the track, leaving her alone.

After a few minutes, she'd unfolded the letter again.

"Darling Fred . . ." The letter had been full of anecdotes, references to mutual friends, a scandal amongst actor acquaintances; and, scattered through the pages, those lightly teasing, thrillingly exciting phrases which turned her gut to water. She'd longed to be there, in London, in Richard's cluttered Chelsea flat, laughing at some malicious rumour, calling up chums to arrange a lunch, knowing that his eyes, full of secret knowledge, were upon her. Wherever they'd gone, to crowded ballrooms, packed theatres, busy restaurants, their eyes would meet and they would laugh: delicious, private, knowing laughter. He'd always been able to make her laugh, had known just how to amuse her, to drive

away the sudden onslaughts of depression which dogged her; unlike Diarmid who, head in book, might not even notice that she was ready to tear Foxhole down, stone by stone, in furious, desperate boredom.

As she'd read the letter, hearing his laughter, excited by his carefully worded persuasion, she'd known that she'd give in, agree to another visit, but this time she'd known too that it would be different. She hadn't wanted to admit to this knowledge.

"Just a few days," she'd said aloud to the doves, "not long"—but, as she'd talked to them, she'd been making plans. Even Diarmid, too honourable himself to be suspicious of others, might be surprised to hear that she would be making another trip to London so soon. As for Brigid . . .

Frummie remembered how she'd stood up suddenly, then, scattering the doves, thrusting the letter deep into her pocket.

She'd thought: Don't think about Brigid. Deal with that later. She's quite happy with Diarmid . . .

She hadn't realised that "later" would prove too late; that Diarmid would prove so stubborn or so determined to keep his daughter or that the battles would be so savage. Diarmid had been inexorable in his position of strength. His care and love for Brigid had been irrefutable but, oh! how he'd exacted his revenge for his own humiliation and pain. He'd written: *"Do you really consider yourself to be responsible enough to have the care of a child? You've abandoned her once for your lover. How can I be certain you might not do it again?"* Frummie shivered and opened her eyes. Forty years ago she'd sat here in the morning; now, it was late afternoon and the seat was in shadow. She took up her mug and reached for the letter. Puzzled she looked about, fumbled in her pocket, even peered under the seat before she came to her senses.

"Old fool!" she muttered contemptuously. "Stupid bloody woman!"

She stood up stiffly, wincing a little, and, as she crossed the courtyard, the telephone began to ring again.

CHAPTER 14

It wasn't until Humphrey had gone back to London that Brigid felt able to give her mind more fully to Louise.

"What was all that about?" he'd asked, when she'd at last replaced the telephone receiver. "Jemima, was it?"

"Mmm. Nothing much. Shall we have a drink while I get some supper?"

She'd been unwilling to spoil the golden mood of the long, happy day by discussing Jemima's fears for Louise. Humphrey was not the sort of man who took an interest in her girl-friends' problems. He had no real understanding of the deeper psychological processes and he quickly became impatient with drawn-out analyses of other people's anxieties.

"We probe about too much these days," he'd say. "Everyone wants to be a counsellor, amateur or otherwise. It isn't always good to delve about in our inner psyches; sometimes it's better just to shut up and get on with life."

Brigid felt that he probably had a point. Despite her own private soul-searchings, her attempts to understand her own feelings and come to terms with her sense of failure—how else could a mother leave her daughter unless that daughter was negligible?—in the end she'd had to get on with her life. Humphrey, because of his love for her, had been sensitive to these emotions, patient, loving, kind, but she rarely imposed other people's emotional problems upon him; especially when he had only a short leave period. So she'd pushed Jemima's anxious warnings to the back of her mind and concentrated on their precious time together.

She'd noticed Louise's safe return, kept a watching brief from a distance, but it wasn't until she'd seen Humphrey off on the train and driven back to Foxhole that she was able to think about the things Jemima had told her. Dropping her bag on the table, hanging her car-keys on a hook on the dresser, Brigid glanced at the telephone to see if there were any messages. The red light glowed steadily and she turned away, relieved. It had been a private terror, whilst Humphrey was home, that Jenny might ring and leave a message and that he might listen to it. So great was her fear that she'd actually switched the answerphone off each time they'd gone out, just in case. Now, it no longer mattered.

With a sense of desolation, Brigid sat down suddenly at the table, resting her head in her hands. There was none of her usual pleasure, no contentment in being here this afternoon. Her peace had vanished, shattered by Jenny's news of possible disaster, by the prospect of Humphrey's long absence, and now, it seemed, she had Louise to worry about too.

"She looks really odd." Jemima's voice had sounded anxious. "Terribly tired and not with it."

Odd, the sensations her sister's voice engendered in her. First there was the tiny but insistent twinge of resentment: however hard she tried she could never be wholly, unconditionally friendly. Brigid could hear that cool note in her own voice, disliked herself for it, but could never quite achieve a genuine warmth. Was it because Jemima approached her with caution? There was a faint anxiety beneath the cheerful greeting, a wariness that could not be disguised. Perhaps, if they'd known each other much sooner, whilst they were still children, this antagonism might have been overcome. Of course, it would be a great deal easier if their mother was not so open in her favouritism—but that was hardly Jemima's fault. She neither sought such approval nor seemed particularly happy with it, and tried hard to form a bond with her elder sister. Now and again there had been evidence of affection between them, a blossoming of sisterly feeling, which had pleased them both. Yet it seemed difficult to sustain it. No sooner had it put forth its fragile blooms than some blight annihilated it. This usually took the form of a remark from Frummie—some slighting observation, some show of partisanship, which roused all the old requirement for self-protection.

Brigid thought: It's me, really. I'll never come to terms with the fact that she left me but wouldn't leave Jemima. I can't seem to overcome my jealousy.

Blot came to sit beside her, resting his chin on her knee, and she pulled his long ears and stroked the silky, rounded dome of his head.

"I'm a twit," she told him—and he wagged his stumpy tail encouragingly. The telephone rang and she sat for a moment, almost too nervous to answer it, afraid it might be Jenny with bad news, seizing the receiver only seconds before the answerphone clicked into play.

"Thea," she said with relief. "How are you? . . . Yes, so I was, wasn't I? With Louise. Only Humphrey's been home . . . Yes, absolutely fine . . . That would be good. I'd like to . . . Yes, of course I'll ask her but she hasn't got much holiday left now . . . I'm sure she would. I'll phone you back . . . I will. Love to the girls and George."

Brigid hung up and stood for a moment, thinking.

"She's quite sure her husband's having an affair," Jemima had said. "She suspected it for a while but now something's made her certain and she's behaving very oddly. I'm worried about her."

Apart from the usual antagonism it had irritated Brigid to discover that Jemima knew such intimate details about Louise's life.

"She's *my* friend," she'd wanted to say—and had been disgusted by such a childish reaction, the old familiar fear threatening her confidence.

She shrugged it away but it clung persistently. After all, it *was* odd that Louise had achieved such intimacy so quickly with Jemima. She'd never seemed the type of woman to spill confidences and this was such a very personal problem. Brigid frowned thoughtfully. Of course it was possible that she'd been too preoccupied with her own terrors, as well as by having Humphrey at home, to notice that all was not well with Louise. Grimacing guiltily to herself, Brigid shook off the deadening threat of inadequacy. The important thing was to see Louise and give her the opportunity to talk, to share her fears. At least she now had a good excuse to go across to the cottage and remind her about Thea's invitation. Louise hadn't seemed too keen when it was first mentioned but she might have changed her mind. Feeling slightly nervous, Brigid went out into the bright, cold evening.

LOUISE WAS sitting at the table in the big living room, painting. She frowned at the sound of Brigid's knock, accompanied by a call of "It's only me." However, at the familiar sight of her, tall and casually elegant, her short fine blonde hair pushed back behind her ears, Louise felt an easing of this strange, new, tight tension in her chest and was able to smile at her: but she did not stop painting.

"How clever." Brigid approached to look. "What delicate little pictures."

Louise did not respond. It might be a trap. She must be very careful, even with Brigid, but she continued to smile.

"I haven't seen you for a day or two." Brigid hesitated, then pulled out a chair and sat down. "I've been making the most of having Humphrey home."

Louise nodded; she knew all about that. You needed to make the most of every second, every single, tiny second, because otherwise . . . She realised that she was still nodding and blinked, frowning. Had she spoken? Betrayed herself?

"Louise?" Brigid was looking at her curiously. "Are you OK?"

She felt the need to giggle but knew that she mustn't. Not yet. She nodded again. Yes, she was quite OK. Never been better. Only she needed to be very, very careful.

"Shall we have a cup of tea?" Brigid had stood up again and was filling the kettle.

Louise smiled a wider smile. She recognised that note, a brightness in her voice, that gave Brigid away. Careful! If she opened her own mouth toads might jump out, just like in the fairy story; toads that might turn into terrible, frightening words, and let loose all those things that were waiting behind the door in the wall. The door must stay shut. She leaned with all her might against it, feeling it pressing against her back. Oh! how heavy it was; how tired she was. She'd like to sleep and sleep but she mustn't break her vigil even for a second.

"Thea just phoned." Brigid was making tea. "She's invited us over for lunch. I know you were wondering if you had the time to come too. What do you think?"

Louise stopped smiling. Danger was here, all about her. She remembered Thea; she was nice, strong and good, but she was connected, somehow, to all the dreadful things that were waiting behind the door. No, she could not see Thea. She shook her head.

Brigid stood the mug of hot tea near at hand on a little round mat. The mug had a picture on it but it was not her own mug; perhaps Brigid didn't know that she always brought her own mug so as to feel at home . . .

"I wish you'd come with me." Brigid had sat down again now, and was smiling at her.

Louise smiled too. She picked up the mug, holding it close so as to look at the picture.

"I thought you might like to see Oscar again. And Hermione."

Hermione . . . Louise's hand trembled. The danger was close, so close now, and she couldn't move; not a muscle. The door was opening, ever so slightly, and someone was trying to slip through. Someone small, with long bright hair . . . Oh! she must press against it, slam it closed, but they were so strong . . .

With a convulsive movement she flung herself backwards, the hot tea spilled over her wrist, across her book, and Brigid leaped to her feet with a cry. She took Louise's mug, forcibly wresting it from the clenched fingers, set it down and ran to get a cloth. By the time she'd wiped the table, blotted the book, dried Louise's hand and wrist, her heart was hammering and her throat was dry.

"There," she murmured. "There we are. My God, you did give me a fright. Are you OK?"

Louise's eyes were blank, but very bright, and she was smiling. The door was closed again, shut tight, but it had been a very near thing. Nobody must guess; nobody must know. She stared back at Brigid, an idea hovering, and her smile became fixed. Was Brigid dangerous too, now? Had she seen something when the door opened? But what? She must be lulled back to safety. Louise nodded and then sighed suddenly. She felt so tired; so very tired.

Watching her, Brigid shivered. There was something terribly wrong here and she needed help to deal with it.

"I have to go," she said gently. "Will you be OK? I'll be back soon. Why don't you try to rest? You look very tired."

Louise pushed her paints aside and leaned her elbows on the table. The door was closed, slammed shut and she could rest, just for a moment . . . not for long, no, but for a moment or two. She put her head on her arms and her eyes closed.

Brigid stepped quietly back. Looking round, she took Louise's car-keys from the other end of the table, picked up the black leather handbag, and moved silently to the door. Outside she took several very deep breaths and went quickly across to Frummie's cottage.

FRUMMIE, WATCHING *Casablanca,* was pleased by the unexpected interruption. She knew the film by heart and the evening stretched emptily ahead.

"Hello," she said, reaching for the remote control. "Missing Humphrey? Like a drink?" She caught sight of the handbag and her spirits fell. "Are you going out?"

"No. It's Louise's." Brigid dropped the bag on a chair but still held the car-keys. "I'm really worried about her. She's behaving very strangely."

"How do you mean?" Frummie was intrigued. She hauled herself out of her chair, impressed by Brigid's expression; she looked quite frightened. "What's happened?"

"Jemima telephoned." Brigid perched on the sofa's arm. "She said that Louise had called in, quite unexpectedly, and that she'd been . . . well, distracted and peculiar. She suspected her husband of having an affair and decided she'd phone him up. It seems that she asked him some kind of trick question which convinced her that she's right. Jemima said she looked terribly tired and then simply fell asleep. She slept for hours, apparently, and then woke up quite normal and very bright, but seemed puzzled to find herself in Salcombe. Jemima offered her some supper and tried to persuade her to stay but she wouldn't. She says she wasn't absolutely certain that Louise knew who she was and seemed to think that Jemima knew Martin. That was two days ago."

Frummie looked thoughtful. "I've seen her about," she said. "She looks fairly normal."

"She wasn't just now." Brigid shivered. "She was just sitting there, painting. She wouldn't speak, just kept nodding and smiling. I made her a cup of tea and she picked it up and then . . . she sort of flung herself backwards. It was so sudden and . . . violent. The tea went everywhere. But she didn't make a sound and the tea was really hot. I'd just poured it out. She hardly seemed to notice."

"How extraordinary." Frummie laid a hand on Brigid's shoulder. "And frightening. Like a fit, or something."

Brigid looked up at her anxiously. "I'm not sure I should have left her alone. I brought her bag and her car-keys, just in case."

"Very sensible. But what do you plan to do next?"

"I think we should telephone her husband," said Brigid firmly. "Louise's not well, I'm sure of it, and he ought to know. I don't want to go through her belongings but I'm hoping there's a number somewhere."

She looked so unusually helpless that Frummie took charge.

"That sounds reasonable. Look, what about a drink? Just

to fortify ourselves? You've had a shock, by the look of you."

"That would be good." Brigid nodded gratefully. "There was something so . . . weird about it. Scary. Yes, a drink would be nice."

Frummie was already dealing with it. "Shock can push you over the edge, you know. I saw a lot of it after the war. People can be terribly brave and then all of a sudden, they crack. She's probably been worrying about it for a very long time but trying not to let it show."

"Probably." Brigid shivered again. "I hope she's OK on her own. You don't think she might do something silly?"

Frummie smiled her down-turned smile. "Depends what you mean by 'silly.' Here, take this. Let's not get too melodramatic."

"I'll feel better when I've talked to Martin." Brigid put the keys on a small table, beside the lamp, and took the glass. "Thanks."

"Will you? Why?"

"Why not?" Brigid looked at her mother curiously. "He's the one to deal with it, isn't he?"

Frummie shrugged. "It depends. If he's having an affair he might not be all that interested."

"Not *interested?* He's her husband!"

"Is he?"

Brigid stared at her and then laughed. "Sorry. Have I lost the plot or something? What are you talking about?"

Frummie sat down again. "It's just something Louise said. That evening when we'd had supper with you she came in afterwards for a nightcap. She talked about infidelity and then said something which made me think that she's not actually married to this Martin or whatever his name is. Of course, she'd had a bit to drink but, even so, I think she was speaking the truth."

Brigid closed her eyes for a moment. "But even if she isn't married to him," she argued, "he still has the right to know."

"Of course." Frummie raised her eyebrows. "Why not? I'm just warning you that he might not be that interested."

"But they've been . . . together," she chose the word carefully, "for at least three years."

"The trouble is," said Frummie slowly, "that when a man or a woman falls in love, or becomes infatuated with someone outside their own relationship, they can become so involved with the drama of this new life, so wrapped up and besotted by it, that their normal responsibilities seem utterly unreal. They crave the new experience so desperately that they can become quite useless to their former partners."

"Well," said Brigid bleakly, after a minute of silence. "You should know."

Frummie bit her lip. "I do know," she said evenly. "That's why I'm warning you."

"But what are you suggesting?" asked Brigid angrily. "Even if Martin chooses to renege on his responsibilities, Louise must have other people, family, who care about her."

"I'm not saying that you shouldn't telephone him. I'm just suggesting that this might not be as straightforward as you think it is."

"I'm going to telephone." Brigid set her drink down. "I'm going to do it now."

She opened Louise's bag and brought out a diary. Frummie watched her with unusual compassion as she sat, holding the little book, unable actually to open it.

"You'll have to, you know," she said gently. "There's no other way. We know he's not at home. Do you have her home number, by the way?"

"Yes." Brigid glanced at her quickly. "Do you think I should try that first?"

Frummie shook her head. "No point. Get on with it. I'll do it if you feel squeamish about it."

Brigid opened the book almost distastefully and looked at the scribbled entries in the "Notes" section at the back. "I always put odd numbers and addresses at the end," she said, almost conversationally. "Don't you?"

"Sometimes. Any luck?"

"No. Not yet. Lots of bits and pieces." She turned a few pages. "Oh, hang on. The letters MM and a long number."

"Martin's mobile?" hazarded Frummie. "Well, give it a go."

Brigid stood up and went to the telephone. She dialled carefully, listened for a moment and then spoke. "I'm hoping I've reached Martin Parry. This is Brigid Foster. Could you give me a call?" She gave her telephone number and replaced the receiver. "Not answering," she said. "I've left a message."

"Fair enough. But perhaps you'd better go over to the house, in case he phones back."

"Yes, I suppose so. I hadn't thought of that." She hesitated. "What should I do with Louise's bag?"

"I'll take it back. Don't worry. I'll be discreet."

"And the car-keys?"

"I think, just for a while, we'll 'lose' the keys."

The two women stared at each other.

"Yes," said Brigid at last. "I think that would be best. And . . . thanks. I'm sorry if I was a bit—"

"Nothing to apologise for. I'll come over, if you like, once I've taken her bag back and checked up on her."

"That would be . . . nice. You could have supper, if you like. Louise too, if she'll come."

"Thank you. I'd like that. Finish your drink and hurry away. It would be irritating if he left a message."

"Yes." Brigid swallowed the rest of her wine, smiled rather wanly and disappeared.

Frummie sipped her own drink more calmly, her face preoccupied. The door which Brigid had closed began to open very, very slowly. Frummie set down her glass, put the bag behind a cushion, reached for the keys, and sat quite still. Louise slipped inside and, holding the door shut behind her, put a finger to her lips.

"Someone is looking for me," she whispered. "She's in my cottage. I can hear her. I fell asleep, just for a minute, and she got in. May I stay with you until she's gone?"

Frummie got up and went across to her, taking her by the arm.

"Of course you can, my dear," she said. "How nice. Now

sit down. No, not there. Here. And I'll get you a drink. Do you like *Casablanca?* Of course you do! I've just been watching it."

Louise looked at her fearfully, with a terrible sadness in her eyes. "She's looking for me, you see. Only I don't know what to say to her."

"We'll deal with that later." Frummie was quite firm. "There." She picked up the remote control and pressed the button. "Now sit still and relax. You're quite safe with me."

Louise relaxed, as a child might in the care of some higher authority. "Thank you," she said politely and, turning her gaze on the screen, she sank gratefully into the corner of the sofa.

CHAPTER 15

Back in her own kitchen, Brigid felt a measure of calm returning. It was warm and quiet here, and Blot wagged a welcome from his basket.

"That was so scary," she murmured to him. "Whatever can be wrong with her? Is it a nervous breakdown because she's found out about Martin?"

Blot stirred about in his basket, settling himself contentedly. He rather missed Humphrey each time he went away—Humphrey had a generous way with biscuits and treats—but he was warm and comfortable, and pleasantly weary. Brigid bent to pat him. When she'd returned from seeing Humphrey on to the train she and Blot had walked along the O Brook, past Horse Ford and up on to Down Ridge, arriving home two hours later, muddy and tired but reconciled to the idea of six months' separation. Even the spacious timelessness of the moor, however, had been unable to soothe or quieten her fears about Jenny's troubles or help her come to terms with the news about Humphrey's father. Now there was Louise to worry about too. Brigid hadn't been made particularly anxious by Jemima's report. She'd dismissed it rather patronisingly, deciding that it was just another of Jemima's attempts to attract attention.

"The trouble is," Jemima had said, "I think that it's partly my fault."

"How on earth could it be your fault?" she'd snapped,

preoccupied by Humphrey's departure, his father's request for a home, Jenny's bombshell. "How can any of it have anything to do with you? Don't be such a drama queen."

Brigid gave Blot a final pat and stood up. The real truth was that she'd been jealous that Louise had told Jemima things that she, Brigid, knew nothing about, and she'd reacted by snarling like a bad-tempered dog. She'd behaved exactly the same way with her mother when she'd discovered that Frummie knew that Louise wasn't married and had talked about infidelity. "Well, you should know," she'd said bitterly.

Brigid, remembering the look on Frummie's face, felt an urge to burst into tears of frustration.

"And we were getting on so well," she said miserably. "She was being so . . . comforting. Oh *hell*. Why can't I be a cow and enjoy it? She's hurt me a million times and doesn't give a damn."

The telephone bell, shattering the silence, gave her such a fright that she stood for a moment or two, her hands pressed to her heart, before hurrying to answer it, convinced that it was Martin Parry.

"Just to say I'm back safely, love." Humphrey sounded determinedly cheerful. "A good journey, no hold-ups. Are you OK?"

"Of course," she lied. "Absolutely fine. It was lovely to see you."

"It was great. And I'll be home in a fortnight for nearly a week." He didn't add: "before I go off for six months." After all, they both knew that and there was no point in raising the subject now.

"We'll make the most of it," she promised. "How's everyone at your end . . .?"

She'd just replaced the receiver when Frummie put her head round the door.

"Sorry," she said. "I did knock but I could hear your voice and guessed you were on the telephone. Was it Martin?"

"It was Humphrey." Brigid laughed, resigned. "I can't tell

you the fright the phone ringing gave me. I was all worked up ready for Martin. It was terribly difficult behaving as if everything is utterly normal. Have you seen Louise?"

"She appeared just after you'd gone. Said that someone was at her cottage, looking for her."

Brigid stared at her mother, the smile dying away from her face. "How horrid."

"It was rather. I got her settled down and made her a drink."

"And what's she doing now?" Brigid looked alarmed. "Should you have left her?"

"Don't worry." Frummie grinned guiltily. "She's sleeping. I put a couple of Mogadons in her wine."

"*Mogadons?* You're joking?"

"Don't look so panicky. A couple of Mogs won't hurt her. I thought it was best to keep her sedated while we decided what to do."

"But supposing she's on some kind of medication, couldn't it be dangerous?"

"It'll knock her out for a bit, that's all. She could do with a good sleep, by the look of her. Don't fuss, darling. She'll be fine. I don't think she should be left alone tonight, though. She'd better stay with me."

Brigid felt a wave of relief. "Are you sure? Won't you be . . . well, frightened?"

"I think she needs looking after. When she gets a lucid moment I'll try to find out what's going on. It could be this thing with Martin but I have the feeling that it's more than that."

"But what?"

Frummie shook her head. "It's just a feeling. Let's wait and see what Martin says. He might be able to throw some light on it."

"But supposing he doesn't call back? He might not pick up the message. We can't just do nothing."

"We'll give it until the morning. You could try the number again later. When she comes to, I'll bring her over and we'll have some supper. Will that be OK?"

"Of course it will. Let's hope Martin telephones before she wakes up. After all, he could be here before morning, even if he's playing golf in Scotland."

Frummie gave her an odd look. "I don't think we should count on it. I'm going back now, just in case she wakes. See you later on."

Brigid shook her head and went to the fridge for some wine. Surely, once Martin heard about Louise's condition, he would set out at once?

Praying that he would telephone, Brigid began to prepare some supper.

LOUISE WOKE and sat for some minutes in silence, puzzling as to where she was. Part of her, a tiny part, didn't much care; was content to sink into a comfortable, mental oblivion. In a different corner of her mind, however, some tough, insistent voice prevailed. It warned her to shake off this all-too-welcome apathy; to continue the fight to keep the past separate from the present. It pricked her onwards, refusing to let her rest, and now there was something else that worried at her; which threatened to fuse the two together. Martin. It was her fear of losing Martin which had started this whole disintegration: beginning before the holiday, crystallising into awareness on the train and culminating in the telephone call.

She sat up straighter, forcing her weary, unwilling mind to concentrate. She'd almost forgotten the telephone call; it seemed so long ago since she'd spoken to him and he'd been evasive, cool, and, foolishly, fallen into the trap she'd set for him. How long ago? This morning? Yesterday? She raised her arm weightily, as if it were a log, and stared at her watch. Ten past seven. Frowning, she let her hands drop heavily into her lap. She could remember a conversation with Jemima but had no idea whether it was before or after she'd talked with Martin. What difference? She shrugged, tried to laugh, but it was too great an effort. What mattered was that her suspicions were grounded in reality. Martin was having an affair and might leave her just as readily as he had left Susan. How could she live without him; without his ability to envelop, to control, to fill the space which stretched back into the past so that she could rest against him? He'd stood between, protecting her, and without him she was vulnerable. Already her past was coming closer, so close that occasionally it collided with her present, sending her spinning out of control.

She said aloud: "It's all the *striving*. I'm too tired."

There was a movement in the shadows behind her and she jumped nervously, staring anxiously.

"But the trouble is," Frummie said, "that one simply cannot give up." She laid a hand on Louise's shoulder, smiling down at her. "Sometimes, though, you can let others carry the burden for a little while."

"Oh, hello." Louise spoke quite naturally but with a certain amount of relief. "I couldn't think where I was for a minute. You know, I think I'm going mad."

"Oh, I doubt it. Not just yet. You popped over to see me and I gave you a drink. I suspect you haven't been eating or sleeping much and it rather knocked you out. You've slept so heavily that I expect you've had some rather odd dreams."

"Yes." Louise shivered a little. "I think I have. It's very strange . . ."

"Don't try to remember them," said Frummie quickly. "No future in that. Real life's quite enough to deal with at the moment."

Louise chuckled with genuine amusement. "You're so right. I'm sorry to have fallen asleep on you. I suppose I ought to go and leave you in peace."

"Oh, but we're having supper with Brigid. Don't you remember? She's invited us both."

"I *do* remember . . ." She hesitated, thinking back . . . Brigid coming in, making tea . . . and something else . . .

"Well, there you are then. Look, I think we should be getting a move on. She'll be expecting us and we don't want the supper to be ruined."

She began to help Louise up, talking, joking, so that the memories, disjointed and insubstantial, faded and she smiled back, following her out of the cottage and across the courtyard.

• • •

BRIGID WELCOMED them in, hiding her misgivings. She shook her head at Frummie's silent query—no, no telephone call—and smiled at Louise.

"Thanks for coming," she said. "I always feel at a loose end when Humphrey goes away."

"Louise's only just woken up." Frummie sent her daughter a comforting wink. "I think my cocktail was rather too much for her but she's feeling better now."

Brigid knew that she was being told that the strange mood had passed, that Louise was herself again. Nevertheless, there was a muted, vulnerable quality about the younger woman which touched Brigid's compassion.

"Thanks," she murmured to her mother, trying to make up for that bitterness, earlier. "I'm really glad you're here."

Frummie smiled her down-turned smile, made some joke about doing anything for a free drink and offered her assistance with the supper.

"It's all under control." Brigid's voice was stronger, quite cheerful. "I hope you're both hungry. I'm starving but then I've had a long walk."

Whilst Frummie answered her and Brigid poured drinks, Louise sat quietly, her face thoughtful. Tiny reverberations echoed in her mind. Brigid's first remark had the force of *déjà vu*. She'd heard something like it before. *"I've been making the most of having Humphrey home"*—and she'd agreed that you had to make the most of every moment, remembering . . . remembering. She was jerked back into the present. Frummie was giving her a drink, raising her own glass, and Louise shook away the cobwebby miasma which clogged her concentration and lifted her glass in response.

"Have you been up the O Brook as far as the Horse Ford?" Brigid was asking her. "Blot and I went way up on the moor this afternoon. He got soaked."

She was ladling tomato and red pepper soup into bowls, taking hot rolls from the Aga, and the delicious smell filled Louise with a sudden, inexplicable happiness. She felt safe, warm, comforted, here in this kitchen with these two women. She could concentrate on this, relax into it. Happiness bubbled inside her and she smiled at Frummie and tasted her soup with relish.

The sudden shrilling of the telephone bell shocked them all. Brigid knocked over her glass and said "Damn" whilst Frummie, with a suddenly trembling hand, reached for her napkin to staunch the red, spreading stain. Louise paused, watching, as Brigid stood, and seized the receiver.

"Hello." Her voice was expressionless but warmed rapidly into friendliness. "Thea! No, no, I'm fine . . . yes, we are, actually. I've got Mummie and Louise over to supper. I'm going to see you tomorrow, aren't I? . . . Oh, oh, I'm sorry . . . Oh, poor Hermione . . . Well, they do, don't they? Quite out of the blue. I'm sure she'll be fine in the morning . . . It sounds beastly, poor little girl . . . Don't worry about me. We can meet any time . . . Honestly, Thea. Just concentrate on Hermione. Let me know how she is when you've got a minute . . . Fine. 'Bye."

She replaced the receiver with a quick nod of relief at Frummie.

"That was Thea," she said, somewhat unnecessarily. "I was going to see her tomorrow but apparently Hermione isn't well." Louise laid down her spoon with a clatter and Brigid glanced briefly at her. "She's very listless, apparently. She's got no energy at all and she's terribly pale. Like alabaster, Thea said. She thinks it's probably a passing bug so she's put her to bed. Poor Hermione. Thea says she's all floppy, like a rag doll." Louise pushed back her chair and Brigid glanced at her again, puzzled by her fixed expression. "I'm sure she'll be fine in the morning . . ."

"No," said Louise. She stood up, placing her chair neatly at the table. "No. She won't be fine in the morning." She shook her head, trembling, biting her lips together. "Tell her," she gestured towards the telephone, "tell her to call the doctor."

Brigid stared at her across the table. Louise's face was filmed with perspiration and her lips shook. She grimaced suddenly.

"Tell her!" she screamed. She grabbed at the back of her chair for support. "Tell Thea that she'll be *dead* in the morning. Phone her and make her get the doctor. Get an ambulance."

Frummie touched her hand and Louise stared down at her, blinking as if to get her into focus.

"Meningitis," she said quietly, her eyes blank, looking past her into another world. "It's meningitis. She'll be dead in the morning."

Frummie stood up swiftly, putting her arm about Louise. "Telephone Thea," she said to Brigid, who stood transfixed with horror and fear. "Quickly."

With trembling, fumbling fingers, Brigid obeyed.

"Thea?" Her voice shook and she cleared her throat. "Thea, listen. About Hermione. Louise says . . . she thinks it could be meningitis . . . I know, but she's very definite that you should call a doctor or get an ambulance . . . Yes, I would . . . After all, it's better to be sure, isn't it? . . . OK. Will you let us know? . . . Right."

She turned back, watching, as Frummie gently pushed Louise down into her chair, still holding one of her hands.

"So that was it," she said gently. "My poor child."

Louise looked at her. The madness had passed and her face was tired and sad. "She was dead in the morning, you see. I hadn't realised that it might be . . . serious. She was so white and listless but I didn't do anything. I thought she'd be better by the morning." And she leaned forward, her forehead resting on the table, and began to cry.

PART TWO

PART TWO

CHAPTER 16

Six weeks later, sitting in the July sunshine on the platform of the Old Station House, Louise watched Hermione playing with Oscar on the grassy track below. Although her heart still ached with an intolerable loss, the weighty, crushing sense of guilt had, at last, miraculously lightened. Three years ago, those two enemies, loss and guilt, had been too strong for her and she had taken refuge in denial. She'd learned that survival was only possible if she pretended that the agony was happening to somebody else and, after weeks of rage, despair and destructive madness, she'd stepped right away from it; become a different person. Martin had offered her the opportunity and she had taken it; after all, there was nothing else left: her child dead and her husband driven away by her anger and guilt. Martin was her passport to a new life, allowing her to bury her past wholesale, and to reinvent herself. She had done it with astonishing success until Martin himself had begun the process which exposed her. In facing up to his betrayal, the façade had crumbled with frightening rapidity. It was Thea's telephone call which had taken her, finally, to the edge of the abyss but this time it had been possible to stare into it. The two women, the sense of sanctuary in the old longhouse, the warm, sunny peace in the courtyard—all these had sustained her, protecting her, refusing to allow her to plunge back into the yawning pit of despair, keeping vigil until she was in some measure restored.

"Where does one go from a world of insanity? Somewhere on the other side of despair . . . A stony sanctuary . . . The heat of the sun and the icy vigil." Gradually she had been able to talk; a thin, unwilling trickle of words which spread into a babbling tide of confused sentences, swelling at last into a flood of poured-out pain. During Hermione's convalescence from a virus, she too had been healed. Past and present still merged but now it was a gentle meeting, no abrupt collisions which unhinged the mind, although she sometimes imagined that it was her own child who played there, on the long-disused railway track, where oxeye daisies leaned and bees hummed amongst the wild flowers.

Her own Hermione would have been much the same age: six years old, nearly seven. For a brief moment Louise could see her: the long fair hair, caught back with clasps, wisps framing the small rosy face; the intent bright look, eyes wide and blue, fixed with friendly curiosity on some object or toy; smooth chubby limbs, jumping, dancing, relaxed in sleep. Louise closed her eyes against the stab of pain. What a shock it had been, to hear the name again; to see the child staring up at her so trustfully; and in such a remote and unlikely place. How carefully she had avoided young mothers, small children, and all those heart-rending reminders of her loss. Martin liked young, professional people, unfettered by family, and she had been buffered by his small circle of close friends. No contact was necessary which might impinge upon her protective bandaging from pain. He had been captivated by her; challenged by her desperate unhappiness. He was convinced that he, and only he, could mend her. He had carried everything before him in his determination and she had allowed herself to be swept away. Now, some other—younger—challenge had displaced her.

When he'd arrived at Foxhole, summoned by Brigid, Louise had been too ill to confront him sensibly. He'd been uncomfortable, embarrassed; not his usual style at all. Even in her weakness and exhaustion she'd guessed that her particular kind of challenge was no longer interesting to him. He'd been there; done it. Even a relapse was not stimulating enough to reignite his own particular need. No doubt he had a different, more challenging lame duck. Carol, perhaps? She'd heard that Carol had an eating disorder, the result of a disastrous marriage which had culminated in a bitter divorce. She hadn't had the strength to question him but she'd noticed the restlessness beneath his solicitousness. It was Frummie who'd suggested that she should stay at Foxhole, rather than return to London, and he'd agreed rather too readily. The strength of her own relief had taken her by surprise and she'd moved thankfully into Frummie's spare bedroom. She'd slept, talked, wept, talked again and slept. Incoherent, violent words had spilled out of her, exhausting her, and afterwards she'd liked to sit in the sun in the courtyard, her mind wonderfully, peacefully empty. As empty as her arms . . .

Louise instinctively crossed her arms over her breast. They'd had to take her dead child from her by force as she'd tried to hug her into warmth, into life . . .

"Where were you?" she'd screamed at Rory. "I *needed* you!"

For three endless, nightmare weeks she'd waited for his return from sea. The news was kept from him until the submarine berthed, by which time she had retreated inside her head to a place he was unable to reach. White-faced, he'd watched her, inarticulate with his own shock and grief; helpless, whilst she destroyed any chance of hope or comfort. She'd known the rules, known that a Polaris submarine is a deterrent and that its whereabouts must be secret; known that bad news is kept from its men because they can do nothing about it and they must remain ready for action. She'd known these things and had accepted them—in theory. In fact it was—to her—intolerable, agonising, that for three whole weeks he was living in a world which he believed still held his daughter. It was unimaginable that he had lived normally, utterly unconscious, whilst Hermione died and was buried. The other wives, the chaplain, Rory's fellow officers had been so kind, but she'd felt utterly isolated, quite alone; as alone as Hermione, in her tiny patch of quiet earth. She'd haunted the churchyard until her mother had come and taken her away from Faslane, taken her home—except that there was no longer any such thing as "home." Home meant Hermione: her voice, her toys, her laughter and tears; her drawings stuck haphazard on the kitchen notice board, her picture-books on the floor, her tricycle in the hall, Percy the Parrot propped in her highchair, tucked in with her at night. He had gone with her, keeping her company at the last . . . And yet here he was, being offered to her. Automatically Louise held out her arms, accepting the toy.

"Mummy's bringing the tea," said Hermione. "I'll help. You can look after Percy."

The toy was something to hold on to, to fill the emptiness, as did Hermione, herself, who was so generous with her affection. Strange, that this child no longer filled her with fear. The rage and the madness had passed away and only grief remained. "Well, it's time you mourned," Thea had said— and her matter-of-factness had been comforting. And Rory? Some long-subdued nerve throbbed painfully and her heart ached. He'd gone away, in the end, on exchange to the Canadian Navy as a staff officer in Ottawa. Her mother had never forgiven her.

Thea was arriving with a tray and Oscar was panting up the ramp to the platform, hoping for a biscuit. Louise smiled at them, able now to contain her feelings with a new patience. The need to pretend and deny was past; but what lay ahead?

"Tea," said Thea. "Tea and then a walk along the track. What do you think?"

"Yes," said Louise gratefully. One step at a time was quite enough to be going on with. "That sounds perfect."

BRIGID, TAKING a break from an afternoon's work which consisted of lining curtains, came slowly downstairs with Blot clattering behind her. She passed through the long, low, sunny rooms, glancing out into the courtyard, deciding to have her tea in the sunshine. Her younger son, Michael, and his girlfriend, Sarah, had been home for the weekend and she was still missing them. It had come as a shock when she'd realised that it was unlikely she'd ever have time alone again with either of her sons. She'd been so thrilled at their growing relationships, clearly serious at last, that she hadn't foreseen that a certain part of her own life was coming to an end as theirs expanded; that she must step back and make room for the two girls with whom her boys were in love. Often it was necessary to bite her tongue during telephone conversations, to put the other side of a case when she was longing to be motherly and protective, to explain, instead, how Emma or Sarah might be feeling. Of course there would be odd moments, during occasional holidays or weekends, when she'd have the chance to be on her own with Julian or Michael but those long, lazy days, those family Christmases, those silly private passwords and games were receding into the past. Her children were making their own traditions and she must learn to stand aside whilst keeping a loving welcome always ready. So much time and energy, so much love and learning had gone into those long years of motherhood, and now, between a morning and a morning—or so it felt— they were over. It seemed that mothers of daughters had a more extended role but she knew that she was lucky to be allowed any part in her boys' lives and tried hard to be grateful and undemanding. It wasn't always easy, when she loved them so much, to practise detachment. She'd thought that the early separation, when they'd gone away to school, might stand her in good stead but this was a different kind of self-denial. Odd that the last of the parenting skills should be the most painful: the final act of letting go.

As she went into the kitchen Brigid remembered that there was the remains of some sponge cake to be eaten with her tea, out in the sunny courtyard. Her spirits rose at the prospect of these simple treats and, whilst the kettle boiled, she went outside, stretching her shoulders and blinking at the brightness. The swallows swooped above her head, carrying food to their babies who jostled snugly in the nests among the beams in the barn, whilst the richly coloured blooms of surfinia and diascia trailed riotously from the hanging baskets on the granite walls.

These hanging baskets were her great luxury and Brigid looked at them with pleasure. Without a greenhouse, it was impossible to bring on bedding plants quickly enough to make an early show and so Liz, at MGM Nurseries, made up the baskets for her. Each year, as soon as it was warm enough, Brigid drove to Loddiswell, collected her summer garden and transported it back to Foxhole. The sheltered courtyard was transformed to an almost Mediterranean luxuriance; a small lush oasis hidden in the stony harshness of the moor.

The doves murmured cosily, drowsing in the heat, and bees lumbered heavily, droning. It was a perfect afternoon and, on a sudden impulse, Brigid left the courtyard. The door to Frummie's cottage was open and music drifted from the living room: Glenn Miller's "A String of Pearls."

"Hi," she called. "Are you there, Mummie?"

Frummie came out, a dishcloth in her hand. "Hello. I was just making some tea. No time to stay for one, I suppose?"

Brigid suppressed her instinctive reaction to the inference that she was always too busy to be friendly: she was trying very hard to be less sensitive.

"To be honest I was going to suggest that you had one with me in the courtyard. It's such a glorious afternoon and I've got some cake."

Frummie raised her eyebrows as if surprised—though pleased—at such an unexpected invitation. "I'd like that very much."

"Good. Come over when you're ready."

She hurried away before Frummie could make any observation about the cake being a leftover from Michael's visit and went into the kitchen to make the tea. When she brought the tray out, Frummie was already sitting on the bench, her face lifted to the sun.

"Heaven," she murmured. "Absolute heaven. I think I must have been a lizard in a previous existence. It simply can't be too hot for me."

She wore a long, sleeveless cotton dress, loosely belted, and leather sandals. Brigid looked at the finely lined skin, opened her mouth to ask about sun block and shut it again.

No use talking to Frummie about the fear of skin cancer. She considered the present climate of fear, which spread miasmically around almost anything relating to normal life, completely paranoid. Despite her fair colouring, she was brown as a nut; Brigid, pouring the tea, envied her inasmuch as she never seemed to burn.

"You look as if you've been on holiday on the Continent," Brigid said.

Frummie opened her eyes. "Speaking of which," she said, "I do think that it was quite dim-witted of Martin to come home flaunting such an amazing suntan. Did he really think that Louise would believe he'd got that kind of colour from plodding round St Andrew's for a fortnight?"

"I don't think she was in any fit state to notice." Brigid sat back comfortably with a sigh of content, Blot curled by her feet in a pool of sunshine.

"But he didn't *know* that she wouldn't be." Frummie crumbled some cake, tasted it and nodded appreciatively. "I do dislike people who underrate one's intelligence."

"Either that or he simply didn't care." Brigid shook her head. "He was so awkward about it all, wasn't he? It was terribly embarrassing."

"I warned you about that. He's moved beyond it and he's living in a different world. His concentration is elsewhere."

"Clearly." Brigid tried not to speak sharply, knowing that they were edging out on to thin ice. "But surely he could have made an effort when he saw the state she was in. He was rather like a spoiled child who's cross because his fun is being threatened."

"The man's a wanker." Frummie closed her eyes.

"Honestly, Mummie . . ."

Frummie snorted, hunching an impatient shoulder. "No good being mealy-mouthed. Louise's well out of it. She's coming on splendidly. And I have to say that at least he's being generous about it, financially speaking."

"I should think so!" said Brigid indignantly. "He goes off on holiday with another woman. Seems quite indifferent to his wife—"

"Mistress. They're not married."

The interruption threw Brigid off her stride. "Yes, I know. You did tell me. But I just don't see Louise as a mistress. And, after all, they've been together for three years."

"Perhaps you'd prefer the modern word 'partner,'" suggested Frummie suavely. "Hideous, *I* think. So businesslike and boring. Sounds like a company instead of a relationship. Mistress is *much* better."

"Well, anyway . . ." Brigid had lost her thread and paused to drink some tea. "She's going up to London, isn't she? To get it sorted out?"

"She is indeed. I must say I'm very happy to let her stay but she needs to make some plans of her own."

"It's been really good of you," said Brigid almost shyly, expecting a sharp rejoinder; Frummie was not a gracious receiver of compliments. "More than a month. It's a long time with someone you don't know terribly well and it was so awful at the beginning."

"She needed to talk. To go over it again and again. Poor child. She was carrying so much guilt, never mind the terrible grief and pain. She's come through splendidly."

"I hope she doesn't have a setback when she sees Martin again. Do you think she's over him too?"

Frummie looked thoughtful. "I don't think there's been much *room* for him," she said. "She's had too much to deal with and she hasn't had the energy to work out what she's feeling about him. She's gone back into a past which didn't contain Martin and she's been coming to terms with it. His turn comes next."

"What a ghastly tragedy. I wonder what happened to her husband. Imagine what it must have been like for him! His whole world vanishing overnight."

"Louise hasn't got that far. At least, she hasn't mentioned him to me. Only that he went on an exchange to the Canadian Navy."

"If he'd been with her at the time, they might have worked through it together. She couldn't forgive him for not being there. Oh God, how appalling it must have been. Poor Louise! And then to be confronted with Hermione."

Frummie set down her cup. "If the older girls, Julia or Amelia, had been with Thea instead nothing would have happened. It was the name that triggered it. It might have happened any time or anywhere. Once she suspected that Martin was no longer standing between her and the past she became vulnerable."

"I wonder if she and Martin might get back together. This other woman could just be a bit of a fling."

"Unlikely. Timing is so crucial. If Rory had been at home when their child died I doubt they'd have ever parted. If Martin had been around when Louise finally cracked they might have been able to make a go of it. As it is, I think the dislocation is too great."

"It's frightening, isn't it? So precarious. Small things can make such huge differences."

"The difference between a 'yes' or a 'no.'" Frummie sounded sad. "Between a 'sorry' or remaining silent. Between writing a letter or making a telephone call rather than waiting for the other person to make the first move. Life never waits and we are so profligate."

Brigid stared at her, longing to ask her if she had regrets, if it were her own experiences that made her sound so sad, but Frummie's eyes were closed again, her face turned towards the sun, and Brigid was unable to frame the question.

CHAPTER 17

Later that evening, Brigid walked up to Combestone Tor. The granite slabs, folded and heaped haphazard, were stained with a sunset glow and a thin, sickle moon hung in the east. Below her, Blot, a dark, dense shadow moving over the short turf, investigated the stony crannies whilst a raven flapped slowly westward with a hoarse croaking cry. Perched on an outcrop, Brigid watched his flight. The immensity of the landscape—peaks and summits of blue and lavender and gold, receding into the mysterious, insubstantial, vaporous distance—was having its usual soothing effect. Here in these airy spaces, high above a shadowy mosaic of moorland and fields and valleys, she was filled with a surging, singing joy; thin hands linked about her pointed knees, straight-backed, her cheeks stroked by a cool current of air, she felt a quivering, exciting tingling in her veins: that long-familiar delight which was the physical manifestation of brief, true union with nature. As the brilliant light faded, sheep grazing on distant slopes metamorphosed into dim, pale, bulky boulders; hawthorn trees dislimned into spectral, twisting, curious shapes. In the valley the rising mist, white as milk, drifted above the river, sliding and curling along the steep-sided combe.

Here, for this moment, remote, separated from the well-worn pattern of the days, she felt all the real possibility of the existence of another, greater design: some loftier, nobler composition which might be attained, lived, accomplished. Here, as the barn owl, numinous and unearthly, drifted on blunt wings above the feathery, plumy tops of Combestone Wood, she was absorbed, overwhelmed, with an unnamed longing which sprang from some deep intuitive source: a longing for something almost forgotten, dimly seen, lost beneath layers of numbing, mind-coarsening cares and desires. True contentment of spirit, the promise of an unshakeable inner peace, trembled tantalisingly beyond her reach, ephemeral—but *there* . . .

A scrabbling beside her on the rocks, something cold and wet thrust against her cheek—and the magic swiftly faded, along with the dying light—yet a quiet joy remained. Blot whined, demanding action, and Brigid stood up, reluctant but resigned, and began the descent. On the moorland road sheep were settling for the night, making the most of the day's heat still locked in the warm tarmac. Keeping Blot to heel, skirting the woolly, immobile bundles, she walked quickly, the lights of Foxhole glimmering among the rowan trees. Across Saddle Bridge, Blot now scurrying ahead, and up the hill she went, joy still beating in her heart.

It sustained her as she passed down the track and into the house and, even when she heard Jenny's voice on the answerphone, she was still so enraptured by her private delight that she could not quite take in the words.

"I suppose it could be worse. The receiver's letting us keep going because it will be easier to sell as an up-and-running business but it seems that there's a twelve-thousand-pounds shortfall. Oh, Brigid, I simply don't know what to say. You'll be getting a letter any day now. I was hoping to see you but I daren't leave the place at the moment. Sorry to have missed you."

Brigid stared at the unwinking red light. She had managed to convince herself that no news was good news; that Jenny and Iain had found some solution. The crisis with Louise, as well as Humphrey's departure for the Bahamas, had helped to distance her; to lessen the fear. Twelve thousand pounds. She shook her head: it couldn't be true; she must have misheard. Quickly she pressed the button, holding it down so that it overrode the "No new message" response. "*. . . but it seems that there's a twelve-thousand-pounds shortfall. Oh, Brigid . . .*" Grim-faced, she wiped the message, opened her address book, dialled a number. "There's no one here at present to take your call . . ." No doubt Jenny and Iain were avoiding angry creditors—and who could blame them?—but there was no telephone at Iain's mobile home and no other way of contacting Jenny. Brigid left a short message, trying to keep her voice friendly, asking for Jenny to call her as soon as possible, and then went to pour herself a glass of wine.

Twelve thousand pounds? How did one raise such a sum? Mortgage, of course, but what would Humphrey say? Her joy evaporated, enmeshed in impotent fear, Brigid kneeled beside Blot, hugging him, needing his warmth, feeling miserably, frighteningly alone.

JEMIMA SWITCHED off the engine and cursed beneath her breath as a tall figure appeared from the back of the cottage and stood waiting. The fact that he stood so—arms folded, face expressionless—indicated that a great deal of placating would be necessary.

"I'm so terribly sorry." She almost fell from the car in her eagerness. "A frightful muddle. Someone was supposed to be here to let you in. I only got the message half an hour ago. I am *so* sorry."

He was thawing very slightly, arms dropping to his side, taking a step or two towards her, and she smiled, registering the fact that he was drop-dead sexy in a casual, indifferent kind of way. Briefly she wished that she'd changed out of her old jeans and had had the time to put on some make-up. She held out her hand to him, smiling warmly, unconsciously breathing in and straightening her shoulders.

"I'm Jemima Spencer. The wretched woman who was supposed to be meeting you has only just telephoned. Some domestic drama, I'm afraid. Have you been here for hours?"

She knew he hadn't but she could see that this abject business was working and decided to stay with it. He was looking at her appraisingly as he advanced across the grass and she had a moment to weigh him up: tall, tough, with a wide curling mouth, brown eyes and very short red-brown hair.

She thought: Ohmigod! He's gorgeous!

"Not too long." He wasn't giving too much away. "But it's already been a rather trying day."

"Oh dear." Not that this was her fault but sympathy seemed in order. "Have you had a long drive?"

He shrugged, watching her finding the key. "Not too bad. The traffic's bloody awful."

"Saturdays in late July, I'm afraid," she said ruefully. "The A38 is hell. Is your . . .? Is Mrs. . . .? Sorry. I should have checked before I rushed out but my one thought was to get here. Janet said it was a couple."

"She's right. It *was* a couple. Now it's just me. My partner broke it to me last night that she wasn't coming with me."

"Shit!" Jemima stared at him. "How awful. I'm so sorry."

"Yes. So," he shrugged again, "I decided that I might as well carry on as planned. It gives her a chance to move out in peace and it gives me a month to recover." He was following her into the cottage now, but was pulled up short by her cry of dismay.

"Oh, I don't *believe* it."

"You sound like Victor Meldrew. What's the problem?"

He was peering over her shoulder as she stared despairingly at the mess in the kitchen: unwashed dishes on the draining board; the remains of food on the table; a general air of disorder.

"This is awful." She turned to him, genuinely distressed. "I'll kill Janet when I get hold of her. She didn't say that she hadn't been in to clear up, only that she couldn't let you in. Nothing's been done, I'm afraid. I am just *so* sorry."

He was frowning, looking past her, and she watched him anxiously, wondering if he would lose his temper, report her, storm out: he might do all three. It wouldn't impress her boss to lose a month's rent, especially at the top height-of-summer rates.

"It won't take long to put right," she said rapidly.

"Honestly. Perhaps you could go for a walk? Or just sit in the sun? There's a nice little garden area with chairs . . ."

"Forget it," he said resignedly. "I might have guessed that it was going to be one of those days. We'll do it together, it'll be quicker."

"That's . . . that's really good of you." She looked at him gratefully. "I can't tell you how sorry I am."

"Forget it." He laughed briefly. "Good job Annabel's not here. She doesn't take kindly to this sort of thing and she likes to see heads roll if mistakes are made. Can't stand inefficiency. I'll wash up. OK?"

"Yes, of course." She watched him as he rolled up his shirtsleeves, feeling an odd need to defend herself. "Well, in that case I have to say that I'm relieved that she isn't here." She hesitated. "I'm not usually inefficient. This has never happened to me before."

He glanced at her quickly, eyebrows raised, and then smiled. "I didn't mean to imply that you were. Anyway, if I'm honest, I found the whole perfection bit rather wearing. Self-righteousness isn't exactly my bag. Is the stuff in this cupboard? Oh, yes. Will there be hot water?"

"Damn!" She pulled herself together. "Probably not. It's money-in-the-slot stuff and visitors who leave cottages in this condition aren't usually too free with their pennies. I'll check."

When she returned he'd already piled the dishes neatly together and was throwing the rubbish into a black sack.

"I'm well trained," he said, seeing her surprise.

"So I see," she said. A pause. "I think Annabel must be a bit of a twit," she added casually.

He smiled. "Thanks."

"I'll be changing the beds," she said, suddenly shy. "We'll have a cup of coffee later, if you like. At least there's some milk in the fridge."

"Great," he said. "Or perhaps a pint. Is there a decent pub round here? It seems seriously remote, if you know what I mean. Rather end-of-the-world-ish. Glorious views but a bit short on human habitation. Since I shall be on my own I'm hoping there's a relatively local hostelry."

"Yes," she said, after a moment. "There is, actually. The Pig's Nose at Prawle is only ten minutes away."

"Great name," he said, putting in the plug and turning on the tap. "Any chance you could show me where it is? Or are you . . . otherwise engaged?"

"No," she said, trying not to grin foolishly. "No, not otherwise engaged. I'd love to."

Humming under her breath, she went away to find the clean laundry.

LYING AWAKE, staring into the darkness, Louise allowed the tide of her thoughts to wash gently in and out of her consciousness. No more need for vigilance; those years of watchfulness were over. It seemed impossible to have buried a whole past so deeply, yet she had managed it. It was another life which had happened to someone else, to a different person who could be shut away, ignored, denied. Now, painful though the memories were, she let them come. At first she had been obsessed with reliving the tragedy itself but lately other images passed on the screen of her mind, scrolling slowly before her inward vision, carrying her back in time: Smugglers Way; the view across the Gare Loch to the mountains beyond; walking through the woods, pushing Hermione in her buggy, to the little shop in Rhu village; waiting on Rhu Spit with the other families to watch the submarines sailing or arriving.

From the beginning she'd found the homecomings difficult: even when she'd missed Rory so much that the weeks stretched like months and life seemed hopelessly empty, she'd been unable to pick up the threads with the easy cheerful jokiness which other wives used as an aid to readjust. She discovered that his actual presence—the disturbing reality of his warm, blue eyes; the impact of his vitality—was a shock to her. She'd reacted with a silent shyness which frustrated her but which she was incapable of overcoming. He'd never let it worry him, allowing time to reattune, adapting his pace to hers until the strangeness passed. He'd always known when that moment had arrived, when the old familiarity was warming her into relaxed, loving normality, and at that point he'd slip an arm about her.

"So that's that," he'd say, as if putting the weeks of separation and any other obstacles firmly behind them. "Now! Where were we?"

A whole world of meaning was encapsulated in that "Now!" It implied that real life was about to resume; that everything which had happened between their last goodbye and this "Now!" was utterly unimportant. She was his love, his life, what truly mattered. That small phrase "Where were we?" was a password which carried them into their own, private world. Hermione had become a vital part of that world; she'd helped with the adjustment: carrying them over the difficulty with her delight at his homecoming, demanding his attention, making them laugh with her enthusiasm. Even so, once she had been put to bed and they were alone together, the shyness still hung between them, a fragile but obscuring curtain, until that moment of recognition. "So that's that. Now! Where were we?" His arm about her shoulders, his cheek against her hair, oh! the comfort of it.

Hot tears slid from Louise's eyes, trickling over her temples and into her hair. She'd given him no opportunity on that final occasion; no chance for healing, loving words. Three weeks were too long to bear such agony alone. She'd projected the unbearable weight of guilt on to him: if he had been at home it might not have happened; he might have been suspicious, insisted on calling a doctor. Rory had always been overanxious where Hermione was concerned. By the time he arrived home she, Louise, had already begun the long journey into denial and it was too late to return. Not even the familiar password could have called her back: she'd been beyond his reach.

How had he managed? Now that she could no longer blame him or resent him for his absence, she must deal with this new pain. How had he felt?

"You're not the only one," her mother had shouted at her, worn down by her own grief and shock. "Other people are suffering too, you know. How can you behave like this?"

She could remember her mother's furious expression, the tears of anger and sorrow in her eyes, but at the time it was as if it were superimposed over the persisting picture of the silent child in the bed, unnaturally still, alabaster pale. Beside that image nothing else had seemed particularly real. Perhaps if she'd remained in the flat at Smugglers Way, if she'd been in their own home when Rory had arrived back from sea, things might have been different. She had spent the days after the funeral there, between Hermione's room and the graveyard, until the other wives had begun to fear for her and had contacted her mother. She'd put up one brief fight, one manic struggle to stay with what remained of her child, but she'd been physically weak with sleeplessness and lack of food, and easily overborne.

Poor Rory! His horror had been unbearable, exacerbating her own guilt, so that her only resource had been mental escape; flight into oblivion. How could there be a way back when she was already denying the past? Unfortunately her relationship with her mother had never been a particularly strong one—she was a demanding, managing woman—and at length she'd sought refuge with her oldest friend who'd had a compassionate grasp of the problem. It was while she'd been with Helena that she'd met Martin. He'd been like some great elemental force, a tsunami, sweeping everything before the overwhelming tide of his determination. She'd submitted to it, grateful to be relieved of thought or will.

"How can you?" asked her mother, stony-faced. "What about Rory? Have you given him a thought?"

Rory. She'd dared not look back along that dark road; there was too much horror. Martin had been beside her, watchful, guarding her, and her mother had turned away in disgust.

"Don't expect me to approve," she'd said. "Rory's more of a son to me now, than you are a daughter. He's absolutely broken-hearted but he won't pressure you if you don't want to see him. He's talking of trying for an exchange to the Canadian Navy but I can see you're not interested."

It had been as if there were a wall of glass between

them: her mother's mouth moving, shaping words, twisting with dislike; her eyes glancing, sliding, narrowing with contempt. Martin had intervened and made an end of it. And Rory?

Louise raised her hands to her cheeks, blotting away the tears. How could she have hurt him so? Rory, who had been so kind, so understanding, and who had loved them both so much. His image rose before her: ruddy, vivid, vitally alive. His voice murmured in the darkness: warm, flexible, full of love.

"So that's that. Now! Where were we?"

Louise turned on her side, pulling the quilt over her head, and allowed the storm of tears to possess her.

CHAPTER 18

"We've got a friend coming for drinks," Jemima told Magnifi-Cat casually. "You'll like him. This is not a subject for ne-gotiation, so please remember to stay put in that chair and then he'll have to sit beside me on the sofa. And don't climb on him and get hairs all over his clothes until we know whether he likes cats. OK?"

MagnifiCat stared at her contemptuously with half-closed eyes, yawned and gave his flank a quick lick, unim-pressed with her strictures.

"Of course," sighed Jemima gloomily, "he'll simply go straight out on to the balcony. Everyone does. The view gets them every time. Pity I can't get the sofa on the balcony. I should have offered to cook for us instead of agreeing to go out to supper. The problem was, it looked a bit keen. Oh, well! He'll have to bring me home again afterwards, won't he?"

MagnifiCat stood up, arching and stretching, and settled himself again with his back turned pointedly towards her. He was not fond of the male of the species and had his own inim-itable ways of making his presence felt. He'd had plenty of experience and had honed his performance to near perfection. He was a first-class judge of character. First there was the nervous, awkward specimen, who, anxious to ingratiate and please, put itself out to be friendly. MagnifiCat would humili-ate this type with a haughty look, bristling under a deferential pat, leaping from the determined show of affection. There was

the confident specimen—the most difficult of all, this type—
who was unfazed by hostility and could remain cool even if
hissed at, although a quick well-aimed stab with a claw could
usually wipe the self-satisfied smile off its face. Then there
was the type who feared cats but was too afraid of losing
Brownie points to admit it. This type preferred to keep its distance and MagnifiCat took enormous pleasure in rubbing affectionately round its trousered legs, jumping on to its lap, and
generally making a nuisance of himself whilst enjoying the
grim, rictus smile on his victim's face. Finally there was the
true cat-hating specimen. Nothing could be done here but to
exchange that fierce, cold, inimical stare which made it quite
clear to both protagonists exactly how the land lay between
them. Naturally, it took Jemima—poor, simple human that
she was—much longer to sum up these contenders but if only
she'd followed his example her life would have been much
simpler. MagnifiCat, resigned to her thick-headedness, settled
himself to sleep.

Jemima prowled to and forth: sitting down, standing up
again, checking the drinks tray. It was important that the
room looked casually charming; not too perfect, as if she'd
been cleaning and polishing for his benefit; nor too untidy
lest he should think she was a slut. Annabel, after all, was a
perfectionist and, though he had said he was tired of it, yet it
might be foolish to present him with too great a contrast.

She thought: I wonder what she looks like?

She stared at herself in the big ash-framed looking-glass
which hung over the bookcase, pushing her hands up into
the thick, fair hair, wondering if she should have tied it back.
She wore a black, raw silk kurta-style tunic and loose
trousers which flattered her rounded and not-too-tall figure
and emphasised her golden tan. She glanced at her watch
just as the bell was rung and she jumped nervously, standing
for a moment, hands clenched into fists, before hurrying to
answer the door.

"Hi." He looked very poised standing there, very cool,
and she heard a faint stammer in her voice as she invited him
in. He followed her along the passage to the sitting room but

did not go immediately to the window. Instead he looked about with that same calm, unhurried glance.

"This is seriously nice," he said. "What a place!"

"It's good, isn't it?" She tried to sound almost indifferent. "I'm very lucky to have got it."

"I should think you are. How clever of you not to have covered up all this lovely wood with carpet. Goodness! That's some view! I bet you had to pay extra for that."

"I had a little legacy from my papa." She followed him out on to the balcony. "It's rather special, isn't it?"

"Rather." He smiled down at her and she looked away, trying to control her tendency to grin madly back at him. "It must be wonderful at night with all the boats lit up."

"Would you like a drink?" She felt so jumpy, so out of control, that she needed to be occupied.

"Why not? A drop of whisky would go down well." He was still leaning on the balcony, looking over the harbour. "It was a very good idea of yours that I should come across on the ferry so that I don't have to worry about driving. It's odd how places look so different from the water, isn't it? What's that ruined castle I saw?"

"That's Fort Charles," she told him. "It was used by the Royalists in the Civil War. I think it was even besieged."

"I'd like to have a good look at it," he said. "I suppose that's possible?"

"Oh yes. You could catch the South Sands Ferry. It takes you past Fort Charles and the battery and then you're met by the sea tractor so you can get on to the beach. There's a wonderful lifeboat station there."

"Sounds fun. I might do that."

"I don't know if you're interested in National Trust properties but there's Overbecks Museum, as well, just above South Sands."

"That would have suited Annabel," he said. "Not really my scene but I might have a look at it. I suppose you've seen all these sights so many times that it's not worth asking you to join me on this Magical Mystery Tour?"

"Not that many times." She tried not to sound too keen.

"Like you say, places look quite different from the water. It would be fun. I ought to get on the river more often."

"You should have a boat." He looked at her in an oddly measuring way. "Are you a sailor?"

"Not much of one," she admitted, wondering if Annabel was. "But only because I haven't had much opportunity, not because I don't like it. Are you?"

"I haven't had the opportunity either," he told her. "Never had much to do with the sea except childhood holidays. I think I might be tempted to try it if I lived here, though."

"Well," she was suddenly shy, afraid of reading too much into his words, "let's have a drink, shall we, and you must meet MagnifiCat."

"MagnifiCat?" He sounded puzzled, leaving the balcony reluctantly, but at the sight of the large, furry pile curled in the basket-chair he burst out laughing. "Oh, what a poser."

The hair on MagnifiCat's neck lifted a little and he sighed: Type B: confident, cool, tricky. He ignored the smoothing, stroking, male hand, pretending to sleep on.

"He's feeling antisocial," said Jemima apologetically. "Never mind. Here's your drink."

"Thanks." He raised his glass. "Here's to a rather different holiday than I imagined. You know, I think I might enjoy it after all."

"Yes," said Jemima, after a confused moment. "Good. I'll drink to that."

MagnifiCat burrowed deeper into the cushion, eyes still firmly closed.

He thought: Here we go again.

As RACHMANINOV's music brought *Brief Encounter* to an end Louise sat in silence, moved as usual by the film, and wondering what Frummie was thinking. She'd been unusually silent throughout—generally the soundtracks were punctuated by her pithy observations—and even now, as she rewound the video, she didn't speak. Surreptitiously blowing her nose, Louise supposed that it was possible that the film had unlocked Frummie's painful memories or transported her back to an unhappy period of her life. After all, in the fifties Frummie must have been a young woman, with a small child, so there were certain poignant similarities. Except, of course, that Frummie had succumbed to her own particular passion and fled with her lover, leaving her child and her husband. Perhaps she was struggling with remorse, wishing she'd resisted . . .

Louise thought: I'm being silly and sentimental. I always was a sucker for a good old weepie. Still, I hope she's not feeling too sad.

Frummie stirred, lifted the remote control and plunged the television screen into blackness.

"It's extraordinary," she said, "but each time I watch that film I find myself utterly unable to connect with it. I simply cannot recall anyone who behaved like that. All those stiff upper lips, fearfully wearing! The only thing that I remember are those wonderful fires in railway station waiting rooms. Now that's certainly true to life."

"Oh, Frummie." Louise began to chuckle. "And I was sitting here trying not to intrude on your memories. How prosaic you are. I think it's a lovely film. I always want to cry buckets."

"Have you ever thought," asked Frummie, "how much more romantic and splendid our own lives would be if we lived them to music?"

Louise looked at her, puzzled. "How do you mean?"

"Well, think about it. When we're watching films or plays how much of our emotional response is actually created by the music? How affected would we have been by those two somewhat anally retentive people if it hadn't been for dear old Rachmaninov thundering away in the background?"

"I hadn't thought about it," said Louise uncertainly. "But what about Shakespeare at the theatre? Or any stage play, for that matter? We don't get background music then but we're still moved."

"Ah, but in the theatre you get the atmosphere, that exciting current that flows between the actors and the audience. It's essential for the rapport to be developed for any stage production to be really successful. The emotion has to be live and real and raw or it doesn't work. It flops. But the cinema and television need aids to recreate that magic, so they use music. Even the old black-and-white silent films knew that they needed the pianist sitting in the pit. If you think about it, it's the music that really rouses the emotions, whether it's fear, compassion, grief."

"I wonder if that's true." Louise thought about some of her favourite films: *Death in Venice* without Mahler; *The Deer Hunter* without Samuel Barber. "Actually, I think you might have a point."

Frummie snorted. "Of course I have a point. And what I'm saying is, I think we'd all feel much nobler if we had an orchestra around when we're living those really dramatic moments of our own lives. I'm sure it would be much less of a dreary struggle if Brahms or Mozart was accompanying our own private dramas. We watch all these plays and films and are moved by suffering and fear or great romantic passion, yet our own lives we imagine to be rather pathetic and dreary. I've always had a fancy to die to some great dramatic musical theme but I can't quite decide what it should be."

"Wagner?" Louise began to enter into the spirit of the thing. "Beethoven's Ninth?"

Frummie frowned thoughtfully. "The thing is, that it needs to be long enough to see you through. One might not be able to keep nipping out of bed to keep restarting the tape."

"You need one of those remote controls for your radio," Louise told her. "You just point it at it and it would keep playing."

Frummie looked at her, impressed. "Do they make them for radios, now?"

"They do indeed. I'll get you one."

"Of course one might not be even strong enough to do that." Frummie looked faintly irritated by these complications. "How difficult it all is."

"It would be frustrating if the music stopped at the wrong moment." Louise was amused at the idea. "I suppose it would have to be something powerful and dramatic."

"On the other hand I might prefer something sexy and terribly evocative," said Frummie. "Something that really invokes a memory. Nina Simone, perhaps. Someone with a gravelly voice that plucks the heartstrings right out of your chest, so that you're way back there in that dim, shadowy cellar and you can see the little, round tables with their half-empty glasses, and ashtrays spilling over, and a velvet evening bag dumped down amongst the wet sticky rings. You can smell the grey smoke curling in the thick atmosphere, which you could cut with a knife, and you can hear the rich beat of the bass and the hush-hush of the drum. There's a black singer in a low-cut dress who's sitting at a piano. One of those old prim French uprights. Her eyes are closed and her head's thrown back so that you can see the long, rippling black column of her throat. She's singing about love and lust and betrayal and she's singing *your* story because you know that the bastard sitting opposite is going to tell you, later on, that he's leaving you for the bitch you saw him with that morning. But you'll go back to his room with him, anyway, and cling to him and give him what he wants because you love him more than anything else in the world and you can't see straight for lust. That's what she's singing about and everyone knows it."

There was a silence. Presently, Louise looked at her.

"It sounds terribly poignant and real," she said. "And I have to admit that it's not much like Trevor Howard and Celia Johnson."

Frummie gave a crack of derisive laughter. "Not much. But that's the way it was for me."

"I thought you were dreary, respectable and middle class," suggested Louise, trying to disguise her own emotion with a lighter tone.

"I was." Frummie smiled her down-turned, derisive smile. "Oh, I was, darling. That's why it was so bloody painful."

"Not Mozart then." Louise wished that she had the courage to give the older woman a hug. "So be it. Nina Simone it is. And I'll come and sit with you so that the music doesn't stop."

"I'll hold you to that." Frummie was getting to her feet with the usual grimace of pain. "It might take a while, though. I don't give up easily. I hope you'll have the time to spare."

"You've given me the time when I needed it," said Louise lightly. "You say the word and I'll be there when it's your turn."

"Supper," said Frummie. "Before we get maudlin. And a drink. But we've got a deal."

"We have indeed. I'll be there. With Nina Simone."

"And a bottle," added Frummie.

"And a bottle," agreed Louise.

CHAPTER 19

Each morning—and often in the long, dark watches of the night—Brigid woke to the grip of fear. It twisted her gut and stampeded her heart into a choking racing beat. Twelve thousand pounds. No word had come from the Bank although she had managed, at last, to speak to Jenny.

"I've been trying to raise the money myself," she'd said, "but I don't have any security. We put everything into the business, you see. I just didn't imagine anything like this would happen to me. I thought of all sorts of other disasters but not this one. Bryn was so keen on it. It was his baby. It's bad enough, him running off with another woman, but to cheat and steal . . ." She'd paused, as if words were beyond her.

"And what can I do?" Brigid asked herself desperately on this particular morning, after a disturbed and unrefreshing night, as she flung back the quilt. "I want to scream at her. To say, 'I don't give a shit about Bryn. How the hell am I going to tell Humphrey?' But she's lost so much, it would be too cruel."

She thrust her long, narrow feet into moccasins, dragged on her dressing gown and went downstairs. Blot wagged a sleepy greeting from his basket by the Aga and she bent to pull his silky ears.

"I know it's early," she told him, "but I can't sleep."

Blot watched her for a moment and then settled himself

again. Brigid stood at the window watching the sun rising away over Combestone Tor, remembering the evening she'd sat there. How quickly the peace and joy had faded in the face of her fear. For a brief moment she'd glimpsed something which she'd believed to be enduring, some strength that would sustain her through any crisis. Yet at the first threat to her wellbeing it had vanished, leaving her alone. Or was it simply that she lacked the courage to hold on to it; to continue to believe in it, despite the storms that buffeted her security?

"It's Humphrey," she said aloud, as if she were justifying her lack of faith to someone. "It's having to tell Humphrey that I went behind his back and agreed to something which I know he'd disapprove of because he doesn't like Jenny. It seemed so mean to penalise her because Humphrey finds her irritating. She's been such a good friend and I felt I owed her my loyalty. And now Humphrey will say, 'I told you so.'" She laughed bitterly. "God, if that were the only thing he'd say! He's going to be so angry. And hurt, as if I care more about her than I do about him, which is just not true. But it might look like that. I risked his future for her. We'll have to remortgage or pay it out of his gratuity which means, either way, that he won't be able to retire."

She turned away from the window as the kettle began to boil. It was possible that Humphrey might not want to retire full time—although as a commander of fifty-three, with no likelihood of further promotion, he would certainly be leaving the Navy after this posting—but the point was that now he wouldn't have any choices. He'd often discussed what he might do when he came out—he had several local charity projects in mind—but his idea had been to diversify. He was looking forward to being out of uniform and free of rules and regs. Brigid made coffee, her heart weighted with misery. She could not decide whether she should warn him or wait for the letter from the Bank. For some reasons—cowardly ones—it would be easier telling him whilst he was so far away, yet it seemed so unfair to give him this shock by telephone or letter. If she could only find some way through without his knowing anything at all about it . . . and on top of all this muddle and anxiety she had Humphrey's father arriving in four weeks' time.

"His name's Alexander," Humphrey had said rather awkwardly. He was still feeling guilty that Brigid should be left to deal with this alone. "I don't know if I've ever told you before."

"Probably. I don't remember. You always refer to him as 'Father.'" She'd been seized by a moment of panic. "He won't expect me to call him 'Father,' will he?"

"I doubt it very much." Humphrey had sounded faintly amused by the idea. "He's not at all conventional."

She'd looked at him curiously. "That sounds oddly ominous. What do you mean?"

"Oh, nothing in particular." He'd hastened to reassure her, not wishing to alarm her. "He just doesn't look at things the way most people do."

"Are you basing that on the fact that he remarried so quickly after your mother died or have you been hiding things from me?" she'd asked suspiciously. "Come on, Humphrey. It's bad enough as it is, without you hinting at anything more sinister. Look at what 'things,' for instance?"

"It's difficult to define." Humphrey had been on the defensive. "It's not anything weird. Just the way he sees life in general. He comes at it from a different place than most people. He's entirely unmaterialistic and rather penetratingly honest."

Brigid had frowned, confused. "I've never imagined him like that," she'd said. "The way you talked about his going off made him sound a very selfish person."

"He is. But that's the kind of thing I mean. He didn't think about how I might feel or how it looked or anything. He just did his own thing. But when you confront him his reasons can be . . . well, disconcerting, to say the least."

"*Did* you confront him?"

"Not sensibly. I was too young and still too upset about Mother dying. I remember he asked me how it would benefit me if he stayed single and I said that it looked bad and that people would get the wrong impression."

"What did he say?"

"He asked what people I had in mind and why their opinion was important. I couldn't think of a sensible reply. So then he asked me again how it would benefit *me* and I couldn't think how. After all, I was nearly twenty-one and about to go to sea. It sounded so childish to insist that he stayed put because it gave me a sense of security but I resented his insensitivity. Everything happened all at once: Mother dying, me going off to sea, Father going away. There seemed nothing solid to hold on to and I felt he should have understood that."

"And he didn't?"

"That's the point. He said he did. And then he said, 'But does it matter?' That's what I mean when I say he doesn't behave or react like other people."

"Then he should get on well with Mummie," she'd said rather crossly because she was feeling nervous. "Thank God it's only for three months."

Brigid finished her coffee and put the mug in the sink. Suddenly she was possessed with a great weariness; an inability to deal with the problems life was presenting; a need to escape. She went quietly out of the kitchen and back upstairs. Crawling into bed she pulled the pillows into a nest about her and almost instantly plummeted into a heavy sleep.

JEMIMA, TOO, had woken unusually early. She lay for some moments, luxuriating in a sense of true relaxation; her limbs heavy with a kind of boneless immobility. It was impossible to move; even her eyelids were weighted with sleepy content; her mind working with a slow, satisfying happiness.

She thought: I love him. Oh God, I really do.

Excitement surged, shattering her torpor, and she rolled on to her stomach, closing her eyes tightly, hugging herself, lest she should lose even a second of this sudden moment of delight. She had several meetings, now, to tell over, reminding herself of special exchanges, heart-stopping glances—but he was playing it cool, very cool. A morbid curiosity led her into conversations about Annabel, which made him moody, but she simply couldn't help herself. This was a completely new experience for her. Hitherto, she had been uninterested in her companions' partners: they belonged to a different world in which she had no interest. This, she told herself, was because she'd never been in love with any of the men whose paths had briefly marched with her own. Now it was different and she needed to know what qualities had drawn him to Annabel, dwelling on it with the kind of painful insistency with which one presses the tongue against a nerve-jumping tooth. His moodiness, the drawing together of his brows, instinctively set off a flutter of fear in her gut, yet still she could not resist. Once he'd overcome his initial reluctance, however, he'd been quite lyrical in his praise. As he described Annabel, Jemima's own private reactions became soundless grace notes to his glowing recital.

"She works in IT," he'd told her. "She's a very bright girl. She got a first at university"—*She would.*—"and was offered several really good positions with top companies. She was head-hunted for this job"—*Naturally!*—"and she's had a lot of promotion. You can tell that she's being groomed for something pretty special"—*Who could doubt it?*—"and they think very highly of her. That's where the trouble really started"—*Aha! Now we're getting to it!*—"and I should have seen it coming. The chap who's training her clearly fancies her. Well, I can't blame him for that"—*Oh, of course not.*—"but it came as a bit of a shock to find that she fancied him too. Enough to break up our relationship so . . . well, so brutally"—*She must be an absolute bitch.*—"but I suppose I've just been stupid . . ."—*No you're not. You're absolutely gorgeous and she's a silly cow.*—"You're very quiet. Sorry. This must be all rather boring for you. I got a bit carried away."

She'd caught at her self-possession and shaken her head. "Don't apologise. It's a terrible shock, I can see that." *Keep it low-key. Casual.* "I expect she's pretty attractive, as well as clever?"

He'd smiled. It had such a sadly reminiscent quality, his gaze drifting beyond her to some past, precious memory, that she'd had to hold her clenched fists under the table lest he should see the jealous spasm which made them tremble, and her smile had slipped into a fixed grimace. You asked for it, sweetie, she'd told herself grimly. And now shut up. I know you want to ask what she looks like in detail but don't even go there.

"To be honest, she's rather gorgeous"—*Shit! I don't want to know this.*—"and a bit of a clotheshorse. She's so slender that she looks good in anything"—*It's too late to sit up straight and hold your stomach in, so forget it.*—"and she's tall too. Very, very, dark colouring—but, hey, who cares about Annabel? Let's talk about you. Much more interesting."

"That's true." She'd regained her poise quickly, assuming a jokey sophistication, hiding her sense of insecurity, and his good humour had been restored. He'd almost missed the last ferry.

Jemima rolled on to her back, chuckling to herself. It wasn't her fault he'd caught it. She'd kept a surreptitious eye on her watch, thinking up all kinds of delaying tactics, until he'd glanced at his own watch. She'd had mixed feelings about his determination to get back across the harbour but had kept calm, waving him off cheerfully. He'd telephoned her later . . .

The indolent, relaxed mood had passed and she sat up, yawning, pleased to see the sunshine, listening to the gulls and the familiar water sounds: the diesel on a fishing boat chugging out to sea, the rhythmical dipping of oars, the lapping of the tide against the ferry pier. Later, they would meet for a drink and then she'd drive him out to Bolberry Down for a walk along the cliffs, followed by supper at some pub. This time, he'd probably be too late to catch the ferry. Pretending that she would have done it anyway, Jemima slid out of bed and began to drag off the sheets. She pottered to and from the airing cupboard until the bed was freshly made; clean, crisp linen; plump, downy pillows. Humming, she flung the blue and cream patchwork quilt across its surface and smoothed it carefully, thoughtfully. Smiling to herself, she pushed the blue, heavily figured cretonne curtains right back and leaned for a moment from the open window, looking up the estuary, beyond the Bag, where gorse and heather bloomed gorgeously, gold and purple patches of colour on the headland.

It was nice, the way he let her drive him about—"You drive like a man," he'd told her. "And from me that's a compliment. I don't like being driven"—and encouraged her to decide what they should do. She liked the way other women looked at him; it made her feel good in a possessive, strong, sexy kind of way.

"I must admit," he'd said on one occasion when the pub was crowded and they'd had to wait for a table, "that it's good to be with a woman who doesn't fuss all the time."

"Fuss?" She'd looked surprised, as if she'd never heard the word before; a light "Whatever can you mean? What's to fuss about?" tone in her voice. And when he'd answered, "Oh, I was just thinking about Annabel. She could be a bit heavy sometimes if things weren't absolutely just so," she'd said, "Oh, right," with just the correct amount of amused indifference; a sort of "What? Oh, *Annabel.* Yes of course," carelessness and made a point of being positive and jolly whenever things were a bit iffy; like the pub kitchen running out of lobster just when she'd said that she'd set her heart on it or it starting to rain when they went for their ferry trip to South Sands. He'd smiled at her, that smile that made her heart behave like some crazy yo-yo, and told her he couldn't remember when he'd enjoyed himself so much. "Me, too," she'd answered—but still jokey, so that he'd slipped an arm about her and murmured, "You're rather special, aren't you?"

"Rather special." Jemima straightened up and turned back into the bedroom; fair-haired, not dark; size fourteen, not a clotheshorse; no university degree, no IT qualifications—but "rather special" all the same.

She made a rude face at an imaginary presence. "Eat your heart out, Annabel," she said—and went to take a shower.

CHAPTER 20

The house looked just the same and yet she might have been seeing it for the first time, so unfamiliar was it. No, not unfamiliar, that wasn't quite accurate. It was, rather, something glimpsed in a dream—or so long ago that it aroused curiosity rather than any deeper emotion.

Louise thought: It's unreal. Smugglers Way is real. Foxhole is real. But this place no longer seems to have any importance for me.

She was confused: disorientated. On the journey back to London she'd imagined several reactions but not one of curiosity. Three years of her life had been spent here yet the events of the last six weeks had cut down like a bright sword, dividing her from her previous existence; but not from all of it. Just as she had cut herself off from her life with Rory and Hermione, denying its existence, so now it was her time with Martin which seemed to have happened to someone else. It was a different Louise who had stood here in the kitchen, climbed the stairs, worked in the garden. She stared around at objects which had once formed the backdrop of her life; a well-known tapestry of belongings which set the scene for her life with Martin. Where was the Louise who had lived among them? Who was she?

The front door opened and closed with a bang. She stood quite still, waiting. His footsteps, muffled by the rug, thudded quickly along the hall and he came briskly into the kitchen, his arms full of carrier bags, his face creased in a faint frown of abstraction. The change of expression was ludicrous. He almost jumped away from her with a gasp of shock.

"Sorry," she said quickly, automatically. "I'm a bit early. Of course, you wouldn't have recognised the car."

"I thought you were coming by train." It was an accusation. "You said you'd telephone from the station."

"Yes, I did." How strange to be here with him again. "But I decided to drive, you see. Does it matter?"

Watching him, she could almost read his thoughts. He'd been expecting her to arrive by taxi, giving him time to prepare himself, and he was wondering if she'd seen anything of an incriminating nature.

"You'd forgotten that I have a key. Well, I *do* live here."

Not any more, sweetie. He might have spoken the words aloud, so clearly were they written in his narrowed, unwelcoming eyes. He turned from her, dumping the bags on the table, giving himself time.

"How brown you are," she said lightly. "You're looking tremendously well."

He sighed. "OK. Let's not do the subtle hinting bit, shall we? No, I didn't pick up this tan on the golf courses of Great Britain. But you knew that, didn't you?"

"Not at first," she said slowly. "I suspected things but it wasn't until I met the man on the train . . ." And I saw the woman with the child, she thought, her heart quickening.

"What man?" He was staring at her impatiently. "What are you talking about?"

"It doesn't matter." Suddenly she didn't want to be here. Slowly, painfully, she'd regained her grasp on reality and she didn't dare let loose her hold. "Honestly, Martin, it really doesn't matter."

"Oh, please." He closed his eyes. "Don't talk yourself into being a martyr."

"I'm not. At least, I don't think I am. It's just that things have changed. I know I haven't been able to explain to you yet—"

"I know, I know. I should have come down to Devon

again but to tell you the truth, sweetie, it wasn't exactly my scene. The erring bastard giving his faithful beloved a nervous breakdown and a built-in audience watching the reconciliation scene."

"Frummie's not a bit like that." Louise stopped abruptly. "Look, Martin, I just want to tell you how I feel."

"Oh, I'm sure. Well, let me do it for you. I shouldn't have slipped off to the Med. I shouldn't have been touchy on the telephone; I shouldn't have been so lazy about coming down to Devon to visit you more often—"

"You shouldn't have been having an affair with Carol in the first place."

His eyes snapped wide open with shock. "You *did* know, then?"

She looked at him thoughtfully. "Did you really imagine I was taken in by your slagging her off all the time?"

"But you said you only suspected."

"So I did." She shrugged. "I imagined you had better taste."

He flushed a dark, patchy red and she looked away from him, shocked by the surge of fierce pleasure she felt at this cheap hit.

"She's young," he said, wanting to hurt; to retaliate. "Twenty-three."

She looked at him compassionately. "Well, that's great, then," she said. "If that's what you want, Martin—"

"Don't be so bloody patronising," he shouted. "I picked you up from nothing. Just remember that. You didn't know what day of the week it was. Your life had collapsed and you were nothing. *Nothing!* All you had were your clothes. Even your mother had given up on you."

"That's absolutely true," she answered. "You were very good to me, Martin. You looked after me."

"Too right, sweetie. And a lot of looking after it was, in the early days, I can tell you."

"Martin, let's not do this. I'm grateful for all that you've done for me but I want to say that it's finished. No, wait. Not because of Carol or anything you've done or haven't done but because I've been able to come to terms with what went before. You protected me from all that but now I need to face it and I can't do that here or with you."

He stared at her, puzzled, suspicious. "So what brought this on?"

Louise hesitated. No point is telling him that his infidelity had begun the process: he wouldn't understand and he would see it as an accusation. After all, it wasn't important any more.

"I think it was simply time," she said slowly. "The shock of Hermione's death numbed me. I couldn't face it. Maybe I've been protected from it until I could bear it. I don't know. The point is that it's happened and things are different."

"You mean you don't care about me any more?"

He'd seen his advantage and seized it quickly. Now it could be all her fault.

"I'm still very fond of you," she said levelly. "Do you want me back?"

His face was a study of conflicting emotions: irritation, anxiety, caution. She laughed suddenly.

"Can't we be honest? I want to go and you want to be free of me. Does there have to be blame? Condemnation? I don't know what I shall do but I think I have to be alone."

"You're not staying at that setup in Devon?"

"I can't stay with Frummie indefinitely," she said. "I'm thinking of taking a winter let. I don't like to look too far ahead at the moment."

His expression softened, responding as always to need. "Will you be OK? Look, you don't have to worry financially just yet. You'll need a car, for a start. It's expensive to hire long term. I'm sure we can sort something out between us."

"That's very good of you, Martin," she said sincerely. "I might need a bit of a loan to start me off but I shall find a job as soon as I can."

"Are you fit enough to work?"

She shrugged. "Depends what the work is. But I shan't be a burden on you for any longer than is necessary."

"Oh, honestly, sweetie. As if that matters. I don't want you to be silly about this."

"Thanks." She smiled at him. "If we can be friends that's what really matters. I'm not out of the wood yet."

Quite suddenly the old current of ease and familiarity was flowing between them again. He came swiftly across to hug her. "Friends," he said warmly. "Now tell me how you really are."

"YOU'RE LOOKING better," he told her later.

He'd made tea for her, properly, in the blue flowered teapot. Martin hated mess and was not a natural kitchen dweller. They sat in the sitting room, with the French doors open to the small, pretty garden, amongst the elegant comfort of Rose and Hubble chair covers and curtains, rosewood furniture and his precious pieces of Meissen. His mother had left him some property, along with a comfortable amount of money, and he would wait months for the right painting or figurine or bureau with which to complete his setting. He was fastidious, careful in his choice, and yet his generous warmth lent life to the otherwise sterile beauty of his rooms.

Louise, smiling at him, was remembering the married quarters at Smugglers Way: the flat-roofed blocks, rendered with grey, pebble-dash concrete, the uniformity and lack of imagination of the decoration and furnishings. She had a mental picture, suddenly, of the Fablon tacked to the side of the bath and was pierced with an anguished longing.

"What is it?" He was refilling her cup, watching her with his old, familiar tenderness.

"Oh, Martin." She shivered a little, responding almost unconsciously to his sympathy. "It's so hard, this going back."

"My poor girl." He sat beside her, putting an arm about her, rocking her slightly.

She leaned into him, comforted by his warmth and strength. At this moment it seemed that it might be easy to let it all go again, to turn blindly into this protection; to cocoon herself from the painful, prising fingers of memory. He too might be drawn back to her, his love roused again by her new dilemma. Sitting there together, she knew that they were both aware of the faint *frissons* of passion which speeded her breathing and tightened his embrace. She longed, suddenly, for the simple, uncomplicated release of tension which love-making would bring: the insistent, thought-denying excitement and the peaceful aftermath of spent emotion. Yet, even as she imagined it, she knew that it was no longer an option. This moment of tenderness between them was only possible because each of them had tacitly withdrawn: they were both emotionally free and so could now meet in this uncomplicated atmosphere of affection. They could not go back and any future relationship they might forge must remain uncomplicated by physical attraction.

She leaned away so as to be able to look up at him. "It must have been very difficult for you, Martin, at the beginning. Yet you handled it all so well. How did you know what to do for me? No one else did. Not even my own mother."

He was distracted from his growing sexual need by the question, releasing her, moving away slightly as he considered it.

"The one thing that was clear to me," he said, "was that you needed time. The shock was cataclysmic. People with horrific physical injuries are given plenty of time for their bodies to recover and it seemed that you needed the time for your emotional and spiritual side to heal. I think that it was probably wrong of me to encourage you to ignore it so completely but then I wasn't certain what was happening inside your head, you see. I never quite knew whether you were coming to terms with it in your own way but I felt that you needed to be given the chance to be quiet."

"Dear Martin. I *did* need space. I couldn't . . . couldn't bear to think of it. Of Hermione. I was mad, Martin, mad with grief and guilt and . . . I couldn't bear the emptiness. The reason for living had gone and the world was . . . just nothing. If Rory had been there . . . No." She shook her head. "I don't mean that. Not that it was his fault. I've done that bit too: blaming him for not being there. I mean that if he had been there, so that we'd been dealing with it together, then it might not have felt so empty and I might have thought I could go on living for him. But he wasn't there. For three weeks I was all alone with this terrible aching emptiness and when he got back it was too late. I was set in despair. Rock hard. Impermeable. He couldn't get through to me. My mother could see that I was simply destroying everything around me and she was terribly angry. I can see why she was so desperate but she and I never could communicate properly."

"She was . . . not particularly wise or tactful."

Louise gave a short laugh. "No. Tact was never her strong suit but she was upset too, so I suppose we mustn't be too harsh."

"I could never quite understand why she simply left you at Faslane alone after the funeral." He looked at her quickly. "Can you talk about this now?"

She nodded. "I think so. You have to grasp the fact that we just didn't get on. She desperately wanted a son, you see. It was years before she conceived and then, after all the excitement, I was a girl. Later she had a miscarriage. It was a boy and I think she never quite forgave me for living whilst he had died. My father died in his forties and she and I simply drifted apart once I went to university. It was very sad but we had nothing in common. Not until I met Rory. She adored Rory. In her eyes he could do no wrong and he was very sweet to her but she was disappointed that Hermione was a girl. 'A man like Rory needs a son,' she said, as if I'd done it on purpose to thwart him—or her—and she never really cared much for Hermione. When we moved up north to Faslane it was a long trip for her to make and, since Rory was at sea so much as well, we hardly ever saw her. She came to the funeral, of course. 'You can have more children,' she said, and I knew she was still hoping that one day I would produce a grandson for her. You can understand her fury when it seemed that she would lose Rory. He was the nearest she'd ever got to a son of her own."

"I have to admit," said Martin, after a short silence, "that I never really took to your mother."

Louise smiled. "I think the feeling was mutual," she said.

"So what happened, down there in Devon, to bring all this to a head?"

"I met a child," she said slowly, "a little girl called Hermione." She felt him stiffen beside her. "I think that the floodgates were already beginning to give way and she was the weak part in my defences. Through her, everything else came flooding back."

"And the final breakdown? I thought it was me. That awful telephone call—"

"No," she said quickly. "It was a part of the process, I suppose, but it wasn't that simple, Martin. What happened was that Hermione became ill. The symptoms sounded just like meningitis and quite suddenly it was like history replaying itself. It was the last straw."

He was staring at her with horror. "She didn't . . .?"

"No," she said. "No, she didn't die. I warned Thea who called a doctor and Hermione was taken to hospital. It was just a virus, not meningitis after all. She didn't have septicaemia like . . . like my Hermione . . ."

He put his arm about her whilst she wept, holding her closely until she sat up straight, pushing back wisps of escaping hair, smiling at him.

"I *am* better," she reassured him, "but I still get bad moments. It's right for us to part, isn't it?"

A long silence.

"Yes," he said at last. "I think it is. If we stay together you won't grow out of it."

She was touched by his wisdom. "It's not that I don't care about you." She needed to reassure him. "You do understand that, don't you?"

He touched her cheek with his finger. "Sweetie," he said gently, "I know you needed me and you are still very fond of me but you never really loved me, you know."

She stared at him, shocked. For a brief moment she wondered if he might be protecting himself against any subsequent accusations regarding Carol but the next minute she had exonerated him. They were beyond that tit-for-tat small-mindedness.

"Of course I loved you."

"No." He shook his head. "It's Rory that you love. Then, now, and all the time between. I knew it but there was nothing to be done about it. You couldn't have stayed together. Not then. It was a tragedy but it couldn't be helped."

"Don't. Don't say that. Don't you think I feel guilty enough already?"

"It's not your fault. The whole thing was like some ghastly explosion, shattering your lives, and you and Rory were victims, damaged by the fallout."

Rory. She saw him so vividly it was as if he stood beside her; heard his warm, flexible voice.

"So that's that. Now! Where were we?"

"I daren't think about Rory." She was seized by panic. "I'm simply not ready yet. I can't bear to think about how much I hurt him. I haven't got that far. Talk to me, Martin. Tell me your news while I drink my tea."

Her hand trembled on the cup but she was able to banish her fear and control the uprush of misery whilst his voice flowed gently, drifting somewhere above her head, calming and soothing her as it had done so often in the past.

CHAPTER 21

When the letter finally arrived it lay on the kitchen table for most of the day before Brigid read it. Her visitors were slow to pack up and vacate the cottage, leaving her barely enough time to clean and dust and polish, find the clean linen, put milk in the fridge, before the incoming holidaymakers were bumping down the track. These were regulars, old friends, so it was necessary to pause, to welcome them and make them some tea, before leaving them to unpack and settle in.

"I must say, you earn your money," observed Frummie, who was ostensibly reading a book in a deckchair in her garden but actually watching the proceedings with amused irritation. She was missing Louise; feeling edgy and at a loose end. "Making them tea and chatting for hours. More like arriving at a hotel than a holiday let."

"I've known them for years." Brigid paused, annoyed by the instinctive need to justify and explain. She knew very well that Frummie was making an oblique reference to the well-worn theme that her daughter had no time for her. "They've just driven all the way from Carlisle."

Frummie shrugged. "There are tea shops on the way, I imagine."

Brigid suppressed an urge to smack her hard. "I'm sure there are but they've become friends over the years. It seems the natural thing to do."

"Oh well, that's all right then. It's just seeing you so tired, dashing about all day preparing for them, it seems rather a lot for you to have to entertain them too."

"Well, it's part of the job, isn't it? Anyway, it's all done now and I can relax. I thought I might go and have a drink before I think about supper."

"Is that an invitation?"

Brigid's heart sank. She was longing for the absolute quiet and privacy of her kitchen—or the sunny peacefulness of the courtyard—but she knew very well that it was a test: if she could do it for these visitors, she could do it for her mother.

"Would you like a drink?" She tried to make the unexpected possibility of Frummie's company sound like a pleasant surprise. "I've got some rather nice Australian Chardonnay Humphrey bought before he went away. I put a bottle in the fridge this morning so it should be just right. We could have it in the courtyard. It's too hot to be indoors."

"That would be very nice." Frummie was feeling very slightly ashamed of herself. "If you're absolutely sure?"

"Of course. I'll go and get it. See you in a minute."

In the cool dimness of the hall she closed her eyes in frustration and swore beneath her breath. She longed to sit in a chair, with her shoes off, her head on a soft pillow, and simply sleep. If only she could *sleep*. In the kitchen, Blot's tail thumped on the cold flagstones but he did not move. He lay on his tummy with his legs stretched fore and aft, a spreading, inky puddle on the grey slate, and she massaged him lightly with her foot, too weary even to crouch down to stroke him.

"Glasses," she murmured to herself. "Bottle opener. God, I am so *tired*."

She glanced at the letters, lying on the table where she had tossed them earlier, and fear trickled icily into her heart. She moved the topmost envelope carefully aside so that she could see the letter from the Bank more clearly and stood quite still, staring at it. For this brief moment nothing existed outside this warm, shadowy kitchen: the clock's measured tick, striking like blows upon her undefended head; the dog stirring about, seeking a colder space; the white envelope, sharp and clear upon the grainy wood. The whole of time and space seemed to be pressing down upon her, a weighty inverted triangle, and she was pinned by it, unmoving, immobile with fear.

"Don't open it." This was her first reaction; her instinctive instruction to herself. Could she read it and still sit in the courtyard with her mother, acting as if nothing had happened? Dread gathered in her heart and churned in her gut. Might it not be worse, though, if she were to be simply guessing at the contents? After all, it might not be as bad as she feared. Without further thought she picked up the envelope and ripped it open. Edging the letter out, she glanced at the first few lines and quickly refolded it.

> . . . and I regret to inform you that it might be necessary to call in your guarantee . . .

She stood holding the folded sheet, staring at nothing in particular . . . Might be necessary. Only *might* be necessary. She shook the paper out and read it quickly, as if by hurrying over the words she could render them less frightening.

> . . . The partners are attempting to sell the sailing school and, should they succeed, the outstanding debt might be met out of the proceeds. However, it is only fair to warn you . . .

"Are you there, darling?"

Frummie's voice echoed in the hall and Brigid quickly folded the sheet, sliding it beneath the other envelopes.

"In the kitchen," she called. "I seem to have mislaid the bottle opener."

By the time her mother appeared in the doorway, she was standing at the dresser drawer, smiling ruefully, bottle opener in hand.

"Stupid of me," she said, marvelling at the cheerful tone which sounded so unforced. "I think I'm losing my marbles."

"As long as that's all." Frummie smiled her down-turned smile. "Better than losing the corkscrew."

"Could you take the glasses?" For some reason it was

terribly important to get her out of the kitchen. It was necessary to be outside, in the fresh air and the sunlight. "I'll bring the bottle."

"Splendid. I nipped back to collect some rather nice new nibbles I found in the deli in Ashburton. You must try them."

Brigid took the wine from the fridge, holding the icy, slippery bottle tightly in her cold, trembling hands, and followed her mother out into the courtyard.

DRIVING THROUGH the narrow lanes, singing to her *Saturday Night Fever* tape, Jemima was tingling with happiness. The warm air, laden with late summer scents—rich red earth, pale lemon honeysuckle, sweet dried grasses—carried a languorous, end-of-season fullness which drugged the senses. Tall rosebay willowherb grew beneath the hedgerows where the prickly arching brambles still displayed delicate pink blooms. Soon black, luscious fruit would hang there and the willowherb would be a mass of downy, plumy fluff. Autumn was only a week or two away.

Singing loudly ". . . *uh, uh, uh, uh, staying alive, staying alive . . .*" Jemima gave a delicious shudder as she drove towards their rendezvous.

"I'm not going to like going back," he'd said. "Not one bit."

Afraid to give herself away too much she'd made no answer, although she'd wanted to cry, "Don't go, then. Stay here. Stay with me." She'd learned that he played his cards very close to his chest and she'd tried hard not to pry. Apart from any other reason she'd seen that her nonpredatory approach appealed to him. This was fairly normal behaviour for Jemima. So far she'd compartmentalised her life very satisfactorily and, usually, it was her partners who pressed her to become more involved. She'd been quick to see that her independence appealed to him; a show of indifference excited him.

Jemima frowned a little. Such games were fine for a while but it was difficult to sustain a constant awareness and soon it might become wearisome. If this were a mere holiday flirtation then these rules would be perfectly acceptable but already she was wanting something more.

"For heaven's sake," she muttered, "it's only three weeks. Twenty-two days to be exact," but she knew that it had taken hardly more than two meetings to fall in love. The real thing. What did it mean, after all, this longing and burning, the twist of the gut, the need to be with him? She couldn't concentrate, couldn't eat. When he telephoned, her heartbeat crashed in her ears and strangled the voice in her throat, yet she was loving every minute of it; even the terror and the uncertainty made her feel vitally, painfully alive.

She made a face, grinning at her thoughts. What a drama queen! She stretched back from the wheel, loving the whole sensation of this warm, drowsy, sunny early evening: liking the cool, crisp scrape of her cream linen overshirt against her skin, the sleeves rolled back over her firm, brown arms, the glinting gold of her bangles, her hands confident on the steering wheel. Her cotton capris were honey-yellow, her bare feet thrust into tan leather dekkies. She felt strong, attractive, positive.

He was waiting for her; the door to the cottage open. The development was built about a courtyard, which shared its parking facility with all four converted barns, but each unit had a small private garden, looking out over plumply curving fields which sloped away to the invisible sea. Latticed, wooden fencing ensured visual privacy for each attractively paved area which was carefully designed to keep noise interaction to a minimum. These apartments were expensive and generally booked by young couples with no children or older retired people. She parked next to his convertible and climbed out, trying to swallow down a sudden attack of nervousness.

"You look great," he said. "I like your hair like that."

"Thanks." Would he give her a hug; kiss her? "It's been too hot to wear it loose."

She slipped past him, not waiting for longer than a second or two for the hoped-for touch. This was the rule she had made for herself, knowing that if she once gave way she would betray her feelings utterly. He was so spare; so economic in his movements, his speech, his emotions; but she could match him. She guessed that Annabel had been very contained, very private, very controlled—and he'd liked it. Very well. She wouldn't be an Annabel clone but she would adapt a little, just a little: cool with unexpected displays of warmth; casual with tempting hints of passion.

He followed her out on to the paved area, where some wrought-iron chairs were placed about a matching table with an umbrella set in its centre. There was white wine in an ice bucket and smoked salmon, curled into thin rolls of brown bread and butter.

"Well!" She raised her eyebrows. "So you can cook as well."

"As well as what?"

"As well as looking gorgeous," she answered lightly, enjoying the role reversal element.

He chuckled, lifting the bottle. "You ain't seen nothing yet."

She looked at him swiftly. "So I should hope," she said challengingly—and smiled secretly at the slight, very slight, surprise in his eyes.

"Had a good day?" He recovered quickly, pouring the wine.

"Pretty good. I've taken on a bungalow near Thurlestone. The owner has died and the son lives in London. He wants to let it but doesn't want the hassle although he wants to keep it for his own use for a month each year. The good thing is that he came direct to me. Heard of me from a neighbour I look after who does much the same thing. My boss will be pleased about that. Lots of lovely Brownie points."

"Something to celebrate then." He raised his glass to her. "I suppose, outside farming and the tourist trade, there aren't that many jobs down here?"

She sipped slowly, hiding the quick upbeat of hope. "It depends what field you're in, I suppose. The West Country needs doctors, teachers, lawyers, just like any other part of the country."

During the short ensuing silence, Jemima congratulated herself on her calm, almost indifferent response.

"Well, that must be true," he said at last. "Naturally. But what about IT, for instance?"

"Oh, Devonians can use the Internet too," she said lightly. "Just about. Or did you think computer literacy stops at Bristol?"

"Of course not." He frowned impatiently. "I didn't mean to sound patronising but I suspect that it would be difficult to find the kind of work I do down here."

She thought: How do I handle this one?

"Of course, I don't quite know what you do." She smiled at him, a friendly, open look. "Are you thinking of moving?"

He held her gaze with his own; a thoughtful, level glance.

"I have to say it's crossed my mind once or twice during the last few days."

She wanted to laugh madly, jump up, fling her arms wide. "Ah. Well, I really couldn't say. I suppose you'd need to make a few enquiries? Find a few contacts?"

"I suppose I would." He was smiling at her, amused by her calm reaction. "I might need to come down for a few weekends whilst I was . . . checking things out."

She shook her head. "That could be tricky at this time of the year. Devon's pretty busy until the end of September."

"You think I might find it difficult to find a bed?"

"You might be lucky. With a little help from your friends."

"Or one particular friend?"

She thought: Ohmigod! This is it. Go for it.

"You're just after my view," she said. "Admit it!"

"That and a few other things," he said—and stretched out a hand to her.

She waited a second or two and then took it in her own. "I'll give it some consideration," she said.

CHAPTER 22

Travelling back to Devon, Louise was aware of a sense of disorientation, switching between happiness and despair. In these last few agonising months she'd learned that the past could not be simply tidied away and forgotten but now, for the first time for years, she felt that the future could be approached with a measure of confidence, even with hope. She was no longer in hiding, in denial, but trying to confront her life truthfully, as a whole. Hermione, Rory and Martin were a part of that life, yet she had lost them all and she must learn how to come to terms with it. As she drove back to Foxhole, memories slid in and out of her consciousness. She let them come: walking through the woods amongst the banks of flowering rhododendrons; watching Hermione, long fair hair in bunches, playing on Rhu Spit with the other naval children; the view across the Gare Loch; going to the Royal Northern Yacht Club with Rory. They'd been locked away for so long, these memories, that they came with a new freshness that surprised, filling her with wonder whilst they stabbed her to the heart. Hermione. Singing breathlessly to herself as she played with Percy; gabbling unintelligibly on her toy telephone; riding her tricycle in small circles round and round the kitchen. Tiny feet with curling toes, chubby wrists and starfish fingers, pearly teeth in a rosy face. Oh, the pain of it; the terrible finality of death.

"What will you do?" Martin had asked anxiously. "Where will you live?"

"With Frummie," she'd answered, "until I can find a little place to rent. I shall need a job first."

"Will you . . . go back?"

She'd smiled at his wariness. "To teaching? What else could I do?"

"Can you cope, d'you think? For heaven's sake, sweetie, don't try to take things too fast."

She'd been a nursery teacher before she'd married Rory; she'd always adored small children, longing for a family of her own.

"I think I could," she'd answered. "I have to start again, Martin. I have to become independent."

"I know. I can see that, but don't try to do it all at once. I shan't stop your allowance just yet."

"Dear Martin. But it would be quite impossible now to be dependent on you. I shall be grateful for it for a little while longer but I shall look upon what I take from you now as a loan. Anything else would be quite wrong."

"Fine. That's fine. But you might . . ." He'd hesitated, unwilling to be pessimistic, anxious lest she should be hurt or worried by the implication, yet feeling the need to warn her. "You might have the occasional setback."

"I've accepted that. Don't worry. I know I'm not out of the wood just yet. That's why I shall stay with Frummie for a bit. Apart from anything else I know she likes having me there. She hates being alone, poor old soul. She's got her old friend Margot coming to stay in October so it's like a cut-off point for me. I hope I can settle myself by then."

"Well, you can always count on me, you know."

She'd grinned at him. "You think Carol would be pleased to see me back again?"

He'd smiled too, refusing to rise to the bait. "We're friends. Whatever happens."

She'd hugged him thankfully. "Bless you. It's so important to me. You're giving me space and it's what I need. I'm truly grateful, Martin."

"Forget it. But I insist that we get you a little car. You can't afford to hire one indefinitely and you'll need wheels of your own. No, nothing over the top," he forestalled her protest, "just something small, reliable and economic. A little parting present. Shall you continue to call yourself Parry? I know we agreed that it was the simplest arrangement three years ago but how do you feel now?"

"For a bit longer, if that's OK." She'd felt oddly nervous at the thought of so definite a change.

"Take all the time you need," he'd said, "but just stay in touch."

It made it easier knowing that Martin loved to be needed; that in allowing him to help her she was also giving him pleasure. He was certainly right, however, regarding setbacks. At present she had to struggle against panic attacks and periods of melancholy juxtaposed with a growing sense of freedom and waves of relief. Soon, she hoped, the latter would outweigh the former until she found herself on a solid footing; yet she needed to test herself. She wondered if it would be possible to find a job in a nursery or pre-prep school, part time to begin with, so that she could see how strong she was. Perhaps it might be necessary to admit to her past and her more recent breakdown and, if that were so, would anyone be prepared to let her work with small children? Perhaps she should be thinking of some other kind of career? The creeping shadows of depression and anxiety curled about her mind and she tried to thrust them away, concentrating on the more immediate future: Foxhole, with Brigid and Frummie looking forward to her return.

"I'm so glad that you're coming home," Brigid had said with warm, characteristic generosity. "As long as you can cope with Mummie . . .?"

"Of course I can. I can't tell you how I'm missing you all."

"Well, she'll be delighted to have you back again, I can tell you. She's missed you dreadfully."

Louise had felt a glow of comfort and confidence at these words. How lucky she was to have these kind friends, to be allowed this necessary space of time to heal and recover.

"Tell her I'm on my way. I should be there just after lunch."

Foxhole: her stony sanctuary with Brigid and Frummie, and Blot, waiting for her. This was all she needed to concentrate on; all that was required of her at present. Gently, slowly, the shadows receded, panic subsided and balance was restored, yet she sensed their presence, waiting, watching.

"One day at a time," she hummed to herself, caught behind a large motor-caravan which was negotiating the narrow lanes with caution. "One day at a time."

It was still necessary to fall back on devices to distract the mind, although no longer from the reality of the past. Now it was a means to prevent panic and fear wrestling her into despair. Well, she had plenty of experience here. She began to recite aloud:

> "The Centipede was happy quite,
> Until the Toad in fun,
> Said, 'Pray which leg goes after which?'
> And worked her mind to such a pitch,
> She lay distracted in the ditch
> Considering how to run."

The motor-caravan slowed, flashed its rear trafficator and trundled heavily into the car park at Venford Reservoir. Louise sighed with relief and pressed her foot down on the accelerator, her attention fully concentrated on Foxhole and her home-coming.

BRIGID HAD had a trying morning. Waking with the now-familiar panic attack in the early dawn, she'd made herself some tea which she'd taken back to bed and then fallen into a heavy slumber, waking with a violent start at twenty to ten. She'd dressed hastily and hurried down to release Blot into the outside world. He'd gone off looking faintly reproachful, despite her promises of walks later, and she'd made more tea, yawning heavily, pushing her short blonde hair behind her ears as she examined the morning post. The *Dartmoor News* had arrived and, discarding the other letters as unimportant, she settled at the corner of the table, turning to Kate Van Der Kiste's article on letterboxing with her golden retriever, Rex. Amused, temporarily distracted from her worries, she gave a groan of irritation at Frummie's familiar tapping on the front door, going reluctantly to open it, turning the enormous ancient key, trying to smile.

"You're late this morning." Frummie nipped past her, bright and shiny as new enamel. "I came over earlier but I couldn't get any reply. You used to be such an early bird."

Brigid followed her into the kitchen, biting back a sharp retort. "I've just made some tea. Would you like some?"

"Tea? At this hour? No thank you, darling. Coffee wouldn't go amiss, though. I've been making a cake for Louise and I was hoping that you might have some cream."

"Yes, I've got some cream." She took out her small cafetiere, knowing that Frummie liked fresh coffee and could rarely afford it for herself. "She's very grateful to you for letting her come back."

"Hasn't too many options, from what I can gather." Frummie perched at the table, watching her make the coffee. "She needs more time. I know what it's like to need a bolt hole."

Brigid glanced at her quickly, defensively. "You've always been welcome with me and Humphrey."

Frummie smiled her down-turned smile. "That's what I mean. I've been lucky. Don't think I don't appreciate it."

Embarrassed, Brigid shrugged. "It's good of you to have her. I'd be horrified at the thought of a guest staying for an indefinite time. I'm very fond of Louise but even so . . ."

"Ah, but you are happy alone," said Frummie. "So is Jem. I'm not, you see. You have to like yourself a little to be able to spend time alone. I've never liked myself very much."

There was a short silence.

"I . . . I haven't really thought about it." Brigid pushed the cafetiere across the table, reached down a mug from the dresser. "I suppose I haven't had much choice, with Humphrey being in the Navy."

"There are always choices. In your case you've chosen to accept the separation cheerfully, making the best of it. But you could have chosen to make everyone's life hell whilst making a martyr of yourself or you could have chosen to manipulate him so that he gave it up. Or you could have chosen to get out. I'm sure you know naval wives who have exercised each of those choices."

Brigid stared at her. "Yes," she said slowly. "Now you mention it, I do."

Frummie shrugged. "Mind, it's not always that simple." She pressed the plunger down slowly with obvious satisfaction, and poured the hot black liquid. "Do you worry how you'll manage when Humphrey retires?"

Brigid sat down again and picked up her mug of tea. "Yes," she said, refusing to give her instinctive need for self-preservation time to prevent such an admission. "Yes, I do. It's going to be a big learning curve for both of us. He's looking forward to it."

"But you're not."

"I didn't mean it to sound quite like that." She glanced at Frummie. "I've just got used to doing things my way. When Humphrey's home, it's great. He's fun to have around and we enjoy being together but it's as if it's not quite real. It's because it's always a holiday, I think. We have this lovely time and then he goes away again. I don't know what it's like just to live with him—day after day, month in, month out. We've never done it. Now, suddenly, it's going to be like that. Twenty-four-hours-a-day stuff. It frightens me."

Frummie sipped her coffee appreciatively. "Delicious." A pause. "Won't he get a job?" she asked.

Brigid hesitated. They were moving on to sensitive ground. "He hoped the cottages would bring in enough income for him not to have to get a full-time job. There are some charity things he wants to do—the Barn Owl Trust and things like that—but he'll probably get bored very quickly and need something more time-consuming."

"And I've buggered up the system by taking one of the cottages."

"No," said Brigid quickly. "No, honestly. Anyway, you pay rent . . ."

Frummie laughed. "But not nearly the amount that you'd get by letting it out to visitors."

"Please, Mummie. Don't let's go into all that again. You know that we're very happy to have you here."

"Odd, isn't it?"

"What?"

"That my bolt hole has now become Louise's bolt hole."

"Yes. I suppose it is. She . . . doesn't expect you to support her, does she?"

"No, no. Don't worry about that. Martin is going to help her out until she can get back on her feet."

"That's nice of him."

"Well, it suits him too, doesn't it?"

"How d'you mean?"

"He wants shot of her so that he can concentrate on this new woman. So he helps her to go. Of course, she wants out too. Their choices are complementary, if you see what I mean. Lucky, isn't it?"

"You're such a cynic."

"Possibly." Frummie swallowed the last of her coffee and stood up. "That was perfectly delicious. By the way, have you read the paper yet? There's been another murder, Plymouth this time. This is the third and no suggestion that the police have any clues at all. Another woman on her own, walking her dog. Shocking, isn't it? Ah, and here's the cream. I must get back to my cooking. Thanks, darling. For my coffee and for the cream. I'll buy you some when I go out later."

"There's no need, honestly."

She stood up to see her out just as the telephone rang. Frummie disappeared and Brigid picked up the receiver.

"Hi." Jemima's voice bubbled with wellbeing. "How are you?"

"Fine. I'm fine."

"I was wondering if I could buy you lunch? I'm coming over to Totnes, which is a kind of halfway house between us. How about it?"

For the second time that morning, Brigid denied her instinctive reaction. "I'd love it," she said.

"Great!" Jemima sounded truly delighted. "Where shall we meet? What about Effings? Gorgeous food and lots of lovely treats to buy afterwards to take home."

"Fine. What time. One o'clock?"

"Make it earlier if you can. It'll be crowded by one and we won't get a table."

"Half twelve?"

"Great. See you then."

Brigid replaced the receiver and glanced at her watch; just time to take Blot for a walk, shower and change. She went through to the lean-to and called to Blot as she pulled on her boots. Moments later they were crossing the field to the river.

EFFINGS WAS busy. Squeezing past the customers at the delicatessen counter, breathing in the exciting scents of delicious food, Brigid was relieved to see Jemima sitting at one of the tables. She waved cheerfully, smiling as Brigid finally came to rest opposite.

"Bank Holiday weekend and market day all rolled into one," said Jemima, almost apologetically. "I only thought about it after I'd set out."

"I've had to park down on Steamer Quay and walk up," said Brigid, somewhat breathlessly. "Sorry I'm a bit late."

"It's not a problem. I wanted to see Gus Mallory at Studio Graphics about a brochure and I was here in plenty of time. Have a glass of wine while you think about what you want to eat."

"That would be nice," said Brigid gratefully. "Something cold and white and some water as well. Thanks." She looked around her, liking the atmosphere which was a mixture of delicatessen and French bistro: shelves packed with preserves and hand-made chocolates; the cold counter with its array of cheeses and fruit tarts. The three other tables were full and she looked with a sudden pang of real hunger at a neighbour's plate of bresaola and his companion's bowl of steaming, herb-scented soup.

"So," she said, when the order had been dealt with, "how are things with you? You're looking fantastic."

Jemima glanced at her in surprise. She was not used to such unqualified praise from her sister. "I'm feeling pretty good." She thought: Be careful. We've been here before. It's like Tom Tiddler's Ground. One false step and we'll both be back to square one.

Brigid thought: Puddle-duck. Will I ever really be able to call her that with true affection? I wish I could.

She felt an overwhelming need to confide in Jemima, to tell her about Jenny's disaster and her own terrors, but the deep-seated prejudice made it impossible to frame the words.

"You're looking tired." Jemima was watching her, concern on her face. "Are you OK? Has all that business with Louise been getting you down?"

"It has a bit." Brigid grasped thankfully at this ready-made reason. "It's been rather scary. And, of course, Mummie insisted on trying to cope without a doctor or any sensible advice."

"But she's OK? Louise, I mean."

"Yes." Brigid admitted it almost reluctantly. "She's certainly over the worst. She's coming back this afternoon. Mummie's putting her up for a while until she finds her feet. I think it's pretty good of her, actually."

"But she loves it, doesn't she? Anything rather than be alone, although she's very fond of Louise, of course."

Brigid looked at her sister curiously. "Would you feel like that?"

Jemima's eyes widened with a kind of horror. "You must be kidding. I couldn't do it. Not for any real length of time. A few days, perhaps. A week. Not indefinitely. Not unless it was someone terribly close to me. I need my space."

"That's how I feel." Brigid frowned. "She makes me feel inadequate. Guilty, almost."

Jemima chuckled. "Why? Frummie's a terribly lonely person. She hates being on her own. She'd rather have someone she actually dislikes with her than be alone. I hear she's got Margot coming back for a while in the autumn. They'll drive each other mad, Frummie knows that, but it's better than being alone."

Brigid looked shocked. "But that's terrible. Anyway, I'm just across the courtyard." She laughed a little, bitterly. "Of course, I've never been enough for her."

Jemima watched her compassionately. "It's not quite that, is it?" she suggested gently. "The point is, you have your own life: your children and their families and Humphrey. You've got your work and the cottage to see to and your own friends. Frummie hasn't got anyone of her own—no one who shares her life with her, her very own person to do things with or sit about with or cook for. Other people are kind but if you haven't got your own person it's simply not the same. You have to depend on other people asking you and then you feel beholden."

"Do you feel like that?"

"No." Jemima shook her head. "But I'm like you. I like my own company. Frummie doesn't. That's why she tries to get out as much as she does. Driving into Ashburton so as to have a chat with Meg in the gift shop or joshing with Anne and Bar in the second-hand bookshop. Sitting for hours in the Café Green Ginger. Anything to be out amongst people. She can start up conversations and be part of the human race. She needs the buzz, the contact. It's how she feels alive."

"You know that she shouldn't be driving?"

Jemima bit her lip. "I know you're cross with me for paying her car tax and insurance but she was so desperate at the thought of being stranded."

"With me at Foxhole."

"No, Brigid. Don't be like that. It's not you or Foxhole. It's the whole scene. Frummie is a totally urban animal. She loathes the countryside; she hates the quiet emptiness of the moor. She likes bustle and noise and lights. Imagine if you had to live in a noisy city all the time, even if you had Humphrey with you. How would you feel?"

The wine arrived and Brigid was spared the necessity of answering. She smiled her thanks and took the menu automatically.

"Have a look at the chef's specials," said Jemima, indicating the blackboard on the wall behind her. "His antipasto is very good. Or the home-made pâté. The difficulty is knowing what to choose. Oh, and you must try some of the French lemon tart afterwards so leave a bit of space."

"I can't imagine," Brigid said, when they'd ordered and were alone together again, "why she ever married Daddy."

"Novelty?" offered Jemima. "He was different from anyone she'd ever met. And Foxhole out in the wilds of Dartmoor. Real *Wuthering Heights* stuff. There was something romantic about it all. But when the chips were down she simply couldn't cope."

"She left me," said Brigid angrily. "How can you leave your own child?"

"We don't know the whole circumstances." Jemima was shocked by the expression on her sister's face. She thought: Help me, someone. I can't do this. Oh hell. I wanted this to be fun. To bond with her. Shit!

Brigid said, "She didn't leave *you* when she bolted."

"No," said Jemima gently. "But the difference was that your father wanted you. Mine didn't put up a fight for me so she took me along with her."

The sisters stared at each other.

"I missed him terribly." Jemima's lip trembled. "He was such fun and I loved him so much but, in the end, they used to row all the time. I tried to stop them, to make them laugh. You know? To lighten things up and stuff? But it never really worked. What really hurt was that he never made much effort afterwards to see me. Frummie wouldn't have stopped him but he couldn't be bothered. God, it hurt! It still does. I think it's why I've been so cautious about relationships. I don't seem to be too good at them. It's probably because I'm always waiting for things to go wrong so it's easier not to get too involved."

She thought: Until now. Oh, God! Until now. Shall I tell her? Dare I? Will she knock it?

"I was lucky to have Humphrey." Brigid, in her compassion for her sister, felt the need to justify her good luck. "He was so kind to me and he made up for it, if you know what I mean."

"But not completely."

"No," said Brigid, after a moment. "Not completely. I suppose nothing ever truly makes up for it. You have this uncertainty deep down. Like you said just now, there's that fear that something might go wrong."

"I didn't realise," said Jemima carefully, "that you felt it. You seem so complete, so in control. There's nothing muddly about your life. Not like me."

Brigid thought: I could tell her about Jenny and the mess I'm in but I suppose I ought tell Humphrey first. Shall I tell her?

She hesitated, sitting back in her chair as Mike arrived carrying platefuls of mouth-watering food, and, by the time everything had been sorted out, the moment had passed.

CHAPTER 23

It was odd to come jolting down the drive and see a car parked outside "her" cottage; odd to park opposite, remembering that she was not on holiday but beginning a whole new life. This was for real. Her stomach turned in terror and excitement and she sat for a moment, assailed again by familiar fears, unable to move. Now that the need to concentrate on driving was over, the world slid gently out of focus; distorted, frightening. Recovery and achievement seemed impossibilities conceived by a much stronger will than she possessed. She held on to the wheel, fighting down this crawling, paralysing impotency, wishing she'd stayed with Martin. How could she have imagined that she could conquer guilt and loneliness and loss?

Frummie came out of her garden through the little gate, passed along beside the low stone wall and bent to look in at her. Louise stared at her blankly, panic bubbling in her throat. Frummie, who knew a great deal about these enemies to mental health, reached to grasp the hand still clenched upon the steering wheel.

"I thought you'd be late," she said. "There's been another murder and I watched the local news at lunchtime to see if they've managed to catch the murderer. I saw the queues on the M5. Lucky you made an early start. You've missed the worst of it and you're still in time for tea."

Tea. There was comfort in the word: warmth, peace, familiarity. Somehow she could not quite release the wheel but hung on to it grimly, feeling that without it she might fall, disintegrate. Frummie's thin hand was warm, tough. She stared at it.

"I can't do it," she said, her eyes fixed on the two joined hands, hers and Frummie's. "I can't . . ."

"Yes." Frummie's voice was calm, unemotional. "Yes, you can do it. Let go of the wheel, Louise, and hold my hand."

Slowly, very slowly, she released the wheel, holding on instead to Frummie's hand, easing herself out of the driving seat until she was standing upright. She trembled, shaking with reaction.

"I thought I was better," she cried angrily, near to tears.

Frummie smiled. "And so you are," she said. "Much better. You've driven yourself to London, had a gruelling session with your ex-lover, made a commitment to the future and driven back again. For God's sake, girl! Be proud of what you've done and don't be wanting the impossible. Could you have managed all that a month ago?"

"It takes me by surprise," she mumbled, allowing Frummie to lead her through the garden. "I'm feeling fine . . . and then it hits me."

"It's the next step," said Frummie, settling her on the sofa. "You've stopped denying the existence of the past but now you've got to let it become part of your memory and your life. It's painful and frightening but you have to learn to accept it. Don't try to fight depression and fear with violent physical or mental exercise. But don't give in to them either. Just think. Oh, here they are again, and look past them, as if you were looking over someone's shoulder at something beyond. Fix your mind on what's beyond."

"But how do you do that?" Louise stared at her in perplexity, longing for some kind of formula, but confused and pessimistic. "How can you see past something so . . . so *huge*?"

"You have to practise it. You mustn't let them be important, you see, or you simply feed their power. Don't pretend they're not there by flinging yourself into some manic busyness, they'll simply reappear when you're exhausted, but just look past them as you might look past a tall person sitting in front of you at the theatre. You know he's there but he doesn't prevent you from watching the action. Have something positive to look at—your next possible achievement, for instance, or something as simple as a cup of coffee. Something cheerful but attainable."

"Does it really work?"

"It works in so far as it makes it possible to exist with personal tragedy and still achieve and make a worthwhile contribution."

"But how do you *know?*"

Frummie thought: Shall I tell her the truth? That I went through something similar when it sunk in that I'd lost Brigid. Or might it spoil her sense of security here at Fox-hole? Better not.

She said, "At the end of the war, there were an awful lot of people who were suffering just like you are. Reacting from the shock of loss, grief, guilt and the future stretching emptily ahead. I had one or two very close friends who had breakdowns and suffered from clinical depression. It's a tried-and-trusted remedy, I promise you."

"And you think it would work for me?"

Frummie smiled at her. "Try it and see. Ready for that tea now?"

"Oh, yes." Louise sighed, settling back against the cushions, relaxing a little. "I'd love a cup of tea. I stopped twice but the motorway cafés were heaving so I just grabbed a can of something and drank it in the car park."

"Terrible places. I'll put the kettle on and then you can tell me all about Martin. If you feel you want to, that is."

"He's been so kind." She shook her head rather sadly. "He always was, really. The problem is that he only feels fully alive when he's mending someone. I think I'd become unrewarding so he looked about for a new challenge."

"I should have thought that you were something of a challenge, just at present," observed Frummie drily.

Louise chuckled, recovering rapidly from her attack of

terror now, strengthened by Frummie's stringent presence. "He was tempted," she admitted. "We both were. I remembered how comforting he was just as he was beginning to wonder if I might be interesting again."

"And what happened?" asked Frummie curiously.

"Martin said that if I stayed with him I'd never grow out of it. He's right, of course. I knew it—but I was tempted."

"He's very wise," said Frummie after a moment or two. "I have to say that he's gone up in my estimation."

"He's a good man," agreed Louise. "He's funding me until I can support myself. I'll pay him back, of course. I've got to think where to live and whether I can go back to teaching."

"Well," said Frummie, "lots there to plan for and to keep the blues at bay."

"Yes," said Louise. "Yes, there is, isn't there? Oh, Frummie. It's good to be home. But what's this about another murder?"

"A woman in Plymouth." Frummie frowned anxiously. "Rather too close for comfort. It's the same pattern as the other two but in broad daylight this time, and the police say that the murderer is getting overconfident. Still . . ."

"It's horrid." Louise shivered. "I'm glad I'm staying with you."

Frummie decided that it would be unwise to unsettle her further; she needed to be confident and cheerful. "I expect we're all quite safe here," she said. "Let's have that tea."

JEMIMA SAT on her sofa, MagnifiCat curled beside her, listening to the rain drumming on the balcony, watching the drops pocking the smooth surface of the water. The silvery, shining curtain almost obscured the further shore and the sudden cloudburst had sent holidaymakers hurrying from the beach to seek cover. The sun was already breaking through the stormy purple clouds, shafts of shining light glancing to the sodden earth, so that the still falling rain gleamed and sparkled whilst a rainbow arched above the harbour.

"September tomorrow," she murmured, smoothing his soft coat. "Summer's nearly over."

She could feel his deeply contented reverberations beneath her hand and, for a brief moment, she felt an echo of her old contentment and that serenity of spirit which she'd taken for granted—before love had taken her by surprise. Since then, anxiety gnawed at her peace of mind.

"Can you really imagine settling here?" she'd asked him, playing devil's advocate and cursing her foolishness even as she did so. "It can be pretty dull in the winter, you know?"

"Can it?" He'd arched an eyebrow. "Doesn't it depend on one's company?"

She'd been flustered but determined to make her point. "I didn't quite mean that. The South Hams can be rather different when the holidaymakers have gone home and it rains for weeks on end. It's a big change from London. No cinemas or theatres a tube-ride away."

"There are other forms of entertainment." He'd refused to take her too seriously.

"That's true but, to be honest, I'm surprised that you came down here on holiday in the first place. From what you've told me about Annabel, it sounds as if the Maldives would be more her scene."

His expression had changed slightly, as if some inner retrospection were taking place, and she'd felt a pang of fear. How stupid to encourage him to think about Annabel, to dwell on the past!

"I have to say that you're right," he'd admitted. "The truth is we went skiing for a few days at Easter and Annabel caught some kind of virus. It really pulled her down. And then there was a lot of pressure at work so she was offered some extra leave. We decided to keep it really simple and try Devon. Neither of us had been here before and the brochure was quite impressive. We knew that in July it would be terribly hot in Europe and we didn't want to make arduous journeys so we picked this very quiet place where we could just chill out." He'd shrugged. "I wonder, now, if she ever really intended to come with me at all. I'd been doing a lot of overtime so I was able to squeeze an extra week and we were really looking forward to an extended break." A pause. "At least, *I* was."

"I'm sorry," she'd said wretchedly. "I didn't mean to drag it all up again."

"Oh, forget it. I feel a bit sensitive because she made such a complete fool of me. I really had no idea that she was having it with this other guy. It's because I wasn't in control, I suppose. I felt so helpless. She just came in that evening and said, 'Oh, by the way, about the holiday . . .' and I was just utterly gutted. I pleaded with her, you know? Crawled and begged." He'd shoved his hands in his pockets, his mouth grim and hard with self-contempt. "I really wish I hadn't done that."

She'd thought: So do I. I wish you hadn't cared that much. But you did. Do you still? That's the big one.

Now, feeling MagnifiCat's soft warm fur under her fingers, the rhythm of his deep, quiet breathing, she tried to regain her own sense of peace. Quite suddenly she remembered Brigid's expression when she'd said "She left me!" and remembered her own shock at the pain and the bewilderment on her sister's face. It had never occurred to her that Brigid had harboured resentment all these years because she had been abandoned, an unwanted child. Terrible though the disclosure had been, she felt that some vitally important first step had been taken and that she and Brigid might at last be able to develop a real relationship. She'd put herself out on a limb, telling of the heartbreak of her father's indifference, but she'd learned that it was necessary, sometimes, to display one's own weaknesses, to put weapons into other people's hands, in an attempt to give courage, to engender a sense of sharing. Sometimes she'd been badly hurt when they'd been used against her but some deep conviction persuaded her that she must be prepared to sacrifice her pride for future good. This had been one of those occasions. She'd described her own hurt at her father's betrayal and how it coloured her approach to relationships. She wished now that she'd gone further but her confidence had deserted her. Nevertheless it had been a start; a foundation laid on which the future might build. She'd had the feeling that Brigid, too, was withholding something; some problem which she could not share. Yet what could it be? She was so secure; so sure. Had it simply been the strain of seeing Louise through her breakdown which gave her that fine-drawn, rather gaunt look? Perhaps it was the anxiety of Humphrey's father's proposed visit? Brigid valued her privacy and it would be hard, coping with her father-in-law, along with Frummie.

"Put them together," she'd advised, trying to make Brigid laugh whilst they sat comfortably over their coffee in Eff-ings. "Pair them off and wash your hands of them."

"If only I could," Brigid had answered. "Mummie's been too preoccupied with Louise to make overmuch of it but she's hinted that it's rather high-handed of Humphrey to leave his father to us whilst he lives it up in the Bahamas. She can't say too much, of course."

"You're both very generous to her."

Brigid had flushed. "So are you."

"Oh." She'd shrugged it off. "I buy her booze and pay her car tax, neither of which she ought to be having. I know you buy her all sorts of treats which she couldn't possibly afford. Decent coffee and nice cheese. Logs in the winter. Plants for her garden. I know you do it very casually, she's told me so. Tactfully and quietly. Trying to save her pride. But she's very grateful really, you know. She's just so bad at showing it."

"She doesn't have to show it." Brigid had been crimson with embarrassment. "It's cheaper to buy things in bulk and with Humphrey away I couldn't possibly use it all myself. And I didn't mean to be sharp about the car tax. I just hadn't really taken it on board. How much she hates being stuck out in the country, I mean. I love it so much myself, you see . . ."

"Never mind. She's got a busy winter ahead, what with Louise and Humphrey's father. And Margot, of course. She'll be too busy to give it a thought." She'd hesitated. "How are the boys?" she'd asked—and watched Brigid's face smooth into love and pride.

They'd talked about Michael's forthcoming engagement then, and parted at last, having made a plan for supper for the four of them at Foxhole.

Jemima thought: I will tell her. But later, when I've got something more definite to tell. Oh, *please,* God, let it work. I love him. I really, really love him.

The rain had stopped and she got up and went out on to the balcony, leaning her bare arms on the wet rail, smiling to herself in the sunshine.

PART THREE

CHAPTER 24

Brigid sat in the courtyard, a large writing block on the table before her, watching Blot stalking a magpie. The doves perched, heads cocked, twittering anxiously at this intruder who was so clearly unmoved by their distress. He hopped cockily, not even troubling to fly so as to avoid Blot's pursuit, running a few steps, and then turning back to inspect the bread which had been put out for the robin. Blot was trying not to appear intimidated by this large thief and, in an effort to save face, burst into a volley of sharp short barks accompanied by a determined rush across the cobbles which sent the magpie flying up into the branches of the rowan tree. Pleased by this success Blot sat down and scratched vigorously whilst the doves cooed their approval from the stable roof.

The entertainment over, Brigid turned her attention once more to her letter. She had almost decided to write to Humphrey, explaining the whole wretched dilemma: almost but not quite. This letter was a practice run: an attempt to put it all into words. If it could be done in a reasonably acceptable way, then she might write it out properly and send it. On the other hand . . .

Brigid laid down her pen and stared at nothing in particular. Mentally, she'd examined every method of approach; no avenue was unexplored, no stone unturned. She could write to him—but imagine his reaction on opening a letter from home only to read such news! The shock of it! It was this aspect which made her hesitate. She might telephone him, except that the idea of stumbling through the whole story at long distance was appalling. How did you start? "Oh, by the way, before you hang up . . ." "I meant to tell you about this when you were home but it slipped my mind . . ." She might get a flight out so as to tell him face to face—but on what pretext? He was working, at sea a great deal of the time, so what excuse could she give for her sudden decision to leave Foxhole—she who loathed holidays—so as to visit the Bahamas, knowing he would be too busy to spare her much time? She could pretend some drama which would necessitate his being flown home but imagining his expression when he discovered her duplicity made her shudder. If only it hadn't been Jenny . . .

Brigid swore violently beneath her breath, so as to relieve her desperation, and hastily arranged her face into welcoming lines as one of the visitors from the cottage appeared in the courtyard entrance. This couple, quiet and contained, were having their first holiday in the Dartmoor National Park.

"And I hope their last," Brigid had said grimly to Louise the previous evening. "They didn't realise walking would be so unpleasant, apparently."

"Unpleasant?" Louise had looked surprised.

"Shit," Brigid had explained succinctly—and burst out laughing at the expression on Louise's face.

" 'We have to watch where we're putting our feet, dear,' " she'd mimicked in refined accents, " 'because of the mess. It's everywhere. Horses' dung as well as sheep's droppings and dogs' mess. And even cowpats. We didn't know there would be cows.' "

"You're kidding?"

"No," Brigid had said morosely. "Not kidding. I'm not at my best with city dwellers who regard the countryside as their personal playground. I think they expected some kind of sanitised theme park with the locals dressed in smocks and saying 'Oh-ar' when poked with a stick. Never again. I shall be booked up next year. Not that I think they'd want to come back."

Now, she smiled at Mrs. Prout and called "good morning." At least they hadn't been able to complain about the weather. The Bank Holiday had been unusually hot and the fine weather seemed set fair.

"I just thought I'd mention, dear," Mrs. Prout raised her voice, a wary eye on Blot lest he should rise and savage her ankles, "that the water's a funny colour."

Cursing silently, a smile on her lips, Brigid stood up. "Really? How d'you mean . . .?"

"It's a kind of brown colour, dear." Mrs. Prout glanced about for dog-turds and advanced a few cautious steps. "It's got a cloudy look to it."

"I'm sure it's nothing to worry about," said Brigid, accustomed to many variations of water colour from their private supply. "It's spring water, you know, so it might be anything."

"Anything?" Mrs. Prout looked alarmed. "How d'you mean, dear?"

"Well, it's probably just a bit peaty. Nothing to hurt you, honestly. I've lived here all my life and I've never had a problem with it."

"Mmm." Mrs. Prout looked unconvinced. "Hubby's not too happy with it, you see, dear."

"Perhaps you should drink mineral water, just until it clears," suggested Brigid desperately. "And boil everything else. It will soon clear itself, I'm quite certain."

"If you say so, dear. I'll tell him. Only he thought perhaps a call to the Water Board . . .?"

"But it's a private supply, you see. Spring water. It's not piped."

"Fancy. No one told us that."

"It's been tested, don't worry. It's perfectly safe to drink. But we do get this discoloration occasionally."

"Well, we'll keep an eye on it. We're off to the coast this morning, anyway."

"I'm sure it will be normal by the time you get back," said

Brigid with determined cheerfulness. "Have a lovely day."

"I'm sure we will. See you later, dear."

Brigid sat down again and picked up her pen. How far had she got? . . . *and somehow I couldn't find the courage to tell you face to face. I didn't want to spoil those last few days together.* Yes, well, so far so good. She rolled up her shirt-sleeves a little further, tilted her cotton hat against the sun and scribbled a few more words. *The real problem is that it's to do with Jenny and I know we never see eye to eye about her. Not that that's any excuse for not telling you the truth* . . . So how to go on from there? To explain her loyalty and sympathy for her old friend whilst not ever believing that she was taking a serious risk? Phrases and sentences jumbled in her head . . .

"Good morning, darling. You look very industrious."

Brigid's fingers clenched on her pen. "You made me jump," she said. "Are you off somewhere?"

"Louise's driving me down to Holne to the mobile library," said Frummie. "You've got a book, remember? Steve ordered it for you specially. I'll take it back for you."

"Book?" Brigid tried to remember. "Oh, yes. Yes, he did. Look, could it wait until next time?"

"I'm sure it's due back. Do you want me to look for it?"

"No. No, really. I've no idea where it is at the moment. Do you think you could explain to Steve? I know he'll understand. It's just that I want to get this done."

"Oh, very well. If it's that important . . ."

"I'm sure it's not due back yet. I only had it out a fortnight ago. Don't worry about it and tell Steve I'll see him in a fortnight. Enjoy yourself."

"Oh, I shall. I always enjoy a chat with Steve. Louise and I have decided to have lunch in the Church House afterwards. Would you like to join us?"

"Can I see how I get on?"

"Yes, of course. Just turn up. If you can tear yourself away from your magnum opus."

"I will." Brigid ignored the sarcasm. "See you later."

Presently the Prouts' car drove slowly away up the track,

followed after a short interval by Louise's. Brigid let out a deep sigh. Solitude closed in peacefully about her and she could feel her muscles unknotting, her body relaxing. The shutters of her mind opened gently, allowing thoughts to flow freely, unimpeded by panic. She wrote for a while, phrases coming easily, explanations forming clearly, reasonably, until, pleased with her lucidity, she put down the pen and began to reread the letter. The sound of an engine approaching alerted her and she looked up, listening. Could the Prouts' progress have been impeded by some giant dropping in the road? Had her mother forgotten one of her books? Her nerves, so gloriously freed from anxiety, began to tighten. The engine idled for a moment and was switched off. A door slammed. Silence. Brigid frowned, listening intently. Who was it and what were they doing? Suddenly she thought about the recent murder and was gripped with a spasm of uncharacteristic terror.

Footsteps approached and a figure appeared, pausing at the entrance to the courtyard, looking round with an open, almost childlike interest. He was tall and one of the thinnest men that Brigid had ever seen. His long legs were clothed in rather disgraceful sailcloth trousers and he wore an ancient tweed over his checked shirt. His shoulders were wide, his arms hanging with an angular sharpness, scarecrow-like. As his gaze came to rest upon her, she rose to her feet, as though his glance had drawn her up from the bench, and they gazed at each other in amazement.

"You're Brigid," he said—and his face creased into a thousand lines of delight. "This is very good. So very good."

He advanced towards her, a thin, strong hand outstretched, and, automatically, she held out her own hand which he took, holding it tightly, bending slightly to peer into her face. A white, fierce bristle of eyebrow was drawn down over his keen grey eye and he grimaced.

"You're not expecting me. My dear girl, have I made a mistake? Got the dates mixed? I do hope not. So like me to get off on the wrong foot. I'm Alexander. Humphrey's father."

. . .

"Brigid's not looking well," mused Frummie, as the car crossed the cattle-grid and approached Saddle Bridge. "She's lost weight and she's got a drawn look. She doesn't concentrate on what you're saying. Have you noticed it?"

"I'm afraid that I've been too wrapped up in myself to notice anything much," admitted Louise. "Can it be that she's missing Humphrey?"

Frummie wrinkled her nose dismissively. "Unlikely. Anyway, not more than usual. No, it's not that kind of thing. She's jumpy and distracted. Something's on her mind."

Louise, herself distracted by the gold and purple splendour of heather and gorse blooming riotously together, slowed the car to allow a group of ponies to cross, leaning from the window to watch a foal pressing shyly against its mother's flank. She put the car in motion again, thinking about Brigid.

"Can't you ask her?" she suggested.

Frummie frowned. "Brigid's a very private person," she said, almost defensively. "It's not quite that simple."

Louise, thinking of her unhappy relationship with her own mother, wondered why such barriers should rise between those who should surely understand each other best. It was odd that Frummie should have been so intuitive and caring to *her* whilst she seemed to delight in needling and upsetting her own daughter.

"Could I help?" she wondered aloud. "Do you think she might confide in me?"

"It's possible. I've always thought that Brigid seems very fond of you. Perhaps, if a moment suggests itself. Nothing too obvious."

"Of course not. I'll be very tactful."

"Well, then." Frummie shifted more comfortably in her seat, as though a problem had been taken care of, and looked out of her window. "What a splendid day! Such a good idea to have some coffee at the Café Forge before the library van arrives. We can have a chat with Chloe if she's not too busy.

She won't have gone back to college yet. Such a pretty girl, isn't she, and such fun? Of course, you haven't met Steve, have you? You'll like Steve. He always knows what books to suggest for me and he has such clever children. His son is doing a PhD, you know . . ."

As she talked, Louise wondered how someone who enjoyed people so much managed to survive in this isolated environment. She tried to imagine Frummie as a young woman, fresh from London, attempting to adapt to these bleak, wild moors with only a small child for company. Diarmid, she'd gathered, had been much absorbed by his research and Frummie thrown back on her own resources. She was not a particularly maternal woman and it was evident that she preferred the company of adults to babies and tiny children. She rarely made references to her great-grandson and tolerated Brigid's enormous pride in him with a kind of patient indifference. Louise found herself wondering about Diarmid; what kind of man he must have been, what qualities he'd possessed to lure the young, urban, fun-loving Frummie into marriage. How had he felt when she'd left him?

She thought: What a muddle we make of our lives. What terrible mistakes we make.

Rory's face appeared briefly before her inward eye and she winced with pain.

"So that's that. Now! Where were we?"

What madness had possessed her so that she had allowed herself to lose him: him, who had always been her comforter? Had it really been necessary to be so destructive?

"There seems to be even more people about than usual, have you noticed?" Frummie's voice was comfortingly matter-of-fact. "That's because it's Bank Holiday week. Schools start back next week, thank goodness. Let's hope there will be a space in the café's car park."

One day at a time. She hummed the words over and over in her head whilst she drove into Holne and parked the car. One day at a time. One hour. One minute. Frummie was watching her quizzically and Louise smiled reassuringly.

"I'm fine," she said, as if in answer to a question. "Really. Let's go and have some coffee."

BRIGID, STARING at Alexander, had the sensation of them both being set in time, like flies sealed in amber, whilst the universe whirled about them. She was fixed, immobile, shocked out of her own troubles and faced now with a new one. For one brief moment, which seemed like eternity, she was utterly helpless. His grip tightened, guided her back to her seat, forced her down.

"Sorry," she murmured—and suddenly the whirling slowed and the world settled about her once more. The doves strutted, cooing gently, and Blot wagged round Alexander's legs as he settled her on the bench and sat down beside her.

"I blame myself," he said. "I should have telephoned. A warning shot across the bows."

"It's just . . ." Brigid realised that she was still holding his hand and released herself. "It's only that I didn't think it was just yet. You arriving, I mean. I thought it was another week. Or something . . ." She felt awkward, embarrassed, hearing the unfriendliness, the lack of welcome in her voice. "Did Humphrey write to you, explaining?"

"D'you know, I rather think he did." He sounded quite cheerful, rather as though they were discussing someone else's situation. "And now he's gone . . . to the Bahamas, was it?"

"Yes." She still felt helpless. He was so large, so very *real*. There was a vitality which emanated from him, a force which rendered her powerless. She waited to see what might happen next.

He was looking about, fondling Blot's ears, quite at ease, his long legs disposed with an unconsciously elegant casualness.

"I've imagined it, you know." The fierce bright glance lanced her briefly. "I came pretty close. Didn't get the position of the cottages quite right. Humphrey explained it very well, though."

"I didn't realise . . ." She hesitated, unwilling to expose herself—or Humphrey.

"That he wrote to me?" Another keen look. "Well, not too often, you know. Just enough to stay in touch but not much more."

Loyalty demanded that she should defend Humphrey but there had been nothing condemnatory in Alexander's statement. It was the truth; no more no less.

"He doesn't get much time for writing," she said feebly.

"Doesn't he? Of course, I've no real idea as to what his duties are."

She realised that he was not expecting her to be trivial. Well, that made things a little easier.

"The trouble is," she said, "that the cottage has visitors in it. I wasn't expecting you for another ten days."

"Is that the cottage?"

"Yes." She was confused by his unexpected responses. "Yes, it is. It's a holiday let, you see. That's why Humphrey wrote. To explain that it was occupied until the last week in September."

"And who lives in the other one? This blank wall must be the back of it. How sensible of you to leave both walls without windows. It gives you privacy, doesn't it? I expect you value that with visitors about all the time."

"Yes, I do."

"Might I see inside your house?"

"Yes, of course." With instinctive politeness, Brigid rose to her feet. "I should have offered you some coffee. Would you like some?"

"Later. That would be quite delightful." He rose too, smiling down at her, and she found herself smiling back. His force was irresistible: innocent, warm, focused. "You're much more beautiful than I'd expected."

She gaped at him, suddenly distressed that he might be trying to flatter her, surprised at her whole reaction against it; at how much she was already valuing his directness.

". . . but far too thin," he was saying, his brows suddenly

drawn together as he sized her up dispassionately. "Are you usually this thin?"

She laughed, relieved, wanting to say, "You can talk!" but instead, "Probably not," she admitted. "It's been too hot to eat."

"Has it?" He was following her into the cool hall and she suddenly realised how difficult it would be to lie to Alexander.

"There's not much to show," she said lightly, ignoring his question. "These longhouses are rather odd. One room leads to another. Three rooms down and three rooms up."

He stood in the hallway, looking through the two rooms, as if he were reconciling them with his own ideas of the house.

"Must be rather gloomy in the winter," he observed.

"Well, yes." She was startled. Most people enthused over the house's character and charm. "It's damp and cold too. I'm used to it, I suppose. I've lived here for most of my life. The kitchen's the best room. Come and see it."

"And the bedrooms lead off one another, too?"

"Yes." She answered more reluctantly, sensing danger, not wanting to admit to the boys' quarters. "So how about some coffee."

He was looking about the kitchen with that interested air, taking in all the clutter of her life: the things that defined her. The flowered china on the dresser and the watercolour paintings on the walls; the brightly painted Henny-Penny on the working surface, the ivy-leafed geraniums in pots on the deep windowsill and the well-worn cookery books leaning together on their shelf. It seemed to her, in the brief few seconds of silence, that he was learning her, understanding her, seeing far more than she imagined might be possible in such a short time. She pushed the kettle on to the hotplate, feeling oddly nervous, thrusting her hair behind her ears—then changed her mind and reached for the cafetiere . . .

"It can't have been easy," he was standing quite close to her, "with two small children."

She frowned. "Easy?"

"The sleeping arrangements. Upstairs. Very little privacy, I should imagine."

"Oh, I see. No, it wasn't . . . easy." She stared up at him almost desperately, willing herself to stop there. After all, she wasn't obliged to tell him everything. A short silence. "In fact," she found herself adding, despite herself, "we converted half of the barn to make some extra space."

He smiled at her. "What a splendid idea. I must admit that I'm ready for that coffee. It's the smell of it, isn't it? Like frying bacon. Quite irresistible. Shall we drink it in your nice courtyard?"

"Yes, of course," she said. "Why not?"

She put mugs and the cafetiere on to a tray—"No milk for me," he told her, "or sugar"—and then, taking the tray, he carried it out into the sunshine with Brigid following, dazed and helpless in his wake.

CHAPTER 25

"Brigid's got visitors," said Frummie, peering through the windscreen. "No wonder she didn't turn up for lunch. I wonder who it can be? I don't recognise the car."

Louise smiled privately at Frummie's blatant curiosity, wondering what her next move might be so as to satisfy it. She parked behind the unknown car: a small blue hatchback.

"They know where we are if they need me to move," she said. "But I think there's room to turn."

"Not if the Prats come back," said Frummie. "They'll get blocked in. I'd better just go and warn Brigid."

"Good idea," agreed Louise amiably, chuckling at the name. "Then you'll be able to see who it is, won't you?"

"You're not too old for a smack, you know," said Frummie, grinning wickedly. "You could come too, if you like."

"No, thanks. There's nothing of the Elephant's Child in *my* make-up. But take care Brigid doesn't pull your nose for you."

Laughing to herself, she turned away whilst Frummie headed purposefully for the courtyard.

It was empty, except for the doves, although a tray stood upon the table. Her curiosity now well and truly roused, she trod lightly over the cobbles and stood for a moment just inside the front door, listening. Voices drifted from the kitchen: Brigid's, rather anxious, clipped as if with breathlessness, and then a deeper voice with a hint of amusement beneath its attractive drawl. She knocked sharply on the door, yodelled her familiar call and nipped across the hall and into the kitchen before Brigid could have any opportunity of forestalling her.

A tall man rose courteously from the table as Brigid pushed back her chair and turned round. Frummie spoke to her daughter but her attention was riveted on the guest who stood waiting for an introduction.

"I am so sorry to interrupt," she said mendaciously, "but I just wanted to say that we might be blocking your visitor's car." She smiled blindingly at him. "If the Prats come back"—"Prouts," corrected Brigid automatically—"he'll be stuck."

"This is Alexander Foster, Mummie," said Brigid, not in the least taken in by her unruly parent's stratagems. "Humphrey's father. Alexander, this my mother."

She hesitated, never quite certain as to which sobriquet her mother might wish to be known.

"How do you do?" Frummie advanced, hand outstretched, smiling. "I'm Frummie. Freda, really, but Frummie to friends and family. How very nice to meet you at last. I'd begun to believe that you didn't really exist."

Alexander swept aside Brigid's embarrassed apologies and took Frummie's hand in his own.

"That's quite understandable. I've left it very late to become part of the family and I'm touched by my welcome." He glanced briefly at Brigid, who was staring wretchedly before her. "It's been far more than I deserve."

"Well, that's probably true," agreed Frummie candidly. "You haven't shown a great deal of interest, have you?"

"Mummie, *please!*" cried Brigid, scarlet now with humiliation—but Alexander shook his head, smiling at her.

"She's quite right," he said gently. "I arrived without warning and you've given me coffee and made me a delicious lunch."

"I thought you weren't coming for another week or two," said Frummie. "Have you changed your plans?"

"I seem to have mislaid my son's letter," he answered.

"This was the original date, you see, but things are somewhat confused. I shall have to find somewhere to stay."

"That won't be easy," Frummie told him brightly. "Not during Bank Holiday week."

She glanced at Brigid, who stared back at her coldly.

"Brigid was explaining that to me when you arrived," he said. "I'm afraid it was foolish of me to turn up unannounced."

"Well, you could sleep on my sofa," she said, "until the Prats"— "*Prouts!*" said Brigid furiously—"leave. It's only a few more days, isn't it, darling?"

"They go on Saturday," agreed Brigid unwillingly, "but don't forget that Louise has the cottage booked for the next fortnight."

"But Louise doesn't need it," exclaimed Frummie cheerfully. "She's very happy with me."

"I thought," said Brigid carefully, "that we'd agreed that it might be sensible for her to be on her own again. Just to break her in to it a bit before she has to leave us. Wasn't that the plan?"

"She's coming on splendidly," said Frummie. "She doesn't need breaking in."

"Nevertheless," Brigid was beginning to sound desperate, "I feel we should ask her. She always books the cottage for that fortnight and she's paid a deposit. We can't be quite so high-handed as to assume she doesn't want it."

"I'm causing a great deal of trouble," said Alexander apologetically. "Please forgive me. I'm sure that I shall find somewhere to stay. Although, if your friend finds that she doesn't need the cottage, after all, I should be delighted to have it. Naturally, I shall pay the normal rate."

"Please." Brigid looked as if she might burst into tears. "Please try to understand that I'm not trying to be difficult. And I don't care about the money. It's simply . . ."

She faltered, confused, unable to express her true feelings. It had been a pleasant interlude and she was surprised at her unwillingness to see Alexander leave. Nevertheless, it was simply out of the question to offer him the cottage without consulting Louise and there still remained the problem of the three days between and, at any moment, her mother might just suggest that—

"What about the stable wing where the boys sleep?" cried Frummie. "It's the obvious solution. Just until the weekend. What do you think, darling?"

Brigid bit her lip, schooled her lips into a smile and looked at Alexander.

"The problem is that it's not self-contained," she said rapidly. "That's why I hadn't offered it. There's the playroom— well, it's a sitting room now—and two bedrooms and the bathroom and loo. But there are no cooking facilities, you see."

"Does that matter?" asked Frummie. "Couldn't you muck in together for a few days? I tell you what. I'll go and have a word with Louise. See how she feels about the cottage. If she's willing to stay with me then I'm sure we could all cope together until Saturday. Shan't be long."

She hurried out and there was a silence.

"You've made a conquest," said Brigid bitterly.

"She seems very . . . generous with your accommodation."

Brigid glanced at him quickly. He was watching her, smiling a little, his eyes warm with affection. Suddenly she wanted to burst into tears.

"It's not that I want you to go," she said stiffly. "It's just not that simple. And she always makes me look . . . ungenerous."

"Not to me," he said. "Tell me what you want to do, Brigid."

"I want you to stay," she said, and caught her breath, astonished at her uncharacteristically unguarded response. "But I'm not good at having people in the house with me. I'm a private kind of person and it makes me nervous."

"Supposing," he said thoughtfully, carefully, "supposing I were to buy a little camping stove. Do you think I might manage in the boys' quarters?"

"We could have supper together," she said, anxious to show friendship. "Anyway, I expect Mummie will be only too pleased to look after you."

"Well then. Shall we try it? If it's just until Saturday. If Louise wants her cottage that's perfectly reasonable and I'll go off now and find a hotel. But if she doesn't?"

"I expect," said Brigid, with a return to her normal self, "that Louise has already been talked out of her cottage. But yes. If she doesn't then we'll give it a try."

JEMIMA WOKE first. Watery reflections danced upon the wall, shifting and wavering, shot through with sunshine. She could feel his warmth, radiating beside her although he was turned away, his long bare back exposed, his face almost hidden. She longed to touch him, yet feared to wake him. Resting on her elbow, she stared down at him: smooth pale skin patched with tiny, golden freckles across his shoulders; red-brown hair, tousled, beginning to curl a little, needing a trim; an angle of determined bristly jaw; lips swollen with sleep crushed against the pillow. He had become so important to her, so necessary, that it was impossible now to imagine how she had lived before his arrival. They'd spent every spare moment together—"Some of us have to work," she'd said as he'd begun to demand more and more of her time—but during this last week since the Bank Holiday weekend she'd spent the minimum amount of time in her office.

"I'll catch up later," she'd promised herself, "after he's gone back to London"—and now this moment was upon her. Today, when he woke, after some breakfast, he'd be driving back to London. He'd already packed up at the cottage, spending the last night with her in Salcombe, planning to leave early.

"Must you go on Friday?" she'd asked, sinking any pride left to her after this last glorious week. "I know you've got to be out on Saturday morning but you could stay with me."

He'd shaken his head, smiling at her. "No, no," he'd said. "I remember the roads when I came down. It was hell. Imagine what it must be like on the Saturday after the Bank Holiday week!"

"Fridays are terrible too," she'd argued. "Wait until Sunday."

"I shouldn't think there's a good day to travel," he'd said. "I expect Sunday is as bad as Friday or Saturday. But, anyway, I need to get back in time to sort myself out for Monday. I don't know yet how Annabel's left the place."

She'd tried not to plead with him—reaching desperately after the cool composure, the quirky humour which attracted him—and had managed to agree, lightly, that perhaps it was best after all. She'd been rewarded by his affectionate reaction, his ready admittance that he was hating the thought of going back.

"I shall have terrible withdrawal symptoms," he'd said. "I've been here too long. It seems more like home than . . . home."

She'd made certain that he'd spent as much time as possible at the flat with her; subtly showing him how good it could be together, hoping to erase the memories of Annabel. Impossible, of course, to wipe away five years in barely four weeks, but she'd done her best. She was also hoping that returning to an empty, depleted flat might underline all that he was missing.

Jemima leaned closer, almost touching him, but not quite. If he were to wake they might share a few moments in love-making but then he would be gone. All the time he remained asleep she could keep him. She slipped carefully from the bed and went out into the hall and into the kitchen. Pouring some orange juice into a glass, she drank thirstily, refilled the glass and carried it into the sitting room, closing the door gently behind her. MagnifiCat came to her, stepping carefully, then drew away from her, fastidiously.

"You don't like the smell of him, do you?" murmured Jemima, drawing her hand down over his head. "Well, you might have to learn to love it. You're just being difficult."

He twined and weaved about her bare ankles as she went out on to the balcony, leaning as usual on the rail. Below her a sleek, modern ketch, with a woman at the helm, was approaching the anchorage. As she turned the boat into the wind, her companion on the foredeck threw the anchor over the side. The water rose and sparkled in the sunshine as the chain payed out and the boat came to a rocking, swinging rest, the sails crumpling gently on to the deck. They called to one another cheerfully as they tidied up, coiling ropes, checking fenders, and presently the woman disappeared below—probably to cook some breakfast. Jemima watched them, wondering whether they'd sailed round from Dartmouth or from a further port; envying them their easy companionship, their evident pleasure at this delightful landfall. How romantic to sail into Salcombe; to be a part of this charming scene. She sighed a little. Soon her legacy would be gone and she would no longer be able to afford this place which had become so special to her. Yet how could she bear to leave it? It was going to be an impossible act to follow. Perhaps it would have been more sensible to have put a deposit on a more affordable flat; something which she could have continued to maintain. Of course, if there were *two* salaries coming in then there would be no problem . . .

She thought: Anyway, if we were together I don't think I should mind too much where we were. We could buy a little cottage and do it up together. Ohmigod! I *want* him. I want to do all those corny things I used to despise—be together, decorate rooms, have babies . . .

"Oh!" She gave a small startled yelp as his arm encircled her waist. "My God! Don't *do* things like that."

"Sorry. Really sorry. I didn't hear you go. You should have woken me."

She saw that he was dressed—no more lovemaking then—and shaved. How quick he'd been. In his chinos and cotton shirt he looked casual enough but, somehow, more London casual than holiday casual. There was a whole new look about him: sharper, distanced.

"I needed a drink," she said casually, suppressing her instinctive desire to fling her arms about him and beg him to stay. "I had no idea what the time was, to tell you the truth."

"It's later than I meant to be." He too was staring out across the harbour. He sighed, turned back to her with a quick shrug. "How on earth am I going to do this? Leave you, I mean?"

Her heart ricocheted about, bouncing off her ribs, up into

her throat. Yet, even now, some deep instinct warned her to be cautious.

"I shan't be going anywhere," she said lightly. "You can come back any time you want to."

"Promise?" He kissed her for a long, breathless moment, then hugged her tight. "Like next weekend, for instance?"

"Next . . .?"

"You did say any time? Is that too soon for you?"

"No. Oh, no. That's . . . that's simply great. You're sure?"

She thought: Don't ask that, you silly cow. Don't put doubts in his mind.

"Quite sure." He was kissing her once more—but quickly now. "Do I get coffee before I go?"

"You certainly do." She could be bright again: wacky, fun, flirty. He would be back; in seven days he would be back. "You could even have toast, orange juice."

He was shaking his head. "No. I never eat when I'm travelling."

"Fine." She must remember that, along with all the other tiny, vital things she'd learned about him. No mumsy attempts at persuasion. No fussing. "Coffee it is."

He held on to her, now that she was making no attempt to detain him. "It's great to be with a woman who doesn't make everything into a drama," he murmured. She raised her eyebrows as if to say "So what's there to make a drama about?" and, releasing herself, went into the kitchen, leaving him to lean on the rail, having a last look.

On her own, the door pushed almost closed, she punched the air with both fists, cheering silently, applauding her own performance, exulting in its success. Laughing at herself, she reached for the coffee. "Oh, God," she prayed, "make him really miss us!"

CHAPTER 26

Louise locked the car door and glanced about with an air of satisfaction: only two cars, parked at the further end of the car park, and one of those about to depart. During these last few weeks she'd developed a passion for the quiet path which bordered the peaceful waters of Venford Reservoir. The woods sheltering and silent, the rippling lake, the majestic stands of rhododendron engendered a mysterious, magical atmosphere; a fairy-tale scene. So enamoured had she become that she almost resented the presence of other holidaymakers who shouted back and forth to one another as they made their ways, single file on the shingly root-crossed paths, and whose dogs ran to and fro, barks and voices alike ringing across the drowned valley, shivering the silence into echoing fragments. She'd taken to arriving early and late, avoiding noisy family parties, so that she might walk alone in the rosy, glowing dawn or in the violet, shadowy dusk.

Now she crossed the road, skirting the iron palings, letting herself in through the gate, stopping to look at the rugged granite mortarstone with its three deep, rough holes. The ground under her feet was dry; soft brown needles carpeting the hard, sterile earth beneath the fir trees which towered above her. She paused to watch a robin flitting among the branches of the rhododendron and walked on, watching the reflections; cloudy shapes of gold and scarlet trembling across the surface as a cat's paw of wind ruffled the water.

This evening, alone again, away from the companionship of Foxhole, she let the thoughts of Rory drift into her mind. He'd been in her thoughts all day but now she allowed him to come close to her. She experienced once more the reality of him: his shape and smell. Unbearable longing, need for him, squeezed and twisted her heart. His humour, his passions, his vitality and courage filled her senses. Painful though these memories were she recognised the necessity of facing them, dealing with them and then letting them go. Not denying but allowing them to take their rightful place in her past along with all the other experiences which had made her what she was now. Rory and Hermione. Sitting down on the wooden bench she could see them as clearly as if they were superimposed upon the peaceful scene before her. Rory and Hermione playing together: Rory racing her on Rhu Spit, letting her win, or walking patiently beside her little wooden tricycle with the pony's head, listening to her chatter: sleeping on Sunday afternoons, a film, unheeded, reeling silently out on the television screen, whilst he stretched full-length on the sofa, newspapers strewed about the floor, Hermione sprawling crab-like across his chest, her long fair hair in his mouth, her blue eyes sleepy. His pride in her: "These drawings are jolly good, you know, for a three-year-old." His irritation: "Does she always have to throw a temperature an hour before Ladies' Nights or on Saturday evenings just when the surgery has closed for the weekend?" The bedtime stories with him sitting on the bed, legs stretched out comfortably whilst she leaned against his arm, sucking her thumb, her eyes fixed on the book. His voice, flexible, savouring the words: *"The world is so full of a number of things, I'm sure we should all be as happy as kings."*

Shutting her eyes, she saw the picture: a drawing of a small boy dressed in crown and ermine and, above his head, a rainbow of smaller scenes: a pig with a flower in its mouth, a sailing ship, a snowman in a top hat. It was titled *Happy Thought*.

Tears slipped from beneath her closed lids, grief dragged at her heart, and she wrapped her arms about herself lest she should fall apart.

The stealthy rustle, the sharp cracking of a dry twig in the wood behind her, made a faint impression on her sorrow. She frowned a little, still staring out over the water, not turning, and, as the memories faded, she wiped the back of her hand across her cheek.

"Look past despair," Frummie had advised. "Concentrate on something good and positive."

First, however, she must come to terms with loss; she must accept the pain of it, learn to live with it. Now, at this moment, all she could think about was the self-destructive madness which had allowed her to drive Rory away. Why had she not seen that he could have saved her; realised that together they might have been able to survive such horror? Resolutely she dragged her mind away from these negative questions. Memories were one thing, further self-destruction another. At least now she could tell the difference and slowly, if she persevered, the memories would lose their stinging, painful power. She must hold on to that.

A blackbird, startled from its perch, flew out of the trees, its staccato, warning cry stuttering over the water. Louise stood up, hugging her fleece around her. She'd been sitting for longer than she realised and it was growing darker. She began to walk back, deliberately concentrating on other, lighter thoughts. What music, for instance, would Frummie consider suitable accompaniment for an evening walk amongst these shadowy woods, beside the glinting water? Sibelius, perhaps? Grieg? One might easily imagine trolls behind the trees. She wouldn't ask her, though, guessing already at the sharp retort. For Frummie believed that these solitary walks were the height of madness and refused to be convinced that they were necessary.

"It's much too risky at the moment," she'd said. "All those women were on their own. I know that they were all in cities or large towns but you shouldn't go out alone, at least not so late in the evening."

Louise knew that Frummie had a point but sometimes she simply had to be alone, to have time to remember, to work through her feelings, to stretch and grow emotionally. She'd been very willing to yield up the cottage to Alexander—she enjoyed Frummie's society, needed company—but she also had an absolute requirement for periods of solitude. This evening, however, her serenity was disturbed. Some deep atavistic instinct was pressing against her preoccupation. Turning her head slightly she fancied she saw a movement in the woods, away to her left. The depth of her fear surprised her; it being the measure of her reviving love of life. Not too long ago she'd have been too sunk in misery to care much about survival. Now she was jumpy—and it was all Frummie's fault. Hands in her pockets, she chuckled at her fears—after all, it was most likely a fox, or a deer—nevertheless, her footsteps quickened and her breath came a little faster. Beneath the silent trees the shadows crept stealthily, reaching down to the path. The water, clear and cold, drained of all colour, stretched away to the further darkening shore.

There *was* a figure, too tall for any animal, skirting the furthest tree-trunks, slipping along inside the fence. Louise began to hurry, panic rising in her throat, measuring the distance to the gate, praying now for some noisy holidaymaker to break the silence with his cheerful shouts. There was a stumbling noise away to her left, a muffled crash, and Louise began to run, stumbling over the roots across the path, dragging open the gate, fumbling for her keys. One other car remained in the car park; the same which had been parked there earlier, surely, although it was too dark now to identify it.

With trembling fingers she unlocked the door, scrambled in and pushed the key into the ignition. The engine wouldn't start. Teeth chattering, quickly, desperately, she locked the other door and then her own before trying again. This time the engine purred into life and, gasping with relief, she slammed the gearstick forward and jolted across the car park, turning out on to the road, racing back towards Foxhole.

"YOU'LL BE glad to get into the cottage," Brigid was saying to Alexander, serving her rather special pudding, Brettle cream, on to his plate. This was their third shared supper and if the food were rather more extravagant than Brigid would have cooked for herself she was not admitting to it.

"I shall be very glad," agreed Alexander, looking with delight at his generous helping—despite his thinness he had a terrific appetite—and then smiling at her. "It will be a great relief."

Brigid experienced the slight shock which was now becoming familiar at the devastating honesty with which Alexander answered questions. He had no concept of the mendacious verbal interplay which greased the wheels of social intercourse. She remembered Humphrey's words: *"He's unmaterialistic and penetratingly honest."* Well, the latter was certainly true. She hadn't wanted Alexander in the house with her but now, contrarily, she needed his reassurance that he had been quite happy with her; that they had both enjoyed this brief time of odd intimacy. He had been careful not to invade her space and to make himself as unobtrusive as possible.

"You'll need to use the fridge, of course," she'd said, "or your milk will go off."

"I shan't bother with milk," he'd replied. "I drink my coffee black and I have some dried milk for an emergency."

"What about breakfast?" she'd asked anxiously, trying to make up for her previous lack of hospitality. "Don't you eat cornflakes?"

"I shall have toast," he'd answered. "You've lent me this very nice toasting-machine and Frummie has given me a pot of her home-made marmalade."

"Has she?" She'd stifled the retort *"She would!"* knowing it to be childish, attempting a more adult approach. "You'll enjoy it. She makes very good marmalade. Better than mine. Well, do say if you need anything and do feel free to use the courtyard."

He'd been surprisingly nice to have around; finding it unnecessary to engage in idle chitchat but passing her with an inclination of his head and a smile, seeming to be happily occupied, utterly at peace. His peacefulness fascinated her. She'd never met anyone who was so serene; so apparently at one with himself. Remembering Humphrey's remarks about him she began to understand that such contented self-sufficiency might be seen as selfishness, a lack of interest, perhaps, in his fellow men, but she was beginning to be curious about Humphrey's mother. The usual conversational opening gambits, however, were utter failures; he simply didn't recognise them.

"I was so sorry to hear about Agneta's death," she'd begun—hoping to lead on to some interesting disclosures.

"Were you?" He'd stared at her, surprised. "But you didn't know her at all. You didn't even know *me*."

She'd been silenced by such a prosaic response, unable to continue her probing. She'd murmured something platitudinous, too embarrassed to recover her poise quickly. He was entirely unafraid of silence and on one occasion they'd sat together in the courtyard for a whole hour, neither of them speaking. Even when he'd put down his book he'd made no attempt at conversation but had merely sat staring straight ahead of him, relaxed and perfectly at ease. She'd begun to learn that the only way to communicate satisfactorily was to be as straightforward as he was. This was not nearly as simple as it might at first appear. Sitting down again, with the Brettle cream within reach, she decided to make an effort.

"Does it seem odd to you," she began, "that we should meet only now? After all, Humphrey and I have been married for nearly thirty years. Weren't you curious about me?"

"I was very curious," he answered at once. "But I had to be content with what Humphrey was prepared to allow me."

"Allow you?"

He looked at her, a keen, penetrating look. "He wrote to me, you know. Humphrey is very punctilious. He doesn't approve of me but he was always very filial in that respect. He told me about you but I was not invited to your wedding."

It was odd how, after years of partisanship for Humphrey's mother, Brigid wanted to justify that decision; to explain how Humphrey had felt.

"He was very upset about his mother's death," she said.

"And he felt unwilling to meet Agneta. It was all very difficult."

"Humphrey was devoted to Elizabeth, and she to him," Alexander said calmly. "He made his feelings quite clear."

"And it was so quick." She was gaining confidence. "Your remarrying, I mean. He thought that it was—"

"Insensitive." He supplied the word for her. "And what did you think?"

"I thought so too." She took a deep breath. This honesty was heady stuff. "It wasn't just that you remarried so quickly after his mother died. Humphrey wasn't very old. He felt that you'd abandoned him."

"He was very confused." Alexander was getting on with his pudding. "He was very loyal to Elizabeth but what he wanted was for me to take over where she left off. At that time he was still very immature. He relied heavily on her advice and she liked to be in control of his life. I was delighted when he chose the Navy. She tried to stop him joining. Did you know that?"

"No." Brigid was fascinated by these disclosures. "I had no idea."

"She attempted to persuade him out of it, but he held firm, and I was very impressed with his courage. It was the first time he had ever stood against her wishes. She accused me of encouraging him, which was quite true. I felt that it would free him from her tyranny."

"Tyranny? That's a very strong word."

"She had a very strong claim on him. It was the infamous claim of the weak, sick, older person upon the strong, young one. She used his affection as a weapon, you see. Humphrey was afraid of sickness, afraid that she might die. She used his fear to bind him more strongly to her."

"I had no idea," Brigid said again. She had quite forgotten her pudding. There was no rancour in Alexander's voice, no hint of self-pity; he was simply stating the facts quietly and calmly, which made it all the more impressive. "But then how could he love her so much?"

"Silken cords are just as effective as a coarse rope.

Humphrey had no idea that he was being manipulated. She explained that everything she did was for his own good and he never doubted her. He accepted her values and she dedicated her life to him, a happy, willing martyr. She was very sweet and gentle, easily wounded. She suffered in silence— but it was a very loud, imposing silence. They were very close—until he joined the Navy. For the first time ever he discovered something which he loved as much as he loved her. When she saw that he was adamant she tried other tactics. She hoped he would become disillusioned and then she planned to buy him out. She died before that could happen."

"Do you think he might have given in?"

"It's possible. He'd never crossed her before and he was finding it very hard to deal with her studied disinterest and tiny gibes. She allowed him to see that she believed the rules and regulations to be rather childish and pointless in peacetime, as if he were playing soldiers, that kind of thing. He was hurt by her amused indifference but resented my approval."

"But why?"

"I had never allowed Elizabeth's views to compromise my own. She soon realised that she could not manipulate me and, as he grew up, Humphrey gradually accepted her assessment of me. I was abroad a great deal. I worked as an engineer for a paper-making group which had mills in Sweden. I was a kind of troubleshooter and I was often away from home. It was inevitable that Humphrey and his mother should become very close. Her resentment infected him and, by the time he was at Dartmouth, my approval was unimportant, almost an irritant."

"Yet he didn't want you to move to Sweden."

"He was shocked by Elizabeth's death. It flung him into a kind of limbo from which he sought desperately for another mentor. He thought he needed someone to take her place. In my view he needed to stand on his own two feet, make his own decisions and fight his own battles. Even if he could have accepted me it would never have worked. It was time he grew up."

"It sounds rather brutal."

"The world is a brutal place. The armed forces especially so. I could see that his passion for the Navy would help him to overcome many obstacles but that I might only weaken him."

"And you wanted to move to Sweden anyway?"

He smiled a little, accepting the implication. "My company was opening a new mill and wanted a works engineer. It was a splendid opportunity. We each had the chance to make a new start."

"And Agneta was part of your new start?"

"I'd known her for some years and we decided that it was foolish to waste any more time simply for the sake of convention . . . You haven't eaten your pudding."

Brigid looked at her plate, conscious that she had been taking great liberties, surprised by her temerity. It was time for a change of subject.

"No," she said. "But you have. Help yourself to some more while I catch up. Tell me about Sweden."

CHAPTER 27

"It's simply asking for trouble," said Frummie, "and I've no patience with you, roaming about the moors when it's nearly dark."

She banged a handful of spoons on to the draining board whilst Louise stood meekly holding the dishcloth. Her abrupt, frightened arrival, the previous evening, in the middle of a *Morse* video, had upset Frummie considerably. She'd listened to Louise's account of her walk and had been all for telephoning the police.

"But what could I say?" Louise had asked, recovering rapidly now in the bright, cheerful living room, ready to laugh at her terrors. "It might simply be some poor innocent soul taking a stroll. And I couldn't possibly describe the car. It was one of those small hatchbacks like yours. Or Alexander's or mine."

"Nevertheless there have been three murders. Three! If he's innocent he won't have a problem."

"Who?"

"The man who was walking about in the wood. Why walk in a wood in the dark when there's a perfectly good path? Thank goodness Brigid's got Alexander with her. I'll telephone her so as to warn her to lock up properly. How she could bear it alone all those years with Humphrey away I simply can't imagine."

She'd been irritated further by Brigid's refusal to become

frightened and had remained slightly grumpy for the rest of the evening, despite a long telephone conversation with Jemima, who'd been much more conformable. Louise, realising that part of Frummie's annoyance was merely relief that she'd come home safely, had been frightened enough to adopt a genuinely repentant attitude which did nothing to allay the older woman's acerbic comments. Next morning, it was clear that she was still suffering from anxiety and breakfast had been a subdued affair.

"I won't do it again," said Louise, picking up the spoons, feeling about ten years old. "Honestly, I won't. Not so late in the evening. I sat down on one of the benches and I just didn't realise how late it was getting."

"I still think we should have alerted the police." Frummie wasn't giving up easily. "It was our duty."

"I will if you want me to." Louise put the spoons into the drawer. "It's just that I can't tell them anything positive. I don't know the make or the colour of the car—or anything really."

"It's too late now," said Frummie, with a kind of self-righteous satisfaction. "The car will be long gone. And so will whoever it was who was in the woods with you."

Louise dried plates guiltily, racking her brains for some distraction. "The Prouts are supposed to move out this morning," she said cunningly, hoping to deflect Frummie's train of thought. "Alexander should be able to settle in. Brigid will be pleased, I expect."

Frummie's brow cleared a little. She was looking forward to having Alexander in a more accessible location, imagining little suppers together and jolly lunches at the pub.

"I wonder if she needs any help," she said thoughtfully. "Changeover day is always a busy one. Of course, Alexander might need some help too. Perhaps he'd like to come over for lunch. I doubt he'll have time to bother about food."

"That's true," Louise agreed enthusiastically, relieved by this change of direction. "Have you remembered that Thea's coming for coffee?"

"I have," Frummie swooshed water vigorously around the bowl, "but I doubt she's coming to see me."

"No, well . . ." Louise felt a faint confusion. She felt that, as Frummie's guest, she should be tactful regarding her own visitors. "The girls are with friends for the day and George is visiting his mother so she's on her own for once."

"So you said. Well, I shall leave you to get ready for her while I go and see if Brigid needs help." She dried her hands, moving to look out of the window. "The Prats are already packing up by the look of it. I'm just going upstairs to change. See you later."

Presently, she went out, crossed the courtyard and entered the house with her usual call. Brigid was sitting at the table reading the *Western Morning News*.

"Good morning, darling. No more murders, I hope? I still think we should have telephoned the police, you know."

Brigid, who had glanced up briefly from an engrossing article, did a double take. Frummie was wearing a very smart white shirt tucked into a pair of narrow-fitting tartan slacks. Her silvery-fair hair was newly washed and her make-up had evidently been applied without the assistance of the spectacles which she was too vain to wear. Brigid stared at this unexpected vision whilst her mother returned her surprised gaze coolly.

"The Prats are packing their car"—"Prouts," corrected Brigid automatically, still staring—"and I wondered if you might like a hand with the changeover."

"That's very kind." Brigid attempted to disguise her reaction, to pretend that there was nothing unusual in her mother's suggestion or attire, and then decided to use the Alexander-technique. "You're looking very smart this morning."

"Oh." Frummie drew down the corners of her mouth and shrugged dismissively. "These old things? Had them for years."

"I don't think I've seen them before."

"Probably not. But you're hardly intimately acquainted with the contents of my wardrobe, are you, darling?"

"No." Brigid was nonplussed. Clearly, honesty was not necessarily the best policy when applied to her mother. She tried a new tack. "How's Louise this morning? Has she recovered from her shock?"

"Yes, she has. But please don't encourage her to wander round the moor in the evening. I've given up trying to persuade *you* to be sensible, though I hope you might just think about it more carefully now."

"I'd rather wander round the moor at night than round the streets of Plymouth. Or any city, for that matter. All these murders have been in the towns."

"Very likely, but that doesn't alter the fact that Louise was badly scared last night. I don't think she's by any means strong enough yet to cope with a real fright. It's foolish to risk it."

"Of course." Brigid was contrite. "I have to say that I hadn't considered that aspect of it. She *is* OK?"

"She recovered very quickly," Frummie admitted. "But she was certainly shaken by it. I don't want to take any chances."

"I can quite see that. I didn't mean to be . . . uncaring. I expect she'll be more cautious now, anyway. Look, I'd better go and see the Prouts. She's nervous about coming over here in case Blot attacks her."

They both looked at Blot, who lay fast asleep on his back in his basket. His front paws were drawn up on his chest as if he were begging, his ears flopping like bedraggled plaits across his blanket.

"Yes," murmured Frummie. "A truly fearsome spectacle. I can see why she's terrified of him."

"He's been in the river," Brigid explained. "It was glorious early this morning. Quite autumnal."

There was a silence.

"You'll be careful too, won't you?" Frummie looked unnaturally strained. "About where you go, I mean?"

"Of course I will." Brigid was touched by her obvious anxiety. "I promise." She tried for a lighter note. "At least we've got a man about the place now. I'll go and get the Prouts on their way and then he can move in. Why don't you sit and read the paper? I'll give a shout when I'm ready to start."

• • •

THEA ARRIVED alone, waved to the Prouts—who stared at her suspiciously—and joined Louise at the little table in the garden.

"Are they going or coming?" she asked, sitting down. "They look rather fraught."

"Going," answered Louise, pouring Thea a glass of elderberry cordial. "To everyone's relief. They weren't Brigid's most successful visitors."

"Poor Brigid." Thea took a cotton hat from her capacious carpet bag and set it on her red-gold head. "She's worked so hard all these years, you know, and she tends to take it rather personally if people aren't happy. I wish I knew if having Humphrey at home will be good for her."

"Good for her?" Louise shifted a little, folding her cotton skirt above her knees, stretching bare legs to the sunshine. "How d'you mean?"

"He's been away so much. And she has a need for solitude, doesn't she?"

"I don't know her nearly as well as you do," Louise reminded her. "But she certainly doesn't have a problem with being alone."

"Quite. Now I don't mind my own company—after all, I became inured to it as a child in the wilds of Shropshire—but, given a choice, I like to have all my people round me. Dear old George and the girls, and his mother, and any friends and relations who might drop by. I love him being retired and being able to potter about and do things together."

"You don't think Brigid would enjoy that sort of thing? She and Humphrey always seem very happy together."

"Oh, they are." Thea sipped her cold drink, considering the matter. "I just wonder if she wouldn't find total togetherness just a touch claustrophobic. Perhaps it might be better if Humphrey had to work part time for a while until they adjust to it."

"I think the cottages are their pension plan. Or some of it." Louise bundled her hair off her neck and sat with her hands clasped behind her head, face tilted back, eyes closed. "Goodness, it's hot."

"Mmm." Thea was still brooding on Brigid and Humphrey. "We've been very lucky. George inherited the Station House from his mother so that he's never had to think about buying a property and, being a bachelor all those years, he's saved and invested. George is very careful with money. Brigid inherited this from her father so it's a rather similar situation, except that with all the conversion work they had to raise a mortgage, so I suppose it's possible that Humphrey might have to carry on working for a while when he comes out of the Navy. Especially now that Frummie's occupying one of the cottages."

"Will Humphrey want to retire? He can't be much more than fifty. It seems terribly young."

"As a commander, assuming that he isn't going to be promoted, he has to retire by fifty-three. George made captain and had to retire last year at fifty-five. Even with all his savings he might have to look for a job to help with the girls' education. Poor old George! That's the disadvantage of marrying and starting a family in your forties. At least Humphrey doesn't have that problem."

"It seems odd—you with such young children and Brigid having a grandchild. Yet your husbands being contemporaries."

Thea laughed. "His friends thought he'd gone quite, quite mad when he married me. After all, I'm twenty years younger than George. They're all very nice to me, although Humphrey thinks I'm rather peculiar."

Remembering his remarks at the dinner party a few weeks before—*"One of the nicer sorts of nutter"*—Louise hesitated. Thea grinned at her evident discomfiture.

"It's not a problem. I'm very fond of Humphrey but he finds it difficult adjusting to the age gap. I'm not much older than his oldest boy. Julian was at Mount House when it was a boys' preparatory school and now it's co-educational and my two girls are there, although they don't board. It's those sorts of things. He sees me and my children as a different generation yet George is his contemporary."

"Doesn't Hermione go to Mount House too?"

"Yes, she's at The Ark. The pre-prep. She absolutely loves it. Well, they all do. It's a terrific school and they'll be heartbroken when they have to move on."

"What age is the pre-prep?" An idea was forming in Louise's mind.

"Three or four, I think they start. And then they can move over when they're eight. Why?"

"I was wondering. I think I told you I taught small children before I got married, didn't I? Well, I shall need to get a job as soon as I can and it suddenly occurred to me that The Ark sounds rather nice."

Thea shifted her chair into the shade. "Do you feel ready to start again?"

A little pause. The doves wheeled overhead, shiningly, startlingly white against the heavenly blue, diving and turning in their aerial dance: the Prouts stood together, surveying the neatly packed contents of the car's boot-space with satisfaction.

Louise took a deep breath. "Sometimes yes. Sometimes no. But I'd like to be doing something and I'd like to be doing it with children. Thank God that the absolute terror of being near a small child has passed. But I do get the occasional panic attack."

"I think you should talk to Charles Price," said Thea thoughtfully. "He's the headmaster. I'm sure he'll help if he can. Two of the staff are naval wives, I know that."

"I'd have to tell him the truth."

"Yes, of course. But you needn't feel nervous about it. He's such a nice person I'm sure he'd be terribly understanding."

"It would be a start," said Louise, "just to talk to someone to find out where I stand. I'm probably no longer eligible to work with small children. Rules are very strict these days."

"I'll speak to Charles Price," promised Thea, "and when term starts again you can come with me to meet Hermione and have a look around."

"Thanks," said Louise gratefully. "If you feel it's a sensible idea, I'd be really pleased to make some kind of move. In more ways than one. I have to think of somewhere to live too. Frummie's got a friend coming for October so I've got a cut-off point. Quite a challenge."

"Yes," said Thea, not convinced for a moment by Louise's cheerful, determined tone. "Yes, it is. But you don't have to face it alone. We all want to share it with you."

"That's . . . very kind." Louise fought down a weak desire to burst into tears. "Gosh, it's getting hot. Oh look, the Prouts are off. Doesn't Brigid look relieved?"

Brigid was standing on the track, beaming wildly, her hand raised in farewell. On a sudden impulse, Louise and Thea waved too; standing up to cheer the travellers on their way, shouting "Goodbye, goodbye," so that Brigid glanced round and laughed, shaking both fists in the air in a gesture of delighted thanksgiving. Frummie joined her and they went into the cottage together.

"I'll make some more cordial," Louise said, getting up. "All the ice has melted."

Thea pulled her hat forward a little, relaxing in her chair, watching the doves. A movement on the extreme edge of her vision alerted her. Away to her right, across the field which sloped down to the river, someone was moving along the hedgeline which bordered the road. This was Foxhole property and Thea wondered if whoever it was might have wandered from the footpath and was lost. She sat up a little, staring intently, but the person was standing quite still now, gazing towards her. Louise came out, carrying the tray, and when Thea looked again the figure had disappeared.

CHAPTER 28

It was much later, in her workroom, that Brigid found the unfinished letter to Humphrey. She picked up the sheets, staring at the words she'd written three days ago, before Alexander had come wandering into the courtyard; into their lives. Even now, he was moving into the cottage—with Frummie's assistance. Still holding the sheets of writing paper, Brigid let her gaze roam round the room, resting almost unseeingly on the familiar objects which created the atmosphere and formed the shape of this small cell at the heart of her stony sanctuary. Alexander's arrival, his extraordinary personality, had dominated her thoughts, occupying her mind to the exclusion of everything else. He was such a shock. Prepared to dislike him, with a lifelong partisanship on Humphrey's behalf, she'd been taken by surprise and he'd disarmed her almost immediately.

Brigid frowned a little, moving towards the window, her fingers trailing lightly across the material stretched out upon her work table, the letter still held in her other hand. No, "disarmed" was not the true word here: "disarmed" implied an intention on Alexander's part and she was convinced that there had been no such intention. He was too direct, too open. Dealing only in facts, he appeared to be indifferent to praise and blame alike which gave him a tremendous inner strength. This was his attraction, the lodestone which drew her towards him. His was no febrile charm but a real power consisting of serenity and courage borne of that inner strength; a power of which he seemed unaware.

She leaned upon the sill, staring out of the window towards the unevenly piled granite of Combestone Tor. The sun, now at its height, flooded the landscape with a brilliance which flattened and drained it of its mystery; the heat pressed down, suffocating, enervating. Even the waters of the West Dart were subdued to a distant muffled murmur. Brigid withdrew into the coolness of the room. Her former ideas, received learning accepted unthinkingly from Humphrey's point of view, were now to be questioned. His mother had not been quite the saintly, hard-done-by, gentle creature she'd imagined. She had been manipulative, controlling Humphrey by working on his childish affection and warm-heartedness, exploiting his loyalty. Other remarks, made over the years, held different meanings now. "Poor Mother felt things so keenly. She was such a sensitive soul that it wrung my heart to see her when she was hurt." *She suffered in silence—but it was a very loud, imposing silence.* "She did so much for me; she made so many sacrifices." *A happy, willing martyr.* "I felt I had to make up for Father's thoughtlessness." *Humphrey gradually accepted her assessment of me.* "Of course, she was never really out of pain, it was terrible sometimes to see her." *Humphrey was afraid of sickness, afraid that she might die.* "Father always got her back up when he was home. I was quite relieved when he had to go away again." *Her resentment infected him.*

He was twenty-three when they'd married. One of the bonds between them had been the experience of a difficult parent: it had become a joke between them. They'd grown up together, each strengthening the other. Had she been the mentor Humphrey had hoped he might find in his father once his mother had died? The Navy and marriage had between them forced Humphrey into adulthood; what might he have been like if his mother had lived? Freed from her influence he'd developed into the cheerful, determined man she knew and loved. He was not, by nature, weak or gullible. Perhaps Alexander had been right in his decision to make certain Humphrey stood on his own two feet, however brutal the method.

Still slightly shocked by her capitulation, her readiness to change sides, Brigid looked again at the letter in her hand. *"The real problem is that it's to do with Jenny and I know we never see eye to eye about her. Not that that's any excuse for not telling you the truth . . ."*

At the reality of the words, fear scraped in her throat and her gut clenched in a spasm of terror. It seemed impossible that she could have forgotten this problem which destroyed her peace and threatened her future. She simply had to concentrate on it; deal with it before the Bank lost patience and seized the cottage. Somehow she must find the words and phrases to complete the letter, explaining exactly what had happened and trusting that Humphrey would understand. Ignoring the worm of fear crawling in her gut, Brigid sat down at the corner of her work table, clearing a space, picking up the pen and blank sheets of writing paper which she'd flung down soon after Alexander's arrival. She sat for a moment, idly imagining a scenario in which she might tell him her problem; ask his advice. The thought of sharing it was so tempting that she had to prevent herself from hurrying downstairs to find him. She shrugged hopelessly. Even if she didn't consider it disloyal to tell him before Humphrey knew the truth, the idea was still nonpracticable. He would be busy, unpacking his few belongings, settling in; and then again Frummie would be with him, helping.

Brigid rolled her eyes in silent impatience. The sight of her mother, dressed as if she might be going out to lunch rather than volunteering to clean a cottage, was still vividly before her. It was clear that she was very taken by Alexander, considering him worthy of her mettle and attracted by him too. Brigid shuddered slightly. Quicksands lay ahead which must be carefully navigated. It would be too embarrassing if Frummie were to make a fool of herself. He had accepted her offer of help so politely—though pointing out that he had very little to be unpacked—accepting her offer of lunch graciously but with a private smile for Brigid, clearly noticing

and understanding her anxiety. It was odd how protective
she'd felt towards Frummie: protective and furious. She
couldn't have borne it if Alexander had been amused by the
smart clothes, the unskilfully applied make-up, the ornate
bracelets clanking on the skinny, fragile wrists. Yet she'd
been scorched with humiliation at the sight of her mother
frisking to and fro like some elderly chorus girl. She'd been
glad to go away; to leave them to it.

The house had welcomed her as always; cool and shadowy after the bright, hot sunshine. She'd kicked off her
shoes, enjoying the sensation of the flagstones sharply cold
beneath her bare feet, stopping to crouch beside Blot, who'd
been fast asleep, an inky puddle in the gloom. The peace and
silence enfolded her, restoring her, and she'd decided to do
some work. It was only when she'd been fiddling at the table
that she'd seen the letter.

She thought: And even now I'm putting it off. Allowing
myself to be distracted. Procrastinating.

She smoothed out the sheets, read through what she'd
written, picked up her pen and began to write.

WHEN THEA had gone, Louise continued to sit for a while,
deep in thought. Presently she went inside, put the tray on
the table in the kitchen and sat down beside the telephone.
Her call was answered very promptly. Martin's voice was
comfortingly familiar.

"Martin," she said. "It's me. Louise."

"I can still recognise your voice, sweetie," he said. "How
are things?"

"This isn't a difficult moment?"

"If you mean 'Is Carol around?' the answer is no. She's
having a lie-in."

For a second or two the mental picture, with its associa-
tions, was so powerful that Louise was unable to speak:
Carol asleep, relaxed and untroubled amongst the rumpled
sheets where once she'd lain with Martin. She swallowed,
frowning, trying to concentrate.

"Are you OK?" His voice was anxious.

"Of course. I just wanted to talk something through with you. The thing is, I've been thinking of starting work again. I can't stay with Frummie much longer and I don't want to be dependent on you either. Even if I can work with children again, it's unlikely I shall fall into something this term and if I'm not earning I won't be able to find something to rent. I might have to take a fill-in job—waitressing or something like that."

"Look," he said urgently, "don't do anything in a hurry. Just don't. I'm not worried about how long it takes. If it weren't for me you'd be here still, wouldn't you? You'd have come back home and we'd have gone on as usual."

"Oh, Martin," she said warmly, "it's nice of you to put it like that. But don't forget that I've changed too. I'm not certain it would have worked any more."

"Probably not, but you'd have had the time and space to find out where you were going. Because of Carol it means that you're doing it down there instead of up here. Just don't jump into something without thinking it through. Give yourself time, sweetie. Promise?"

"Yes. But I have this cut-off point with Margot coming. I should be able to get a winter let—a cottage or a flat for six months. I've got to make the break sooner or later, Martin. I need to feel independent."

"I can see that. But just don't take on anything too permanent all at once."

"No, I won't. My real difficulty is that I think I might have to pay three months" rent in advance but I doubt I'd get paid until the end of the first month. Would you sub me? I could pay you back once I'm working . . ."

"Look, sweetie, if we'd been married for the last three years I'm sure you'd be able to claim all kinds of things. If you find a job and a flat I'll pay for you to go in and sort yourself out. After that you're on your own. How does that sound?"

"It sounds fine. Bless you, Martin. You're a terrific comfort."

"It's not a problem. Stay in touch."

She replaced the receiver, sat indecisively for a moment and then made up her mind. She collected her car-keys, hesitated over whether she needed a jacket and went out again. Frummie was lifting a box from Alexander's car and Louise paused beside her.

"I'm going to Ashburton," she said. "I want to go to the chemist and I think I'll grab a sandwich while I'm out."

Frummie raised her eyebrows. "I hope you don't feel that Alexander and I need to be alone?" she asked.

"Of course not. It's just I feel a bit . . . oh, you know. Restless. Twitchy. I need some exercise. Don't worry. I won't go off into the lonely wild. I'll stick with the crowds."

"Make sure you do," said Frummie sharply. "See you later."

Louise drove up the track and pulled out on to the road. There were the usual number of cars crammed into the lay-by beside the O Brook and, as she passed over Saddle Bridge, one of them, to her irritation, pulled out behind her. She hated being followed over the moor; she liked to be able to relish the glorious spectacle of the hills unfolding to misty horizons, the stony peaks, the deep-sided combes and wooded valleys. The rowan trees by the bridge were bright with berries, stonechats perched, swaying on the bracken, and the warm, exciting scent of gorse drifted on the faint currents of air. The car parks at Combestone Tor and Venford were packed with holidaymakers: families with children making the most of this last weekend of freedom before the new school term. The waters of the reservoir lay calm and unruffled in the noonday heat and it seemed impossible now, in bright sunshine, to imagine that sudden nightmare panic which had sent her fleeing from the wood. Perhaps, after all, it had been Pan, the god of fields and woodland, who waited behind stone and tree so as to ravish unsuspecting travellers. She chuckled, slowing to allow some sheep to cross the road, glancing in her mirror as she applied her brakes. The car following was idling some way back and she pulled away again, glad not to be pressured into driving too fast.

She clattered over the cattle-grid and picked up speed,

heading for Ashburton, hoping it wouldn't be too crowded. The small red car continued to follow her out on to the Poundsgate road and along beside the river to Holne Bridge. Here there was the usual weekend crowd of canoeists, putting on wet suits, unloading canoes from their cars and vans, and Louise sat in a queue of cars, waiting to cross the bridge, watching them and occasionally glancing in her mirror at the car behind. The driver, the only occupant, was wearing Ray-Bans and a baseball cap. His arm, in its rolled-up shirtsleeve, rested on the window-ledge and the fingers of his left hand beat a rhythm on the wheel. Louise felt a tiny pulse of recognition and wondered if he was the man who had come to Foxhole recently to clean windows. The car looked familiar . . .

She pushed her hair back impatiently, hot and wanting to get on, disliking the smell of diesel fumes and the noise of idling engines. Mentally she reviewed her conversation with Martin, remembering the sudden need to communicate. If only she could effect some change in her circumstances. Despite the descents into fear she was quite certain that she needed to make a new effort but it was odd—and deeply unsettling—how the prospect of the future could be alternately exhilarating and terrifying. Suddenly, without warning, she was possessed with an overwhelming longing for Rory: the need to feel his arms round her, to hear his voice in her ear. *"So that's that. Now! Where were we?"* She stared straight ahead, biting her lip, her eyes wide and staring against tears.

Suddenly the road was clear again; she was passing over the bridge and in another five minutes was approaching the town. She drove into the car park, peering for a space, spotting a car on the further side which was backing out. Feeling lucky, she parked, checked for some change and strolled over to the pay meter to collect a ticket. The small red car was not so fortunate. He pulled in, waiting behind a row of cars, watching until Louise had locked her car and walked quickly away towards the shops.

LATER, AFTER some lunch at the Victoria Inn and a trawl around the shops, Louise went back to the car park, put her shopping on the passenger seat and drove off. By the time she arrived back at Foxhole it was nearly four o'clock. Frummie came out to greet her and Louise climbed out, surprised and faintly alarmed.

"Is everything OK?"

"Yes." Frummie gave a sigh of relief. "I'm just glad to see you back safely."

"I only went to Ashburton, you know." Louise reached into the car for her shopping and locked the door. "Oh, and I stopped on the way home to climb Combestone Tor in the company of about four hundred tourists."

"You may well joke," said Frummie grimly, "but another woman was attacked last night at Buckfastleigh."

Louise stared at her. "Oh, no. How do you know?"

"It was on the lunchtime news. Luckily some young chaps going home from the pub heard her screams and went to her rescue. Her attacker ran off but the girl was able to describe him. She thought that she'd seen him about. The police say that it sounds as though he spies on lone women, watches their movements and then strikes. They think it's related to those three murders."

"How horrible." Louise shuddered. "Oh, Frummie, supposing it was him last night . . ."

"We might just tell them about it. It's not far from Venford Reservoir to Buckfastleigh, after all. Anyway, I'm very glad to see you home again and, for the time being, no more evening walks for you or Brigid."

"No," agreed Louise. "Absolutely right. No more evening walks."

CHAPTER 29

"I'd love to see you." Jemima was on the telephone talking to Louise. "Come and have lunch. Or supper. I can look through my files and see if we've got any winter lets that might suit you . . . No, not this weekend. It's just hectic, I'm afraid . . . Oh, just lots of different things. There's a private viewing at the Cove's Quay Gallery . . . David Stead. I love his watercolours so I'm hoping to do that. And then I've got a friend coming for supper and a lunch with Mandy and Ness. It's terribly muddly. But next week sometime would be great . . . Tuesday? For lunch? . . . OK. About one o'clock? Great. See you then."

She replaced the receiver and let out her breath in a gasp of relief. It was not in her nature to dissemble and she was finding it difficult being quite so discreet. Yet this time, her new love affair was so important, so precious, that she'd become quite superstitious, deciding that if she told anyone about her feelings and her hopes it might all disappear; vanish as if it had never been.

Sometimes she wondered if she'd imagined it. Now that he was back in London, that her life had resumed its more ordinary quality, it seemed impossible to believe that she'd actually lived through those few blissful weeks. Yet on Friday he would be here again.

"Friday," she said ecstatically to MagnifiCat, who was eating his supper. "He'll be here in forty-eight hours. Two days."

MagnifiCat continued to eat, unimpressed by the treat in store, unmoved by her transports of delight. His tail twitched dismissively, contemptuously. Jemima wandered into the sitting room and lay full length upon the sofa.

"I'm missing you," he'd said. "It's awful here. She's taken so much."

"How beastly." She'd wanted to show support, and it was so tempting to bad-mouth Annabel, but she'd managed to restrain herself. "It must be awfully depressing."

"Well, it is."

She'd imagined him looking round the deserted flat, familiar objects and pictures gone, and her heart went out to him.

"She's left a note."

"Oh?" It had been difficult, at a distance, when she couldn't see his expression, to know quite how to play it. She was by no means confident of her ability to hold him once he was back in his own territory. His and Annabel's territory. Fear seized her and she'd wanted to scream, "Well, read it then. What does the bitch say? How's the girlfriend from hell?" but she'd been too afraid. He'd sounded pretty low—which in itself was disappointing. Why should he care any more? Hadn't they got a pretty good relationship going between them? Why should he feel it so much after these last few weeks together?

She'd had to hold herself in check, tell herself that it wasn't quite that simple. Going back to the flat was bound to resurrect old memories, open old wounds. A month-long holiday romance was hardly to be compared with a five-year-old relationship and it was unrealistic to expect him to be unmoved as he confronted the break-up.

"She's explaining why she's taken certain things," he'd said, "and suggesting that we discuss them if I feel it's not fair. She's trying to be civilised about it. There's an address and a telephone number and she's saying we could meet for a chat."

"Well, that sounds . . . OK." It didn't sound OK at all. It sounded absolutely all wrong. "Don't go," she'd wanted to beg him. "Please don't go. It's over. Finished," but he'd been talking about how important it was that they should remain friends and she was unwilling to show herself in a selfish, jealous light. At least there had been no question of his changing his mind about the weekend.

"Can't wait to see you again," he'd said. "Seems like weeks already and I only left a few hours ago. Salcombe seems like paradise compared with this place."

Jemina had been able to raise her game, then, to joke a little, tease him a bit, so that he'd forgotten Annabel and her letter and had talked, instead, about his plans for making some enquiries about IT jobs in the southwest.

"You're sure you wouldn't mind sharing your flat?" he'd asked.

"I'd consider a trial period," she'd answered lightly, glad that he couldn't see her face, her wide, delighted grin. "Anyway, it's MagnifiCat you have to persuade, not me."

"Don't tell me that our future depends on that neurotic fleabag," he'd said cheerfully. "God!" His voice had changed, deepening, not at all steady. "I really miss you."

She'd taken several deep breaths lest her own voice should betray her. "Me, too," she'd said. "Honestly."

"Well." She'd been able to sense him glancing about, bracing himself to deal with the depressing situation; his new status. "I'd better see what I've got here and get myself sorted. I just wanted to say 'Hi' before I got stuck in. Give me a call, won't you?"

"Course I will," she'd said. A tiny pause. "Hey. Not long till Friday."

"No." His voice had brightened a little. "Not long till Friday. Talk soon."

She'd made herself wait until the next evening, praying that he might phone first but taking her courage in both hands and dialling his number on Saturday evening.

"At least she left the television," he'd said—he'd sounded just the least bit surly—"and a couple of videos. Big deal!"

She'd felt a nervousness at the pit of her stomach, a tightening of the muscles as if she were bracing herself for some kind of contest.

"Was it worse than you thought, then?"

"If it wasn't nailed down then she tried to take it," he'd said bitterly. "I didn't notice, not to begin with, but she's taken all the ornaments, all the paintings and most of the books. I still can't believe it."

"Have you . . . spoken to her?"

"Not yet."

She'd cast about for some kind of comfort but her mind had remained obstinately blank. "I'm so sorry," she'd said at last. How feeble it had sounded—and how hurt he must feel. "It seems very unfair. I mean, they must have belonged to you both, jointly."

"I must say that that was my view of it."

"Well, perhaps you can sort it out with her." She'd said it tentatively—she who hadn't wanted him to go near Annabel. "Surely she'll be reasonable?"

"If she was reasonable, she wouldn't have taken them in the first place."

"No, well . . ." There hadn't been much she could say to that.

"Sorry, love. I'm in a shitty mood to be honest. I don't want to take it out on you. Look, I'll give you a buzz tomorrow. I'll have pulled myself together by then. OK? 'Bye then."

The next twenty-four hours had stretched themselves interminably, giving her time to imagine every conceivable scenario, from his being unable to stand it another second and rushing back to Salcombe, to forgetting her completely in the upheaval of his new situation. It seemed, in this fraught, tense state, that every single one of her friends and relations decided to talk to her during that period of time. She'd wanted to scream at them, trying to concentrate whilst wondering if he were trying to get through, her eyes fixed desperately on her watch until she could hang up with relief, only for the bell to ring again almost immediately with some other well-meaning and utterly time-wasting prattler on the other end of the line. By the time he'd telephoned, late in the evening, she'd hardly dared to pick up the receiver.

"How are you?" she'd asked, trying to pitch her voice between cheerfulness and concern.

"OK." He'd sounded resigned. "Sorry about last night. It hits me every now and again, if you know what I mean. Being here brings it all back. Anyway," he'd sounded as if he were making a great effort, "how are things with you?"

Remembering, Jemima smiled to herself. She'd made an effort too, trying to cheer him, make him laugh—and she'd succeeded. She'd hung up, her confidence restored. He needed her. As the week progressed his mood improved. Once back at work he'd sounded more balanced, more positive. He'd been making those enquiries about jobs and had sounded quite hopeful: there would be quite a lot, he'd hinted, to talk about on Friday. She stretched, excited and nervous, and gasped as MagnifiCat landed heavily on her stomach, purring heavily, full of delicious rabbit. She stroked his soft fur with long sensuous strokes, her eyes closed, imagining delightful scenes for the weekend ahead, waiting for Friday.

"BRIGID'S WONDERING if she should suggest that Michael and Sarah should come down to meet you." Frummie looked at Alexander inquisitively. "How do you feel about it?"

"Confused," he answered calmly. He laid the newspaper courteously to one side and watched Frummie taking notes on the contents of his breakfast table. "I like a good old-fashioned breakfast," he told her, lest some detail might have escaped her. "Sausages, bacon, toast and marmalade. All those years abroad, I never got out of the habit."

She was entirely unabashed. "I was never one for more than a cup of black coffee," she said. "So how do you manage to stay so thin?"

"Much the way you do, I imagine. It's genetic."

"How do you know that I don't diet madly?"

He smiled. "Because you look quite right with your thinness. Now Brigid is too thin."

She settled down on the chair opposite, enjoying this opportunity to be intimate with him. The big kitchen-living room was full of sunlight, and various cooking utensils lay carelessly abandoned on the worktops, yet a faintly impersonal atmosphere clung to the room. Perhaps Alexander did not have enough luggage with him to stamp his personality upon the house—or perhaps it was simply too early. Although he had allowed her to assist with his moving in, he had been quite intractable in refusing to permit her to unpack for him. There were some books on the windowsill, and newspapers littered the big square table, but there was very little other evidence to give clues to the kind of man he was. No doubt all would be made clear in time. Meanwhile she was very ready to discuss Brigid's thinness.

"Why shouldn't that be genetic, too? Diarmid was thin. Well, lean and rangy. Brigid's just like him."

"You don't think she's too thin?"

"Well . . ." She wriggled impatiently. If she said "yes" he might ask her the reason and if she couldn't give one it might sound as if she didn't care about her daughter. If she said "no" it might be the end of this little session. Anyway, he was right: Brigid *did* look rather gaunt. "I've noticed that it only needs the loss of a pound or two for Brigid to look peaked. It might be Humphrey going off. It's quite a long spell, this time."

"Isn't she used to it by now?"

"Yes." Nettled by his obstinacy she took a more direct line. "Of course she wasn't too happy about you being here, you know."

He seemed unruffled by this oblique accusation. "I can well imagine it. So you think I am the cause of her weight loss?"

Frummie shrugged. "A contributory factor," she said airily. "There might be other reasons. Brigid and I are not particularly *en rapport,* you know."

"I had suspected as much." His thoughtful tone robbed the words of any sting. "It's odd, isn't it, how much easier it often is to relate to people other than one's own flesh and blood?"

She looked at him approvingly. "You're so right. Why should it be, I wonder?"

"Probably guilt. But I might think this way simply because it happens to be my own personal experience. Humphrey and I will never be able to be close. He mistrusts me and I feel guilty about certain decisions I took relating to his upbringing. My guilt and his mistrust stand between any other feelings of love and anxiety which we might feel for each other. Yet because of our relationship we cannot treat these feelings lightly and circumnavigate them as we might with other people less important to us. Precisely because he *is* my son I am unable to connect."

Frummie regarded him with amused surprise. She hadn't expected such honesty so early in their growing friendship. "It's exactly the same with me," she admitted. "I feel guilty because I ran off to London and left Brigid with her father. She resents me for abandoning her and my guilt makes it impossible to relate naturally with her as I do to Jemima, my other daughter. I feel her resentment. It's fatally easy to dislike people that you hurt."

"It's because they are a constant reminder of our weaknesses and failures."

"Is that why you stayed away?" she asked curiously.

"We stayed in touch," he answered carefully, "but he made it clear that I was not to be a part of his new life. I went abroad when his mother died, you know, and remarried quite quickly. Humphrey felt that he was forced to build a new life for himself, that I had abandoned him. He was very proper in letting me know everything that happened in it but made it clear that I had no right to participate in it. All my letters went to his BFPO address."

"It doesn't sound like Humphrey." Frummie shook her head, her brow wrinkled. "He's such a friendly, open person."

"Is he?" He was watching her almost eagerly. "You like him?"

"Oh, tremendously. He's been terribly kind to me, you know."

"I'm glad." Alexander turned his chair aside, crossing his

long legs. "I'm very **glad. And so** Brigid is thin because of me and not because of **Humphrey.**"

"Well, I didn't quite say that." Frummie felt a strange empathy with him. "She and Humphrey have been terribly happy together, have no fear about that. I think, if you want the truth"—"Yes," he said soberly, "I want the truth"—"that their early bond was based on the fact that they'd both been abandoned, if you see what I mean. They were a bit like the babes in the wood. Humphrey and Diarmid got along famously together. They might have been father and son . . ."

She paused, aware of her tactlessness. Alexander was staring ahead of him. "I envy him," he said gently—and she felt a pang of anguish for him.

"Is that why you came back?" she asked. "To make certain?"

He sighed, a long indrawn breath. "Yes," he said at last. "Humphrey wrote to me some months ago, telling me about this posting and that he would soon be retiring. Agneta had died and I wanted to come back to England. Everything seemed to work together. I decided to ask if I could stay."

"Were you surprised when he said yes?"

"Not terribly." He looked amused. "I knew that you were here, you see, and I traded on Humphrey's sense of fair play."

She laughed, throwing back her head. "You don't pull any punches, do you?"

He chuckled too. "I had nowhere to go, you see. I counted on his filial feelings. I'm sure you know exactly what I mean?"

"I do indeed." She was delighted with him. "And was it the truth?"

"Was what the truth?"

"That you had nowhere to go. I understand that it wasn't the real reason. You've told me what that was—but was it the truth? That you were homeless?"

He hesitated for a moment and she watched him curiously, strongly attracted to him. "It was the truth," he said at last. "I'd sold up in Sweden but there was a three-month gap before I could take up my new residence. It seemed as if I were being led here, if that doesn't sound too fanciful. It was true, though, that I had nowhere else to go."

"I see. Well, it was the same for me. My husband went off with a much younger woman and I was left with nothing and nowhere to go. I loathe the country but, at that moment, Foxhole was a sanctuary for me. Of a sort."

" 'There is but one safe thing for the vanquished; not to hope for safety,' " he murmured. "It must have been very hard for you."

She parried the keen, penetrating glance with a bitter thrust of her own. "A touch of the Prodigal Mother, you feel? Forgive me, daughter, for I have sinned? Well, it was. Like you, I counted on Brigid's loyalty and Humphrey's generosity but it stuck in my throat, I can tell you. They were both so damned noble about it. Determined that I shouldn't feel my humiliation or the weight of their kindness. I threw it back at them whenever I got the chance. I went to the Social Security and got Housing Benefit and insisted that Brigid had a rent book. How she hated it." She stared at him, her mouth set in a bitter line. "Each time I give her the money and watch her initial the book I feel a stab of pure satisfaction *here*." She struck her breast lightly with a clenched fist. "He left the whole lot to her, of course. Diarmid, I mean. Not a thing for me. God, how I grew to hate him!"

"He wouldn't let you have her?"

Her face relaxed slowly into an expression of resigned despair. "No," she said. "No, he wouldn't let me have her. I really believed that he'd let her go. I simply couldn't imagine him coping, you see. He was so . . . distracted by his bloody work—bound up in it. But he dug his heels in. He saw how he could strike back at me and, of course, I had no chance against him. Back then, forty-odd years ago, no judge in his right mind would have found for me, the erring wife, against Diarmid's noble uprightness."

"And Brigid?"

"Brigid loved her father. And Foxhole. We should never

have married and I knew it very soon after the deed was done but, by then, Brigid was a poor little casualty of my passing lust and poor judgement. Diarmid would have stuck it out. To be fair—though it's something I try to avoid—I believe that he loved me after his own quiet, unemotional fashion. But it was impossible. I loathed the screamingly dull emptiness of the country and Diarmid was not, by nature, a companionable man. He was gorgeous to look at, frighteningly bright, terribly well read, but I'm a frivolous, partyloving person. I like gossip and fun." She paused, not looking at him, touching the toast rack gently with one finger, turning it round and round. "The man I'd lived with in Paris and London before I met Diarmid wanted me back and, after a while, short visits, a weekend here and there, simply weren't enough. One day I just went. I told myself that Brigid would be allowed to join me but my own desires were stronger than my love for her." She smiled her self-mocking, down-turned smile. "Might as well be honest about it. That's how it was at the time. I was allowed to see her here, but he refused to let her come to me in London. I think he was afraid I'd run off with her. I would have done, too. But here, the whole scene was impossible. Brigid nervous. Me brittle. Diarmid louring in the background. Of course, she had no idea that her father was withholding her from me and I couldn't bring myself to make her party to our rather sordid battles." A shrug. "In the end I stopped coming here. I stayed in touch with cards and letters but it simply didn't work. I married Richard and then Jemima came along." She paused again. "I'm not a particularly maternal woman, you know, but I love my children in my fashion. Jemima was like her father and terribly easy to love. Everyone adores Jemima . . . Well, everyone except Brigid."

"That's understandable."

"Is it? It's hardly Jem's fault that I left Diarmid and he behaved so unreasonably. I left Jem's father too."

"But you took her with you."

She frowned at him. "It was a completely different set of circumstances."

"Does Brigid know that?"

"I've no idea, I imagine so. I've never talked to her about it."

"So how would she know?"

Frummie shrugged irritably. "Perhaps she doesn't. I can't discuss it with her. The obstacles between us are too great. Her resentment and my guilt. You said it yourself. Because she is my daughter I can't communicate properly."

"We must content ourselves with the knowledge that they have made each other happy. My son and your daughter."

She glanced at him sharply. "Yes, that's true. But you won't make any attempt to see Humphrey?"

"I think not. Why upset the applecart at this late date?"

"What about your grandchildren? And a great-grandson now, don't forget."

Alexander smiled at her. "Do you think their lives would be significantly enhanced by my sudden appearance?"

"I don't know." She felt oddly uncomfortable. "I've told you, I'm not madly maternal so I don't have this belief in the sanctity of family. My grandsons have done splendidly with the minimum interference on my part."

"Then I expect they'll manage without mine," he said amiably. "And now that you know what I have for breakfast are you going to help me clear it up? Or was your visit purely an inquisitive one?"

"Oh, sheer nosiness, I assure you. And I hate washing up." She grinned at him, relieved by the change of atmosphere, grateful to him for the lighter touch. "So where will you go when you leave here? Have you bought a house somewhere?"

He stood up, shaking crumbs from his jersey. "I shall go north, to the Borders." He answered patiently, amused by her persistence. "And now that you've satisfied your curiosity and have no intention of being useful, you might leave me in peace. Oh, and when I've cleared up, I shall be writing letters and then going for a walk. After lunch I shall sleep. I'm telling you all this in case you feel the need to drop in again later for further information on my habits. Perhaps we might have a drink this evening before supper."

"Perhaps we might." She was quite unmoved by his directness. Standing up she hesitated for a moment, as though about to make a further comment, but decided against it. "Come over at about seven, if you feel like it," she said lightly—and slipped out, closing the door behind her.

CHAPTER 30

Brigid was sitting in the courtyard, watching the harvest moon rise over Combestone Tor. In the normal course of events she would have been up there, on the Tor, much earlier in the evening, watching the moon rise away to the east, but Frummie had been so anxious for her safety that she'd been obliged to remain at Foxhole. She'd considered inviting Louise to go with her but she'd known in her heart that it wouldn't be quite the same. Moonrise was one of those magical, heart-stopping moments that must be experienced alone. Huddling herself into her fleece, shivering a little in the chilly air, she wondered if Humphrey would ever truly understand these strange but very real needs. He'd never been home long enough for his tolerance to be put to the test but she could imagine how, to a man as prosaic as Humphrey, her unusual requirements might easily become a source of irritation.

She crossed her arms beneath her breast and hugged herself, feeling the tension rising and spreading, stiffening her spine and tightening her muscles. How long, she wondered, before he received the letter? What might be his reaction? How would he deal with it? If only it hadn't been Jenny . . . She dragged her mind from its weary circling and forced herself to think of other things: of her children and of the wonderful and utterly unexpected telephone call from Geneva.

"We thought we might come home for Christmas, Mum. Do you think you could cope?"

"Oh, darling, how wonderful." She'd been almost speechless with delight. "Of course we can cope. Josh's first Christmas . . ."

This had been her instinctive reaction. Afterwards she'd wondered what atmosphere might prevail, with Humphrey home and the need to find twelve thousand pounds as well as her deception as a bone of contention between them. Even the peaceful beauty of the scene before her—the moon, framed between the end of the longhouse and the wall of the cottage, pouring its brilliance down on the Tor—could not distract her from her anxiety. Since she'd posted the letter her whole world had become slowly drenched in fear. It coloured everything: stealing peace, corroding joy, draining her of energy. It had been a miracle that for three short days Alexander, by his sheer presence, had kept her fear at bay. His serenity had communicated itself to her, protecting her. Having him with her in the house, seeing his tall, thin figure, passing between his quarters and the courtyard, had given her some kind of insulation. Childlike, she'd felt that nothing could really harm whilst he was near.

Brigid's face crumpled a little. She remembered the few lines of a poem she'd read recently . . .

The night is very silent, the air so very cold,
I wish I were a child again and had a hand to hold.

The deep silence was disturbed by a distant sound; a car, up on the road, climbed the hill and rattled over the cattle-grid, slowing as it approached the end of the track. It sounded as if it had stopped, the engine idling for a moment before it was switched off, and Brigid straightened a little, listening, hands clasped between her knees. She could hear the doves, shifting and murmuring in their cot, and this tiny, domestic sound made her suddenly aware of the emptiness beyond this small encircled yard: the moor, like some great dark sea, rolling away on all sides whilst shadows crept stealthily across the cobbles. Up on the track there was the sound of a stone rolling, a slithering brought up short, a muffled curse. Blot, curled at Brigid's feet, sat up, ears pricked, and growled softly. Brigid swallowed in a dry throat, unlocking her laced fingers, every muscle straining in her attempt to hear more clearly.

Blot stood up, growling deep in his throat, and she caught at his collar. "Stay!" she whispered fiercely. "I said *'Stay!'* Carefully, slowly, she pushed herself to her feet, still grasping his collar, and began to edge towards the house. As she moved into the line of the entrance between the two cottages she stared into the darkness, keeping herself out of the moon's relentless shining. Beyond the deep shadow of the buildings the track, bright in the moonlight, was empty, yet she had the distinct impression that she was not alone. She felt quite certain that out there, just off the track, waiting in the bracken, was a living, breathing presence. Blot began to bark, a high, warning baying that shivered her blood into icy trickles and made her legs tremble. She gained the door, hauled him inside and slammed it shut, turning the heavy key, crashing the bolts into their housings. Loosed at last, Blot leaped up, barking wildly, whilst Brigid ran into the two living rooms, dragging the curtains together with shaking hands. She raced through the kitchen, closing and locking the lean-to door and, back again in the kitchen, fastening the intercommunicating door whilst Blot continued to hurl himself at the front door, screaming with rage.

As Brigid reached for the receiver the telephone sprang into life, startling her so that she knocked it from its rest and it hung on the end of its cord, banging gently against the dresser. She seized it.

"Hello," she said, her voice small and frightened. "Hello, who is it? Oh, Humphrey." She felt quite weak with relief, yet what could he do, so far away?

"I've had your letter." His voice couldn't have been less comforting. "What the *hell* did you think you were doing, Brigid? My God! I still can't believe that you could be so *stupid*. And for Jenny, of all people. How could you have even considered it? With her track record? And without even mentioning it to me. Have you any idea . . .?"

His rage had a chilling effect upon her. Her hand was an icy claw, clutching the receiver, and she shivered uncontrollably, her teeth chattering as she listened to his relentless fury.

". . . so what do we do now? Have you any suggestions as to how we're going to find twelve thousand pounds? Hello? Are you still there? And why is that *bloody* dog making that row?"

"There's someone out there." His rage and her fear between them had reduced her nearly to tears.

"What do you mean, 'out there'? Out where?"

He sounded impatient, irritated at this distraction, totally unsympathetic. She tried to pull herself together, unwilling for him to think that it was some ploy to defuse his wrath.

"I heard someone out on the track in the dark so I came inside. There's someone going round attacking and murdering women."

"Oh, for God's sake . . ."

"Yes, I know it sounds melodramatic. But there *have* been three murders and a woman was attacked last week in Buckfastleigh . . ."

"In Buckfastleigh?" His voice was calmer, sharper.

"She was saved by a couple of young men going home from the pub. The police have warned women not to go about alone. Mummie's paranoid . . ."

"And there's someone there now?"

"I was in the courtyard watching the moonrise. I heard a car on the road and then it stopped and I thought I heard someone walking down the track." She felt exhausted. "And then Blot started."

"Get off the phone and get hold of the police. Are you locked in?"

"Yes. Look, I'm really sorry about everything—"

"Shut up and do as I say. And then phone Father and get him over with you. For God's sake be intelligent and don't go outside. And don't let Blot out."

"Humphrey—"

"Do it now. I'm hanging up."

The line went dead and at the same time there was a hammering on the front door. Brigid gave a cry of terror.

"Brigid!" Alexander's voice echoed through the thickness of the wood. "Are you there, Brigid?"

She stumbled out of the kitchen into the hall. Blot was whining now, his tail wagging furiously, and she drew back the bolts, turning the heavy key with still-trembling hands. Alexander, Frummie and Louise all burst in together, crowding round her, slamming the door shut and locking it again.

"I saw someone creeping about outside," Frummie was explaining, "so I phoned Alexander and he came over and we contacted the police. And then we heard Blot barking . . ."

Alexander's arms were round her, almost carrying her back into the kitchen, pushing her down into a chair. Louise's eyes were wide and frightened but Frummie seemed almost to be enjoying herself.

"My poor darling," she said, slipping an arm about her daughter's shoulders, giving her a hug. "Don't worry. We're all together now. What do you think? A drink, perhaps? You look white as chalk."

"Tea." Alexander was smiling at her reassuringly. "Hot and sweet. And don't tell me you don't take sugar."

"I heard him," said Brigid, her eyes enormous with fright, speaking directly to Alexander. "I heard him on the track."

"Where were you?" asked Frummie sharply.

"In the courtyard," said Brigid. "Watching the moon rise."

Frummie put down the kettle with a bang. "Can I believe this?" she asked of no one in particular. "After everything's that's happened, you sit all on your own, out in the dark—"

"It wasn't dark," said Brigid defensively. "The moonlight was nearly as bright as day."

"Oh, really!" Frummie brought her hands together in a sharp clapping movement which set all her bracelets jangling.

"It doesn't matter." Louise had taken charge of the tea-making, Frummie being temporarily distracted. "We're all together and no one is hurt. The police will be here soon."

"There speaks someone who has only recently come to live in the country." Frummie's underlying anxiety was being discharged in immense sarcasm. "This isn't London, my dear Louise. Of the two police cars available to cover this huge area, one of them will probably be in Okehampton and the other in Salcombe. It will be at least an hour—and only then if we're really lucky—before we see a policeman."

"In which case," said Alexander calmly, "we might as well make ourselves comfortable. Apart from anything else, I'm sure he's long gone. Whoever it was."

"I'm sure he has." Louise took up this encouraging cue. "We all made such a racket and there was good old Blot sounding like the Hound of the Baskervilles. He's got quite an impressive bark for a small dog."

Brigid watched them as they made tea, found the milk, put out the mugs. Was it possible that Humphrey had telephoned, after all the agonising waiting and wondering, only to be distracted by this newer drama? It was an extraordinary anticlimax. What had he actually said? Her weary mind refused to be cajoled into providing answers; she could only remember his angry voice. She took her tea and drank obediently. The telephone rang and Frummie snatched up the receiver.

"Hello. Who is it? . . . Who? . . . Oh, *Humphrey*. My dear boy, how are you? . . . Oh, did you? . . . Yes, yes, that's right. Three murders and an attack . . . Don't worry, we're all here with her and the police are on their way . . . No, she's quite all right. Well, she's looking rather peaky and under the weather, if you want the truth"—"Mummie!" cried Brigid wretchedly, *"please!"*—"and much too thin but we can't talk now in case the police need to contact us. Have we got a number for you? . . . Good. We'll phone when the police have arrived. 'Bye."

"You might have asked," said Brigid crossly, "if he wanted to speak to Alexander. Or to me."

"We mustn't block the lines," said Frummie airily, "and he sent you his love. He can speak to his father any time."

"Did he?" Brigid looked at her quickly.

"Did he what? Oh, send his love. Yes, well, he actually said, 'Tell her I love her.' Rather sweet, I thought. I didn't realise that he'd phoned earlier. He was terribly worried about us."

Brigid placed her mug carefully on the table and squeezed her hands between her knees.

She thought: Oh, thank God, thank God. He said he loves me. It'll be OK.

She opened her eyes and saw Alexander watching her but, before he could speak, there was the sound of a car on the track and a blue light, flashing intermittently, filled the kitchen with its glare.

It was nearly midnight when Brigid telephoned Humphrey.

"Everyone's gone," she said. "The police took statements and had a good look round but whoever it was had long since disappeared. Everyone's gone back to bed."

"Have they left you on your own?" he asked, almost accusingly.

"They all wanted to keep me company," she said quickly, placatingly, "but I'm sure there won't be any more trouble. He'd be crazy to come back after all the row we made. The police are going to maintain a bit of a presence, apparently. Which means a car going along the road once a day, I should think."

"Well, for God's sake be careful."

"Oh, I shall be," she assured him, warmed by his anxiety. "Alexander says he'll move back in if necessary."

"Yes, well, I know you'd hate that."

Brigid opened her mouth to say that she'd liked having his father about—and closed it again. Intuitively she knew that this was not the moment to suggest that they might have misjudged Alexander.

"Let's see how it goes," she said. "I imagine we're OK now—and I've got Blot."

"Mmm." He didn't sound too impressed.

There was a tiny silence, humming across the thousands of miles between them.

"I'm sorry," she said awkwardly, "that the timing was so awful."

"Oh, I don't know," he said drily. "From your point of view it must have seemed heaven-sent. I expect you're probably too rattled now to want to do much more than go to bed."

She thought: I could say that I'm exhausted. That it's been very scary and I'm still in shock. It would postpone having to explain and by the time we talk again the heat would have gone out of it. I could do that.

Instead she said quickly, "I can't tell you how sorry I am. About all of it. I completely misjudged it and I should have talked to you first."

"So you said in your letter." His voice was cold but it was clear that his rage had passed. "The point now is: what do we do about it?"

"I've thought about it over and over again," she said miserably. "I suppose the only thing we can do is to add it to the mortgage."

"Great," he said heavily. "Well, that's my retirement plans out of the window."

"Oh, Humphrey, I'm so sorry—"

"Oh," he said irritably, "it's not that I particularly object to working a bit longer. It's just that it would have been nice to have a choice. I wanted the time to think about things. My gratuity would have dealt with most of the mortgage and the cottage would have kept us going. Now I shall have to look around. The Bank won't object, I expect, but if they ask about my retiring from the Service next year you'll need to tell them that I shall be getting a job, otherwise they might not be quite so happy about it."

"I'm sorry." She couldn't think of anything else to say.

"The trouble is it's not going to be easy, finding something down there. You'd better start looking out for bursars' jobs, that kind of thing."

"You see, it all sounded so unlikely to go wrong. And, to be fair, if Bryn hadn't decided to syphon off the money and disappear it wouldn't have crashed. They were making a real success of it."

"So you said in your letter," he repeated coolly. "But you might have guessed that anyone Jenny picked up with was likely to be suspect."

"Oh, I don't know." She couldn't help herself. "You seem to have a lot of time for Peter. She picked up with him first and, if I remember rightly, it was he who started having an affair, not Jenny."

"OK. OK." Irritability was back in his voice. "So you've supported your old school chum and now I'm going to have to pay for it. The question is: how?"

Remorse took hold of her again. "Oh, darling, I *am* so sorry." Her voice was ragged with weariness and worry. "I'll do everything I can to help."

"Yes, I know." Irritability softened into a kind of impatient affection and she felt relief flood through her. "OK. Let's stop the bitching and decide what to do. But not now. You sound bushed. Go to bed and we'll talk again soon."

"Tomorrow?"

"No, I'm at sea for a few days. I'll call as soon as we're back in. And, Brigid? Take care of yourself, OK?"

"Oh, Humphrey . . ."

"Look, I love you. We'll manage somehow. Get on to the Bank tomorrow. Now, go to bed and try to get some sleep but call the police if you hear or see anything the least bit unusual."

"Yes, I will." She wanted to weep: remorse, gratitude, anxiety weakened her. "I love you too."

"Then take care of yourself and go to bed," he said—and hung up.

She sat down at the table, resting her head on her folded arms. The worst was over. There would be moments of reproach on his part and guilt on hers but the real worst was over . . . Her eyes closed and, for the first time in weeks, she relaxed, allowing her thoughts to spin into welcome, unanxious oblivion. In a few moments she was fast asleep.

CHAPTER 31

Louise, driving from Foxhole to Salcombe, was thinking about Frummie; how she'd changed since the arrival of Alexander. There was a sharpness to her, a bright, shiny quickness, so that she seemed to dart to and fro like a little bird, alert, cocky. She hummed as she flitted about, breaking into song, preening in the smart new clothes which had suddenly appeared, pecking at her food, taking tiny sips of wine or water. She never alighted anywhere for very long but was up again, hopping off to some new task. The videos had lost their power of attraction, her attention too easily distracted, and only late in the evening would she sit, broody and quiet, clucking secretly to herself.

As she drove down from the moor, through the back of Holne and turning right at Play Cross, it occurred to Louise that perhaps Frummie hadn't changed at all. It was simply that, with the advent of Alexander, certain characteristics were showing themselves more clearly. Behind the cruel ravages of old age, she could see the younger Frummie: the Frummie who had sat in the jazz cellar, obsessed by love and driven by jealousy. It was as if she'd grown young again. Louise, touched by the metamorphosis, teased her a little whilst encouraging her.

"You look great," she'd say. "Where's the party?"

Frummie merely smiled her self-mocking smile and uttered some witty retort. She was aware of her foolish vanity but was, nevertheless, enjoying herself. Life had offered her an unexpected opportunity for fun and she was seizing it with both hands.

"I wonder," Louise had said naughtily, "how Margot will like Alexander?"

Frummie's inaccurately rouged lips had stopped smiling, the bright blue eyelids had dropped calculatingly. "I could put her off," she'd said thoughtfully. "After all, it's more important that you have a roof over your head than Margot has a holiday."

Louise had felt rather shocked at this reaction, wishing she hadn't joked about it. "Poor Margot," she'd said lightly. "She'll have been really looking forward to it. You couldn't disappoint her at this late date."

Frummie had made a face, shrugging a little, and Louise felt the first stirrings of anxiety. It was clear that she must remain positive and forward-thinking. Yet it was becoming impossible now to discuss her future with Frummie, who was busily thinking up new reasons why she should not yet implement her plans to find a job and move out. Even with Brigid she felt uneasy. Having promised Frummie that she'd talk to Brigid, she'd made a very real attempt to discover what was occupying her thoughts—but it had been surprisingly difficult to be natural with her. The old ease was absent and Louise saw quite quickly that Brigid had no intention of unburdening herself. It was evident too that Brigid was feeling deeply embarrassed by her mother's behaviour. Here, Louise could sympathise. She knew that people were likely to react much more sensitively towards their own relatives and that Brigid had a horror that her mother might be looked upon as pathetic or ridiculous. Despite attempts to reassure her, Brigid had remained gloomy, preoccupied—and then, that evening, all these small confusions had resolved themselves in the greater drama. Their sanctuary had been invaded and they'd all drawn together to protect themselves.

Now, a few days afterwards, everyone seemed more balanced and, although the smaller tensions had discharged into a larger anxiety, yet a calmer atmosphere prevailed. Brigid seemed to have overcome some private worry whilst Frummie was quite above herself now that her fears had been realised. The reality of the man on the track, the arrival of the police, the seriousness of the situation seemed to invest her with an importance which oddly neutralised her former terrors. Everyone was obliged to take her very seriously and she was making the most of it. As for Alexander . . . Louise smiled to herself. Alexander seemed as unchanging as the eternal verities.

"Frummie's very fond of you," he'd said, when she'd explained how hard it was to find the courage to leave; to break away on her own.

"She's been wonderful to me," she'd answered warmly. "Like a mother. Much more so, in fact, than my own mother. I know I have to go but I love being here with her. I feel so safe."

"I expect that's why you need to go," he'd answered—and she'd frowned after him, puzzling at his odd remark.

Once on the A38 she accelerated, looking forward to seeing Jemima.

"I might be late back," she'd said. "If there's no reply go and have some coffee in The Wardroom and I'll come and find you."

Louise drove carefully, concentrating automatically whilst part of her mind wrestled with the problem of work and accommodation. She tried to take Frummie's advice; looking beyond panic and despair at some more positive future. At present, however, there was nothing to fix her gaze upon. Thea had telephoned Charles Price who, though he had expressed a great willingness to meet Louise, had warned that there were no vacancies for staff at Mount House's pre-prep school. He'd suggested that Louise should visit The Ark and then they could have a talk.

"After all," Thea had said to her, "you never know when a vacancy might come up and then you'd be first in line."

She'd agreed, telling herself that an opening now would have been a miracle, trying not to feel too downcast, whilst looking forward to seeing the school and meeting Charles

Price. Meanwhile, she must explore other avenues. It was hardly likely, after all, that there would be teaching vacancies so close to the beginning of term; she'd set her sights too high and must be prepared to content herself with something outside teaching. Her other enquiries to playgroups and schools had been fruitless but her name and telephone number had been filed. The important thing was to remain optimistic. There were other jobs, and maybe Jemima might be helpful in finding her a suitable winter let. The ones she'd seen advertised in the local paper were demanding frighteningly high rents.

There was still a lot of holiday traffic and she was glad to leave the dual carriageway at Wrangaton, driving through the lanes again, noticing the turning of the year: milk-green hazelnuts ripening in the hedges; bleached grasses, tall and feathery, fading in the ditches; beech leaves, glossing and yellowing, kindling on the trees. Her heart was comforted by the beauty of the gently rounded hills and placid river valleys; the pale gleam of harvested fields and the scarlet flash of rich, red earth. She drove on the back roads from Kingsbridge, round Batson Creek—where a heron stood in humped, immobile contemplation—into the town, and was lucky enough to find a space for the car on Whitestrand Quay.

There was no reply at the flat and she walked back to The Wardroom, went in and ordered coffee. The café was busy and the veranda tables, to her disappointment, were occupied. She sat down, wondering if she might be competent as a waitress, considering other jobs, not noticing the young man on the veranda who wore a baseball cap and Ray-Bans against the sun which dazzled on the water. He glanced round, saw her, and turned quickly away, but she didn't see him and presently Jemima arrived and hurried her off to the flat.

"YOU'RE LOOKING good." Jemima stared at her critically. "Honestly. No flannel. There was a kind of *stretched* look about you which has gone. Are you really OK?"

"Really OK," said Louise. "Well. Nearly really OK. I have

occasional panic attacks but I'm over all that awfulness. Sorry I frightened you."

"You were pretty scary," admitted Jemima. "We were very worried about you."

"You've all been so good to me." Louise shook her head. "I can't believe how kind everyone's been. Your mother was fantastic. She seemed to understand how I was feeling."

"I'm not terribly surprised about that. Frummie's lived quite a Bohemian life and she's hung out with some unusual people. Not that I'm saying that you're peculiar or anything . . . Oh, shit! I'm going to really put my foot in it, aren't I?"

Louise chuckled, "Don't worry, Frummie said that she saw a lot of nervous breakdowns after the war. She recognised some of the signs. Don't look so embarrassed. I can hack being potty. And talking of looking good, you're looking pretty fantastic yourself. Any particular reason?" She watched Jemima blush, her fair skin washed with scarlet, and her eyebrows shot up. "Goodness! What have I said?"

"Nothing," said Jemima hastily. "Honestly. Look. What about a glass of something? I'm not quite organised with lunch yet but it won't take long."

"Never mind about lunch," said Louise, intrigued. "So who is he?"

"Who?" asked Jemima unconvincingly.

"Oh, come on!" Louise sat down on the sofa beside MagnifiCat. "Don't give me the wide-eyed bit! Is it that chap you were waiting for when I came to supper that evening? When was it? Goodness, was that really last May!"

"It's unbelievable, isn't it?" Jemima seized on the distraction. "Nearly four months ago."

"I can count too," said Louise, amused. "But you can't fool me. Is it him?"

"No," said Jemima. "Anyway, he was married . . ."

"And you said you were strictly mistress material," mused Louise, teasingly. "Don't tell me you've changed your mind?"

"I don't know," mumbled Jemima. "It's not that simple."

Louise burst out laughing. "When was it ever?" she asked.

"Sorry. I really don't want to pry. Well, I do—but I shan't. It's none of my business. And I'd love a glass of wine."

"It's not that I don't want to talk about it," said Jemima rapidly, hating to seem so stuffy. "It's just a bit premature and I have this crazy feeling that if I talk about it before anything's really settled it'll go horribly wrong. I've never been like this before. It's . . . well, it's—"

"Wonderful and terrifying and fantastic and scary. When you're with him you never want him to leave ever again and when he's away from you you're so frightened at the thought of such a commitment you can't believe you'd have the courage to go through with it. But you still wait for the phone to ring, hate it when it's anyone else, and then find yourself being all cool and brittle when it's him and cursing yourself when he hangs up and lie awake all night thinking of all the things you wish you'd said instead. Is that it?"

Jemima was staring at her. "Yes," she said slowly. "That's pretty much how it is."

"It's not new," Louise sighed, "but it gets us every time." She gasped as MagnifiCat landed on her lap, purring loudly. "Good grief! He weighs a ton," she said. "What have you been feeding him on? Whalemeat?"

Jemima laughed. "He's such a tart," she said, relieved to be offered a change of direction. "At least he is when it comes to the ladies. Let's have a glass of something and talk about winter lets. I'm not sure I can help you much, you know. My properties are all in a fairly small radius. And they're not too cheap. It's becoming a bit trendy to spend Christmas round here, especially now that the Royal Castle at Dartmouth is second to Trafalgar Square in popularity for New Year's Eve. So owners can get a pretty good screw for their cottages during the fortnight over Christmas and the New Year, which means that the people who want to let for the whole six months are increasing their rents to make up for that fortnight."

Louise took her glass, looking crestfallen. "Oh," she said, rather dismally. "I thought you could get really cheap cottages between October and March."

"Oh, you can," said Jemima quickly. "There's lots of little cottages about which wouldn't attract this sort of market. The trouble is that my firm specialises in pretty up-market stuff." She leafed through her folder, hesitated, glancing over the details of one particular sheet. "It's a pity you're not into decorating but, anyway, it's only vacant until Christmas."

"What is it?" asked Louise hopefully. "I'm pretty good with a paint brush, if that's what you mean. I did a whole cottage once when we—when I couldn't get anything else. And I made a very good job of it, too."

"It's a small cottage in East Prawle." Jemima was reading the details more closely. "The cottage was taken on some years ago before Home From Home went up market. It's owned by a woman; a civil servant who lives in London. She uses it for three weeks in the summer but we let it out for her for the rest of the year. She's retiring at Christmas but she's asking us to get it redecorated for her. She's rejected one estimate as being too high. Perhaps you could live rent-free in return for doing it up." She looked at Louise questioningly. "Would that be any help?"

"Rent free?" Louise was aware of a trickle of excitement. "Sounds OK."

"It's not very big. In fact, it's a cosy little place, just a bit shabby, that's all. I could come over and give you a hand."

They stared at each other. "It would give me a breathing space," said Louise. "Just until I know where I'm going. Maybe I could find a part-time job . . ."

There's the Pig's Nose at Prawle," suggested Jemima. "They might need someone. But could you manage financially if you can't find anything quickly? Not that I'm trying to pry or anything."

"I probably could." Louise was thinking of Martin's offer of three months' rent in advance. Maybe he'd be prepared to convert that to a loan for her subsistence until she found a job . . . "I'm sure I could," she said firmly.

"Well," Jemima was watching her uncertainly, "if you're sure. It's a bit remote over there, you know, although the cottage is actually end of a terrace on the edge of the village and there's a farm quite near. You wouldn't feel lonely or . . . anything?"

"You mean would I be nervous after all the hype about these attacks? Probably." She shrugged. "But I've got to do it sometime."

"But you don't have to be stuck out in the country," argued Jemima, feeling a certain sense of responsibility. "You could get a place in Kingsbridge or Totnes."

"I'm like Brigid," said Louise. "I feel less nervous out in the country than I do in towns. It's not as though Devon is full of murderers, and I expect he'll be caught before too long. I'll take a chance."

"OK." Jemima was still hesitating. "And you feel . . . strong enough to be alone? You talked about panic attacks . . ."

Louise held out her hands, palms upwards. "But what else can I do? Sooner or later I have to make the break. I can't live with Frummie for ever. Anyway, Margot will be here in a fortnight. It would be the answer to a prayer, Jemima. I can't afford much and I don't want to be too committed in case a teaching job turns up. I have to be ready to lift and shift. I'll go for it if you can convince the owner to let me do it."

"I don't see why not." Jemima shrugged. "She's a tight-fisted old biddy and unwilling to pay the going rate. I bet she'll jump at the chance. What she wants is a quid pro quo and I'm here to see she gets it."

Louise began to chuckle. "And if she's not satisfied with the results?"

"Tough!" Jemima was grinning. "It'll be too late to worry about it. By the time she comes down you'll have moved on. Anyway, I've got no patience with people who want something for nothing."

"Not quite nothing," protested Louise. "Not if I get the cottage for three months."

"True. Anyway, you said you'd done up a cottage or something?"

"Yes. A few years ago but, hey, who's counting?" It was Louise's turn to look for a distraction. "Any chance of seeing this cottage? I feel really excited about it."

"Hang on a sec."

Jemima got up and went into her study whilst Louise sat staring out at the harbour, stroking MagnifiCat. Excitement and panic strove together in her heart and her hands trembled a little.

She thought: I can do this. I can do it.

"There are visitors in until Saturday week." Jemima was back. "But I might be able to show you over the place. Some people are a bit funny about it but I'll ask them. There's no phone so you'll have to wait until I can get over there and leave a message."

"Damn!" Louise looked disappointed and Jemima smiled sympathetically.

"I know how you feel," she said. "Once you've made a decision you want to get straight on with it. I'm the same. Sorry. There's nothing I can do about this one."

Louise looked at her. "I'm afraid I might lose my nerve," she admitted honestly. "It's a big step for me and I don't want time to chicken out."

Jemima sat down beside her. "Look," she said. "I can't get them out until Saturday week but suppose we were to drive over now and have a look at the cottage from the outside? If they're around I'll try and bluff us in. I've got to be back by two thirty, though. We could grab a sandwich at the Pig's Nose and you could ask if they need a barmaid."

"It would be terrific," said Louise gratefully. "Could we really do that?"

"We certainly could. Leave your wine. You can finish it when we get back. Don't forget your bag."

They went out together. The man in the baseball cap and Ray-Bans, wandering around the RNLI museum on the ground floor, saw them go past the door. He stood for a moment, indecisively, and then followed them out into the street.

CHAPTER 32

Towards the end of the following week the clear, bright weather changed slowly into an airless, sultry heat. Thunder grumbled and rolled in the distance and fat, warm raindrops splashed intermittently on the cobbles of the courtyard. There was a breathless apprehensiveness which gave rise to edginess; as if the moor and its inhabitants were waiting for something cataclysmic to happen.

"A thunderstorm would clear the air," Frummie said, coming over to borrow a book. "I feel so unsettled. That might be because Louise's going, of course. I do wish she'd change her mind. I could have put Margot off."

"She can't stay for ever," Brigid answered gently, putting aside the letter she was writing to Julian and Emma, full of Christmas plans. "And poor Margot would have been dreadfully disappointed. Don't you think this is rather a good move? Just three months to see how she gets on. Much better than a longer commitment."

"And she can come back for Christmas," said Frummie. "I've told her that."

Brigid held her peace: no point in saying that, by then, Louise might have made other plans. She knew that her mother was going to miss Louise quite dreadfully but at least she'd have Margot to occupy her for a while, to help soften the blow.

"What did you think of the cottage?" she asked. Louise

had driven Frummie over to see it at the first opportunity.
Jemima had met them there and they'd had a good look at
what needed to be done.

"It's not bad." Frummie was determined not to be too
excited. "Very small. Thank goodness it's not too isolated.
They haven't caught that man yet and I don't like the idea of
her being all alone."

"Jemima says that it's on the end of the village and
there's a farm quite close. I'm sure someone would run over
if she were nervous."

"She could get help quite quickly," admitted Frummie
grudgingly, "assuming someone's around. She's bought a
mobile phone, thank goodness. Do you realise that she's
never lived alone before? Oh, well, she must make her own
decisions. She's inviting us over for lunch as soon as she's
settled."

"I'm looking forward to seeing it." Brigid had deliberately stayed in the background. It was important to Frummie
that she still felt she had a vital role to play: this was *her*
scene. "Is Alexander invited too?"

"Oh, yes." Frummie brightened a little. "And Jemima, of
course. It should be rather fun. I've promised to help Louise
move in. Not that there's much to move, even with all the
stuff she brought down from London. I might stay a night."

"I'm sure you'll make her feel at home. And she knows
we're here, if she needs us."

"It's a pity that it's quite such a long drive. Oh, well. I'll
see you later."

Frummie went away and Brigid sat for a moment, feeling
guilty. She knew that her mother felt that she should have offered the stable wing to Louise whilst Margot was visiting
but she'd felt quite strongly that Louise needed this break.
Frummie, naturally, believed that Brigid simply didn't want
Louise with her for a month and, although she hadn't accused her of selfishness, Brigid felt that it was implied. The
old, familiar frustration settled on her, bringing depression.
Unable to concentrate on her letter she stood up and went

through to the lean-to, calling to Blot, and presently they were crossing the field below the house.

The water tumbled noisily in the heavy, brooding silence, almost drowning the harsh croak of the raven as he flapped with measured wing-beats above the rocky, granite bed of the river, making his leisurely way upstream. Rowan trees leaned along the bank, their twisting, woody roots clinging, claw-like, to the rounded, pitted boulders; their ancient, lichened boughs bright with golden leaves and bunches of scarlet berries. Brigid paused to watch two wagtails, tails bobbing, scuttering over the rocks whilst, further along the bank, Blot scraped excitedly at a rabbit hole.

As usual, this connection with nature soothed and calmed her troubled mind, restoring balance and harmony in her soul. She and Humphrey had now had several conversations and, although he was by no means reconciled to this problem which had shattered his plans for the future, he was coming to terms with it. The Bank had agreed to transfer the loan to the mortgage, and forms were being prepared, but the big question which remained was how he was going to pay for it.

Brigid turned away from the wagtails' dance and gave a gasp of fright as a tall figure moved from beneath the shadow of the thorn. Alexander raised his hands, as if conveying both an apology and a blessing, and prepared to move away but she called to him above the rushing of the Dart and he waited, smiling, as she came towards him.

"I'm sorry if I frightened you," he said regretfully. "I had no intention of trespassing on your privacy."

"But you're not," she said—she who had so needed to be alone—smiling back at him. "I wanted some fresh air . . . except that it's not very fresh, is it? It's so oppressive."

"There is change in the air," he said. "And not only in the weather."

They walked for a short distance in silence, stopping whilst Brigid found a stick to throw for Blot. He raced away through the fading bracken, across the short turf, and Brigid glanced up at Alexander, ready to share her amusement at the sight of Blot's busy, excited figure; the wagging, stumpy tail and flying ears. His face was grave, his gaze fixed on a distant point, and her own smile died as she watched him.

"What are you thinking about?" she asked involuntarily—and cursed her inquisitive insensitivity, knowing how she, herself, hated such questions.

"I was wondering," he answered at once, "why it should be that a woman who has been married contentedly for thirty years should look so extraordinarily relieved when she hears that her husband has sent a message saying that he loves her. Relieved. Not gratified or touched but *relieved.*"

Brigid was silent, remembering that evening when Humphrey had telephoned and the police car had come down the drive with its light flashing.

"You don't miss much, do you?" she asked rather bitterly.

"Not much," he answered equably. "You asked."

"Yes," she agreed, almost irritably. "I asked." She hesitated. "It's a bit complicated."

He looked at her, eyebrows raised. "You're not obliged to tell me your secrets. I was merely replying to your question."

She stared back at him, wondering if she had the right to share her burden with him: wondering how Humphrey would feel about it.

"It's none of my business," he said gently. "Don't feel anxious about it."

"The thing is," she took a deep breath, "that I'd like to talk about it. It would be a relief. Only, it's not just about me."

"I didn't imagine that it was. If you want to tell me then I promise you it would be treated as a confidence."

"Yes," she said gratefully, making up her mind. "Yes, please"—and, as they walked beside the river, she began to tell him about Jenny and the sailing school and her own act of deception. Their steps grew slower as her story unfolded and presently they stood quite still, she talking, he listening, whilst the water flowed beside them and Blot paddled in the shallows.

"I don't know how to make amends," said Brigid sadly, at last. "And it's almost worse now he's beginning to be calm and reasonable about it."

"Do you need to make amends?" Alexander frowned as if puzzled. "You did what you felt was right at the time. You didn't deliberately jeopardise your retirement plans. If you continue to act guiltily Humphrey will respond accordingly and will continue to feel hard done by. That's human nature. Gradually, it will poison your relationship. Your guilt will slide into resentment and his sense of injury will harden into bitterness."

"But you have to admit that it's a bit tough." Brigid was almost affronted at his lack of sympathy—for either of them. "He simply must continue to work now. He can't stay in the Navy and it's not easy finding a job at fifty-three."

"I agree with that but the answer seems obvious to me. Humphrey's a sailor. You have to pay the sailing school twelve thousand pounds. Why doesn't he simply buy the school? Your debt simply becomes a different kind of loan which he can work to pay back whilst giving himself a living."

"But . . . he's not that kind of sailor."

"Not what kind of sailor? Humphrey has sailed small boats and he could learn to teach others and help to run the school. Why not? He'll need a challenge of some kind. He's far too young to retire."

"But I don't know if he'd want to." Brigid was struggling to come to terms with this extraordinary idea. "And it's down in Cornwall."

"Does that matter? He'd get home quite often, I'm sure. More often than he does at present. He could probably do some of the administration work from home. And what happens in the winter? Surely it's much quieter then?"

"I don't know." Brigid was utterly confused. "I've never thought about it. Iain and Jenny are keeping the school running in the hope of finding a buyer. I'm sure they'd be glad to carry on. Oh!" A new thought struck her. "I can't see Humphrey working with Jenny."

Alexander shrugged. "He might feel quite differently about her once it becomes his school. Or she might decide to leave and do something else."

Brigid began to laugh. "You are quite ruthless," she told him.

He looked surprised. "Am I? I don't think so. Doesn't it seem an obvious solution to you? The loan becomes an investment in your own business. Much more satisfactory than adding it to a mortgage and then doing a grinding job to pay it off. Isn't it likely that Humphrey would be more at home running a sailing school, *his* sailing school, than working in an office or as a bursar at a boarding school?"

"Well, yes. But if that were the case wouldn't Humphrey have already thought about it and suggested it to me?"

"He's probably too busy responding to your guilt and feeling aggrieved," answered Alexander bluntly. "He probably hasn't thought it through at all. Why not suggest it to him?"

"Do you know," she said slowly, "I think I will."

"Good," he said lightly. "Very good. In that case I'll leave you to finish your walk in peace. You'll need time to think about it carefully."

"I will," she agreed, rather anxiously. "I'll need to know exactly how to put it to him."

He looked down at her, smiling a little at her serious expression. "And you're sure that was the only reason? For that relieved look?"

"What else could it be?" she countered lightly.

He nodded, as if accepting her evasion. "Well, good luck with the thinking," he said. "And just remember that no one ever sticks to the script, no matter how perfectly you write it in your head. Give him room to manoeuvre. Be flexible." He turned away, hesitated, and turned back again. "Oh, and by the way, don't tell him that this was my suggestion. Put it to him from your point of view."

She watched him stride away, feeling an enormous affection for him, and then walked on beside the river, her head whirling with new, exciting ideas; guilt and depression quite forgotten.

• • •

FRUMMIE, PEGGING out washing, saw him return. She stood for a moment, considering, and then called to him.

"Louise's shopping," she said. "What about some coffee? I'm just having some."

He paused, as if giving it some thought, and then nodded. "That's very kind."

"Come over when you're ready."

She went back indoors, her spirits rising. Alexander was a challenge worthy of her mettle; and she felt invigorated after a bit of a run-in with him. She took out the cafetiere Brigid had given her and her special coffee from Effings, also a present from her daughter, and spooned in a generous quantity. By the time Alexander appeared everything was prepared and set out on the low table by the sofa in the living room.

"Did you enjoy your walk?" she asked, as he sat down beside her on the sofa. "I hate this weather. It gets on my nerves."

"It's better down by the river." He watched her press down the plunger. "There's always a movement of air by water."

"If you say so. I have very little desire to go out into this bleak, inhospitable countryside. I can't think why Brigid loves it so much."

"She is by nature solitary. Its emptiness appeals to her."

"She takes after her father. Diarmid was exactly the same. Just adored it. I've made her promise she won't leave Foxhole's land while this murderer is still at large but it's impossible to make her stay inside." She glanced at him sharply. "And what about you? Are you another solitary?"

He smiled—and she saw in that moment how like Humphrey he was, a much thinner, older Humphrey—shaking his head at the mere thought of it.

"No, no. I'm not cut out to be alone. I like people about me."

She set down her cup, delighted with him as usual, a now-familiar sense of fellowship spreading pleasantly within her.

"Oh, so do I. I loathe being alone. Hate it, simply. It's been heaven having Louise with me. I'm going to miss her terribly."

"But you have a friend coming?"

Her eyes slid sideways, considering him. "Yes," she said. "Dear old Margot. We were at school together. I'm sure you'll like her."

He settled himself comfortably, moving the low table a little so that he could stretch out his legs. "Is that relevant?"

Frummie chuckled. "It will be to her. Margot likes to be liked. I've told her a thousand times that it's a weakness but she can't help herself."

"Not one you suffer from?"

"Certainly not!" she answered indignantly. "Being disliked or even hated can add spice to a relationship. These days everyone needs to be loved. Children require to be praised and lauded for simply existing and adults have to be awarded prizes for being merely adequate. Standards must be lowered lest anyone should fail and excellence is diluted down and shared out amongst footballers, those who acquire wealth through bully-boy tactics or talentless musicians. These are our icons in a society of wishy-washy political correctness. I cannot abide it."

"I believe you," he said. "And do you dislike Margot? Or hate her? Or do you merely tolerate her rather than be alone?"

She was taken aback by his directness. "I'm actually very fond of Margot," she said defensively. "Well . . . most of the time." She began to laugh. "You're impossible," she said. "Truth to tell, Margot is my insurance against a long wet lonely autumn. If I'd known that Louise would be here I wouldn't have asked her."

"But Louise won't be here."

"No." Frummie drank some coffee. "Part of me knows that it's time she made the break but part of me won't accept it. I think it's because I dread being alone again but I'm pretending that I think it's because she's not ready to manage on her own." She stared at him crossly. "So there you are," she said irritably, as if he had wrung the confession from her.

"It seems a sensible plan," he said reflectively. "This short break to test herself. Don't you think so? And you'll have Margot . . . and the rest of us."

"As you say." She shrugged—but felt in some way soothed and relieved by her admission.

"I'm thinking of inviting a friend to stay," he offered.

It was as if he were seeking a reaction—approval, perhaps?—yet it seemed out of character and Frummie looked at him warily, coolly.

"Oh?"

"Mmm." He sipped his coffee. "An old school-friend. Quite a coincidence, isn't it?"

"Shall we like him?" Frummie's lips turned down in her characteristic smile. "Or is that irrelevant?"

Alexander laughed. "Not to Gregory. He loves everyone and likes to feel it's reciprocated. He and Margot should get along splendidly."

"Well." Frummie was intrigued but determined not to betray herself too far. "And when is he coming?"

"Quite soon. Early in October."

"Margot and I must give a little party for him. Brigid will help. I'll get Jemima over and I'm sure Louise will come back for it."

"It sounds just up Gregory's street. Five women to two men, he'll like that."

"And what about you?" she asked lightly. "Will you like it too?"

He turned to look at her smilingly, so that she felt slightly confused and rather foolish.

"Oh, yes," he said gently. "I shall like it too."

CHAPTER 33

When shall I see you again? Jemima did not ask the question. For too many years it had been against the rules and, even now, despite a really fantastic weekend, she could not bring herself to frame the words aloud. She was not secure enough to risk a rebuff; this new love was too precious to lose as a result of a hasty or misjudged assumption. The impossible had happened: she was no longer content to be alone nor considered herself to be by nature a mistress. Now she wanted him with her on a permanent basis; longed to hear him make some kind of commitment. There were moments, very serious moments, among the longer periods of fun and light-heartedness, when he talked about the future, *their* future, and she felt convinced that his intentions were in line with her own. Nevertheless, she was quite unable to broach it openly. Because of the nature of their meeting, her role, it seemed, had been defined. She was destined to be companionable, cheerful, happy. She knew now all of Annabel's characteristics which had annoyed or distressed him and she was too afraid to allow herself to stray into their territory. No. She must remain bright-faced and sweet-tempered, unfazed by inefficiency, laid-back and undemanding; quirky, cool, independent. These were the things about her he loved, the traits which captivated him.

"It will come," she told herself. "It's early days. Don't be greedy. It's a big step for him, just don't rush it."

It was hard, though, really hard to dissemble; to tease and joke and play it cool when she wanted to hold him; to sink into comfortable, relaxed security with him. To say "When shall I see you again?" easily, naturally, as though she had the right.

He rolled on to his back and opened his eyes. "Do I have to go?"

She bit back her instinctive response: an overwhelming desire to cry: "No! Stay with me. Don't ever leave me."

"I'm afraid you do." She made herself smile at his groan, to pretend toughness. "It was your idea to stay over and make an early start."

"Slave-driver," he grumbled. "Admit, though, that it was clever of me to arrange a meeting in Bristol first thing Monday morning."

"Pretty good," she said judicially. "Exeter would have been better."

He gave a crack of laughter, pulling her down on top of him, and she responded willingly but with a brief, backward glance of regret for that past sensation of upward-swooping joy which had revelled in her separateness; which had held her free of sadness and desire. She was careful, however, to be the first to break away, to subdue her quickly rising passion.

"I need some coffee," she said. "And so do you. Thank God you don't eat breakfast."

He lay watching her, arms folded behind his head. "Annabel could never come to terms with that," he said. "She believes that no one can function properly without a good solid breakfast inside them."

She was shocked by the depth of rage which shook her; holding back with difficulty the urge to turn and scream at him; quelling the need to punish him for his insensitivity. Why should Annabel be so readily in his thoughts after such a heart-shaking night of love? No commendation for remembering his habits and foibles: no gratitude for not fussing. Only a reference to bloody Annabel! She kept her back carefully turned towards him as she belted her wrapper and slipped on her espadrilles. Forcing down her rage, she reasoned with herself that she could expect no praise for something which he believed to be her natural behaviour. She had, after all, taken pains to show him that she did not fuss.

"It depends what she means by 'function properly,'" she said lightly. "But perhaps our priorities are different. I've known lots of people who 'function'"—she deliberately stressed the word, giving it a sexy overtone—"extraordinarily well indeed with very little inside them."

He gave another shout of laughter, enjoying the occasional flash of bitchiness, flattered by these latent signs of jealousy, and went away to take a shower. She went into the kitchen, still angry, feeling oddly degraded. In attempting to compete with Annabel, to outdo and undermine her, she'd made herself sound like some promiscuous airhead. Confused and miserable she made the coffee and wandered into the sitting room. MagnifiCat raised his round, flat face and she dropped on her knees beside him, laying her cheek on his warm, soft flank.

"I'm a fool," she told him. "I'm just no good at this. God, I love him!"

Presently she stood up and went out on to the balcony. The harbour was wreathed in curling mist, the opposite shore invisible, the sounds of the sea-birds echoing mournfully, evocatively, in the early morning silence. He was behind her, putting his arms about her, burying his mouth in her hair, and she folded her own hands over his, returning the pressure.

"Magic," he murmured. "You, this place. The whole scene. I can't stay away from you. You've bewitched me, I hope you realise that."

Relief, gratitude, love, welled inside her in an unstoppable tide of generosity and she turned in his arms, slipping her own around his neck. Impossible to remain cool or to give some quirky answer. The kiss was deep, long, satisfying.

"Me, too," she said at last, inadequately.

They clung together until MagnifiCat came winding

round their legs, butting and pressing his head into their ankles, so that Jemima began to laugh and they drew reluctantly apart.

"The coffee will be cold," she said. "And you'll be late."

He sighed. "You're a hard woman," he said as he followed
her inside, "but it's not long till Friday."

The words repeated themselves sweetly inside her head,
or she said them out loud to herself, long after he'd gone,
making it impossible to go back to bed or sleep. She could
only sit on the sofa, MagnifiCat beside her, watching the
cold white mist diffusing into a glowing, golden, cloudy
brightness just as her own private joy was warming the remains of her fear and anger into a deeper love and a more
confident hope.

LOUISE WAS relieved to be making the trip to East Prawle
alone. This would be her first official day as tenant and she
needed the time to be quiet, to have the chance to think
things through, to decide exactly how she was feeling. She
was feeling tired, that much was certain. Ever since Jemima
had suggested the cottage she'd bounced between excitement and terror; determination and lack of confidence. It
didn't help that she was well aware that they were all watching her, anxious lest she should not be strong enough yet to
be alone, ready to encourage her to draw back. Knowing instinctively that she must take this step, she hadn't dared to
show her true feelings, not even to Frummie: especially not
to Frummie. For the first time since her breakdown in
Brigid's kitchen it was necessary to keep a guard on her
emotions. Frummie didn't want her to go. This was very
touching—and she didn't want to go, not really—yet part of
her knew that if she didn't make the break now she might
never have the courage. She could imagine staying on for
ever, finding a job, working from Foxhole with Frummie
looking after her. To begin with it would be just until she
found her feet and afterwards it would be impossible to
leave without hurting Frummie's feelings. Of course, it was
probable that Frummie would be unable to sublet, that

Humphrey and Brigid might not be too happy with her continuing to be a paying guest, but she could imagine that the situation might drift on indefinitely. Margot's arrival, along with the offer of the cottage, had given her an opportunity she simply had to take.

She'd tried to keep Frummie involved, showing her over the cottage, listening to her advice, promising that she'd admit it if she found this new independence all too much, but she was glad to be alone now, to be driving out of Kingsbridge, the little car piled with her belongings, ready to make a new start. Turning right over Frogmore Bridge, climbing the hill, glancing with delight at the estuary winding between quiet, autumnal fields, she was washed through with an unexpected wave of freedom. She felt light, rinsed of anxiety, buoyant. Gradually she allowed herself to give way to excitement, happy anticipation: planning how she would settle in, trying to imagine this new, rather solitary, life. The little cottage was charming, if tiny. Yet it was its tininess which appealed to her: there was a sense of safety in such a small comfortable area; security in its cosiness. It was the last cottage of a higgledy-piggledy terrace which was charming in its nonconformity. The minute porch led directly into the one big living room, with the kitchen, a narrow slip of a galley, screened off by a divider containing cupboards and shelves and a breakfast bar. The kitchen door opened into a long narrow conservatory with a door to a small walled yard. Upstairs was one good-sized bedroom, the bathroom and a boxroom.

She thought: At least it won't take too long to decorate it.

The owner had already sent colour charts and Louise's first thought was to begin with the boxroom. It was Brigid who had suggested that, instead, she should start downstairs with the living area whilst the weather was still fine enough to leave doors and windows open. This made sense—but it was certainly going to be a muddle, trying to live amongst ladders and paint pots with the furniture piled together and covered with dust sheets. Yet even the thought of such confusion in a small space had no power to depress her today.

The high banks and tall hedges were full of colour—yellow and red berries of the white bryony; the dog roses' scarlet hips—whilst on the hillside a farmer was drilling winter wheat, a cloud of seagulls circling in his wake.

She turned right at Cousins Cross, passing through narrow lanes, until she drove at last into the village. Her sense of excitement increased: it was fun to be moving into her little house, to be looking across the green to the cliff path and the sea; smiling to herself at the sign of the Pig's Nose, with the Piglet Stores and Grunter's Café. She parked carefully outside the cottage, as close as she could get to the stone wall which bordered the few square feet of the front garden and, climbing out, paused to look at the tangled mass of chrysanthemum and montbretia which grew beside the few steps which led from the gate to the front door. Toadflax grew on the wall, with stonecrop and aubretia, and she stood in the sun, her hands on the warm dry stone, her confidence growing. She took the front door key from her pocket and went inside. The living room was dim, coming into it from the bright sunshine outside, and she stood for a moment, just inside the door, looking about her. The shabby, chintzy cottage furniture was set around the small Victorian grate, the bookcases on either side of the chimney-piece held a few tattered paperbacks, and an old portable television stood in the corner on a scarred and much-used tea-trolley. Silence filled the room; silence—and the scent of freesias. On the gate-leg table under the window a small pottery jar was filled with them.

Louise stood quite still, her arms locked beneath her breast. Freesias: white and gold in her wedding bouquet: purple and blue for her first wedding anniversary: multicoloured when Hermione was born.

"Trust you," he'd murmured, his lips against her hair as she'd thanked him with a hug, "to love a flower which is so difficult to find. What's wrong with a nice bunch of chrysanthemums?"

"It's a test," she'd said, hugging him more tightly. "Just to see how much you care."

"Well, if you don't know now you never will," he'd answered, kissing her. "Who d'you think I am? Lancelot in search of the Grail? You wait! It'll be lilies and carnations, next time, from the garage. They keep them in nice Cellophane packages in buckets outside."

He'd arranged to have some freesias delivered for her birthday only a week after Hermione had died. They had arrived with a message he'd written a month before, not knowing that when she received them she'd be racked with pain and half mad with grief. *Happy Birthday O Best Beloved's Mama. May there be many, many more and may we spend them together.* He loved Kipling's *Just So Stories* and read them to Hermione, who'd listened entranced. He'd had no idea, when he'd given his message to the florist, that he would never read to her again.

She thought: And I let him go, afterwards, without a kind word or a hug, consigning him to oblivion along with the rest of my life. With Hermione.

Crossing to the table she picked up the postcard which lay beside the flowers. It was a coastal scene of the cliffs just below East Prawle. Jemima had scribbled right across the back.

Welcome, she'd written. *Make yourself at home. See you soon.*

It was sheer coincidence that she'd chosen freesias. Louise propped the card on the narrow mantelshelf and went back outside to unload the car. It was important that the cottage should be made homely; that the chill, impersonal "holiday-let" atmosphere should be warmed into a friendly cosiness. She took her supplies through to the kitchen, filled the kettle and switched it on, and prepared to make the cottage her own. Her books from two cardboard boxes very nearly filled the shelves on either side of the painted fireplace. One of the leaves of the gate-leg table was put up and a wooden chair set beside it. On the table she put her paint box, a notebook and some pencils; her pashmina shawl was draped over the back of one of the armchairs; two pretty ladies, Doulton figurines, were set upon the mantelshelf beside the postcard; an elderly teddy bear, his fur worn and rubbed from love, was propped in the corner of the sofa. As she unpacked some pieces of china she was reminded of her arrival at Foxhole more than four months before; how she had set about making the cottage her own, accompanied by those echoes from the past. This time she had rather more belongings with which to create the desired result—but the echoes were still with her.

Louise paused amid the boxes. The echoes were there but the fear had gone: she no longer had to deny them, no longer needed to be continually clenched in a spasm of rejection. Now she could hear the voices with sadness, remembering, with a gentle grief, all that she had lost, accepting the tragedy as her own and learning to live with it. She sat at the table, holding her mug of coffee, breathing the scent of the freesias. Michaelmas daisies, purple and dark red, leaned at the window and montbretia flamed beneath the wall. A passer-by, glancing in, raised a cheerful hand, and Louise waved back, encouraged by this friendly gesture, already feeling a sense of belonging.

She finished her coffee, her former confidence returning, and began to carry her suitcases up the narrow, twisting stairs.

CHAPTER 34

"I just thought I'd touch base," said Humphrey. "See how you are."

"I'm fine," said Brigid. "Absolutely fine. How's it going?"

"OK. No real problems. We're having a few days at Cocoa Beach while they reload torpedoes at Cape Canaveral."

"That sounds nice." She thought: Once I'd have pulled his leg, teased him and said that it's OK for some. Now I'm afraid to. My guilt makes me treat him with kid gloves.

"It's pretty good," he was saying. There was the *faintest* air of martyrdom, the *slightest* hint of "although how I'm expected to be able to enjoy myself *now* . . ." about it. "How's life at Foxhole?"

"We had an enormous thunderstorm which rumbled round the moor for nearly two days," she said, "and then it all packed up and moved off somewhere else and we're having lovely sunshine."

"Right," he said. A pause. "Have you filled in the forms from the Bank?"

"No," she said. "Actually, I started to do it and then I had an idea."

"Mmm?" Very cool.

"Yes." She tried not to sound cajoling, as if she needed to persuade him into it. Enthusiasm was the keynote here. "Yes. I had this thought that it was silly to put the loan on to the mortgage without thinking a bit more about it. And I wondered if we could simply take over the school and run it ourselves? Since you have to have a job," *don't* sound apologetic about it, she warned herself, "why not work in your own business? The debt becomes ours and we can have more flexibility with it."

"I thought that the debt was ours anyway," he observed drily.

"Well, of course you're right." She sought about for inspiration, trying to remember Alexander's words. "But wouldn't you rather have some control? Be running your own show, rather than just putting it on the mortgage and then having to flog at something boring to pay it off? Remember that the school was doing tremendously well. It only began to fail because Bryn syphoned money off and didn't pay the bills."

"I suppose that it's utterly unimportant that I haven't the least idea how to run a sailing school?" He sounded rather churlish.

"You don't know how to be a bursar," she said bravely, "but you're prepared to have a go at that. You said yourself that you didn't want to work in an office all day."

"I don't. But that doesn't mean that I want to run a sailing school."

"OK." She had the intelligence to back off. "It was just a crazy thought. After all, it's a hell of a haul down to Falmouth and there probably wouldn't be much doing in the winter. It was just a mad moment. I'll get the forms off, then."

"I don't see how it could be done from Foxhole." His voice was irritable. "It would be impossible on a daily basis."

"Oh, well, naturally you'd have to be down there a couple of days a week," she said almost indifferently, as if, now, the idea were purely academic. "Of course, Iain does all the sailing and teaching . . . and Jenny runs the office."

"I can just see Jenny working with me!"

"Quite. I hadn't really thought it through at all. Although I suspect that once the school is bought she'll leave. She's only stayed to keep it as a working proposition. There's been quite a bit of interest, apparently, and she's confident that it'll sell. Not that it's our problem. Anyway, did I tell you that Julian and Emma are coming home for Christmas? Isn't it fantastic?"

"Fantastic," he agreed flatly. He gave a kind of mirthless snort. "Could you really see me running a sailing school?"

"What? Oh . . . Well, yes, actually. You're very good at organisation and you used to adore taking the boys sailing when they were young. I could see it being quite an exciting project actually. And it's such a prime spot. Still, I agree it was crazy. You don't want anything too taxing . . ."

"It's not that," he said crossly. "I'm not quite over the hill. It's just a bit of a shock, coming out of the blue."

"Oh, I can believe that," she said readily. "It took me a while to come to terms with it. It was such a wild idea." She laughed. "Just for a minute it seemed rather fun. Quite a challenge."

"You haven't mentioned it to anyone else, then?" suspiciously.

"Mentioned it?"

"Well, you know." He sounded impatient. "Talked it over. Discussed it."

"Of course not." She crossed her fingers automatically. "Why should I? It just occurred to me whilst I was filling in the forms. By the way, I'll have to send them on to you. They need your signature and you can check them through."

"Right." A pause. "I'd better shoot off. No more murderers hanging about?"

"No. No more murderers. I think we frightened him away with all the noise."

"Well, take care. How's Father?"

"Fine. He's fine. Very quiet. He and Mummie are getting along very well together."

"Good. That'll keep him out of your hair a bit."

"He's not a problem, honestly. Well, nice to hear from you. Enjoy the beach."

"Yes. Well, then . . ."

"Lots of love. Take care."

She hung up quickly, knowing that he was finding it difficult to finish the conversation, and stood for a moment, wondering if she'd overplayed her hand. She was quite sure that his interest was aroused and hoped that he'd now have the time to think about this new idea very carefully. Relaxing a little, taking a deep breath, she took a bottle of white wine from the fridge and poured herself a drink. This feeling of tension between them was horrid, especially with him so far away; if only it could be resolved in a positive, forward-looking way it would be such a relief.

"I'll drink to that," she muttered, with a sigh, and Blot, thinking that she was talking to him, struggled up from his basket and came wagging over, hoping for a cuddle.

As LUCK would have it, when Margot came bumping down the drive, Alexander was just going out. He backed down to his gate, waiting for her to park, smiling in response to her wave of gratitude. He had no intention of stopping but, before he could set off again, she'd wound down her window.

"Hello," she called. "Sorry about that. You must be Alexander."

She was struggling with the door handle, climbing out, so that there was nothing for it but to switch off the engine, get out and introduce himself properly.

"Margot," she said, gripping his hand firmly, beaming up at him. "How very nice to meet you." Alexander murmured something appropriately noncommittal but she was hurrying on. "I've come to stay for a few weeks. Fred and I are very old chums. We were at school together, you know. And we were Wrens together in the war, well, right at the end of the war when we were old enough to join up . . ."

She did not hear Frummie's light step on the path and she turned, startled, as Frummie laid a hand on her shoulder.

"We've got a month, dear," she said drily. "He doesn't have to hear all our secrets in the first five minutes."

"Oh, but the ones that are told in the first five minutes are the only ones worth hearing," said Alexander. "After that, one loses the first flush of truth. Either the teller becomes cautious or he begins to add to—or detract from—the truth according to his own subconscious reactions to his confidant." He smiled sweetly down at Margot. "Already it's too late for us. Never mind." He gave a little bow. "So good to meet you. I'll see you again soon, I'm sure."

He folded his length back into his small car and drove away up the track.

Margot stared after him. "Well," she said, on a long-drawn-out breath. "What a gorgeous creature! Why didn't you warn me?"

"I thought you might overreact," answered Frummie sourly, taking in the rich coppery auburn of her old friend's hair, the rather short skirt, the brightly varnished nails. "You're looking very smart."

"I do feel it's a shame to let oneself go," said Margot serenely. "So easy at our age." Her glance lingered on Frummie's enthusiastic use of blusher, the gold bangles clanking on the skinny wrist and the rather smart plaid trousers. "You're looking pretty good yourself, Fred," she observed thoughtfully. "Rather better than the last time I saw you."

Frummie's lips curled down in her self-deprecating smile. *"Touché,"* she said. "OK. No bitching."

"That's right, lovey," said Margot comfortably. "All's fair in love and war, and at our age we might as well enjoy the battle. I hope you've got the kettle on, I'd kill for some coffee."

"More or less ready. Shall we bring the cases in?"

"Coffee first," said Margot, following her up the path and into the cottage. "You know, he *is* rather delicious."

"So you said." Frummie began to make coffee. "He's got a friend coming to stay."

Margot's eyes brightened; her wizened lips puckered into a wicked smile. "Has he?" she murmured. "One each, then."

Their eyes met. Frummie lifted an eyebrow. "I wonder what yours will be like?"

Margot chuckled. "Like that is it? You never know. He might be even nicer. Where is Alexander going after this?"

Frummie frowned a little. "I don't actually know."

It was Margot's turn to raise her eyebrows. "Don't *know?*

And how long has he been here?" She snorted contemptuously. "You're losing your touch."

"I never was quite as good at worming as you were. Quite shameless!"

"Nonsense. It's perfectly simple. I only ask because I want to know. No, no sugar. I've got my sweeteners in my bag. He's quite like Humphrey, isn't he? Only much thinner."

"There's certainly a look of him. He's a bit . . . disconcerting at times. Very direct. But it's fine when you get used to it."

"And how does Brigid get on with him?"

"Very well. It seems so odd that there's been this silence all these years. I can't see why he and Humphrey don't get on."

"Probably for much the same reasons that you and Brigid don't."

"Yes," said Frummie, after a moment. "Yes, I suppose that's fair enough."

"I wonder where he's going," mused Margot, rootling for her sweeteners.

"He did say something about going north, to the Borders," admitted Frummie, "but I wasn't certain if he were pulling my leg."

"To the Borders?" Margot looked surprised. "Whatever can he be going there for?"

Frummie shrugged. "I've no idea. Maybe he's got a house there."

"Mmm. Could be rather nice, I suppose. Is that where this friend comes from?"

"I really don't know." Frummie was beginning to sound impatient. "I promise you, Alexander's not quite such an easy touch as you might first suppose. He fences very cleverly. Anyway, the friend will be here in a day or two. You'll be able to ask him yourself."

"I shall," declared Margot. "This is all very exciting. I can't thank you enough for inviting me, Fred."

"Better than *I, Claudius?*" Frummie started to grin. Their eyes met and they began to chuckle.

"Oh, much better," said Margot. "Ever so much better. Wait till you see what Harry's sent you. A very nice selection of wine from his wine club."

"I always approved of that boy," said Frummie. "More coffee? Or shall we unpack the car?"

"More coffee," said Margot promptly, proffering her cup. "Well." She breathed a deep, satisfied sigh. "It's really good to be back."

JEMIMA OPENED her eyes, wakened from her doze by the insistent buzz, groped for her mobile and smiled when she saw the number.

"Hi," she said warmly. "How are you?"

"I can't get down after all," he said crossly. "My colleague's been taken ill and I've got to cover for him at a conference in Birmingham. I'm really peed off with it, I can tell you."

"Oh. Oh, I see." Jemima simply couldn't hide her disappointment. It was quite impossible to be quirky and cheerful about it. She stared out bleakly at the grey, wet early evening gloom.

"I know." His voice was suddenly resigned, almost amused. "Shall I swear for you? I promise I've been doing just that all day. It's not Ian's fault, poor sod, but I'm finding it hard to be sympathetic. I was hoping that I might be able to dash down for a few hours, but I can't see my way at the moment. I'm just so sorry."

"Honestly," she said, gaining control over her low spirits, comforted by his own evident frustration, "it's OK. Don't worry about me."

"I'm not worrying about you," he said. "I'm worrying about *me*! If I don't get my weekly fix I get terrible withdrawal symptoms. How shall I manage?"

"You'll have to phone more often," she said, smiling to herself. "More text messages."

"I suppose it will have to do." He sighed heavily but she could sense that he was smiling too. "You sound alarmingly cool about it."

"I'm not really," she assured him. "There's just not much point in making a fuss, is there? I don't want to waste the time we *do* have together, even if it's only on the telephone."

"You really are very special." His voice was tender. "Write me in for the weekend after. In ink. I might have some news for you?"

"News?" She tried to sound unaffected by his tenderness. "What goes on?"

"Oh, nothing definite yet but I hope it will be the next time I see you."

"Be mysterious," she said lightly. "See if I care."

He laughed. "Must go. Speak soon. Take care."

She continued to lie full-length on the sofa, her telephone clasped to her breast, staring up at the ceiling. What could his news be? And why had she been unable to tell him her own, rather less-than-exciting news?

She thought: The timing wasn't right. Not while he was upset about the weekend. It's got to be the right moment. And it might be just what we need to push us over that last bridge.

She grimaced a little, suspecting that she might be a little overconfident about that; wondering if she were, after all, whistling in the dark. A little surge of misery and fear stabbed in her gut and, on instinct, she switched on her phone and dialled a number. Brigid's voice was as cool and clear as always.

"Hi," said Jemima. "It's me. How are you?"

"I'm fine." Brigid sounded encouragingly friendly. "How's life in Salcombe?"

"Oh . . . Much as usual. I was wondering if we might have lunch again. It was rather fun last time, wasn't it?"

"It was great. Why not? Where? Would you like to come over here?"

"Um, probably not."

Brigid's chuckle was sympathetic. "Too many people? I couldn't agree more. Effings again, then? It was really nice there and it's about halfway."

"Great." Jemima was relieved by the solution. "When can you make it?"

They fixed a date and hung up. Jemima continued to lie, stretched out but taut, watching the rain hissing gently on the windows. Might it be possible that she could tell Brigid all her secrets? Would it not merely be confirming the opinion she feared that Brigid had always held? Underline her sister's disapproval? Yet she was sure that recently there had been a lowering of the barriers; a new closeness. What a comfort it would be to share her feelings with her sister.

MagnifiCat came padding softly over the floor and she leaned to pull him into her arms. He lay contentedly, eyes closed, his round, flat face serene, and she settled again, relaxing in his warmth, drowsy, at last, with the rhythm of his purring.

CHAPTER 35

Standing on the half-circle of beach, watching the rising tide, Louise could just see, out of the corner of her eye, the man under the trees. He was half hidden by the rocks at the edge of the cove, and he, too, was watching the small child at the water's edge. She danced lightly on her toes, skipping after the receding waves and jumping back quickly as they washed in again over the sun-warmed sand. Delight flowed in every line of her movement and her long, fair hair flew in a shining cloud about her face, an aureole of bright filaments. Her feet were bare, her dungarees rolled up to her knees, a fleecy jacket open over a T-shirt. She jumped, crowing with delight, splashing amongst the brightly curling foam at the waves' edge, a tiny water-nymph.

Louise glanced about; the small cove was empty. The child seemed to be alone—apart from the man, watching from the trees—and an uneasiness settled on her heart: weighty, formless. A cloud edged across the sun, so that shadows crept along the beach, and a chill breeze sprang up from nowhere, ruffling the grey water which broke more roughly on the shore. A light mist, clinging and vaporous, drifted, hiding the houses on the opposite shore, hanging above the water. The tide was rising quickly, the waves breaking over the rocks at each point of the cove, yet still the child danced and leaped, unaware of the change in the weather. Perhaps her family was round the point, somewhere along the beach which stretched to the ferry steps. Soon she would be cut off: too small to wade in the strong current around the rocks or to negotiate the sharp rocks themselves.

Anxiety pumped inside her and she looked again towards the man beneath the trees. He had moved further round the point towards her, up into the cove amongst the rocks, his gaze still fixed on the tiny figure. She should go down to them, warn them, yet she was strangely unwilling to move. The mist was thicker now, more dense, and a wave, rougher than the others, caught the child off balance and knocked her to her knees. As she tried to rise another wave rushed in, swirling round her, breaking over the bright head, so that she cried out.

Louise tried to shout, to run to help her, but fear seemed to immobilise her, and she saw that the man had turned and was watching her.

"Help her!" she shouted. "*Save* her," but the words were lost amongst the crashing of the waves and she could see, quite clearly now, that the man was Rory and he was watching her with pity and despair.

She gave a great groaning shout, stretching out with her arms, and the crash and splintering of glass woke her from her dream. She sat in a welter of crumpled sheet and rumpled blanket, her face in her hands, whilst the sunshine streamed over her bed and shone on the broken glass and spilled water. Presently she wiped her eyes on the edge of the sheet, still huddled, willing down the panic. The dream slowly receded and she was left with the familiar sensation of loss. Now that she was alone it made its presence felt more keenly and it was hard to look past it; to allow it to exist without the old habit of denial creeping back. She tried hard not to block it by singing, by busy, mind-numbing activity, as she had taught herself so successfully in the past. Now she made herself live with it, accepting it but trying to look beyond it.

Louise pushed the bedclothes away and stood up. The sun was shining—well, that was a bonus—and she paused at the window, staring out over the upland fields, still seeing Rory's face, so distant, yet so familiar—and Hermione, dancing at the water's edge. Oh, how she missed them! Was it really possible that this gnawing aching emptiness might ever be filled? Despair edged close. Look beyond it—but at what? She forced herself to consider the day ahead: more decorating and, if the fine weather held, a walk along the beach and up through the woods to Rickham Common and over Portlemouth Down. These walks calmed her; the long views of rocky coastline and limitless sea bringing a sense of proportion to her troubled heart. There was a quiet comfort to be had in the contemplation of infinity—the vast stretches of the moor had the same effect—and she was aware of a very slow, gentle healing taking place. Later, after her walk and a hot, relaxing bath, she must prepare something to eat, for Jemima was coming to supper. Yes, a good day: full of simple but positive activities.

Louise pulled back the bed covers and crouched to collect the pieces of broken glass. The small amount of water had already run away, disappearing into the cracks between the floorboards, but she fetched a cloth from the bathroom and wiped the floor carefully, looking for tiny splinters of glass. Presently, washed and dressed, she went downstairs, pulling back the curtains in the living room, going into the galley to admire her efforts. The small, lean-to conservatory was proving to be extremely useful, doubling as a dining room and sitting room, now that she had begun work on the living room. Here, the sun shone in from early morning until late in the afternoon, and she'd moved the gate-legged table, the small wooden chair and an old Lloyd loom into its narrow space, leaving just enough room to squeeze past into the yard outside. Here, she could forget the muddle and the dust sheets at least until it became dark. As she laid her breakfast, she wondered how she and Jemima would manage this evening. One more chair could be crammed in beside the table but where would they sit afterwards? The Foxhole contingent had arrived for lunch before the decorating had got underway and, thanks to Jemima, it had been a very jolly party. Louise had been seized by panic at the last moment, all her new-found independence deserting her, her confidence evaporating, as she envisaged preparing something special for the five of them.

"I'm hopeless at cooking," she'd mourned, "especially in such cramped conditions. Whatever shall I do? Would they be hurt if I took them to the pub? Brigid's such a brilliant cook too. I know I'll just mess it all up."

"You've just lost your nerve," said Jemima, "and everything's a bit strange. Tell you what. I'll take you to Effings and you can get some of their home-made frozen meals. They are truly delicious and no one need know."

They'd gone to Totnes together and studied the menu, trying to decide between Lady Booth's haddock gratin with prawns or a spicy lamb curry called Rogan Josh. Finally they'd decided on the Breton rabbit casserole with poached pears to follow. It had been a huge success. She'd tucked away in the freezer a two-portion pack of spinach and ricotta pancakes, as well as some sticky toffee puddings, as an emergency. Perhaps they'd do for this evening. Jemima was blissfully easy to have around: undemanding, good company, making light of difficulties. Brigid had unostentatiously left two bottles of rather good claret behind—"Just a little present to help you settle in," she'd said later, when Louise had telephoned to thank her—and one of these would add a touch of class to the supper.

She heaved a sigh of relief as she poured some orange juice and put some bread in the toaster. Louise liked to be generous to her friends but, just at present, she was trying to manage on very little. Martin had agreed readily to subsidise her, in place of the rent, but she hated the thought, now, that she was living on him. No part-time jobs were available, at least not within an easy driving range, and the one waitressing job she'd considered meant that she'd have been out of pocket at the end of the day.

"It's the one snag with being so far away from any of the towns," she'd said to Martin anxiously. "But I'm still looking. I suppose I'm eligible for social security . . ."

"For heaven's sake, sweetie, stop fussing. Just give yourself this three months. Try to relax into it and make yourself really better. We can hack it if you'll just stop worrying about it all the time. You're living on next to nothing as it is."

"I don't need much," she'd said. "I just don't feel right about it."

"Look, I just know something is going to turn up. OK? Trust your Uncle Martin and enjoy yourself. Please?"

She'd given in, grateful as always for his kindness, but she still kept looking at the "Situations Vacant" columns, hoping to hear from Charles Price, praying for a miracle. She put the toast in the rack, pausing for a moment to enjoy the warmth which already radiated into this little glass room. The last cobwebby shreds of her dream were evaporating, like mist before the sun, yet the longing remained.

BRIGID WAS working upstairs at her big table when she heard Alexander's voice, raised from the hall below. She went out through the bedrooms and on to the stairs, bending to look, calling in reply. He'd obviously been standing near the front door but now he moved further into the hall, into her line of vision.

"I'm so sorry to disturb you," he said, both hands raised in the now familiar gesture which seemed to be both apology and benediction. "I'm going shopping and merely wondered if I could save you a journey. Do you need anything?"

"I don't think so." She descended the last few steps. "I shopped a few days ago. Oh, well, actually, I do need some dog biscuits. Well, Blot does. Shall I show you the box? That would be great, if you really don't mind."

He followed her into the kitchen. "Are you well?"

"Yes, I think so." She smiled at him. "I've spoken to Humphrey."

His eyebrows shot up. "*Have* you? Did he stick to the script?"

"Only partially." She chuckled. "He wasn't particularly

enthusiastic, I have to say, but the minute I backed off he became quite keen. So I continued to back off."

Alexander grinned. "Have you ever heard of Stephen Potter?" he asked.

She frowned, puzzled. "I don't think so."

"Ah, well, never mind. It sounds as if your gamesmanship was first class."

"Do you think so?" She looked at him anxiously. "I've been wondering ever since. I've sent the mortgage forms off to him but hoping that by the time he gets them he'll have given it some thought. His problem will be backing down, won't it? You're quite right in saying that *my* feeling guilty makes *him* feel martyred but it will be hard for him to admit that taking the school over is a good idea—and that it might even be fun. I wish he'd thought of it first."

"I have every confidence in you," said Alexander. "I've no doubt that Humphrey will, in time, believe that he *did* think of it first."

"You *are* a cynic," said Brigid firmly, "even though you always deny it." She sighed. "Oh, I can't tell you just how much I'm praying that he'll be able to do it. It's not just to let me off the hook. I really believe he'd love it."

"I can't quite see him retiring just yet," agreed Alexander. "He's still a young man. Although I can well believe that you need some time together. I hope that will be possible."

"Oh, I hope so too. I just wish I knew exactly how much he'd need to be there." She shook her head. "There's still so much to think about; whether he and Jenny could work together and the logistics of it. Well, we'll simply have to wait and see. I've hinted that there's quite a lot of interest being shown so let's hope he doesn't take too long to make up his mind. And what about you? When's your friend arriving?"

"Tomorrow." Alexander looked mischievous. "His arrival is causing quite a lot of excitement."

"Isn't it just!" Brigid looked severe. "I hope you know what you're doing?"

"Oh, I think so. I'm too old to cope with two women at once any more. I need reinforcements."

"You must bring—Gregory, is it?—to supper. I suppose everyone had better come. It'll be quite a party. Would you like that?"

"It sounds great fun. But I don't want to put you out. He's my guest not yours."

"Oh, I don't think cooking some supper will be too difficult. It's Mummie and Margot who will be the problem."

He watched her with a tender, smiling look. "You shouldn't let them embarrass you. Why should the way other people behave reflect on you?"

She'd spoken jokingly but she might have guessed that he would go directly to the point. "She *is* my mother," she said rather bitterly. "I hate to see her . . . demeaning herself."

"You're too harsh," he said gently. "Frummie is still young inside. So is Margot. So are we all. It's a tragedy that the joy in our hearts no longer matches our wrinkled, saggy exteriors but that doesn't mean that we should extinguish the flame lest other people should be embarrassed by it. Why deprive them of their fun?"

"As long as you don't despise her," she mumbled, flushing hotly. "I know I'm strait-laced and boring but I just wish she'd be more . . . responsible. Jemima's just like her. They don't seem to worry about anything. Or anybody."

"I'm not sure that's quite true. People make mistakes and then it becomes impossible to put them right. Pride or guilt or resentment block the path to reconciliation and seem insurmountable. You're seeing a little of that with Humphrey, aren't you? Your own guilt or resentment triggers off a reaction and it rapidly gets out of hand. It happened between me and Humphrey and between you and your mother. Imagine how your mother feels, having let you down so terribly."

"She could have put up a fight," said Brigid angrily.

"Perhaps she did," said Alexander, "but perhaps your father's pride resisted her too strongly. He loved you and was determined to keep you and protect you. Perhaps your mother discovered the strength of his determination and pride too late."

She stared at him. "She never speaks of it."

He shook his head. "It's had such a long time to become entrenched. Has it really harmed you? Did my decision to remarry really harm Humphrey?"

"I . . . don't know," she said uncertainly. "It's awful to think that your parents don't love you."

"But your father *did* love you. Far too much to give you up."

There was a silence.

"It was because of Jemima," she said at last. "She took Jemima with her when she bolted. Jemima says that's because her father didn't want her. She missed him terribly."

"I rather like your sister," said Alexander thoughtfully. "Have you told her about your problem with Humphrey?"

She looked at him in horror. "Oh, no," she said. "Goodness! Jemima would be horrified."

"Horrified?" He looked surprised.

"Well . . . you know . . ." She hesitated. "I told you, she's like Mummie, terribly laid back and easy-going. She does the craziest things and is . . . well, unreliable, I suppose. She thinks I'm very organised and sensible."

"I think I understand. You mean you don't want to lose face? That because you feel that Jemima is the favoured one you must hold on to your superiority over her?"

"Superiority?" She flung back her head, as though he had slapped her.

"Well, isn't it? You feel in control, capable, in the face of her . . . unreliability. If you admitted this error of judgement you'd lose that sense of superiority. You'd be on an equal footing. Would that be a bad thing? Or perhaps you wouldn't consider it equal, since she was taken and you were left. Perhaps your capability is the only weapon you have with which to fight her."

She stared at him, shocked, pinned by his keen gaze. Was there pity in it? With an effort she pushed aside the overwhelming desire to shout, "But that's not fair," and struggled, instead, towards some kind of honesty.

"I like her," she cried, "I'm very fond of her but she gets

away with everything. She falls on her feet every time . . ." she caught her breath, remembering, and burst unexpectedly into tears . . . "her big, flat webbed feet." She choked on her self-loathing. "I called her Puddle-duck, you know, when she was born. I used to enjoy imagining this fat, white, duck-bodied child with tiny eyes and big flat feet." She looked at him, pushing back her hair. "It helped me to hate her, d'you see. When I saw a photograph of her, well . . ." She shook her head. "You've seen her. She's so pretty, isn't she? As a child she was quite delicious."

He put a handkerchief into her hands and she took it automatically, rubbing her cheeks, blowing her nose, her eyes fixed on the past.

"They came to Daddy's funeral. She was about fourteen then. But she had no idea, no idea at all, how I felt or what I'd been through. She was simply delighted to have found her sister at last. 'Hello,' she said. 'We're sisters. I've always wanted to meet you.' She was so pretty, so sweet. And I felt so jealous, so utterly miserable with Daddy just buried. I hated her. I said, 'I've always called you Puddle-duck.' I wanted to hurt her, you see. I needed her to see the image of her that I'd always had in my mind. But she didn't react. She laughed. I think she was even pleased. She saw it as a delightful, happy nickname. She even told Mummie, but Mummie knew straight away. She looked at me, right through me, and she laughed and I felt mean and small and disgusting. She said, 'And what do you think of my ugly duckling?' Jemima wanted us to be a family but it's always stood between us. She's never dissembled or pretended to be different from what she is. It's just like she's waiting." Brigid wiped her wet eyes. "It's odd, actually. She often quite deliberately tells me things that she knows I'll disapprove of, or displays her weaknesses to me."

"Perhaps," said Alexander gently, "your sister has discovered a very important truth. She sees that we serve others as much by our weaknesses as by our strengths. The only difficulty is that it takes humility and courage to be able to live by it."

"Mummie's always so nice to her," Brigid sounded exhausted, "which doesn't help."

"Your mother also needs weapons," he said. "Perhaps it's time you laid yours down. Show me the dog biscuits and I'll leave you in peace."

After he'd gone, Brigid reflected that any other man, having reduced her to tears, might have made tea or poured a drink and stood by whilst she recovered. The point was that Alexander was not like other men. In the comforting and the apologies, the truth might have become blurred and forgotten. Alexander never took that chance. Brigid drank a glass of cold tap water, tied her hair back with a faded cotton scarf and went upstairs to her work.

CHAPTER 36

Gregory arrived late in the afternoon. He climbed from his car, looking about him with tremendous interest, beaming with delight when Alexander emerged to greet him. They shook hands and then hugged, their words snatched from their lips by a malicious wind which tore over the moor and keened around the cottages. The two ladies watched—discreetly hidden—from the window. The cheerful roar of Gregory's laughter was carried to them and it was clear that the two men were enjoying their reunion.

"He looks rather nice," said Margot thoughtfully. "Don't you think so, Fred? Not as tall as Alexander but not as thin, either. Looks like a man who knows how to enjoy himself."

Frummie slid a sideways glance in her direction. "Well, if he doesn't, dear, he will by the time he leaves Foxhole."

Margot grinned. "Do you think Alexander will ask us over to meet him today?"

Frummie shrugged. "They'll have lots of catching up to do. Anyway, he's probably knackered after driving from London."

"London?" Margot looked at her sharply. "How do you know he comes from London?"

"I asked." Frummie looked faintly discomfited. "Well. Sort of asked. I just mentioned something about him having a long drive and Alexander said that it wasn't too bad just coming from London."

Margot brooded for a moment, watching while Alexander with extensive sweeps of his arm explained to Gregory the setup at Foxhole.

"Of course, that doesn't mean he *lives* there," she said. "Does it? He might have been visiting, on his way from somewhere else."

"Possibly."

A silence, during which time several bags were removed from the car and placed on the track whilst the two men continued to talk.

"I do love Alexander," burst out Margot irritably, "but he can be so infuriating."

"He sees through us," said Frummie, her eyes on the tall, thin figure. "It's impossible to wheedle him."

"That's what I mean," cried Margot. "And yet you can't get anything out of *him*. Have you noticed that, Fred? Quite unfair."

"He's a remarkable man," agreed Frummie. "I've never met anyone quite like him before, I must admit. Definitely a challenge."

"Well." Margot looked at her slyly. "That's an admission, coming from you. Have you found out where he's going when he goes north?"

"Not really." Frummie frowned, puzzled. "I asked him if he had his own place and he said he had. So then I asked him if it were in the country and he said it was and that it was a big place but only a small bit of it was his. I'm paraphrasing, you understand. It took quite a long time to get to the root of it. I said, 'Oh, you mean sheltered housing or something like that.' You know. Just to draw him out. And he laughed and said, yes, it was something like that."

"You didn't tell me all this," said Margot jealously, clearly put out. "How long have you known?"

"I'm telling you now," said Frummie unperturbed. "And he only told me this morning when I popped over to see if there were anything I could do. It was when we were talking about how far Gregory was driving. It just fell rather neatly into place."

"Mmm." Margot craned to watch Gregory follow Alexander into the cottage. "Perhaps he's bought a flat in one of those big old country mansions. You know the sort of thing I mean? It's very fashionable. You get to use the grounds and there's usually one of those electronic thingies on the gate. Very posh. I wonder if it's that?"

"I suppose it could be. I wonder what it would be like."

"Oh, I've heard it can be great fun." Margot sounded suspiciously encouraging. "They have a swimming pool and a sauna and restaurants and hairdressers. It's like a little world all on its own. Suzy and Jim moved into one in Hampshire. I stayed with them for a few days. My dear! Absolutely rolling in it! The lap of luxury. They played bridge and tennis and there were lots of lovely drinks parties. I was green with envy, I promise you. You'd love it, Fred."

Frummie smiled her down-turned smile. "Sounds like you're trying to sell it to me, dear."

Margot laughed, dismissing such a foolish notion. "Don't be silly. I only meant what with Alexander being so fond of you and it all being in the family, so to speak . . . Well, you might get the chance of a visit, that's all."

"I might. If that's the sort of place he means. I can't quite see Alexander in that kind of company. He'd put their backs up in no time at all."

"Of course, Suzy and Jim chose one with a particularly social reputation. It's quite famous. Retired people with lots of money who like to enjoy themselves. Alexander probably couldn't afford quite that sort of place. Maybe it's a slightly less posh one. I'm sure Gregory will tell us, once we get to know him."

The two men had reappeared and Gregory was taking a familiar-looking cardboard box from the back of the car whilst Alexander picked up the remaining suitcase.

"Seems like he's brought some booze with him," said Margot happily. "Didn't I say that he looks like a man who knows how to enjoy himself?"

"You did. What's more important, he looks like a man

who likes to help other people to enjoy themselves. He looks rather fun, I do admit."

Margot glanced at her sharply. "Hands off, Fred! We decided that he was mine. *You* decided. Too late to change your mind now!"

Frummie rolled her eyes sideways. "Who says I'm changing my mind? But it's rather up to Gregory, isn't it? Perhaps Alexander might bring him over later to say hello."

"I think I'll take a bath," said Margot, as if seized by a sudden inspiration. "Is that OK, Fred?" She nipped off towards the stairs with surprising alacrity. "Shan't be long."

Frummie remained at the window, watching the crate and the case being taken indoors. Presently the two men reappeared and Gregory reparked the car, turning it and then tucking it in closely to the wall whilst Alexander watched and gave directions. He climbed out again, locked the door and slipped the keys into his pocket. Alexander followed him through the gate and, as Gregory disappeared into the cottage, Alexander turned towards her and raised a hand in a friendly salute. Frummie laughed aloud, delighted with him, but remained for some time at the window, still half hidden by the curtain, absorbed in her own train of thought.

JEMIMA REPLACED the telephone receiver and gave a howl of frustration. MagnifiCat jumped on to the windowsill and sat watching her, his tail curled tidily around his paws.

"What shall I do?" she asked him. "I can't find anyone to do the Hope Cove cottage on Saturday. No one! Janet's got a stomach upset, Judy's taking her mum shopping and Sally's got something on at school. I'm going to have to do the changeover myself. Oh, what a waste of a morning! Why do people want to come on holiday so late in the season?"

She riffled through her address book, muttering under her breath, trying to be reasonable. At least he was coming for the weekend. Beneath the overriding excitement, anxiety nagged. Was she being a fool in believing that they had a future together? Had she taken too much for granted? She'd gradually convinced herself that she could confide in Brigid;

tell her about this new, exciting relationship and the subsequent unwelcome shock. Carefully, hopefully, she'd persuaded herself that Brigid might understand and share her thoughts and fears, only to be cast suddenly into doubt. Even as she'd walked into Effings she'd still been in two minds about it but, oddly enough, as soon as she'd seen her sister, sitting waiting for her, her anxiety had evaporated and she'd suddenly felt a sure confidence. There had been something open and candid about Brigid's expression; her body language was welcoming, her smile warm. There had been tension, yes, no doubt about that, but it had been on Brigid's side: an uncharacteristic nervousness which had surprised and disarmed.

Jemima, remembering, laughed almost bitterly. How typical that on the day she'd screwed her own courage to the post, preparing to unburden her soul, Brigid had been going through exactly the same mental process. Watching her, Jemima had realised that Brigid was feeling just as she did herself: she recognised in her sister the urgent need to begin before she lost her nerve. Jemima had felt first amazed, then very touched. She could hardly believe that the cool, reserved, sensible Brigid was telling her—*her,* the scatty, disorganised, foolish Jemima—these personal details. She'd almost forgotten her own troubles in hearing Brigid's. It was as if she were discovering a completely new woman; not the Brigid she'd known at all. She was riveted, finding it almost impossible to believe that she should act without Humphrey's knowledge and consent—that she should take such a chance, to risk her little cottage . . . She'd listened, fascinated and then horrified, as the tale unfolded. When she'd heard about Bryn's flight and the unpaid debts, she'd guessed what was coming but she'd easily imagined Brigid's shock and fear and could readily understand how difficult it had been to tell Humphrey.

"What on earth did he say?" she'd asked. "Twelve thousand pounds! You must have been out of your mind."

Brigid had talked on, her hair pushed back behind her ears, her home-made pâté forgotten, sipping occasionally from her glass of wine. When she'd explained about taking over the school, Jemima had felt a thrill of excitement.

"That's a brilliant idea," she'd said at once. "Fantastic! Surely Humphrey will go for that, won't he?"

"It was Alexander's idea," Brigid had admitted. "It was so clever of him to think of it."

She'd recounted her conversation with Humphrey, how she'd practised what she called her "gamesmanship," until they were both laughing. Somehow the tension was released at last and Brigid began to eat her lunch whilst Jemima took it all in.

"Do you mind that he'd still be away?" she'd asked. "Just when you thought you were going to have time together?"

"I don't think I have any choice," Brigid had answered honestly. "I can't drop him in the shit and then complain about it, can I? Actually, though, to tell you the truth I've been rather dreading his retirement."

Another shock! Jemima had stared at her in surprise.

"Dreading it? But why? You always seem so happy together. You have so much fun."

"I know." Brigid had looked worried, guilty. "It's just . . . I have this need to be on my own. I like solitude. It's great to have him home—of *course* it is—but I get a bit twitchy if there's someone around all the time. I know it sounds really weird, doesn't it . . . ?"

"No, it doesn't," Jemima had answered quickly. "It doesn't sound weird at all. I'm exactly the same."

"Are you?" Brigid had looked up at her, toast poised mid-air. "Really?"

"I'd thought it was just me. I've always hated sharing with people and I've never been able to have anyone living in with me long term. I can't relax properly or do my own thing. I'm kind of on edge all the time."

"Yes, that's it." Brigid had sounded almost excited. "That's exactly it. How extraordinary."

They'd stared at one another, pleased at this mutual discovery, as if it had strengthened the bond between them.

"It must be genetic." Jemima had grinned at her sister.

"Though we certainly don't inherit it from Frummie. She'd rather live with anyone than be alone."

"Oh, I know." Brigid's expression had been a mixture of amusement and despair. "At least she's got Margot at the moment. Not to mention Alexander and Gregory to keep her busy."

They'd laughed together companionably, enjoying this new depth of relationship growing between them. Unwilling to spoil it, Jemima had decided to keep her own problems a secret for the moment. She sensed that it would be better to continue to concentrate on Brigid's disclosure.

"So what do you think Humphrey will do next?" she'd asked—and the rest of the time together had passed in speculation and conjecture and Brigid's hopes for the future.

MagnifiCat stretched a languid leg, leaning to lick his flank, and Jemima rested her chin in her hands, watching him, continuing to readjust long-held assumptions about her sister. She still felt certain that it had been wise not to introduce her own dilemma at that point: that it had been right to postpone her own needs until a later date. They would serve to reinforce this new closeness which was building between them. Brigid had offered her a gift of her fears and weaknesses: next time it would be her turn. She sighed deeply. She could confide in Louise but it seemed unfair to burden her with worries when she was just managing to hold her own again. No, she must deal with this one alone for the time being. Of course, it was always possible that the coming weekend might solve all her problems.

A tiny flame of excitement flickered in her gut and a surging wave of happiness buoyed up her flagging confidence. Surely all would be well? If only she could find someone to do the changeover for her at Hope Cove then she could really look forward to the weekend. Two whole days together. She allowed herself to relax into anticipation: to melt with love and expectation. He had sounded very ebullient, very affectionate; teasing her with the news he would be sharing with her.

"I never thought that relocating would be such fun," he'd

said. "I can't believe I'm actually considering leaving London."

"I felt like that once," she'd said, making it sound very casual: a kind of "Been there, done that, bought the T-shirt" kind of indifference, as if he were still catching up on what was *really* cool. "But now . . . well." She'd made it sound like a shrug. "Who needs it?"

"I'm beginning to believe that I don't. I can't wait to see you again."

"That's good." She'd wondered how she could possibly continue to play it so casually whilst all the time her hand was gripping the telephone as though it were a lifeline and her body was clenched in a spasm of need and love. "Not too long till Friday."

"No, I suppose not."

She'd heard him sigh and immediately had felt anxious that she'd been overdoing it, longing to cry, "I love you. I want you to be here *now*!"

"I'm going to see Annabel tomorrow evening," he'd said—and her stomach had instantly curdled with fear; her hands were icy.

"Oh?" The small sharp word had sounded curt; loaded with terror.

"Well, she asked if I'd go over." He'd sounded conciliatory. "There are still things to discuss and she's got some of my stuff. You know how it is."

"Sure." She'd made herself answer calmly, even cheerfully. Yet why shouldn't she show her insecurity; ask for confirmation of his love? Why not give him the chance to comfort and reassure her? Some instinct warned her against it: some deep intuitive sense told her to wait.

"I miss you," he'd said softly. "I really miss you."

They'd talked nonsense for a while; teasing each other affectionately, laughing, making plans . . .

Now, sitting at her desk, Jemima groaned with longing— and tensed her muscles against that trickle of excitement. Maybe she had nothing to fear, after all. With an uprush of her natural optimism she closed her eyes and began to fantasise: he'd have found a wonderful job in Exeter; they'd never be separated again; he'd want to get married, have babies . . . She opened her eyes abruptly.

"Dream on!" she muttered derisively—and, seizing her address book, she began to turn the pages, searching diligently through its scribbled entries.

CHAPTER 37

"I've been thinking about this suggestion of yours."

Humphrey's voice was very nearly truculent and Brigid, her nerves stretched taut with hope and nervousness, was seized by a crazy desire to say, "Oh? Which suggestion was that?" Hysterical laughter bubbled inside her and she took several deep breaths in an effort to control herself. She thought: I'm going mad. The strain is sending me round the bend.

Aloud she said: "Have you? Well, it was just a foolish idea, really. Not properly followed through."

"No, I realise that."

He still sounded alarmingly unfriendly but she instinctively knew that he was having difficulty in introducing the subject. The fact that he had done so raised her hopes, convincing her that he was at least interested. It was necessary to encourage him now, but she must be tactful.

"I'm sure it's terribly complicated," she said, taking care to keep her voice light, not quite dismissive, not too enthusiastic.

"Well, I've been giving it quite a lot of thought." She remained resolutely silent. "I'm beginning to think that I might be able to work something out."

"Really?" The sharp upward inflexion at the end of the word indicated amazement and she grimaced, wondering if she'd overdone it.

"Well, obviously it's not going to be easy."

She thought: Huffy. That's the word. He sounds huffy.

"I'm sure it can't be," she agreed. She simply mustn't be patronising. "I don't even know whether it can be done, of course."

"It occurred to me that if they're trying to sell it there must be some kind of prospectus. Do you think you could get hold of one and send it to me?"

She was silent for a moment, eyes stretched wide, before she hastened into speech. "Of course. I'm sure I can. What a clever idea!"

"Well, not *that* clever."

He was unbending slightly, the chill in his voice thawing into his more usual tones, and she did not waste this small opportunity.

"I was wondering if you could speak to the Bank? They're pestering a bit about the forms. I know it's not really fair to ask you to do it . . ." She let the sentence die away, having subtly indicated dependence, guilt and remorse.

"I can if you like."

It was clear that he was reluctant to sound too eager and she was quick to give him space.

"I know it's not easy with the time difference and, after all, I dropped us in this mess, but they're getting a bit stroppy."

She allowed a touch of pathos, a tiny hesitation to creep into her voice, appealing to his natural chivalry.

"It's probably sensible." He sounded almost his normal self. "I wouldn't mind running a few ideas past them. Just harden up a few thoughts, that kind of thing."

"Oh?" The initiative was now definitely passing from her to him. "Well, that's great, then." A tiny pause. "It sounds rather exciting."

"It could be. I might just be able to turn the thing round. I'd be away quite a bit, though. I don't know how you feel about that?"

Her mind leaped in several directions at once. An answer of "Oh, I don't mind a bit if it sorts out the problem" was neither quite accurate nor was it tactful, yet she could hardly say, "Oh, I can't bear the thought of it!"

"How do *you* feel about it?" She turned the answer back on him, opening herself up to a direct reproach: a "Well, I don't really have a lot of choice, do I?" kind of bitterness.

"Well, we're used to it, aren't we?" he answered, almost cheerfully resigned. "I expect we'd manage. I'm prepared to give it a try if you are. Assuming, of course, that the Bank will agree and I can sort out all the nitty-gritty."

She was humbled by his generosity, feeling guilt, gratitude and an enormous relief all in one huge upsweep of emotion. She answered him from her heart.

"I love you," she said.

There was a short silence.

"I love you too," he said—and he was Humphrey again: warm, human, kind. "We'll have a go, shall we? Give it a whirl?"

"Oh, darling! Do you think you might like it?"

"I was talking to some of the chaps here about it and they were really enthusiastic—rather envied me the opportunity. I expect full retirement could have been a bit OTT just yet."

"You might have got a bit bored." She was deliberately cautious: careful not to take too much for granted. "But I feel so mean for taking away your choices."

"Oh, well. I wouldn't have had the choices in the first place if it hadn't been for you, would I?"

"How do you mean?" She was genuinely puzzled.

"Well, Foxhole is yours, my sweet. You share it with me but, let's face it, you have the right to do what you like with your own cottage."

"I've never thought about it like that. It's you who's made it possible all these years. Your salary paid for the renovations so that they'd support our retirement."

"They still will." He was comforting her now. "I'm only fifty-two. Thirteen years till retirement. Anyway, I might have made a packet out of the sailing school by then."

"Oh, Humphrey."

"Look, you tried to help an old friend. It's not your fault it came unstuck. I've been thinking about it quite a lot and it could just be a stroke of luck for us. I know I'd have to be away quite a bit but we could cope with that, couldn't we? My role would be mainly advisory, I imagine, and administrative stuff, although I have to say that a bit of sailing does have an appeal. It would probably be quite quiet in the winter and I don't see why I couldn't do some of the administrative work from home. As long as the staff in the office is reliable. If anything blew up, I could be down there in an hour or so if necessary. What d'you think?"

"I think it's a wonderful idea," she said warmly. "I really do. If you're absolutely sure?"

"I think I am." He sounded pleased, almost jubilant. "I'll talk it over with the Bank. Oh, and see if you can get hold of a prospectus."

"I will," she promised. "It all sounds quite exciting. Well . . ." She gave a little chuckle. "I think I need a drink after all this. It's come as a bit of a shock."

"I know how you feel. It needs a bit of adjusting to—but I feel sure it should be followed up."

"If you think so." She stressed the "you" lightly; giving him the credit for it. "It's . . . well, it's quite an idea."

"You'll soon get used to it," he told her kindly. "I know it's not how we planned it but I think that it's right for us. I wish I was at home with you. Apart from anything else, it would be so much easier to start negotiations."

"I wish you were here too," she said. "But I'm sure you'll manage."

"Go and have that drink," he said affectionately. "Oh, by the way, how's Father?"

"He's fine. He's got a friend staying with him. A very nice man called Gregory Stone."

"Oh, yes, I remember him. An old school-friend, isn't he? So he's not being a pain in the arse? Father, I mean."

"No, oh no. Not at all. I . . . I hardly see him. Mummie's got Margot staying with her, so they're doing things in four-somes. They're having a ball by the sound of it."

"That's great. Only I'd rather you don't mention my plan

to him just at the moment. OK? Not until it's a bit more settled."

My plan? "Of course not," she said quickly. "No, I quite
understand. Mummie doesn't know about it either. I'll get
hold of that prospectus and send it off to you. And you'll
stay in touch, won't you? Let me know what the Bank says
and things like that?"

"Of course I will. I'll have to speak to them very soon to
let them know why I'm not sending back the forms. I'll ring
as soon as I've got anything to report."

"Great," she said. "Good luck. Love you."

"Thanks," he said. "Me, too."

She replaced the receiver and stood, grinning to herself.
"*My* plan. You'll soon get used to it." She remembered
Alexander's words: *"I have no doubt that in time Humphrey
will believe that he* did *think of it first"* and burst out laughing.
Feeling happier than she had for months, Brigid found Jenny's
telephone number, lifted the receiver and began to dial.

THE WIND was strong and cold, stinging tears to the eyes,
piling up the breakers which pounded thunderously on the
shore, filling the air with a salty, misty spray. The surging
heaving sea was grey, reflecting the rain-heavy clouds which
rolled sullenly before the westerly gale, although an occasional bright finger of sunshine pierced the gloom, to touch
the watery mass with a golden brilliance, so that dazzling
rainbows shimmered above the curling, windblown, white-
headed waves.

They walked in silence, the shingle crunching beneath
their boots, hands resolutely in pockets. Jemima hadn't had
the courage to take his hand, as she sometimes did, and he
made no attempt towards intimacy. He was stunned by the violence of the elemental forces which were sweeping the coast
and he paused at regular intervals to stare out to sea, almost
shocked by the noise: the crashing water, sucking greedily at
the land, and the relentless roaring of the wind. They'd
shouted to one another to begin with but had been obliged to
stop, their words torn from their lips and tossed into the

maelstrom before either could hear what the other had said. Sea-birds screamed above their bent heads, carried and bullied by the squalls which buffeted them unmercifully.

Jemima watched him, almost amused by the effect the gale was having upon him. The weekend had not yet completely recovered from its unfortunate beginnings. She'd been unable to find anyone to help her with the changeover and, on the Friday evening, he'd telephoned, furious and frustrated: he'd got back late from an unscheduled meeting to find that the car wouldn't start and the garage was closed.

"I'll get away as early as I can in the morning," he'd said. "Let's hope that there's nothing seriously wrong."

She'd tried to hide her disappointment, explaining her own problem. "I could leave the key with someone in the museum downstairs," she'd offered—but he'd refused.

"I probably won't be down much before lunchtime anyway," he'd said gloomily. "I'll go and have a pint in the Ferry Inn. Come and find me when you're back."

She'd fumed her way through the morning, hoovering, changing sheets, cleaning and dusting. The new arrivals were over an hour late and by the time she'd left them, her face aching with smiling so falsely, it was well past lunchtime. By the time she found him in the pub, he'd already eaten. He'd been tired, slightly irritable, and she'd been unable to overcome an attack of nervousness. They'd sat in the pub for a while and then wandered round the town, behaving rather like polite strangers, a barrier between them, invisible but most definitely there. Back at the flat the tension had eased a little. In this familiar setting they'd both loosened up. The harbour scene was blessed by autumn sunshine, which warmed the room with its glowing radiance before deepening gently into a crimson-streaked sunset. Gradually the brittleness between them dissolved and presently, after she'd opened some wine, they'd made love with an unusual intensity. She'd had the sense to prepare a simple but delicious supper, and they'd watched some late-night television, but he'd fallen asleep almost as soon as they'd got into bed.

Jemima had lain awake, listening to his regular breathing, feeling his warmth, lying as close to him as she dared without waking him. She suspected that he was coming close to making a commitment and was having an attack of cold feet. She was able to sympathise, in part, but she was aching with the need to be rid of all these estranging moods which beset them. She longed to have the rights—or privileges—of a steady relationship and was becoming weary of cautioning herself to act warily.

They'd made love again in the early morning and she'd slept, then, until nearly lunchtime. The walk had been mooted—despite the dramatic change in the weather—to clear their heads and wake them up. It had certainly achieved its purpose. When they climbed back into the car their heads were ringing with the clamour of the gale and their eyes streamed and stung. They had a drink and some lunch at the Tower Inn at Slapton and drove back to Salcombe, warmed and refreshed.

"You haven't told me your news yet," she said later, putting a tray of tea on the low table and sitting beside him on the sofa. "All this talk about relocating. So what's happened?"

He was unaware of how much it was costing her to raise the subject, or to speak so naturally, and she wondered if he saw her hands tremble as she poured the tea.

"Nothing concrete yet," he said—and her heart swooped dejectedly—"but there are one or two openings which look quite promising."

"Whereabouts?" She was grimly determined to hold on to her initiative, persuading herself that she had the right to ask; yet she kept her voice cheerful, almost jokey.

He frowned a little. "Bristol," he said almost reluctantly, at last.

"Bristol?" She couldn't prevent the involuntary query; the implied disappointment.

He shrugged. "It's a start," he said defensively. "It's more difficult the further west you come."

"I can believe that," she said reasonably. "It's just, from the way you spoke, it sounded as if . . . well, as if something really good had happened."

"There's a faint possibility of something in Exeter," he admitted. "But it's too early to get excited about it."

"Right." She drank some tea thoughtfully.

"It might take a while," he said, "but, hey, let's not give up hope."

He smiled at her, touching her shoulder and then drawing his hand down her arm, and she felt the familiar shudder of excitement deep in her gut. She set down her cup, turning to look at him, pressing her hands between her knees.

"The thing is," she said, "I've got some news myself."

"Oh?" He looked at her quickly, his eyes bright, wary. "And what's that, then?"

"I'm being chucked out of here," she said. "They've given me three months' notice to quit."

"What?" He laughed disbelievingly, shaking his head. "Sorry, I think I've lost the plot. You said this was your place. You said your father had left you some money . . ."

"I said I had a legacy." She kept her eyes on his face. "But I didn't say I'd bought the place. It just enabled me to pay the pretty astronomic rent." She nodded towards the window. "Waterfront properties don't come cheap."

"No, I imagine they don't." His own eyes were blank. "Right. I see."

"The point is," she felt almost angry now, oddly hurt by his reaction, or lack of it, "that we could live somewhere a bit more convenient to . . . well, where the work is, if you see what I mean. I can't go too far from my own patch, of course, but we are rather out on a limb here. We could be a bit more central. Nearer the A38, for instance."

She stopped speaking and silence crashed between them. Violent gusts of wind flung the rain against the glass so that it ran in rivulets, pouring like tears down the cold cheeks of the window.

"Well," she said, after a while, "that seems to have been a bit of a conversation stopper."

"Sorry," he said quickly. "Really, I am. It was quite a shock." He still looked dazed.

"I found it so," she said, almost brutally.

He looked at her quickly. "Sure. God, yes. Look, I'm really sorry."

"Well," she refused to lose her grip, "perhaps it's a blessing in disguise. Like I said, it gives us choices."

He pulled himself together. "Of course it does. You're right. It could make things much easier."

She said, "Your tea's getting cold."

"Right." He sat forward, swallowed the tea. "And I ought to be making a move. This bloody awful weather will really slow me down and I've got to get the wretched hire car back. This hasn't worked out quite like I hoped. Better next time, don't you think? But it's been great . . ."

He talked himself through his packing and his goodbyes, out of the flat and down the stairs. Once he'd gone she stood at the window, staring out at the night whilst the wind tore across the black water of the harbour and raced shrieking overhead. MagnifiCat came winding round her ankles, rubbing his head against her legs, and, drawing the curtains to close out the storm, she turned back into the warmly lighted room.

CHAPTER 38

Louise sat back on her heels, scanning the skirting board anxiously for any glossy dribbles, and sighed with relief. The living room was very nearly finished and she was looking forward to being able to live comfortably again. She'd been lucky to finish the galley and the living room's walls before the stormy weather arrived. Until the change in the weather it had been possible to leave the windows and doors open to the gentle autumnal warmth but now she longed for the comfort of a fire in the evenings. Sitting in the small conservatory was no longer an option but she was cautious about having a fire whilst the gloss paint was still wet. The tiny grate would have to be cleared out each morning and she simply couldn't risk ash settling on the tacky surfaces. She'd had to make do with an old-fashioned convector heater whilst the damp, chilly fingers of the wind poked and pried around the cottage, reaching beneath doors and squeezing through rattling window frames. The draught had whistled round her ankles and played about her ears as she'd sat huddled in her shawl, thick woollen socks on her feet and a hot-water bottle clutched in her arms. A power cut had suddenly plunged her into darkness and sent her stumbling and bumping in search of her torch before she could find the candles and the matches with which Jemima had so thoughtfully supplied her. She'd sat shivering in the flickering light, whilst the convector heater gradually cooled and she grew colder and more miserable until, in the end, it had been sensible simply to go to bed.

Today was bright again; the power restored. The storm had passed away, the last lingering rags of clouds drifting eastwards, and the sun was shining. She stood up, stretching, and went into the galley to wash her brushes. The clean brightness, the fresh smell of paint, pleased her. She felt the sense of satisfaction which comes with the contemplation of the results of hard work and she sipped at her mug of hot soup, her spirits rising. Tomorrow she would begin work upstairs. Meanwhile, she planned to go for a walk. She'd barely been out since the stormy weather had set in and she longed to stride out over the cliffs or along the beach, resting her dust-filled eyes on distant vistas and stretching her legs after days of crouching and kneeling. Her back felt permanently bent with scraping, sand-papering and rubbing down. She'd worked long and hard, and a treat was in order.

As she finished her soup, between taking bites from a cheese-filled roll and peeling an apple, she decided that she would drive down to East Portlemouth, park in the lane above the ferry steps so as to wander along the beach—if the tide allowed—and up through the wood to Rickham Common. This was one of her favourite walks and she decided to take a small picnic with her: a flask of hot tea and a few small rock-cakes would go down rather well up on the cliffs. Fifteen minutes later she was putting the lightweight knapsack in the car, hurrying back inside to collect her fleece hat, and finally setting off. She did not notice the small red car parked beside the village green, nor the man who was standing half hidden by the stone shelter. He wore a baseball cap and Ray-Bans and appeared to be engrossed in the unusual windvane on the roof of the shelter, his head tilted back as he stared up at its crown and the letters EIIR. Once she had passed, however, he walked quickly to the red car and climbed in, turning it so as to follow her through the winding lanes.

As Louise descended the steps which led down to the beach, she was pleased to see that the tide was ebbing. This meant that if she were careful she could get along the beach quite safely, although she might have to scramble over some of the low-lying rocks. She picked her way along, glancing across to Salcombe, wondering what Jemima might be doing, until she rounded the rocky point into Mill Bay. As she crossed the beach she remembered her dream. It was here that Hermione had danced, teasing the waves, and Rory had stood beneath the trees, watching her. For a moment her heart filled with despair and loneliness and she struggled to keep depression from muscling in; wrestling her happiness in the bright day down to helplessness, dragging her spirits down into misery.

Frummie's words slid into her mind and she clung to them grimly. *"Look beyond it."* She climbed the path into the little woodland, concentrating on the view of the sea which lay ahead. The bent and twisted oaks and sycamore, ancient and stunted by the salt spray, seemed unusually quiet and oddly eerie. She had the odd sensation that someone was near at hand, and she was glad to climb out into the sunshine on the common amongst the fading bracken. She walked more slowly now, looking across the narrow mouth of the estuary to Starehole Bay and the Mew Stone on the further side. The silvery silken skin of the sea stretched to a misty, indistinct horizon, and tiny fishing boats bobbed lazily, the slanting rays of the sun gleaming and glinting on their painted decks.

She wandered along the coastal path, watching gannets diving and the smaller terns with their dancing, skimming flight, noticing the gorse bushes still in flower and the clumps of thrift which grew amongst the rocks. Presently, beneath some wind-shaped apple trees, she laid out her waterproof and poured some tea into the plastic cup. The rock-buns tasted good, full of delicious fruit, and the tea was hot and refreshing, and she sat dreaming in the afternoon sunshine until she began to grow chilly. Kneeling, she packed the waterproof and the tea-things into her knapsack, swung it on to her back and got to her feet. The sun was low now, dazzling into her eyes. For a moment she thought she saw another figure on the footpath but when she looked more carefully, shading her eyes, there was no one there. She started back, watching the boats which were now heading for harbour, hugging the channel of the further shore as they crossed the spit of sand called The Bar.

Louise walked quickly, hands in pockets, crossing the common once more, passing through the woodland and down to Mill Bay. As she came out of the trees and began to cross the half-circle of beach, she caught her breath in a tiny gasp of shock. Beneath the trees, half hidden by the rocks at the edge of the cove, a man was standing. So strongly did he remind her of her dream that she glanced involuntarily towards the water's edge, expecting to see the small child dancing. There was nothing there; only the tide washing gently in across the sand. She looked back at him, her steps slowing, feeling suddenly afraid. There was something familiar about him, about the cap and the black Ray-Bans, which made her search her memory, wondering where she'd seen him before. He was slightly turned away from her, staring over the harbour, yet, even as she advanced he moved round the edge of the point, looking at her now. Trembling, poised for flight, she stopped, and in a swift movement he took off his cap, crushing it into his pocket, and removed the tinted spectacles.

She stared at him, heart hammering in her side, fists still jammed in her pockets and, just as it had been in the dream, no words would come and she was immobilised with fear. He came towards her, hesitated and came on until he was an arm's length away. They stared at each other in silence until he shook his head almost irritably, as if dispelling some emotion which had gripped him and paralysed him, and with an immense effort he smiled at her.

"Hello, Louise," said Rory.

THE WALK back to the ferry steps seemed to take hours. The reality of his presence, suddenly after three years of absence, was a tremendous shock and, to begin with, she could neither move nor speak. She stared at him, struggling with a whole variety of emotions: disbelief, delight, fear, guilt. He took the initiative—but then he always had. She was reminded of those returns from sea and her frustration in her inability to cross the barrier which distance and loneliness had erected in his absence.

"I didn't know how to do it," he was saying anxiously, apologising for the shock. "I couldn't think of any other way."

She shook her head, trying to say, "It's OK. I understand," but still the words wouldn't come. She simply did not know how to begin. What words could be adequate after the way she'd left him? Quite instinctively they began to walk back along the beach together. Whilst he talked, trying to build some kind of bridge, she stole glances at him, sliding her eyes sideways, still gripped with shyness—and shame.

"I've been following you." It was a kind of apology. "Trying to get up the courage to speak." He chuckled, a not very convincing sound, but he was doing his best. "Obviously my disguise worked."

He took out the baseball cap, smoothing it and turning it in his hands. His efforts were palpable and she was shaken with an overwhelming tenderness for him.

"I thought I *did* recognise you." She spoke at last but the words were husky, as if her voice were rusty with disuse. "But not as you, if you see what I mean. As someone else."

He turned to her eagerly, encouraging her, stuffing the cap back into his pocket. "You've probably seen me about without realising it," he said. "I followed you once from Foxhole in the car. We were in a hold-up for a few minutes and I wondered if you'd seen me in your mirror. And I was in The Wardroom when you were there having coffee."

She stared at him, shyness forgotten in surprise. "But how did you know where I was? Sorry. I'm being a bit dense, aren't I? I thought you meant you'd seen me by accident . . ." She hesitated, confused.

"Martin told me," he said. "He said that you'd . . . come to terms with things."

He looked uncomfortable but she was too shocked to notice it. "*Martin* told you?"

They stood quite still, staring at each other, and, when he spoke, he chose his words very carefully.

"He stayed in touch with me, you see. He was horrified by . . . such a tragedy and he tried to keep hold of me, if you can understand that."

She looked away from him, surprised to see the children running on the sand and boats chugging into harbour. The brilliant light and the sounds crashed in on her consciousness. It was as if the whole world had narrowed down to the tiny space which he and she inhabited. Now it expanded almost violently around her. The children's voices echoed over the water and the engines of the fishing boats purred rhythmically. The sun was nearly gone, rolling away behind the cliffs.

She said, "That sounds like Martin. He's a mender of people."

"Yes." A silence. "He was very sensible, actually. He made me see, though not all at once, that you needed the space . . ."

She turned back to him quickly, desperately. "I am so sorry, Rory. Oh God, I was so cruel but I couldn't . . . I couldn't . . ."

"I know. Honestly. It's not that I—Look, I'm not asking for explanations. It's just . . . I'm explaining how it was."

His hair was ruddy in the sunset's glow, his eyes the same colour as Hermione's. Her lips trembled. "Yes. I see that. Sorry . . ."

"Well, he kept in touch." They were walking on again now. "There was a point when we both wondered if it would ever change. And then back in the summer he telephoned." A long pause. "I'm out of the Navy now."

"Out?"

He nodded. "I did an exchange with the Canadians for two years but after that it was never going to be the same." He shrugged. "There was never a day when I didn't think of you both."

"Oh, Rory . . ."

He was determined not to take advantage of her emotion.

"So I got a job with an engineering company in Newport. There's a lot of research and I really enjoy it. Martin phoned and said that you'd had a kind of breakdown but that you were . . . on your own again. He thought you might be able to . . ."

"Face reality?" He did not look at her and his expression was wary. She sighed. "That's what it was, you see. At the time, I couldn't face it. The only way I could manage to survive was to deny it. To pretend that it had happened to another person. By the time you got back from sea I was too far along the path of denial. You had to be denied too."

He said bleakly, "I've never forgiven myself for not being there."

She closed her eyes for a moment. "Look," she said. "Look . . . Oh hell . . ."

"Shall we go and have some tea somewhere?" They'd reached the ferry steps and he was smiling at her. She could hardly bear the love in his eyes. "Just so that we can talk. Nothing heavy."

She smiled back. So it had always been: the familiar advance and retreat until she'd been able to cross the final barrier. He'd never pushed, never forced, but had waited patiently to be accepted once more into her life: her life—and Hermione's.

"Come back to the cottage for tea," she said. "You can follow me. Although . . . I suppose you know where it is?"

He nodded, embarrassed. "Martin told me, you see. I'm sorry. It's rather horrid to be spied on, isn't it, but I didn't know what else to do. I didn't think that telephoning out of the blue was a very good idea."

"No, I think it would have been even more difficult." She tried to convey her gratitude for his making such an effort; for his sensitivity. "Come and have some tea, if you'd like to, but I'll have to go down to the end of the road so that I can turn."

"I'll follow you," he said—and turned away to his own car.

All the way back to East Prawle she drove automatically, quite unaware of her surroundings; shocked, excited, frightened. He followed her quickly and efficiently, parking behind her outside the cottage, waiting with hands in pockets whilst she unlocked the door.

"It's a bit of a mess," she said. "I'm decorating it, you see."

He wandered about, asking questions, whilst she boiled the kettle and spoke lightly about the joys of decorating, but both of them realised that the spell was broken. That unexpected meeting on the beach, on neutral ground, out of time, had moved them forward—or backward—unbelievably quickly. Suddenly, here in the small cottage, they were awkward, ill at ease, uncomfortable. Louise talked because she could not bear the silence, dismayed by her brittleness, helplessly groping towards that earlier extraordinary intimacy. Even Rory seemed incapable of narrowing the gap which now yawned between them.

"Are you on leave? On holiday?" She corrected herself, remembering that he was no longer in the Navy. It seemed unimaginable that he should have come outside, abandoned his career. "Where are you staying?"

"In Kingsbridge." He fiddled awkwardly with his spoon. "I've got a long weekend."

She raised her eyebrows. "A *very* long weekend. It's only Thursday afternoon."

He smiled. "My boss is a very nice man. He and his wife, Frances, have been terribly kind to me. It's a bit odd, you know, after the Service, but I'm getting used to it."

"Newport, you said?" They were like strangers again, talking at a dinner party where the hostess has insisted that everyone goes into another room for coffee, so that the intimacy of the dinner table is shattered, irretrievable. "Not too far from your family."

Rory's forebears had farmed in Herefordshire for generations. She'd always teased him that, with his ruddy colouring, he looked more like a farmer than a sailor.

"Not too far." He didn't look at her. "I've got a little cottage in the Wye Valley. It was nice to have somewhere to put our things."

"Things?" she repeated sharply.

"Mmm." Still he would not—or could not—look at her.

"We didn't have much, I agree, moving round in married quarters, but there were our books and lamps and a few ornaments. And Hermione's toys and books." The silence was weighty with memories: pain seemed to flicker between them. "I wanted to keep them. To remember . . . I like to have them around."

"I couldn't bear them," she said at last. "I couldn't cope with the agony of it."

"No, of course not." His voice was warm with understanding. "But maybe . . . Well, I kept them. But I could never find Percy. You know? That parrot she loved so much?"

Did he really imagine she could ever forget?

She said, "He . . . went with her. I . . . couldn't bear for her to go . . . alone."

Swallowing desperately, she stood up, picking up the teapot, refusing to look at him. "I think we need more tea." Her voice was high, almost social. Almost . . . He sat in silence whilst she went into the galley to boil the kettle, his head bowed.

"So you came out to Foxhole." She put the teapot on the table and sat down again, hardly daring to look at him, willing him away from the quicksands of the past.

"Yes." He took a deep breath, as if shrugging off some unbearably heavy weight. "Yes, I came out to Foxhole and drove about hoping to get a glimpse of you. I had a fortnight's holiday and I decided that I'd try to make contact if I could." He laughed. "You can't imagine how many times I lost my nerve."

"But where were you staying?"

"Well, that was so odd." He took his tea. "Stephen, that's my boss, Stephen Ankerton, well, his son runs an adventure school on Dartmoor. When I told him that I was going down he told me to have a word with Hugh and see if he could put me up. Hugh's a really nice guy, well, they both are, and I stayed with him for that fortnight, making odd forays out over the moor in the hope of seeing you. The first time *was* by accident, actually. I was walking by that reservoir, I've forgotten its name, just trying to sort things out in my mind, scraping up my courage, and then I saw you. Sitting by the water on a bench. It was the most incredible shock, actually, seeing you again after all this time."

"Yes," she murmured, recalling her own reaction earlier on the beach. "Yes, I can believe that. Hang on!" She sat up straight, staring at him. "I remember that evening. I was terrified. I saw you in the trees and I ran for my life."

"I know." He looked shame-faced and amused all at once. "I didn't mean to scare you but I didn't have the nerve to show myself. I was such a fool. One evening I actually parked the car up by the bridge and walked down the track. I'd decided that I was just going to hammer on the door and ask to speak to you. Martin had explained the lay-out to me and I was determined to make a move but I turned my ankle on a stone and suddenly all the lights went on and a wretched dog started barking its head off."

"I don't believe it." She was still staring at him, her face alight with unforced merriment. "Don't say you were our murderer?"

"I hope not!" He grimaced, pretending shock, ready to go along with this lighter mood. "Which murderer is this?"

"There were three murders in Devon in the space of six months or so, all women out on their own. And then a woman was attacked in Buckfastleigh. We all began to get a bit twitchy and Frummie refused to allow us to go out on our own. She took it terribly seriously, especially when I got back from Venford that evening all in a dither because I'd seen you hiding in the trees." She began to laugh. "Clearly you'd gone by the time the police arrived."

"I certainly had!" He was laughing, too. "I remember someone opening a window and shouting out, 'Who's there?' and the dog barking fit to bust. And then the chap came out of the other cottage. I was way back up the track by then. I'd already decided that I wasn't going to get much of a welcome."

"No," she said, sympathetically. "You probably wouldn't. Frummie would have probably laid you out cold with the poker before you'd opened your mouth."

"She sounds rather scary," he said lightly. "A pity you couldn't stay with her a bit longer."

"Martin told you?"

"He kept me in the picture."

The awkwardness was creeping back but the brittle coolness between them had melted with their laughter. They had not regained their former intimacy but a different, friendlier atmosphere had been achieved.

"It was probably right for me to go," Louise said. "I was too dependent on her. She was fantastic when I . . . had the breakdown. She seemed to truly understand how I felt. But it was time to move on. So." She shrugged, looking about her. "Here I am."

"And making a very good job of it." He smiled. "It's a nice little cottage. How did you find it?"

"It's a long story," she said cautiously.

"I've got a long weekend."

"Yes." Suddenly her crippling shyness was back. "Yes, you have."

"Well." He put his cup down, pushing his chair back a little. "I'm hoping you might have dinner with me. If you think it's a good idea? I could pick you up but you might prefer to drive yourself over." He was giving her space to manoeuvre; trying not to crowd her.

"Yes," she said. "That would be . . . good."

"Great." She could almost feel his relief. He explained where the hotel was, how to get to it, and stood up. "I'll let you get on, then," he said. "See you later."

He paused, as if wondering how he should take leave of her, and, when she made no move, simply smiled at her and went out, shutting the door gently behind him.

CHAPTER 39

On Saturday morning, as she drove back from Holne, Brigid overtook Alexander on Saddle Bridge. She stopped, leaning over to wind down the window, smiling at him.

"Had a good walk?"

"I've been along the O Brook." He bent to look in at her. "Such an odd name, isn't it? Are you offering me a lift home?"

"If you'd like one." She reached to open the door for him. "I never quite know when to offer lifts. Sometimes people need to be alone. Not that you've much further to go. Were you escaping, by any chance?"

Out of the corner of her eye she saw him smile as he settled himself in the passenger's seat.

"Like you I need moments of solitude."

"Lucky for you that none of your near neighbours are good walkers." She grinned. "Frummie and Margot certainly aren't, anyway. Is Gregory?"

"Good grief, no! A brisk walk to the Tube is all he can cope with, not by nature a countryman at all. He's managing very well under the circumstances but I'm very glad that the two girls are so sociable. He's loving it."

She smiled privately to herself at the idea of Frummie and Margot being referred to as "girls" and made a decision that had been fretting at the back of her mind for some while.

"I was wondering," she said, trying to sound casual, "whether you might like to meet Michael. And Sarah, of course. But especially Michael. I thought it might be rather . . . nice," she brought the word out rather awkwardly, "for you to get to know each other."

"Did you?"

"Well, he is your grandson." She tried not to sound defensive—or hurt. "They don't get down much but I'm sure we could arrange something."

"And what does Michael say about it?"

Brigid was silent for a moment. "What makes you think I've asked him?" she countered.

"Haven't you?"

Brigid swung the car off the road, on to the track, braked and then sat quite still, her hands on the wheel as if holding on to it for support, staring across to Bellever and Laughter Tor.

"Must I meet him?" Michael had asked, slightly irritated. "After all, it's a bit much, isn't it? Just thinking he can wander into our lives at this late date. Dad never got on with him, did he? Don't you think it would all be a bit difficult?"

Alexander was watching her. "I imagine he wasn't particularly enthusiastic," he suggested gently.

She looked at him. "Not terribly," she agreed honestly, "but it's such a shame."

"But why should you think that either of us would add anything to each other's lives simply because we are related?"

She wanted to cry, "But you've added to *mine!*" but was unable to speak the words aloud. She clung to the wheel, her mouth set stubbornly.

"You don't know that you wouldn't," she said at last.

He reached out and covered her thin, brown hand with his own. "We've been very lucky," he said, "but that doesn't necessarily mean that it would work for anyone else. This kind of blessing isn't interchangeable simply by will."

"But you'll meet them some time." She looked at him pleadingly. "I was hoping that you might come for Christmas."

"And do you think that would be wise?"

"Why not?"

Alexander took a deep, slow breath, looking out at the wild beauty of the autumn landscape. "Have you told Humphrey that it was my idea that he should take over the school?"

"No." She frowned at what she perceived to be a change of subject. "No, I haven't. Anyway you told me not to."

"And would you have told him? If I hadn't advised you not to?"

She looked away from him, staring ahead down the track to the roofs below. "No," she said, after a moment. "Probably not."

"Why not?"

"Because . . . he might not have been too pleased at . . ." She paused, searching for a word.

"At my interference," he finished for her. "He would have resented—and quite rightly—my appearing after all these years and giving him advice on what to do with his life."

"Something like that," she mumbled.

"And have you told him how much we like each other? How well we get along?"

She shook her head, watching the cloud shadows fleeing across Yar Tor.

"Is that because you think he would be hurt, knowing how he feels about me, that you have made me your friend?"

"Probably." She pushed her fine fair hair back, twisting it into a knot and then letting it fall on to her neck. "It seems . . ."

"Disloyal?"

She nodded again, her lips turned down as though she might cry, her eyes angry.

"It's so silly," she burst out. "It's such a waste!"

"But you are assuming that Humphrey and I would respond to each other as you and I have done. If that were the case, don't you think it would have happened years ago, when we lived together for nearly twenty years? Can you imagine how you might begin bringing us together?"

Brigid sat silently, her long legs drawn up, her shoulders hunched. It was true that she'd tried to mentally compose a script for just this occasion but each time she'd come up against the wall of Humphrey's feelings: the irritation— "How long have you known him?" sarcastically—and the hurt—"But surely you remember how he treated Mother and me?" plaintively—and had given it up. It was especially difficult, now that she needed to keep their own relationship on an even keel. Humphrey had been so generous about her secret dealings with Jenny that it would be unthinkable to be in any way disloyal to him again.

"Do you really think it would work," he asked, "with Humphrey just home after six months away, wanting you to himself, and with all the excitement and problems of his new career to be discussed? Do you think that's the moment to effect a reconciliation? Try to imagine it with the real protagonists in action, not just as a theoretical consummation devoutly to be wished. Willing something isn't enough. It might not even be right."

"But you will meet him, won't you?" she asked miserably. "And the boys? Sometime, even if not at Christmas? I agree that Christmas might not be the right timing with Humphrey just back, although you'd feel it should be. It's a family time, after all."

"You're being sentimental," he said gently. "There is no reason why Humphrey should like me better on the twenty-fifth of December than on any other day of the year."

"You're such a cynic," she said wearily.

"So you keep telling me," he said. "I prefer the word 'realist.'"

"But you make it sound as if people never grow or change. Frummie and I are getting on better than we ever have before. Why shouldn't you and Humphrey?"

"There needs to be desire on both parts. We both have to want it enough to work at it; to truly want to forgive and love each other."

"And don't you want that?" She stared at him, almost accusingly.

He smiled sadly. "It sounds so easy, doesn't it? We both might think we do but, even if it were true, that doesn't mean that the transformation would be instantaneous. Remember that the pain and resentment is on Humphrey's side, not mine. He has not injured me."

"But you haven't injured him. Not really. You simply encouraged him to be independent."

"That is how I saw it at the time. It is not how he sees it. There are years of received teaching, of very natural resentment, to work through. You have been generous enough to try to understand it from my point of view and to forgive me but *you* are not the injured party."

"But don't you mind that he's misunderstanding you?" she cried. "He's your son!"

He sighed. "I think you place too much importance on the blood tie," he said. "Any man might be my biological son. Any man might be Humphrey's biological father. The accident of the night doesn't guarantee love or affection or loyalty. You've seen that for yourself. The vital thing is that Humphrey stops resenting me. He'll probably be able to do that now."

"Why? Why now?" She was baffled, angry, frustrated.

"Because he has helped me," he answered. "He has sheltered me, offered me sanctuary when I was in need, and so, deep down, has forgiven me. That is so good, so important. Much more important than outward shows of family solidarity for form's sake. It's possible that all his resentment will drain away, diluted and rendered harmless by this single tremendous act of generosity and kindness. Don't let's endanger it by trying to play Happy Families."

Brigid shook her head, still confused but with some intuitive sense that he was right.

"Later, then," she said, refusing to give up entirely for, after all, how could she bear to lose him now? "We'll think about it later when everything has calmed down."

"Forgive me, Brigid dear," he said quietly.

She turned to look at him. "There's nothing to forgive you for," she said. "It's just . . . I love you."

She looked surprised at herself, at the words which had come so naturally, and he leaned forward to kiss her lightly on the cheek.

"And I you," he answered. "Thank you."

She saw that there were tears in his eyes so she started the engine, lest he should feel embarrassed, and drove gently down the track to Foxhole.

"I THINK it must be a nursing home," said Margot. "I asked Gregory but he's almost as much an oyster as Alexander. He agrees with me, though, that we can't quite see Alexander all amongst the fleshpots. There's something just the *least* bit austere about him, isn't there? He seems so disciplined and he doesn't drink too much. He's terrific fun, though. A very nice nursing home, we thought—the sort of place where he's well looked after but retains his independence. You know the kind of thing? He's going to stay with Gregory in London when he leaves here, apparently. By the way, do you know where he goes when he disappears? Two or three times a week he drives off. Always about the same time too: half-past eleven. Odd, isn't it? Gregory told me that he says he's going to do some shopping."

"That's probably because he's going to do some shopping," said Frummie drily, irritated by the fact that she'd never noticed Alexander's habits for herself. "Why not?"

"But don't you think it's peculiar that he always goes at the same time?" persisted Margot. She patted her hair, which seemed to grow more aggressively chestnut-coloured each week, and frowned thoughtfully. "I told Gregory that he should go along for the ride but he seemed quite shocked at the suggestion. The trouble with men is that they have no natural curiosity."

"They leave that to us, dear." Frummie swallowed her pride and asked for information. "Talking of curiosity, what did you find out about Gregory? I saw you giving him the third degree when Alexander and I were making the coffee last night. Does he live alone?"

"Quite alone. His wife died four or five years ago, poor

soul. Two daughters but he doesn't see too much of them. They live in the country—Gloucestershire and Yorkshire. They sound rather bound up in their own lives, which can be a blessing, after all, though I'm sure they're quite delightful. He's got a dear little house in Fulham—but I told you that, didn't I?—and quite a social life. Well, I suppose he would have. They've lived there for twenty years or so. He does make me laugh." She looked slyly at her dear old chum. "I'm very glad you decided which of them we should pair off with, Fred. Gregory and I suit very well. Alexander's a bit too direct for my taste."

"He's a very unusual man," said Frummie, implying that one needed to be rather special to appreciate him and that she'd made her decision on these grounds. "He's not shallow."

"Well, if being devious is necessary to appreciate his finer qualities, then you've certainly got what it takes," observed Margot waspishly. "I'm a simple soul, myself."

"Well, we all know that, dear," agreed Frummie brightly. "And so you're planning to move to Fulham, then?"

"Well." Margot drew in her chin, bridling a little at such a blunt attack. "Not immediately, of course. It's a very big step to take."

"It certainly is," agreed Frummie readily, "but you seem to be getting on so well." She paused, looking solicitous, ready to be sympathetic. "Or isn't he ready for another commitment?"

"Oh, I think he is," said Margot quickly. "Did he say anything to you yesterday in Dartmouth? We rather got separated up, didn't we? I just wondered if . . . you know . . . he mentioned me . . . or anything?"

"I got the impression that he was rather lonely"—"I've felt that too," interjected Margot quickly—"and that he's a man," Frummie smiled reminiscently, as if at some private joke, "who appreciates female company."

Margot frowned, not quite liking such an ambiguous observation. "He has very good manners," she said sharply. "And he's very charming. Of course, some women always misunderstand the well-bred man's social politeness as something more personal. So stupid."

"Oh, I do agree," said Frummie at once. "I think there's something so insecure about that kind of thing. Nothing irritates me more than the sort of woman who imagines a man's in love with her when he's simply being good-mannered."

"Quite," said Margot, a little uncertainly. "Well, then. So he didn't say anything . . . particular."

"He's *very* fond of you," said Frummie. "That's terribly clear." She sounded just the least bit wistful.

Margot brightened visibly; she almost smirked. "Well, that's nice." She appeared, briefly, to be lost for words.

"Any of that delicious whisky left?" asked Frummie casually. "That malt which darling Harry sent? I think we need a drink, don't we?" She raised her eyebrows naughtily, encouragingly. "A little *celebration* you could say?"

"I think we do." Looking gratified, Margot hurried away.

Frummie sighed deeply, licking her lips in absent anticipation, reflecting on the conversation, her mind busy.

CHAPTER 40

Louise finished washing down the walls of the boxroom, gathered up the cloths and the bowl of dirty water and made her way carefully down the narrow twisting stairs. Her back and arms ached and she was looking forward to stripping off her grubby working clothes and luxuriating in a hot shower. She tipped the water carefully away, rinsed and wrung out the cloths and stood for a moment, looking through to the conservatory, watching the sun on the wall. Tiny ferns grew in the crevices, with ivy-leaved toadflax and stonecrop clinging to cracks in the crumbling stone.

"In Devon," Rory had said, "even the walls burst into flower."

She could still hardly believe that he'd been here with her. The combination of familiarity and the unknown was disturbing. For whole periods at a time they'd found themselves plunged back into intimacy, only to be suddenly shocked forwards into the present: cautious again, fearful and withdrawn. Dinner at the hotel had been an extraordinary affair.

"Do you still like duck?" he'd asked easily, casually, as he considered the menu. "It's very good here, so I'm told."

"Yes," she'd said, deeply affected by this tiny evidence of remembrance. "Yes, I do. Sounds great."

She'd watched him whilst holding her own menu up before her, studying him, looking for clues of suffering. He'd hardly changed. His fair hair was as thick as ever, rather dry and unruly. "You've been thatched," she used to tease him. "Your straw needs hedging." His face was more finely drawn, however, and she didn't remember the two lines that were now lightly etched from nose to the mouth which curled slightly, ready to smile.

She thought: Well, he's thirty-seven. And I'm thirty-three.

She was gripped by a sudden aching grief for the three years they'd lost, for the waste of it all, and realised that he was now watching her, a tiny frown between his fair, feathery brows. She'd smiled automatically, wondering if he'd spoken, feeling confused and frightened.

"Duck, then," he'd said cheerfully. "I'll have it too. So tell me again. Frummie is Brigid's mother? And who is Alexander? Sounds like a commune."

She'd grasped this lifeline gratefully, explaining the inhabitants of Foxhole, telling him about Jemima and MagnifiCat. They'd laughed together over his ignominious departure once Frummie had set up the hue and cry until it nearly— very nearly—began to take on the aspect of some holiday she'd been taking whilst he was at sea. She'd found that she was relating her experiences at Foxhole as some amusing story—except that there were gaps: big gaps, torn and painful gaps, where Hermione belonged and where they could not yet go. He'd helped her along, offering her gentle, unthreatening questions which might be laid like planks across the blanks in her narrative, over which she could step, oh, so carefully, on to the firmer ground beyond.

The food, when it came, had proved a welcome distraction, and they were able to change direction, talking instead of his job and his colleagues. He was clearly happy with his work, and his little cottage sounded charming.

"End of terrace," he'd said, almost diffidently, as if he were fearful that he might appear to be presenting it as some kind of inducement. "It's in a very small village but it's the last house and it's backed by a wood. There are some wonderful walks but not much garden."

"Sounds nice," she'd said, trying to sound enthusiastic but not eager.

"You must come and see it," he'd said—and she'd been instantly plunged back into anxiety.

How would it be managed? Could they stay together in the same house, still married, yet strangers?

She'd mumbled something, reaching for her glass and making a comment about the wine. He'd made no attempt to delay her going after dinner so she'd driven away, longing to stay with him but strangely happy.

Now, Louise turned away from the sink, went back upstairs, pulled off her clothes and let the feeling of strain and grubbiness wash away with the hot water. Presently, clean, dressed in jeans and a corduroy, indigo-coloured overshirt, she tied a long silk scarf around her neck and brushed her dark curls into a thick bundle, secured by a scrunchie. As she stood before the age-spotted glass, looking critically at her reflection, she heard his car and watched from the window as he stood looking away from her over the green. The resemblance to Hermione in the turn of his head wrenched at her heart and twisted in her gut. Quickly she ran lightly down the stairs, snatched up her jacket and went out to him, picking up her walking boots where they lay in the small porch. Somehow, it was easier to maintain normality out of doors.

He smiled at her with such a natural, familiar warmth that her terrors slithered away like snakes, vanishing silently down holes and under stones, and leaving her free and light.

"I've brought my boots," she said, "just in case we want to walk."

"Mine are in the back," he said, taking them from her. "I'm relying on you as a navigator. Have you decided where we're going?"

"Not too far," she said, sliding into the car. "Not with you having to drive back to Wales this evening."

He climbed in beside her. "Don't worry about that. It's barely a two-hour drive. We have the afternoon before us."

She began to laugh and he looked at her, delighted at her happiness, watching her with love.

"Honestly," she said, "you won't believe this but I was going to say, 'Have you ever been to Dartmouth?' completely forgetting that you were at the college for three years. How stupid can you get?"

"It's something I try to forget too," he said drily. "And, in answer to your unspoken question, yes, I have, but I'm very happy to revisit it if that's what you'd like."

"You could show me all your old haunts," she suggested mischievously. "All those pubs."

"And all those barmaids," he added, sighing regretfully.

"No chatting up barmaids," she said firmly. "I draw the line at that."

He bent forward and kissed her quickly, drawing back before she could react. "You're no fun any more," he said sadly. "OK, no barmaids."

As they drove off, she could still feel the touch of his lips, warm and firm upon her own. Happiness grew inside her so that there seemed no room to contain it and its warmth must spread into a joy which loosened her muscles and curved her lips upward. She settled in her seat with a contentment she'd imagined had abandoned her for ever.

JEMIMA LOCKED the cottage door behind her and stood for a moment, enjoying the sunshine, waiting for the couple—who were hoping to rent the cottage through the winter—to get into their car and drive away. The sense of satisfaction which she experienced with a successful letting was undermined by a now constant anxiety. She waved cheerfully to the young woman, as her partner turned the car, knowing very well that they'd hoped to spend some considerable time poking round and enjoying the new-found pleasure of ownership. However, until various forms had been filled in and agreements signed, she also knew that the owner would not approve of her surrendering the key. This elderly lady was a very strict landlord and the couple would need to have very good references. Jemima shook her head sympathetically. She'd liked the two young people and wished them every success. Meanwhile, she suspected that once she was out of sight, they'd creep back and wander round the tiny garden, peering in the windows and making plans.

Climbing into her own car, Jemima sighed almost enviously. She wished she felt so excited about the future. She'd passed the weekend alone—well, that was fair enough, he'd been away on some kind of sales conference—but their telephone calls had been frustratingly short and unsatisfying. At least He'd be with her on Friday; he'd been quite confident about that. With mixed feelings Jemima laid her briefcase on the passenger seat, wedging her mobile behind it. However much she was longing to be with him again some decisions would certainly need to be taken.

As she drove out of the village she found that she was remembering, with a certain envy, the happy-go-lucky creature she'd once been: looking back with a kind of disbelief at the Jemima who'd retained that private detachment which, like an extra skin, had protected her from hurt. Now, with it stripped from her, she felt vulnerable, tender, soft. She was kept almost permanently on edge, the ease and warmth of giving and receiving unconditional love withheld. How simple it had been before this plunge into love; how undemanding. She laughed bitterly when she recalled her complacent, oft-used observation that she was mistress material. Now she knew what it was like to ache with a loneliness which only the presence of the beloved could assuage; to know the trickle of fear which accompanied self-doubt and jealousy. She'd learned that she had no desire to play mental games, or to engage in the techniques which kept one of the players always a step ahead, and she was weary with cautioning herself, reminding herself that he was only just out of a long-term relationship and that he needed time.

On top of all this was the shock of losing her home. Of course, it had always been a real possibility that she'd have to leave. She'd been told quite fairly at the beginning that the flat might be needed for the staff of the RNLI, that it was by no means to be a long let, yet, in her usual casual way, she'd allowed herself to live only for the moment, to believe that it was her home. None of this would matter, of course, if only they could be together. Gladly would she sacrifice the benefits, the comfort, the view, to be with him; give them up voluntarily in exchange for his permanent presence.

"I'm really sorry," she'd said earlier in the week when he'd phoned whilst working late at the office. "About the flat, I mean."

"I can see it'll be really tough for you," he'd said, "leaving that view."

"You looked a bit gobsmacked," she'd said tentatively, hoping for a more definite reaction. "Disappointed."

"Oh, well, of course it was a shock but don't pay any attention to that. Everything's a bit on top of me at the moment. My whole life's been turned upside down in the last few months."

Instantly she'd felt remorseful. He'd lost his girlfriend and was trying to build a new relationship, to relocate—and now there wasn't to be even the continuity of the flat.

"I know it has," she'd answered sympathetically. "That's what I'm saying, really. This is just another complication that you don't need."

"We'll manage," he'd said, quite positively, and she'd felt the quick swing from doubt to happiness.

"Of course we will," she'd agreed. "It might even be fun, looking for our own place."

There had been voices in the background and she was conscious of his attention switched away from her.

"Got to go," he'd said, his voice sounding flat, preoccupied, as if he were now utterly focused on something else. "Problems. See you soon."

The minute she'd been cut off from him her fears had returned but now, as she drove carefully through the narrow lanes, her natural optimism edged her thoughts back towards the more hopeful prospect of the weekend. Her spirits began to rise; she relaxed a little. As she pushed a tape into the deck and began to sing, the telephone rang. She dived into a field gateway, tucking the car in as close as she could, and picked up her mobile.

"Oh, hi!" Her voice rang with delight; she simply couldn't hide her pleasure. "How are you?"

"Fine. I'm . . . fine. Well . . . I'm OK."

"What's the problem?" She switched off the engine and the tape, settling herself, face anxious. "You sound the least bit muted."

"Yes. The truth of it is . . ." he paused. "Hell, I don't quite know how to tell you this . . ."

"You can't get down this weekend." She said it for him, not only to help him, not only in a desperate attempt to boost her own confidence by sounding quite cheerful about it, but—worse—as an involuntary gesture to ward off something more terrible; something she couldn't bear to hear.

"No, it's not just that."

OK. So here it was. She shook back her hair, biting her lips. "What is it then?"

"The truth is . . . Oh, shit, there's just no easy way to say this." A pause the length of a breath, then quickly, "I'm getting back with Annabel."

A tiny bird was hopping in the hedge; it darted quickly from twig to twig with a secretive agility. Jemima watched it, concentrating on it, whilst anguish, cold as death, settled quietly on her heart.

"Are you there?" He sounded anxious. "Look, I'm really gutted about this. It's the last thing I'd have imagined could happen. Look." He drew in breath and tried again. "I really thought we could make it together. I did, Jemima. I wasn't just stringing you along. Honestly. It's just that when I saw her again . . . Well, she'd made a terrible mistake, she admitted that, and she said she wanted to come back. I tried to fight it, to give myself some space to think about it, reminded myself about all that I'd be losing with you, which wasn't easy, I can tell you. And then . . . well, she came over last evening and we talked things through. The fact is that I think I should give it another try. Five years is a long time to tear up and throw down the pan . . ."

The bird had hopped out on to the gate, searching for insects. With swiftly stabbing beak it probed into the soft, splintering wood, absorbed, too busy with survival to notice her.

". . . So I agreed to give it another try. She's really upset and I feel that it's only fair after all that we had together . . . Oh *God*, I feel a right shit!"

There was a tinge of melodrama in the sudden outburst; even self-pity. He wanted her to let him off; to make it all right for him. She stirred, summoning courage, and the bird, startled by the sudden movement, flew off, scolding crossly.

"Well . . ." She struggled to keep her voice calm. "Not much I can say to all that, is there?"

"I'm truly sorry, Jemima. You've been so special, you really have. Honestly, I feel an utter bastard."

She wanted to scream at him, "Good! I'm glad! I hope the bitch lets you down again!" but she knew that such a minor relief would be swallowed up in this cold, creeping misery which was reaching out softly, inexorably from her heart and engulfing her whole self. What was the point in cheap victories?

"Thanks for telling me." She tried to infuse some life into the words but the cold weightiness was too much for her; it pressed in, making her voice dull and heavy. "It can't be easy, I can see that. Look, I've got to go. I'm in a very narrow lane and there's a tractor coming."

"Oh, God! This is awful . . ."

"Isn't it," she agreed, "but I really must move the car. We can talk some other time, perhaps."

"God, yes!" He was generous in his relief. "We can stay friends, can't we? I'll want to know where you go and what happens and stuff. I told Annabel how terrific you are and how you saved my life . . ."

"Got to go," she said abruptly, and pressed the off button. She started the engine, letting it idle for a moment whilst she stared blankly ahead. She had a foolish, childish need to be at home with MagnifiCat; to hold him tightly and to feel the comfort of his warmth. Perhaps it might bring her some relief; it might even thaw the icy chill which caused this queer shivering. With a nervousness which was utterly uncharacteristic, she pulled cautiously out into the lane and headed towards Salcombe, driving slowly with the utmost care.

CHAPTER 41

"Thea," said Louise, "I've got a problem. I need some advice."

"How are you?" asked Thea warmly. "How are you liking your cottage? When are you coming to see us? Hermione's been asking after you."

"Has she?" Louise's face relaxed into a smile. "I'd love to come. Or perhaps you could come over here? Thank you for your card. I'm sorry not to have been in touch but things have got a bit out of hand."

"Too much painting," said Thea comfortably. "It's exhausting, isn't it? And then you just need to crash out and stare mindlessly at nothing. Don't worry about it."

"It's not just that." Louise sounded nervous. "Something utterly amazing has happened." She hesitated, as though she were still adjusting to this amazing happening, not able to find the words too easily. "Rory's turned up."

A short silence.

"Goodness!" Thea was clearly startled. "And is that . . . good?"

"It's very good." Louise's voice bubbled up into uncontrollable happiness. "Oh, Thea! I can hardly believe it. It was the most tremendous shock to see him, just standing there. He wants us to get back together. Oh, he hasn't actually said so in so many words but it's clear enough. He's out of the Navy and working for an engineering company in Wales. He's coming down again at the weekend. It's just so . . . peculiar.

Sometimes it's as if we never parted and at others it's so scary. Everything comes back with a rush and I feel paralysed with terror and all the old horror. We can't talk properly yet about . . . about Hermione. Well, he's better at it than I am but it's still so raw and then I have these moments of thinking it could never work because it'll always be between us."

There was a longer silence. The torrent of words seemed to hum and resonate, echoing on the wire between them.

"Right," said Thea cautiously. "But how on earth did he find you?"

"Can you believe it? Martin has been in touch with him all this time. When we separated, Martin and I, he wrote to Rory."

"That's extraordinary."

"Isn't it? I've spoken to Martin who was . . . well, rather sheepish about it. He said it was all such an appalling tragedy that we were bound to do drastic things we might regret and that he felt so sorry for Rory. He always thought that once I'd recovered I'd probably want to go back to Rory and that he was simply giving me space to heal whilst holding on to Rory at a distance. Rory seems to accept that, and he felt that at least he was keeping in touch with me, indirectly. He says that his exchange with the Canadian Navy was his own way of going right away so that he could come to terms with things. Now he's ready to try again."

"And how do you feel?"

"It's like I said: I want to but there's still so much baggage. I'm afraid I might not be able to make it work."

"But isn't it worth a try?"

"I feel so badly about hurting him, you see—just walking away like that, not caring about how he was feeling. Supposing I'm not as . . . on top of it as I think I am?" There was panic in her voice. "I don't want to hurt him again."

"But why should you hurt him?" Thea was calm. "You've done all the resentment bit long ago. You said so. All that bit about him being at sea—you've got that right out of your system now, haven't you?"

"Yes, I have. Long ago." Louise sighed. "He blames

himself. He says, 'I should have been there,' and I'm saying, 'How could you have been? It was your job.' I hate seeing him look so bleak."

"Well, isn't that a start? You've had three years of comfort and care from Martin whilst Rory worked out his own pain. Now, you can comfort him. You can go on together. It sounds the most fantastic opportunity for a second chance."

"Do you really think so?"

"Of course I think so." Louise could hear that Thea was smiling. "The timing is perfect. All things working together for good. You couldn't possibly refuse it."

Louise heaved a huge sigh. "I do want to," she said, "I really do, but those moments of terror really shake me."

"That's perfectly reasonable. Tell him so. I expect he's having them too, but just not showing them. How brave of him to be prepared to try again. He sounds such a nice man."

"He is. I'd like you to meet him. The thing is . . . This sounds really silly. I want to tell Brigid and Frummie but I don't know which one to phone first." She chuckled a little. "I know that sounds truly bizarre but they live so close and I don't want either of them to feel hurt. They've both been so wonderfully kind. Am I being oversensitive?"

"No," said Thea slowly, who knew all about the relationship between Brigid and her mother. "I can see that there might be . . . difficulties. Frummie might crow if she knows first or she might feel hurt if Brigid tells her, given that you recuperated with her—with Frummie, I mean. Your friendship has expanded to include both of them."

"Exactly!" Louise sounded relieved. "Thank God! I thought that it was me. Of course, I could phone one after the other terribly quickly but one might be out or engaged."

Thea began to laugh. "The mind boggles," she said. "Hang on. What about you telephoning to say that you want to see them together and then tell them both at once? If you feel you can manage it face to face."

"Yes," said Louise thoughtfully, turning the suggestion over carefully in her mind. "Yes, I'm sure I can." She was positive now. "That's brilliant. I'll do that. Thanks, Thea.

Sorry to burden you with it. It's just that I got completely bogged down with it."

"And then we'll all meet him," said Thea cheerfully. "One at a time, would you say? Or in groups? You could sell tickets. I can't wait."

Louise began to laugh. "Don't even talk about it. Look, I'm really grateful."

"It's not a problem. Let me know how it goes and don't forget we'd love to see you."

"Thanks," said Louise gratefully. "I promise I'll be over soon. Give Hermione a hug for me."

When she replaced the receiver she felt as if Thea had removed all the terror for her. Odd how, even at that first meeting, Thea had seemed so strong, stretching out a hand to her, holding on to her, whilst the world reeled about them. Some of the serenity which defined Thea rubbed off on those whom she touched, even if only briefly. Feeling confident now, Louise prepared to telephone Brigid but, even as she dialled, she found herself thinking about Jemima. Her telephone had been on answerphone for nearly two days and, although Louise had left messages, Jemima had not returned her calls. She was just deciding that if she didn't hear from her by the end of the day she'd drive round tomorrow to see if she could find her, when Brigid's cool voice broke into her thoughts and put everything else out of her mind.

BRIGID STOOD in the courtyard watching the doves as they swung in a feathery cloud against the sky. The colour of their wings seemed to change as they passed above her head: pure white against the brilliant blue; grey against the creamy cumulus; startlingly white again against a patch of thunderous black. They swooped in perfect accord, as if responding to some instinctive, in-built choreography, and she was moved to joy at their flight. The swallows had gone; grouping together for days before the final migration, sitting in rows along the barn roof, until one morning they'd vanished away, leaving the empty nests as a promise against their return next spring.

As she watched the doves Brigid remembered how she'd

stood here, on the day of Louise's arrival five months before, thinking about Jemima. Then, there had been a disappointed frustration in the knowledge that she and her sister were still estranged; now, she was able to feel a quiet pleasure in the anticipation of a growing friendship: a stepping free from the old disabling resentment. Hard though it had been she'd tried to follow Alexander's advice—no, not advice. Alexander wasn't the kind of man to give advice—to follow, then, his suggestion that she should lay down her weapons; that she should expose her weaknesses. How had he put it? *"We serve others as much by our weaknesses as by our strengths."* It was a new concept and a rather startling one. She'd always been at pains to appear at her best—strong, capable, sensible—with her mother and her sister. Now, it seemed that not only was it not necessary but that the reverse had much to commend it. And it had worked! It hadn't been easy, telling Jemima her secret; exposing her foolishness and showing that her marriage was not quite the faultless, perfect union that she knew Jemima had imagined it to be. More than that, she had known that she might lose the sweetness she derived from knowing that Jemima envied her. Believing Jemima to be their mother's favourite there had been satisfaction in being able to parade her happy marriage, lovely children and now a grandchild as her possessions. Now she had shown that there were flaws, secrets, fears—and Jemima had met these disclosures with a warmth and generosity which gave no indication of any diminishing of affection. It had certainly brought them closer.

When she'd telephoned the evening before Jemima had sounded fatigued, depressed and anxious and Brigid had discovered that there was no longer any desire on her own part to be impatient, to urge her sister to pull herself together or attempt to sort out her problems. In fact, she hadn't asked any questions as she usually did in a kind of "Oh, what on earth's the matter *now*" kind of way. She'd merely played it by ear, sympathetic, friendly, until Jemima had asked if she might come over to Foxhole to see her.

"Of course," Brigid had answered at once. "Lovely. When?" and when Jemima had said "Would tomorrow be

OK?" Brigid had hidden her surprise—and anxiety—and had agreed at once.

"Just us?" she'd asked tentatively, not quite knowing what was in Jemima's mind. "Or would you like Mummie to come? And Margot?" And when she'd answered with horror, "Good grief, no!" Brigid had felt a glow of satisfaction. She feared that it might be an unworthy glow, to be preferred by Jemima above their mother; nevertheless it had been a source of private joy. It indicated the growing trust between them and Brigid was seized with delight at this prospect and with a corresponding fear that she might not be able to live up to any expectations Jemima might have of a confidante. "Come just before lunch," she'd suggested. "I think the mob are going to Exeter so with luck they'll have set off before you arrive."

Now, as she stooped to stroke Blot, she could hear the sounds of activity issuing from the cottages and prayed that they'd hurry up. Margot was now telling Frummie how much colder it was than they'd imagined and, beneath the ensuing duet between the two women, she could hear the lower bass line as Alexander and Gregory strolled out to the car. She decided to slip away indoors, lying low until they'd gone, but, even as she turned, she heard the sound of an engine and saw Jemima's car coming slowly down the track. Cursing beneath her breath, she saw Frummie glance round and begin to wave enthusiastically whilst the other three watched with various expressions of welcome and surprise.

"Shit!" muttered Brigid. "Shit! Shit! Shit!"

Jemima parked the car and climbed out. She looked tired, pale and oddly defenceless and Brigid was consumed with an entirely unexpected flame of protectiveness, just as she might have felt for her own boys. She went forward quickly as Jemima almost visibly braced herself for the greetings which assailed her.

"Darling!" cried Frummie, almost vexed. "Why didn't you tell me you were coming? How maddening. We're just going off to Exeter."

Jemima smiled at Margot and at Alexander and allowed herself to be introduced to Gregory, who beamed at her appreciatively and shook her hand. Behind their heads, Brigid raised her fists and shook them in a gesture of despair and Jemima's lips curved in a spontaneous smile of understanding.

"I've come to have lunch with Brigid," she answered. "I was sure you'd be off jollying, that's why I didn't tell you."

"Brigid didn't tell us either," said Frummie, with a sharp glance at her elder daughter, and—as was always the case— Brigid was certain that her mother knew all her thoughts, worthy and unworthy, and that she was secretly amused by them. "You could come with us. Wouldn't that be rather nice? Make it a real party."

"We could," agreed Brigid calmly, strolling forward, "but we'd have to take two cars." She winked quickly at Jemima and caught Alexander's eye pleadingly.

"Good idea," he said smoothly, rising immediately to the occasion. "In which case I hope Jemima will travel with me and Gregory." He made her a little bow, smiling at her, whilst Gregory made noises indicating his delight at such a prospect. "I've hardly had the chance to get to know her yet."

"On the other hand," said Frummie, with superb poise, "it's *rather* unkind to ruin Brigid's plans. I expect you've been busy all morning cooking something delicious, haven't you, darling?"

"Well . . ." Brigid hesitated, as though she were seriously weighing up the possibilities of going or staying.

"Don't let us oldies interfere," said Margot playfully, patting Jemima's arm. "You two girls have your own little party. Maybe you'll still be here when we get back."

"Probably," said Jemima, brightening. "Very likely."

"Well, then," said Frummie cheerfully, "we'd best be pushing on or we won't get any lunch. See you later, girls. Alexander's turn to drive, I think. Yes? I'll go in front with him so as to navigate."

"THAT WAS terrible," said Jemima, as she followed Brigid into the kitchen, Blot wagging at her heels. "I could really see us being whisked off to Exeter."

"I thought they'd be gone," said Brigid, "They're often away by coffee-time."

"I couldn't have raised my game today." Jemima sat down at the table. "I am definitely not on my best form."

Brigid looked at her. Jemima was dressed all in black: a soft angora jersey with a roll-neck over an ankle-length narrow, tweedy skirt. She wore leather boots and a long, black fleece waistcoat; her hair, bright and shining, fell loose over her shoulders. Although the unrelieved black accentuated her pallor, she looked very striking and Brigid was reminded of a younger Jemima who had smiled with such sweet friendliness at her father's funeral twenty-two years before.

"You look tired," she said gently. "Would you like a drink?"

Jemima sighed and her shoulders drooped. She seemed too weary to make even such a simple decision.

"I don't know," she said. "I've had a permanent headache for the last few days and alcohol seems to make it worse. Pathetic, isn't it?"

"I can't see why. Alcohol isn't a universal placebo. Have some elderflower cordial with some ice."

"Oh, yes." Jemima sat up. "That sounds nice." She bent to pat Blot who sat at her feet, tail wagging. "Aren't animals nice?" she asked irrelevantly. "Much nicer than most people."

"Now that," said Brigid, filling a glass with water, "sounds like someone who has been shat on from a great height. Who's been horrid to you?"

Jemima laughed briefly and fell silent. She watched Brigid add the ice and then took the glass. "Thanks," she said—and sipped a little. "Delicious. To answer your question, several people."

Brigid filled her own glass, took a quick look into the oven and sat down opposite. "Really?" She checked the question which rose to her lips and drank a little of her wine, praying for wisdom. She simply mustn't begin the third degree or show any of that arrogance which assumed that she had some God-given right to deal with other people's problems. She said, "I always thought that Sartre had the right of it when he said 'Hell is other people,' or something like that."

Jemima stared into her cordial. "I've been asked to leave the flat," she said.

"You're kidding?" Brigid was shocked. "But why?"

Jemima shrugged. "Well, it was always on the cards. It was made quite clear when I took it on that they might need it for themselves as a rest area for staff. It's perfectly reasonable but I'd just grown rather to love it."

"I'm not surprised. It's in a beautiful position. Oh, I am *so* sorry. Have you any idea where you might go?"

Jemima shook her head miserably. "Not yet. They're being very kind about it but I've got to look about. All my own places are short winter lets or holiday lets so I've got to start making a real effort. It's going to be a very difficult act to follow." She smiled wanly. "You always said I should have put the money towards a little place of my own and now, you see, you were right."

Brigid felt no particular gratification at this observation, only a very real sympathy. She also had the feeling that there was something more which she had not yet been told.

"I think it's wretched for you," she said. "Look, you can always come here, you know. Don't jump into something that's not right. I know this is out of your patch but at this time of the year that's not so critical."

"That's really kind." Jemima glanced at her gratefully and Brigid saw that there were tears in her eyes. "Thanks." She made an attempt at a chuckle. "It'll be a family commune soon, if you're not careful."

"I'll expect we'll manage. Where do you think you'd like to be?"

"I don't really know."

She seemed so apathetic that Brigid was genuinely worried. Jemima was usually so light-hearted, so optimistic: this weary indifference was most unlike her. Brigid choked down the desire to ask if she had run out of money and sat in silence for a moment, reviewing and rejecting platitudes.

"Give yourself time to think about it," she said at last. "There's always room here. Don't feel pressured."

She could see that Jemima did not trust herself to speak

and cast about for some lighter topic which might give her sister time to come to the point.

"Hungry?" she asked casually. "We could eat if you like?"

Jemima wrinkled her nose. "I'm not terribly hungry," she said apologetically. "I seem to have lost my appetite."

"That sounds worrying." Brigid was determined not to panic but she was already wondering if Jemima was ill; whether she was about to tell her that she had some terrible disease. "Not like you at all."

She took up her glass and drank determinedly, her hand shaking a little.

"I've been dumped," Jemima said suddenly, almost casually. "Really dumped. Not my usual stuff. It was terribly important. I thought we were going to be together and now it seems we're not."

Brigid realised that she was gaping and pulled herself together.

"Oh God, I'm really sorry. How bloody! I had no idea. Who . . .?" She stopped herself. "I didn't know there was anyone special."

"He's been around for most of the summer. He had a very long holiday at one of my cottages and then he came down most weekends. He'd just split up from his girlfriend and we got on really, really well." She paused, biting her lip. "He was going to relocate. We were making plans." Her chin shook and Brigid longed to get up and go to her. "I love him," she muttered. "I really love him and I don't know how to manage now it's over."

She set down her glass and burst into stormy tears, folding her arms on the table and burying her face in them. Brigid pushed back her chair and went round the table to her.

"Poor, poor Puddle-duck." For the first time in their lives she used the name quite genuinely as an affectionate nickname, kneeling beside her sister as she wept, an arm about her shoulders, her cheek against Jemima's hair, waiting for the storm to pass.

CHAPTER 42

"We thought you might be missing Gregory," said Frummie, "so I've popped over to see if you'd like to come for supper. Don't be polite. If you're enjoying the peace and quiet only say the word."

Alexander smiled. "I wouldn't dream of refusing such a generous offer," he said. "Thank you."

"And you needn't think," said Frummie, somewhat waspishly, "that it's because we're having withdrawal symptoms. Margot and I have a great deal to say to each other."

He looked shocked. "Such a thought would never occur to me," he protested. "I have no doubt that your inner resources are . . . unfathomable."

She grinned reluctantly. "If only that were true," she said, abandoning all attempts at pride. "As winter draws on my spirits sink depressingly low. I dread the dreary wet days and endless dark evenings." She hesitated, as though wondering whether to tell him some of her thoughts, and then pressed on determinedly. "Margot's asked me to go back with her," she said, "and I have to say that I'm seriously tempted."

Alexander stretched out his long legs, crossed at the ankle, and waited. He'd lit the wood-burning stove in the small sitting room and had been reading when Frummie had arrived. Now he put his book aside and watched her, preparing to keep one mental leap ahead.

"Well, it would be fun," she said, crossing her bony knees

and resting back against a cushion, her eyes on the flames. "Margot tells me that Gregory has invited us to stay with him in London. I wondered if you would be there?"

"I?" He raised his eyebrows. "Why should I be with Gregory?"

"I just thought that you said something about staying with him on your way north."

"Oh, I see." His face cleared. "Yes, that's true but only as an overnight stop, as it were."

"London's hardly on the route to the north."

"No, it isn't, is it?" He chuckled at her relentless curiosity. "Nevertheless, I shall spend a day or two with him."

"And when will that be?"

"When I leave here," he answered blandly.

Frummie compressed her lips and her foot tapped the air impatiently. "Have you any idea how irritating you are?" she asked.

"Oh, yes, I think so," he answered judicially. "People have been fairly frank about it during the last seventy-odd years."

She laughed. "Wretched man!" she said cheerfully. "I want to ask you something, Alexander. It's rather personal."

"Ask away," he said, amused and intrigued. "I reserve the right, however, not to answer."

"Oh, I'm sure you do," she snapped. She paused, her eyes still on the flames. "Are you going away to hospital? Are you ill? Dying, perhaps?"

He stared at her in surprise and then burst out laughing. "Good heavens, no! What gave you such an idea?"

She looked at him searchingly. "Just a suspicion I had. Not a nursing home, then?"

"Not a nursing home." He met her gaze levelly. "I'm going north to work."

"To *work?*"

"Do you think I'm too old to be useful?"

"No." She shook her head. "Not necessarily. But what work?"

"Ah." He shook his head. "I'm not at liberty to tell you that at present."

She frowned, biting her withered lips, her fingers beating out a silent rhythm on the chair's arms. "Have you heard of Humphrey's latest plan? That he's going to run a sailing school?"

"Really?" Alexander sounded noncommittal. "Well, why not? Sounds quite interesting."

"It's down in Cornwall." Frummie sounded peeved. "Quite ridiculous, in my opinion. Just when he could be here at last, spending some time with Brigid, he has to go rushing off to Cornwall. I think it's rather selfish of him. They'll hardly see each other at all. It would have been such fun to have Humphrey around."

He watched her compassionately. "And what does Brigid say about it?" he asked.

Frummie shrugged. "Oh, the usual thing. That they're used to being apart and he's too young to retire completely. He's buying the school, it seems. He hasn't discussed it with you, then? You didn't know about it?"

He shook his head. "Humphrey doesn't discuss his plans with me," he answered carefully. "Perhaps it's a good idea. After all, if it's only in Cornwall, they'll see much more of each other than they do now. It will give them time to adjust."

"I suppose so." She grimaced. "I was rather looking forward to Humphrey being about."

"Yes," he said gently. "Yes, I can imagine you were."

"You're alike, you know," she said unexpectedly. "Physically and in other ways. You're the kind of people that one can become very easily attached to." She looked at him, her chin up, eyes defiant, hiding her fear of humiliation. "So you don't want any company in the north? No helpmeet to support you through the new job? I have very good references and a great deal of experience."

"It would be impossible," he answered, "but thank you. I feel deeply privileged."

She shrugged again, smiling her own particular self-deprecating smile. "Worth a try," she said, almost cheekily—although her eyes were bright with self-mortification.

Had he guessed how much it had cost to make such an offer? Did he pity her? "You'll stay in touch, though?"

"Of course. But I'm not going for a few weeks yet."

"No, I realise that, but I might hitch a lift with Margot. I'll see how I feel. Once the clock goes back I start getting low. In the depths of winter the sun doesn't climb over the hill until after nine o'clock and it's gone again by three." She shivered. "Have you any idea how much it rains up here?"

"I had the feeling that you and Brigid were getting on much better," he said, answering her obliquely. "You seem less prickly and she seems more confident."

"I think that's true," she agreed, "but it doesn't make the winter any shorter. I was rather counting on Humphrey." She paused and smiled rather bitterly. "Or you."

"It would be impossible," he repeated.

She looked at him curiously, suddenly suspicious. "Is there someone else?"

He hesitated, his eyes softening, sliding past her and fixing on something she could not see. "You could say that," he said at last.

"You're in love." She was unbelievably hurt, shocked by the strength of her jealousy.

"Yes," he said—and his voice held a deep note of joy. "I am in love."

"Well." She tried to laugh, to hide her pain. "I can see that now. I've been rather a fool, I'm afraid."

He saw that it was essential to restore her pride. "I think you've been extraordinarily generous," he said sincerely. "It means a great deal."

"I'm sure it does," she said sharply, getting up. "Always nice to have an extra scalp. Well, I must be getting back. Don't stand up. We'll see you at supper time."

She went out swiftly, before Alexander could make a move, and he continued to sit staring into the fire. After a while he picked up his book again and began to read.

DRIVING BACK from Foxhole a few days later, on a wild autumn afternoon, Louise could feel her confidence growing and expanding, forcing out the last vestiges of fear. She'd been so nervous of this lunch with Brigid and Frummie that she'd been unable to eat breakfast, trying to convince herself that she had nothing to dread, yet feeling the need to prepare herself by mentally writing various scripts which the meeting might require. It was going to be difficult to explain how Martin had approached the situation; how he had attempted to protect her from herself whilst holding on to Rory. She'd realised that Thea might grasp this compassionate but unusual attitude very readily—it was exactly how Thea herself might act—but Louise could foresee problems with Brigid and Frummie. It was odd too that she and Rory were still married. For herself, she'd switched off so completely from her former existence that she'd never thought of it but she could see now that Martin had never intended theirs to be a long-term relationship: it was not the way he worked. It might be seen as strange, however, that Rory had never wanted to free himself.

"But I never stopped loving you," he'd explained, "and Martin always implied that there was a very real chance that you would recover. He always insisted that you were not in love with him. He said that what you felt for him was the sort of thing that some women feel for their gynaecologist who sees them through a very emotional and dangerous time. A kind of trust and affection—and a dependency. Rather special but not real love."

He'd looked at her anxiously, fearful lest she should misunderstand him, wondering if she'd thought he was patronising her, but she was thinking about what he'd said, rather struck with the analogy.

"That was rather clever of him," she'd answered, "and very true. Looking back, there was that doctor-patient feeling about it all. He was always so kind and . . . and sort of watchful. I felt safe with him."

"In a way, I felt it too," admitted Rory. "It probably sounds bizarre but that's how I saw it and why it was bearable. But I'm so glad that you're out of it now."

His warm, loving look had made her feel oddly shy and

she'd wished that she could throw off all her inhibitions and tell him she loved him. Telling Brigid and Frummie was a hurdle, something still in the way, which needed to be got over, rather as if she were clearing the ground in preparation for her new life. She needed their approval, their good wishes; to feel their support. They'd been a family to her and Foxhole had been her home at a time of great need; a stony sanctuary.

> Where does one go from a world of insanity?
> Somewhere on the other side of despair . . .
> A stony sanctuary . . .
> The heat of the sun and the icy vigil.

They were knitted into the fabric of her life and their love was important to her. Rory had understood it.

"They'll all want to meet you," she'd teased him. "Can you face it?"

"I think I might have met Humphrey," he'd said, "a few years back. I expect I'll survive."

As it happened, Louise need not have been frightened. Brigid had been utterly delighted, charmed by the idea of Rory waiting for her and then turning up so suddenly, and Frummie had seemed oddly muted, not her usual biting, witty self. She'd been very positive, however, and rather sweet.

"Go for it," she'd said with a strange intensity. "Don't let him go because you're frightened you might not be really over your grief. We can get glued to the past, staring back at it when we should be looking ahead. Pass through your pain together. Look beyond it and hold on to each other."

"I will," she'd promised, deeply touched. "I really want to. It's just . . . you know."

"Yes. I know." The older woman had smiled her distinctive down-turned smile. "You'll be fine. I know you will. But don't forget your promise."

"Promise?" She'd been momentarily confused.

"Nina Simone," Frummie had answered succinctly. "And

the bottle. Several bottles. Rory can come too if he likes. The more the merrier."

Louise had laughed. "I promise," she'd said. "Say the word and I'll be there. I mean it."

"I'm counting on you," the older woman had said. "By then you might be the only friend I have left."

Before she could answer Brigid had come back into the kitchen with a bottle of champagne and the party had become steadily noisier. When Louise had prepared to leave, Brigid had hugged her tightly.

"Bring him over," she'd said. "He's part of the family now. I hope he can cope with us all."

"Bless you," Louise had said, holding on to her, surprised by the strength of her love for her. "Thank you for everything. We'll come and spend our holidays every spring and autumn just as I always did."

"So I should hope," Brigid had answered. "And don't forget that we want to meet him as soon as you're strong enough."

Now, driving back to her cottage, Louise was filled with a wild joy that matched the roaring, boisterous wind which streamed across the open, airy spaces of the moor; the dying bracken bowed before its lusty breath and the black branches of the thorn shivered and trembled. The waters of the reservoir flung themselves against the stony walls of the bridge and raced in, to dissolve into flying spume upon the sandy beaches. The memories of the last few months crowded in upon her and, as she descended into the shelter of the deep, quiet lanes, her only real anxiety was for Jemima. It was difficult to be wholeheartedly happy when Jemima was suffering so much, yet, typically, Jemima was genuinely happy for her friend, truly pleased at such a healing outcome to the terrible tragedy. She was looking for somewhere to live, trying to be positive, and quietly pleased that she and Brigid had become much closer.

"She's told me that I can stay at Foxhole if I need to," Jemima had said. "She really means it too. She was so sweet about it all. But I need to find my own pad. I can't decide whether it would be too painful to stay in Salcombe, assuming that I can afford a little place somewhere, or whether to go somewhere different." She'd sighed. "I expect it will be a case of going wherever something turns up."

Louise had longed to be of use, keeping her own private joy under control yet looking forward to the weekend.

"Come and meet Rory," she'd said, surprising herself. "I'd really like it if you would. It would make it more . . . well, *real,* if you know what I mean. There are times when I feel I might be on some kind of film set or something."

"Come and have supper with me," Jemima had said at once. "Or lunch. Whichever you prefer. Let's have one last fling with my dear old view. We'll go out with a bang not with a whimper."

It had been a tremendous success. Jemima had clearly pulled out all the stops and MagnifiCat conceived an instant passion for Rory, who reciprocated fully. There had been a great deal of laughter and she and Rory, once the first awkwardness had been smoothed away by some wine, had behaved like the happy couple they had once been.

"Drop-dead gorgeous," Jemima had pronounced on the telephone the next day, "and MagnifiCat agrees. He's the first man he's ever taken to, which must say something about my taste in men."

Louise had glowed with this praise, overwhelmed with her good fortune, yet, even with all this new confidence, she was unable to make that final leap. Rory continued to book into his hotel and she stayed at the cottage, both of them searching for the last action which would carry them over the last barrier into the future.

She drove on, wondering how it might be achieved, her thoughts rushing ahead to the weekend when they would be together again.

CHAPTER 43

On a chill Sunday morning at the beginning of November a small party gathered to see Frummie and Margot off to Salisbury. The grey uniformity of sullen cloud loured down upon the proceedings, leaking a few spots of icy rain from time to time to drip upon the heads of the well-wishers as they gathered on the track. Frummie was in a gay, almost brittle mood now that the actual moment had arrived, although she'd been somewhat subdued during the last few days.

"You'll be all right, won't you, darling?" she'd asked Brigid in a moment of uncharacteristic maternal anxiety on her last evening. "Thank goodness, they caught that awful man. At least we can all feel safe again. But do take care of yourself."

"Of course I shall." Brigid had been touched by this rare display of affection. "I've still got Alexander for a few weeks yet, don't forget."

"Yes, that's true." Her mother's face had drooped into a kind of bitterness, a disappointed expression, which worried Brigid. "And Humphrey will be back soon."

"At the end of November." Brigid had been unable to hide her grin of delight. "Apparently he'd hoped that it might be earlier than he told me at first but he didn't want to disappoint me. It's great!"

"And you're not upset about this sailing school thing? I

know you've always needed your own space and you were anxious about his being here full time after so many years apart, but I'm surprised that he's hurried into something so quickly."

"Honestly, it's fine. I think it'll be a very good balance." Brigid, who had promised Humphrey that no one should know the exact details, hurried away from the subject. "And it'll be lovely to be all together for Christmas, won't it? Julian and Emma with little Josh. And you and Jemima. It'll be a houseful."

"I'm glad," Frummie had said hesitantly, with a certain difficulty, "so glad that you and Jemima are . . . friends."

"So am I. If only we can find somewhere nice for her to live. You wouldn't mind her sharing with you over Christmas if nothing turns up quickly?"

Frummie had shaken her head almost impatiently. "Of course not. If you don't mind her being here."

"I think it would be rather fun." Brigid had been surprised to realise that this was true. "Anyway, we'll see how it turns out. How long do you think you'll be with Margot?"

"Not too sure." Frummie wrinkled her nose. "To be honest with you I can't stand that wretched daughter-in-law of hers, although Harry is a darling. Barbara likes her to know who's boss. I've been spoiled, living here, doing my own thing."

Brigid had been taken aback, and rather moved by this admission. "Well, you can come back whenever you want to," she said. "If it's embarrassing to tell Margot why you're leaving, I'll send you a letter demanding your immediate return. We'll dream up a crisis which only your presence here can solve."

"You'll be my Bunbury, will you, darling?" Frummie had smiled with a genuine affection. "I'm sure it will be fun. We're going to London for a few days to see Gregory, hoping to coincide with Alexander's stay." A pause. "We still don't know where he's going, I suppose?" she'd asked, almost irritably. "I have to say that I find all this secrecy and silence thing a shade boring."

Brigid, surprised by her vehemence, had shrugged. "He says that it's something rather important to him and he's afraid to speak about it in case it goes wrong." She'd laughed. "I suppose it sounds a bit silly, put like that, but I know what he means, don't you? It's almost a superstitious thing, isn't it?"

"If you say so." It was the old Frummie again, cool, dismissive, faintly amused. "Anyway, Gregory's promised us a few treats: the theatre and the exhibition at the Courtauld, and he's taking us to his favourite restaurant. Sounds rather fun. Margot's planning a shopping-fest."

"Which reminds me." Brigid had suddenly flushed painfully, standing up from the table and going to her bag on the dresser. "Your birthday happens when you're away so I thought I'd give you your present now. I thought with all that jollity it might just be simpler to . . . to . . . well, give you this."

Frummie had stared at the cheque, a very generous one, in silence whilst Brigid had watched her in an agony of anxiety, praying that she wouldn't feel patronised, knowing that with no income Frummie would find her forthcoming visit expensive.

She thought: Please don't let her mind or be humiliated. Please let her just take it. Don't let her be sarcastic because her pride is hurt.

Frummie had folded the piece of paper very carefully and slipped it into her pocket whilst Brigid closed her eyes on a silent sigh of gratitude and relief.

"Thank you," her mother had said. "That will be very . . . welcome." She'd looked up, and Brigid had seen tears in her eyes. "You are a very dear girl. Forgive me if . . . if . . ."

"Nothing to forgive," she'd answered quickly. "Absolutely nothing. Just enjoy yourself."

"Yes." Frummie had smiled her familiar smile, clearly relieved to move on from this emotional moment. "I intend to. So tell me some more about this sailing school."

It was the last time they'd been private together. A flurry

of packing had ensued and now, on this last morning, Jemima had arrived to say goodbye. The unfriendly weather kept the farewells short and to the point. The sisters hugged their mother and watched her climb into the car, which bumped away up the track. Presently, Alexander's car had followed it and Brigid and Jemima were alone. They were glad to be back inside, in the warm kitchen. There was a pan of soup simmering on the Aga, rolls heating in the oven, and Brigid poured them both a drink.

"Well," she said, feeling partly relieved that it was over, partly flat and oddly lethargic. "Let's hope they get there safely. Thank goodness Mummie isn't driving."

Jemima smiled sympathetically. "She's somewhat erratic of late," she admitted. "But I can't blame her for clinging to her car. I imagine that it must be hell to give up the independence of driving."

"I know. It's just the worry that she might hurt someone else and be consumed with guilt. Anyway, Margot is a great deal more steady so I'm sure they'll be OK. How's the house-hunting?"

"Oh, not too good." Jemima stood her glass on the dresser and leaned against the Aga, warming her chilled hands on the rail. "There's a little cottage in Kingsbridge. It's tiny but big enough for me and MagnifiCat. And a flat with a bit of a glimpse over the estuary. That's if you stand on your toes and crane your neck. You know the kind of thing? It's a question of making up my mind to it, that's all. Rory said that it was best not to attempt to recreate my flat but to go for something utterly different. He said that it was always a temptation to try to replace something you've really loved with a lookalike. I think he may have a point. He's a really nice guy. Louise's very lucky."

"I like him too." Brigid sat down at the table. "I think it's just so wonderful that they've got back together again. It makes you feel that it hasn't all been entirely wasted."

"It's not easy, though." Jemima joined her sister at the table. "They're still trying to deal with all the emotional baggage and terrified that it's going to blow up in their faces. He feels guilty because he wasn't there when she needed him and she feels guilty because she walked away from him."

"I can understand that." Brigid looked thoughtful, turning her glass round and round. "I can easily imagine that the only way to deal with such a horror is to switch off from it, can't you? And it's probably easier for couples who are separated a great deal, anyway. Louise was used to doing without him, to compartmentalising her life. You can't live for weeks at a time as if he's just popped out for a packet of ciggies. You have to get on with it. OK, he's gone again. This is what I do when he's not here. It's a different·life. You don't forget about him, or stop thinking about him, but it has to be on a different level. I can see how she could switch off completely after such a mega shock."

Jemima was watching her curiously. "I have to say that I've never thought about it quite like that," she said. "But I see your point. you'd go mad, just sitting waiting, feeling lonely."

"Exactly. It's a delicate balance. Loving him, missing him, but making a life which doesn't include him but will allow him back in when he comes home. But poor Louise went several steps further on. Martin must be the most amazing man. I think that he felt that Louise was as healed as she was ever going to be and he'd been attracted by a newer, more interesting problem. I can't help wondering what would have happened if she hadn't broken down when she did. I'm sure Martin had begun to move on."

"Might he have begun to step back from her deliberately, in order to hasten the crisis, as it were?"

Brigid shrugged. "We shall never know. He was very embarrassed when he came here, although I have to say that Mummie didn't exactly help the situation. She was very abrasive. But it was right, the way it worked. If Louise had gone back to him then she might never have struggled free." She hesitated, feeling her way carefully. "And how is it with you?"

Jemima didn't pretend to misunderstand her. "Bloody," she said honestly. "I'm so miserable, I just can't seem to raise my game." She smiled, a tremulously brave smile. "But I'll manage. The thought of moving is keeping me occupied. I was wondering." She took a sip of wine. "I suppose you wouldn't like to come and see a flat with me, would you? It's described as a 'studio,' which means it's seriously small, but it sounds quite fun. No views but a very small courtyard, sitting-out area. Just say if you're busy . . ."

"I'd love to see it," said Brigid warmly. "What fun!"

"Great! Thanks." Jemima looked relieved. "I've got an appointment for three o'clock."

"We'll get on with lunch then." Brigid got up, paused. "But don't forget, whatever happens, you're booked for Christmas. Your great-nephew is looking forward to meeting you."

Jemima's eyes filled with tears. "I can't wait," she said, not looking at Brigid. "It'll be . . . great."

"He's growing so fast." Brigid was fetching bowls, laying the table, pretending not to see. "I'll show you the latest photographs in a minute. I promise you, Puddle-duck, this is going to be the best Christmas ever!"

LOUISE LIFTED the small, cane-seated chair back into its place, manhandled the oak bookcase against the wall, and looked around the bedroom with a sense of enormous satisfaction. It was finished; the job completed. Of course, she couldn't quite take all the credit to herself, Rory had helped, but it was a splendid achievement. Each room sparkled with a bright cleanliness and she felt quite sad at the prospect of leaving this small place which had sheltered her. Nevertheless, her gut twisted with anticipatory excitement as she thought about that other cottage in the Wye Valley.

"You must come and see it," Rory had said, with a lightness of tone which was not in the least misleading. "I think you'll like it."

"It sounds . . . nice."

She'd known that they were both trying to imagine the scene. Would she be going as a guest or as a wife? It was easier, somehow, maintaining the distance here. This was always "the cottage" and the hotel was always "the hotel." Neither ever quite usurped the other's patch. "Come back and have tea at the cottage," she'd say; never "Come back home with me." "Shall we have dinner at the hotel?" he'd ask. Yet he talked about the cottage in the Wye Valley as "home." "When I get back home . . ." he'd say. "I've still got all your books, you know. At home . . ." They'd begun to talk about Hermione: tiny, fearful glances back in time. He was braver than she was: much braver. "Do you remember . . .?" he'd say—and her heart would shrivel with fear, shrinking instinctively from the pain. Yet gradually, as he had always been able to do, he led her back into the paths of peaceful, heavenly sanity, where she could walk quietly, allowing memories to unravel gently from the tiny ball of agony clenched deep inside her.

Yet she knew that "home," the cottage in the Wye Valley, was where she longed to be; where she belonged; the last step—if only she could bring herself to make it.

Louise took a last glance round the room and went downstairs. Standing on the table was the Erica Oller card from Frummie: two enormous, elderly, fur-clad ladies, tottering on tiny feet, parade arm-in-arm along a pavement. The caption: "Cruising for Boys."

Me and Margot, would you say, darling? *she'd written in sprawling, generous letters.* Except that Margot has a beastly cold. The poor dear is not looking her best. Streaming eyes, red nose, sneezing madly, blotchy cheeks, hair like hay, sleeves stuffed with tissues. So can you see it? Determined, however, to make the trip to London. Gregory's managed to get tickets—like gold dust he tells us—for some exciting West End production, clever old thing, so we're going up early. Not before time. The wretched Barbara is like some terrible school matron, prowling about checking that we're not leaving the lights on too late or drinking whisky too early, which tends to bring out the worst in me. How is the handsome Rory? What a sensible girl you were to have found him! Don't lose him again. Remember what I said and all the luck in the world.

Louise chuckled as she reread it, imagining the wicked glint in the eye, the down-turned smile. The mere sight of the writing gave her courage. Humming softly under her breath she finished tidying the kitchen and went into the living room to light the fire.

CHAPTER 44

Surrounded by boxes, Jemima perched on the arm of the sofa idly looking through an old magazine. Why, she wondered, had she kept it? Once she'd started this process of packing she'd discovered that she had the tendencies of a magpie. Unlike Frummie, who preferred to travel light, Jemima realised that she'd hung on to any foolish bits and pieces which could be seen, in one way or another, as representative of her past. In the drawer of her desk she'd found cards from friends, letters, theatre programmes, menus, even a receipt from one of those meals eaten during those halcyon summer weeks. She'd smoothed it out, remembering the evening they'd dined at the Gara Rock Hotel not long after they'd first met; recalling how she'd insisted on paying. He'd accepted gracefully and she'd noted it, making the assumption that Annabel liked to keep her independence. It was still hateful to think of them together. Jemima put the magazine into the black plastic rubbish sack with a groan, and MagnifiCat leaped into the sofa beside her, rubbing his head against her, purring loudly. He disliked this upset, although he was very glad to have her to himself again, and took almost permanent refuge from the upheaval by remaining curled up in the basket chair by the window.

"I wonder if you're going to like the studio," she murmured, pulling him into her arms where he lay contentedly, like some huge, furry baby. "No more balcony for you, but you might like the dear little courtyard. At least you'll be quite safe in it but I'm not absolutely thrilled by the iron spiral staircase. No drinking too much or we'll be breaking ankles."

She gave him a last hug and poured him out in one long sinuous movement on to the sofa and went back to her packing. As she started on another pile of books the telephone rang.

"Hi," she said, expecting Brigid. They'd begun to move some of the small portable boxes in the back of her old estate car, so that, finally, only a small removal van would be required. Brigid was practical, well-organised and knew how to make moving as painless as possible. "All those married quarters," she'd said succinctly. On good days, Jemima had even managed to enjoy the building of her new nest. "Hello?"

"How are you?" His voice was so familiar—yet so utterly unexpected.

She sat down again with a bump on the arm of the sofa. "I'm . . . as well as can be expected under the circumstances."

"Oh, Jemima." It was a caressing, affectionate cry of regret. "Look, I'm phoning to say that I'm just so sorry—"

"We've done that bit. Remember?"

"Yes, of course I remember. Of course I do. This isn't just some kind of conscience-soothing exercise. I feel a shit about the whole business, you know I do. I'm phoning to say . . . to ask if there's any chance of you being able to forgive me?"

She frowned, gripping the mobile, trying to see into his mind. "Oh, I don't do forgiveness," she said lightly. "So why should it matter?"

A pause. "I think I've made the most god-awful mistake," he said quietly.

She took a very deep breath, dropping her head eyes closed. "You *think*—"

"I know it," he said quickly. "It's for sure this ti

MagnifiCat came purring back, winding him

her, climbing across her lap, so that she overbalanced and fell backwards, right into the chair, her legs hanging over the arm. He lay across her breast, pinning her down.

"Jemima?" He sounded alarmed. "Are you OK? I can hear an odd noise."

"It's MagnifiCat," she said. "He's right beside me."

"Oh," he said, with a little chuckle, as if the introduction of the name moved them very slightly back into intimacy. "That old poser. He never liked me much, did he?"

"No," she said slowly, remembering how MagnifiCat had crawled all over Rory, purring loudly with ecstasy. "He didn't, did he?"

"The point is whether you did."

"Did what?"

"Liked me much. Whether you still do? Enough to have me back, that is."

"Have you . . . left Annabel?"

"We're not together."

She thought carefully about this ambiguous remark. "I see. Might I ask who left whom?"

"It was a mutual decision," he said rather too quickly. "We realised that it was just not going to work again. The first break was the right one."

"I see."

Silence.

"I want to come down," he said urgently. "I know we can make it work. Honestly, I believe that. Could we try? Find a place together? Begin again?"

Jemima realised that she'd been holding her breath. She stared into MagnifiCat's round, flat face; his eyes were fixed on hers. She breathed out slowly in a long, long sigh, happiness bubbling inside her. Odd that she'd forgotten what this particular happiness felt like: the lightness, the separateness, that upward swoop of joy. Now that it was back she'd be able to cope so much better with the loneliness and the pain.

"Jemima?" His voice was sharp with fear. "Can we?"

"No," she said gently, sweetly. "No, I'm afraid we can't. " as he burst into speech, "no, it's not revenge or anything like that. It's simply that I'm sure it wouldn't work. All of a sudden I absolutely *know* it wouldn't work. I'm sorry but I'm moving on. Thanks, though, and good luck."

She pressed the button and cut off his protests. It rang again almost immediately and this time she checked the number and then answered it.

"Hi," she said to Brigid. "Did you try just now?"

"I did," said her sister cheerfully, "but it was engaged. Nothing important, I hope?"

"No," said Jemima, smiling to herself. "Nothing important. So when will you be over?" She laughed aloud. "It's funny," she said, "but I shall be quite glad to leave now. Odd, isn't it? Come when you're ready. We'll be waiting for you."

MagnifiCat padded over to the basket chair and leaped in gracefully. He turned round, tucking in his paws, wrapping himself about with his feathery, plumy tail. As he rested his head on his paws, eyes closed, he seemed to be smiling.

Two weeks later Brigid stood at her working table, pinning heavy brocade material, listening to *Book of the Week* whilst Blot, a black shadow, lay curled nearby. Despite the radiator, powered by the Aga in the kitchen below, the room was cold. A northeasterly wind prowled lazily about the house, penetrating and bone-chilling, and Brigid paused, rubbing her icy hands together, aware of her cold feet and ankles.

"Coffee," she said. "Hot coffee. That's what I need. Come on, Blot."

They went down together, his claws clattering on the wooden stairs, and into the sitting room. Now, towards the end of November, Brigid kept the two wood-burning stoves alight day and night, a glowing centre of heat, but, even so, as yet the granite walls and slate floors were cold to the touch. She paused in the hall to pick up the letters lying on the door mat and went into the kitchen, glancing through them, lifting the Aga lid and pushing the kettle on to the hotplate. Her mother's writing, distinctive as always, caught her attention, and she put the other letters on the table and slit the envelope. Perhaps this would tell her that Frummie was coming home. She'd clearly been enjoying herself but Brigid suspected that it would be difficult to extend the stay much longer. Although the night-storage heaters were left on a low heat in Frummie's cottage, it would be necessary to light up the wood-burner and warm the place right through. She found that she was actually looking forward to having her mother home again and smiled to herself as she took out the sheets and glanced over them. Various phrases seemed to jump from the page and with the smile fading she reread them carefully, disbelievingly.

> . . . Please do try, darling Brigid, not to take this personally . . . it's simply that Gregory and I get along so well . . . we have so much in common . . . such fun. He has a tiny villa in Portugal where we shall spend Christmas. Oh, the lovely thought of hot sunshine. You know what a lizard I am . . . It's not that I haven't been grateful, terribly grateful, for the sanctuary you gave me but it's so wonderful to be back in London and darling Gregory is so lonely . . . I can't bear for you to feel in any way upset—after all, you and Humphrey have your own lives to lead and your own exciting new start. I hope you'll wish me luck with mine . . . I shall be in London with him from now on and the address is at the top of the page . . . We shall be back to see you of course . . .

She had no idea how long she stood, holding the sheets, reading them over and over. When she looked up, her face white with shock, Alexander was standing in the doorway.

"You didn't hear me knock," he said, "and I wondered if you were all right."

She stared at him. "It's from Mummie," she said blankly. "I can't believe it. She's bolted."

Her lips trembled and he feared that she might cry. "With Gregory?"

"Yes." She sounded angry. "Yes. With Gregory. I can't believe it. We were getting on so well for the first time ever. And she's just gone off and left me again."

He watched her compassionately but remained silent.

"Silly, isn't it?" she demanded with painful self-contempt. "Silly that I should care? Why should I have believed that she felt anything?" She stared about her, as if she didn't quite know where she was. "I mean, can you believe it? Just in a letter like that. Not even a telephone call. Just a bloody letter. 'Dear Brigid, just to say that I'm bolting again. See you around and thanks for all the fish, your loving mother.' Christ!" She began to laugh, a high, angry noise, and he went to her, taking the sheets of paper from her hand and pushing her down into a chair.

"Shh," he said, as if she were a restive animal. "Be quiet now. Don't imagine things."

"Imagine things?" She stared up at him, hurt, but still angry. "*Imagine* things? I'm not imagining anything. It's all there. Read it if you want to. Why not? It's hardly a secret."

He turned away from her, not wishing to disclose the telephone call he'd had from Frummie earlier that morning. "Look after Brigid," she'd said. "I can't help it. Alexander, I can't spend another winter on Dartmoor or I shall die of it. Just be around until she's read the letter. Please."

"I'll be there," he'd said, unemotionally.

"And don't despise me," she'd said, with an odd, pathetic bravado. "I'm not strong like you. Or like Brigid."

"My dear girl," he'd said, "I've made far too many mistakes in my life to sit in judgement on anyone else." A pause. "And how is Margot taking the news?"

She'd given an unwilling snort of laughter. "Spitting nails," she'd said, "but she'll come round when she gets an invite out to Portugal."

Alexander had chuckled. "Give my regards to Gregory and tell him from me that he doesn't deserve you."

She'd laughed. "I wish it had been you," she'd said—and had hung up.

Now, he made coffee whilst the clock ticked quietly but insistently and Blot lapped from his bowl of water: ordinary kitchen sounds.

"So," he said, putting the mugs on the table, sitting beside her, "tell me."

"She's bolted with Gregory," Brigid said, more quietly. "He's got a house in London and a villa in Portugal. Well, you know all that, don't you?"

"Yes," he answered. "I know all that."

"Well," she shrugged, picking up her mug, her eyes angry, "that's all it takes, it seems."

"But don't you think that your mother will be happier in that situation? She's not a countrywoman. You know that, don't you? If she is offered an opportunity which is suited to her temperament, why shouldn't she take it? You don't need your mother to live next door to you in order to prove that she loves you. You're not a child."

"It's not that!" she cried crossly.

"What is it then?"

"It's . . . it's . . ." Brigid cast around for the truth. Even in her present state she instinctively understood that nothing less would do for Alexander yet she could not admit it. "It's just so humiliating," she said evasively at last. "It's hurtful to go off without any hint of it. She might have telephoned and talked it through. So, yes, that hurts. Especially as I'd believed we were much closer now. But the real thing is that it's so embarrassing for a woman of her age to run off with a man who's even older than she is, just like they were two star-crossed lovers. Oh, it's just so . . ." she shook her head as if lost for words, ". . . so utterly shaming," she brought out at last.

"For her or for you?" he asked.

She stared at him. "Well, for her, of course. What will her friends say? People like Margot and Barbara and Harry?"

"Does it matter?"

Her blue eyes were enormous, dark with shock. "What do you mean? She'll be a laughing stock. It was bad enough before. But now . . . She's seventy-three. Oh, dear God, it's unbelievable. And Gregory seemed so nice."

"He *is* nice. That's why she wants to stay with him. He'll make her life fun and he'll be grateful to her because he's lonely. He's the kind of man who needs company so why not Frummie's? Why shouldn't two lonely old people, who might otherwise be a charge on younger people who have their own lives to lead, get together and be happy?"

Brigid was silent, remembering that last conversation with her mother: the tears in her eyes when she'd said, "Forgive me . . ."

She relaxed, letting the tension flow out of her. "You're right," she said dully. "As you say, why not? Mummie won't care what people say at this late date so why should I?"

"I can't think of any reason," he told her. "Nothing could matter less. I promise you that he will take care of her. Try to be pleased for her. She doesn't love you less because she needs bright lights and sunshine. You gave her sanctuary when she had nothing left. Perhaps you can forgive her for all her hurts now, just as I hope Humphrey will be able to forgive me. Do try, Brigid dear. It will mean so much to her but she'll never be able to ask, you see. She's hurt you too much and her guilt stands like a barrier between you."

"I love her," said Brigid slowly. "I always have."

"Then tell her so and wish her happiness. Do it and see what happens. Why not?"

"Why not?" she agreed, looking at him, trying to smile. "OK. I'll try."

"Have you ever considered," he began, after a short silence, "whether your worries about having Humphrey permanently at home might be rooted in your fear of being abandoned again? You've taken to yourself a sense of inadequacy which is absolutely baseless. Frummie left Foxhole all those years ago—and again now—because of her own weaknesses, not yours. Don't let this continue to colour your life, Brigid dear. Humphrey adores you. This is clear from how he has always written of you in his letters to me. You are utterly necessary to his happiness and to his own confidence. He will never leave you. Are you certain that your anxiety for your future together isn't cloaking this deeper terror?"

"I don't know." She answered him almost fearfully. "It might be. I worry that living together after all these years apart could come as a shock. To both of us."

"I suspect that you are harbouring an almost subconscious

fear of losing him. You tell yourself that he doesn't know the real you—your need for solitude, for example—whilst deep down your fear is that, once he comes to know you, he will probably cease to love you. Perhaps you block this fear by asking yourself how *you* will cope with your lack of privacy, imagining the pinpricks of day-to-day living, whilst refusing to face your terror that it is Humphrey who will find it impossible to adapt."

A silence. "I've been so frightened," she muttered at last.

"I know. Out of all proportion. I could see it on your face that night when Frummie gave you his message. My dear girl, have you no idea how much he loves you? His letters have been full of you. Of his happiness with you and his boys. His pride in you. Your relationship is a tremendous success and your children are happy and well balanced. Accept your part in this achievement. You've been looking through a glass darkly at a distorted, unreal landscape, Brigid. It is time to let the sunshine into your heart."

Before she could answer him the telephone rang. Brigid got up slowly, almost stiffly, still recovering from shock, and lifted the receiver.

"Brigid?" Jemima sounded dazed. "Have you had a letter from Frummie this morning?"

"Hello, Puddle-duck," said Brigid. "I have, indeed." She glanced at Alexander who smiled understandingly and gave a little punch into the air with his fist, as if encouraging her. "No, I didn't have the least idea about it, either . . . Yes, I'm afraid you're right. She's left both of us this time . . . No, I'm sure she didn't see it like that. She probably didn't think it through at all. You know our dear mama. Act first, think afterwards . . . I know. It *is* a shock. I'm still speechless . . . Look, why don't you come over? Would you like to . . .?"

Alexander swallowed his coffee, touched her lightly on the shoulder and slipped quietly away.

CHAPTER 45

Louise was sitting in the conservatory in the winter sunshine waiting for Rory. The gate-legged table had been taken back into the sitting room once the room had been decorated but she'd found a folding picnic table in the small bedroom and she used this for her breakfast and lunch if it was a sunny day. Even with the sunshine, the conservatory was a cold place in late November and she'd carried the convector heater through to help warm it up. She'd cleared her breakfast things away and now she sat, huddled in her shawl, staring at the small leather photograph case which lay before her on the scarred table. Rory must have dropped it yesterday for she'd discovered it on the floor, half under the chair in the sitting room. She'd picked it up and opened it out, glanced at the two photographs and then closed the case again quickly. Placing it on the mantelshelf, she'd left it alone but had been quite unable to eject from her mind's eye the images it evoked. It was as if it shouted aloud to her, wherever she was, whatever she was doing, until at last she'd picked it up and carried it with her into the conservatory.

Rory was bringing her back to life. Just as he had always been the one to reignite their love after long periods of separation, encouraging her with gentle, persistent persuasion out from the cold house of loneliness where she resided in his absence, so now he was gradually drawing her back to warm, busy, terrifying life. He reminded her of the things she had suppressed: denied love, forgotten laughter—and she was grateful to him; unable to make the first moves herself, she needed his insistence, his refusal to give in or be discouraged. She was quick to follow, however, so that, although she rarely initiated any positive statements which related to their future together, yet she always tried to respond quickly to his: showing him by her implicit agreement that he was right, silently begging him not to give up.

"You can get glued to the past," Frummie had said—and she was right. The past continually pressed in with its damaging experience upon the present, a constant reminder of failures, hampering progress.

She thought: But I love him. Oh! I do so love him.

As if empowered by the thought she leaned forward, took up the photograph case and opened it gently. Hermione gazed out at her with that oh-so-familiar look on her small face: a readiness to be delightfully surprised; an interested, absorbed curiosity. She sat astride a wooden, push-along toy with a pony's head whose ears were the handlebars. A chubby hand grasped one of these, the other clasped a teddy to her chest. Eggy Bear. She'd had a problem, at first, pronouncing the letter D—she'd called Rory "Gaggy" at first—and so the teddy bear had started out as Teggy and then simply become Eggy. This was before the arrival of Percy the Parrot, who had stolen her heart and become her most constant companion, although Eggy had always been somewhere close at hand. She'd been a loyal child, even at three years old. She was wearing dungarees, her sandalled feet planted firmly on the ground, her long, fair hair escaping, as usual, from its restraining slides.

Louise stared back at her. Presently it was borne in upon her consciousness that the old, agonising hungriness had abated; that she was able to look at her child with a gentler emotion: a loving sadness. The pain and emptiness had eased into a more tolerable suffering; one she could live with, perhaps, whilst embracing life again. Other images flitted across her mind and now, although tears blurred the picture of Hermione, she could allow them to take their place, admitting them at last.

After a while she studied the other photograph. A younger Louise looked back at her. She was laughing, twisting back her hair with one hand, the other round Rory's waist. He was smiling down at her, that same absorbed intentness in his eyes which his daughter had inherited, his arm about her shoulders. The picture had been taken at a barbecue during one of Rory's leaves and she'd just heard that she was pregnant. He'd been ludicrously happy.

"Anyone would think it was the first baby in the history of the world," she'd teased him.

"As far as I'm concerned it is," he'd answered jubilantly.

Louise stood the case upon the table, so that she could see the photographs, and sat back in her chair quietly, almost contentedly: the house was redecorated, her job here was done. She brooded on what might be her next step forward. A moment or two later, she heard him knock at the front door.

"Gosh, it's cold," he said as she let him in, "but everything looks so sparklingly bright in the sunshine. There's quite a frost."

"I've been sitting in the conservatory," she said, leading him through. "It's not too bad, although I've had to switch the fire on. Would you like some coffee?"

"Oh, yes, please," he said. "That would be . . . great."

His voice trailed off on a lower note as he saw the photograph case and he glanced at her quickly—and then looked away again.

"It was on the floor," she said, "under the chair."

"It must have fallen out of my coat," he said, still not looking at her. "That's the problem with not wearing a proper jacket. You don't have very safe pockets. I like to have it with me, you see."

"Yes," she said. "Yes, I can imagine that."

Constraint lay between them and he searched for some means to banish it. He leaned forward and picked up the leather folder but, instead of closing it and putting it away, he held it open, looking down at it.

"Do you remember?" he asked with a terrible, heart-shaking tenderness. "Dear old Eggy. By the time she could pronounce it properly it was too late. He was always Eggy. I have him still, you know. At home."

Home. The word hung in the air; inviting, so full of promise.

Louise swallowed. "Yes," she said, following his lead, letting him see that she wanted him to release her from this cold restraining hand of the past into the warm present which he inhabited. She sought about for something more positive to say. "And wasn't that photograph taken at the Sewards' barbecue?"

"Yes, it was." He held the frame at an angle so that she might share it. "That was some party if I remember it rightly but you were afraid to drink any alcohol in case it harmed the baby. We'd just heard, hadn't we?" He laughed a little, leading her on again from that tiny shock of memory, always onward. "Do you remember Phil and Jeff? When the flats began to be used as an overspill from the Mess and they moved in next door? Their telephone number was Rhu 007."

"Oh, yes." She was actually chuckling, remembering. "We called them Bald Eagle and Silver Fox. Hermione adored them."

She fell silent but he persevered, refusing to allow her to stop now.

"Wasn't it Phil who bought Percy for her? Brought him back from London, didn't he?"

"Jeannie sent him down for her." She bit her lip, blinking back the tears, clinging to the path he was showing her, away from the shadows and back into the light. "It was just so typical of her kindness. Phil came in with Percy behind his back and asked for Hermione . . ." She spoke the beloved name bravely and then shook her head, unable to go on.

"That's right." He took the story up, stretching out a hand to her, his eyes still on Hermione, as though she were giving him courage. " 'I've brought a friend to meet you,' he said and then brought him out with a flourish . . ."

"And she jumped up," she was clinging to his hand as though it were a lifeline, "and shrieked, 'Pretty Polly, Pretty

Polly.' Do you remember that television programme? She adored it."

She began to cry and he put the photograph case back on the table and took her into his arms, his own eyes bright with tears.

"There could be other children," he said, holding her tightly. "We could try . . ."

After an electrifying moment she nodded, her face hidden against his breast, and he gave a great sobbing gasp of relief, knowing the risk he'd taken. His tears fell on to her hair as he searched desperately for the right words to carry them once and for all across the final hurdle. She spoke first.

"I love you," she said, her face still buried in his jersey. "I didn't really stop. Truly, I didn't."

"Neither did I," he said. "Not for a moment. Oh, darling, it's all over. No more recriminations. No more guilt." He felt her nod and he wanted to weep again, this time with joy and relief and thanksgiving. "So that's that." He took a deep breath, consigning fear and pain to the past; facing the future. "Now! Where were we?" He felt her embrace tighten and he turned her face up to his, smiling down at her. The present was here and now; the next step vitally important— and they must take it together. He felt an absolute requirement for her to share with him the responsibility of this momentous step. It would set the pattern for their whole future. "What shall we do?" he asked tenderly.

She stretched up to kiss him, her arms tightly round him. "Oh, Rory," she said. "Let's go home."

BRIGID GOT into the car, was welcomed almost hysterically by Blot, and sat for a moment, looking with a certain satisfaction at the purchases lying on the passenger seat: two second-hand biographies from the Dartmoor Bookshop, a bottle of claret and a most original present for her daughter-in-law's birthday. It had been a very pleasant morning, browsing in the bookshop with Anne and Barbara and then going to see Meg in Moorland Interiors, hoping to find something for Emma whilst enjoying a chat with her old friend. She'd looked **unsuccessfully** amongst the gifts and home furnishings until **Meg had shown** her the small quilted totebags which she made. **Brigid had** been delighted with them: pretty and original, **this was** exactly the sort of thing which Emma loved. Reminding **Meg** to telephone when her charming Christmas decorations were ready, Brigid had returned to the car park with her parcels.

She backed the car out and drove away through the town. It was bitterly cold despite the sunshine: hoar frost glittered on the branches of the trees and ice cracked in the ditches. After days of rain Brigid's spirits rose at the sight of the beauty all about her.

She smiled suddenly at a gloriously happy thought. In ten days' time Humphrey would be home. "I've got that coral necklace," he'd told her. "Just wait till you see it." There was no underlying echo of fear now at the prospect of his home-coming. In naming her private terror, in exposing it to the light, Alexander had shattered the web of life-long doubt and given her a new, singing confidence which was building deep inside her. Humphrey adored her; he was proud of her; he needed her. He'd sounded so cheerful lately, confident that they'd made the right decision, even positive about continuing to employ Jenny. Jenny was less confident.

"I don't want to leave," she'd said to Brigid anxiously. "I don't know where I could go, to tell you the truth, but I feel very nervous about working with Humphrey. He's never really liked me."

Brigid had made great efforts to reassure her, to point out how invaluable she would be and to explain that Humphrey would need her to show him the ropes and explain the working of the business to him.

"He needs you," she'd told her firmly. "He really does. At least give it a try, for my sake"—and Jenny had agreed, at last, that she would try.

Brigid passed across Holne Bridge, slowing the car so that she could look down at the tumbling, gleaming water, and drove on, turning left up towards Holne and out on to the moor. It was so clear that she could see for miles: granite-topped tors rising out of blue-shadowed valleys, the rugged steep-sided cleave clothed with the bare bones of the trees and the wild stretches of glowing, fiery bracken. Brigid felt the now-familiar sense of peace invading her heart. She'd been so preoccupied with sorting out the problem of the sailing school, encouraging Humphrey in his growing interest in it, assuaging Jenny's fears, that she had not given a thought to whether she wanted all this for herself. Since she had created the problem, it seemed churlish to complain about the solution, but she now looked ahead with growing courage. The shock of learning that her mother had bolted with Gregory had been diluted by Alexander's loving support; resentment purged at last by long, self-releasing talks with him, distraction provided by the excitement and physical hard work of getting Jemima settled into the studio in Kingsbridge. Her growing relationship with her sister was another cause for quiet, deep-down joy. With the shrivelling of her exposed fear, no longer nourished in the dark recesses of her mind, the throbbing poisonous jealousy had flowed gently away, enabling love to develop, and the two of them were discovering all the unique joys of sistership. This was easier, somehow, with Frummie at a distance. Brigid had even managed a cheerful, friendly telephone conversation with her mother, wishing her luck, inviting them both to stay, promising to stay in touch. Afterwards she'd been surprised at the overwhelming sensation of freedom; of calm confidence. The anxiety and feeling of inadequacy had been absent for the first time ever and she was merely conscious of a warm affection for her parent. She'd taken a deep breath of cautious grateful relief. The longing which she'd experienced all those months ago one evening on Combestone Tor might yet be fulfilled; that tantalising, ephemeral promise of true contentment seemed at last to be within her reach. Today, as Brigid looked down upon the shining surface of the reservoir, her happiness was diminished only by the loss of Alexander.

"I'll write to you," he'd promised, "and explain everything. I still can't believe that they'll have me, you see. Not at my age. I still fear that they might change their minds."

She'd longed to question him but had held her tongue, respecting his privacy but deeply puzzled, almost hoping that his fear would be realised and that he would have to come back to them. Yet, even as she thought it, she knew that he was right in regards to Humphrey's reaction.

"When's the old boy going?" he'd asked. "Before I'm back? Oh, well, it's probably all for the best. I can't see us really hitting it off at this late date and it will be wonderful to be all on our own again. I expect he'll be down one of these days, now that he's back in the country."

She'd realised that he was far too bound up in his new, exciting future to want to bother with a man he hadn't seen for nearly thirty years, and had let it pass. Yet she still continued to hope that at some point there would be a reunion.

Brigid drove carefully down the track, parked the car. She collected her shopping, crossed the courtyard and went into the house, Blot like a shadow at her heels. The warmth was like a living presence coming to welcome her, the heat of the stoves, now permanently alight along with several night-storage radiators, beginning at last to make some impact on the old longhouse. She stooped to pick up the letters, still clutching her parcels, and went into the kitchen. Leaving her shopping on the table she began to look through her letters, leaning against the Aga. Although she'd never consciously seen it, she knew Alexander's writing at once and she put the other letters on the dresser and tore open the envelope. At first the address did not catch her attention and it was only after she'd read a few lines that she glanced back to the top of the page. She frowned. An abbey? Was it after all a converted barracks of a place, sold off to the wealthy, as Frummie had once suggested?

So here I am, Brigid dear, just as I've imagined for so many months. I am Roman Catholic, you know, and, although I lapsed when I was a young man, twenty years ago I felt the need to return to the fold. I used to come here on retreat twice a year and soon I knew that once Agneta was gone—she was ill for years, did you know that?—this is where I'd want to be. I'm too old to be a postulant but after the most rigorous searches and, finally, a truly Bechers Brook of a Scrutiny, I have been allowed to join the order as a secular order regular. This means that I live with the community and I make myself useful in the office and the library. You have to prove beyond all reasonable doubt that you are not seeking some kind of nursing home and show that you will not be a liability, mentally or physically, and, most importantly, that you have a deep, genuine longing for God.

To my amazement and intense joy these dear Brothers are reassured regarding these things and I am allowed to make my home here. You can understand, perhaps, why it was so difficult to discuss all this at Foxhole. It is not always easy for friends and relations to be sympathetic towards the life I have chosen but you, Brigid dear, living in your stony sanctuary amongst the wild, empty spaces of the moor, might come to terms with it more easily than most.

I used to go down to Buckfast Abbey to Mass several times a week and I've bought you some lavender plants to remember me by. I know that traditionally it is rosemary for remembrance but I hope that you will like the lavender just as much. I left it in a corner of your barn, being too overcome with emotion at the last to give it to you. You are the one thing I regret leaving behind me but I feel privileged to be your friend and so glad to know that my son has had you beside him all these years. I shall look forward to hearing from you and I shall write to you often. Be happy, Brigid dear . . .

She stood quite still, staring at nothing in particular, whilst the pieces of the puzzle slid into place. A sudden sense of loss numbed her mind and she could only think "I shall never see him again" and was faintly surprised at how unutterably bleak

the future looked without him. Presently she saw that there
was a card enclosed and she drew it out with unsteady fingers.
A dove with wings outstretched, held the olive branch in its
beak. She read the verses several times before they made any
impact upon her.

> No Heaven can come to us
> unless our hearts find rest in today. Take Heaven!
> No peace lies in the future which is not hidden
> in this present little instant. Take peace!
>
> The gloom of the world is but a shadow.
> Behind it, yet within our reach, is joy.
> There is radiance and glory in the darkness
> could we but see, and to see, we only have to look.
> I beseech you to look.
>
> And so, at this time, I greet you.
> Not quite as the world sends greetings,
> but with profound esteem
> and with prayer that for you now and for ever
> the day breaks, and the shadows flee away.

Brigid rubbed her wrist across her eyes and went back into
the hall and out into the courtyard. The lavender plants were
grouped together just inside the barn and she crouched beside them, rubbing the flowers between her fingers and sniff-
ing them. She would keep them indoors and plant them in
the beds beneath the windows in the spring. Gathering them
up, she carried them back to the lean-to where she placed
them on a tin tray on the windowsill in the sunshine.

Blot stood at the door, tail wagging hopefully, and she
smiled, taking the hint, kicking off her shoes and pushing
her feet into gumboots, taking down her warm jacket. Outside in the courtyard she stood for a moment, watching the
doves executing their dazzling dance against the clear, pure
sky, listening to the distant music of the river, knowing that
now he would always be a part of it. Her sense of loss subsided and she felt his presence as if he stood beside her,

strong and comforting. Her heart beat fast with love and hope—and gratitude. Alexander had helped to free her so that now she need no longer look through a glass darkly but could face the future with a clear, steady gaze. The words he had sent her echoed in her mind:

> And so, at this time, I greet you.
> Not quite as the world sends greetings,
> but with profound esteem
> and with prayer that for you now and for ever
> the day breaks, and the shadows flee away.

When she'd returned from her walk she would sit down and write to him; a long letter, telling him everything. A sudden joy broke inside her at the thought of this new and very special relationship which would sustain her during the years ahead. Meanwhile, for the first time for many months she had Foxhole to herself, its other inhabitants were gone: Alexander settling into the monastic life; Frummie in London with Gregory; Louise starting again with Rory. So many things had changed between May and November. She had a sister now—and in ten days' time Humphrey would be home. Smiling to herself in the sunshine, whistling to Blot, Brigid strode away towards the shining stones of Combestone Tor.

THE CHILDREN'S HOUR

Early autumn sunshine slanted through the open doorway in golden powdery bands of light. It glossed over the ancient settle, dazzled upon the large copper plate that stood on the oak table, and touched with gentle luminosity the faded silk colours of the big, square tapestry hanging on the wall beneath the gallery. A pair of short-legged gum-boots, carelessly kicked off, stood just outside on the granite paving-slab and, abandoned on the worn cushion of the settle, a willow trug waited with its cargo of string, a pair of secateurs, an old trowel, and twists of paper containing precious seeds.

The tranquil stillness was emphasized by the subdued churring of the crickets, their song just audible above the murmur of the stream. Soon the sun would slip away beyond the high shoulder of the cliff, rolling down towards the sea, and long shadows would creep across the lawn. It was five o'clock: the children's hour.

The wheelchair moved out of the shadows, the rubber tyres rolling softly across the cracked mosaic floor, pausing outside the drawing-room. The occupant sat quite still, head lowered, listening to voices more than sixty years old, seeing chintzes scuffed and snagged by small feet and sandal buckles, an embroidery frame with its half-worked scene . . .

Hush! Someone is telling a story. The children group about their mother: two bigger girls share the sofa with the baby propped between them; another lies upon her stomach

on the floor, one raised foot kicking in the air—the only sign
of barely suppressed energy—as she works at a jigsaw puzzle. Yet another child sits on a stool, close to her mother's
chair, eager for the pictures that embellish the story.

"'I'll tell you a story,' said the Story Spinner, 'but you
mustn't rustle too much, or cough, or blow your nose more
than is necessary . . . and you mustn't pull any more curlpa-
pers out of your hair. And when I've done you must go to
sleep at once.'"

Their mother's voice is as cool and musical as the stream,
and just as bewitching, so that the children are lulled, familiar lands dislimning and fading as they are drawn into another world: the world of make-believe, of once upon a time.

In the hall, outside the door, Nest's eyes were closed, pic-
turing the once-familiar scene, her ears straining to hear the
long-silent words, her fingers gripping the arms of her
wheelchair. The telephone bell fractured the silence, breaking the spell, a door opened and footsteps hurried along the
passage. She raised her head, listening until, hearing the
clang of the receiver in its rest, she turned her chair slowly
so that she was able to survey the gallery. Her sister Mina
came out onto the landing and stared down at her.

"At least the bell didn't wake you," she said with relief.
"—Were you going out into the garden? I could bring some
tea to the summerhouse. It's still quite warm outside."

"Who was it?" Nest was not deflected by the prospect of
tea. Some deep note of warning had echoed in the silence, a
feather-touch of fear had brushed her cheek, making her
shiver. "On the telephone. Was it Lyddie?"

"No, not Lyddie." Mina's voice was bracingly cheerful,
knowing how Nest was inclined to worry about the family's
youngest niece. "No, it was Helena."

Their eldest sister's daughter had sounded uncharacteristically urgent—Helena was generally in strict control of her
life—and Mina was beginning to feel a rising anxiety.

She passed along the gallery and descended the stairs.
Her navy tartan trews were tucked into thick socks and her
pine-green jersey was pulled and flecked with twigs. Silvery

white hair fluffed about her head like a halo but her grey-green eyes were still youthful, despite their cage of fine lines. Three small white dogs scampered in her wake, their claws clattering, anxious lest they might be left behind.

"I've been pruning in the shrubbery," she told Nest, "and I suddenly realized how late it was getting so I came in to put the kettle on. But I got distracted looking for something upstairs."

"I should love a cup of tea," Nest realized that she must follow Mina's lead, "but I think it's too late for the summerhouse. The sun will be gone. Anyway, it's too much fuss, carrying it all out. Let's have it in the drawing-room."

"Good idea." Mina was clearly relieved. "I shan't be two minutes. The kettle must be boiling its head off."

She hurried away across the hall, her socks whispering over the patterned tiles, the Sealyhams now running ahead, and Nest turned her chair and wheeled slowly into the drawing-room. It was a long narrow room with a fireplace at one end and a deep bay window at the other.

"Such a silly shape," says Ambrose to his young wife when she inherits the house just after the Great War. "Hardly any room to get around the fire."

"Room enough for the two of us," answers Lydia, who loves Ottercombe House almost as much as she loves her new, handsome husband. "We shall be able to come down for holidays. Oh, darling, what heaven to be able to get out of London."

It was their daughter, Mina, who, forty years later, re-arranged the room, giving it a summer end and a winter end. Now, comfortable armchairs and a small sofa made a semi-circle around the fire whilst a second, much larger, sofa, its high back to the rest of the room, faced into the garden. Nest paused beside the french window looking out to the terrace with its stone urns, where a profusion of red and yellow nasturtiums sprang up between the paving slabs and tumbled down the grassy bank to the lawn below.

"We'll be making toast on the fire soon." Mina was putting the tray on the low table before the sofa, watched by attentive dogs. "No, Boyo, sit down. Right down. *Good* boy. There's some cake left and I've brought the shortbread."

Nest manoeuvred her chair into the space beside the sofa, shook her head at the offer of cake and accepted her tea gratefully. "So what did our dear niece want?"

Mina sank into the deep cushions of the sofa, unable to postpone the moment of truth any longer. She did not look at Nest in her chair but gazed out of the window, beyond the garden, to the wooded sides of the steep cleave. Two of the dogs had already settled on their beanbags in the bay window but the third jumped onto the sofa and curled into a ball beside her mistress. Mina's hand moved gently over the warm, white back.

"She wanted to talk about Georgie," she said. "Helena says that she can't be trusted to live alone any longer. She's burned out two kettles in the last week and yesterday she went off for a walk and then couldn't remember where she was. Someone got hold of Helena at the office and she had to drop everything to go and sort her out. Poor old Georgie was very upset."

"By getting lost or at the sight of her daughter?" Nest asked the question lightly—but she watched Mina carefully, knowing that something important was happening.

Mina chuckled. "Helena does rather have that effect on people," she admitted. "The thing is that she and Rupert have decided that Georgie will have to go into a residential nursing home. They've been talking about it for a while and have found a really good one fairly locally. They can drive to it quite easily, so Helena says."

"And what does Georgie say about it?"

"Quite a lot, apparently. If she has to give up her flat she can't see why she can't live with them. After all, it's a big place and both the children are abroad now. She's fighting it, naturally."

"Naturally," agreed Nest. "Although, personally, if it came to a choice between living with Rupert and Helena or in a residential home I know which I'd choose. But why is Helena telephoning us about it? She doesn't usually keep us informed about our sister's activities. Not that Georgie is much of a communicator either. Not unless she has a problem, anyway."

"I think Helena has tried quite hard to keep Georgie independent, and not just because it makes it easier for her and Rupert," Mina was trying to be fair, "but if she needs supervision they can't just leave her at their place alone. Anyway, the reason for her telephone call is to say that the home can't take Georgie just now, and would we have her here for a short stay?"

Nest thought: Why do I feel so fearful? Georgie's my sister. She's getting old. What's the matter with me?

She swallowed some tea and set the mug back in its saucer, cradling it on her knee, trying not to ask: "How long is a 'short stay'?"

"What did you tell Helena?" she asked instead.

"I said we'd talk it over," answered Mina. "After all, this is your home as much as mine. Do you think we could cope with Georgie for a month or two?"

A month or two. Nest battled with her sense of panic. "Since it would be you who would be doing most of the coping," she answered evasively, "how do *you* feel about it?"

"I expect I could manage. What I feel is," Mina paused, took a deep breath, "or, at least, what I *think* I feel is that we should give it a try." She looked at her sister. "But I suspect that you're not happy about it." She hesitated. "Or frightened of it? Something, anyway." She didn't press the point but stroked Polly Garter's head instead, crumbling a little of her shortcake and feeding her a tiny piece. Nogood Boyo was up from his beanbag in a flash, standing beside her, tail wagging hopefully. She passed him a crumb and in a moment all three dogs were beside her on the sofa.

"You're hopeless." Nest watched her affectionately as Mina murmured to her darlings. "Utterly hopeless. But, yes, you're right. I've been feeling odd all day. Hearing voices, remembering things. I have this presentiment that something awful might happen. A hollow sensation in my stomach."

She laughed a little. "But this is probably just a coincidence. After all, I can't think why poor old Georgie should be cast as a figure of doom, can you?"

She leaned forward to place her mug and saucer on the tray and then glanced at Mina, surprised at her lack of response. Her sister was staring into the garden, preoccupied, frowning slightly. For a brief moment she looked all of her seventy-four years, and Nest's anxiety deepened.

"Your expression isn't particularly reassuring," she said. "Is there something I don't know about Georgie after all these years?"

"No, no." Mina recovered her composure. "Let's have some more tea, shall we? No, I'm simply wondering if I can cope with Georgie, that's all. I'm only a year younger. Rather like the halt leading the blind, wouldn't you say?"

"No, I wouldn't," answered Nest sharply, not particularly comforted by Mina's reply. "You don't burn out kettles or go for walks and forget where you are."

"Just as well." Mina began to laugh. "There wouldn't be anyone to find me up on Trentishoe Down." A pause. "What made you think it was Lyddie?"

"Lyddie?" Nest looked at her quickly. "How d'you mean?"

"The phone call. You asked if it were Lyddie. Has she been part of this presentiment you've had all day?"

"No." Nest shook her head, grimacing as she tried to puzzle it out. "It's difficult to explain. More like a very strong awareness of the past, remembering scenes, that kind of thing." She hesitated. "Sometimes I'm not certain if it's what I actually *do* remember or if it's what I've been told. You were always telling me stories, interpreting the world for me. Giving people names of characters in books. Well, you still do that, of course."

Mina smiled. "Such fun," she said, "although a little bit tricky when you called Enid Goodenough 'Lady Sneerwell' to her face. Poor Mama was horrified. I was praying that Enid hadn't a clue what you were talking about. Still, it was a sticky moment."

"It was fright," Nest excused herself, laughing at the

memory, "coming upon her unexpectedly after everything you'd said about her."

"Lady Sneerwell and Sir Benjamin Backbite. What a poisonous pair the Goodenoughs were." Other memories were connected with this thought and Mina bent to stroke Nogood Boyo, her face momentarily grim.

"I was remembering the stories," Nest was saying, "earlier when I was crossing the hall. I was thinking of us all down the years. Sitting on the sofa listening to *Naughty Sophia* and *Hans Brinker,* or the *Silver Skates.* Do you remember?"

"And *A Christmas Carol* on Christmas Eve while we decorated the tree. How could I forget? So. Not Lyddie, then?"

"Not particularly. At least, I don't think so."

"Good." Mina fed Captain Cat the final piece of shortbread and dusted the crumbs from her knees. "So what do we do about Georgie? Are we up to it? Perhaps we should ask Lyddie what she thinks about it?"

"Why not? Let's clear up first, though."

"Good idea. By then she'll have finished work for the day and we won't be interrupting her." Mina put the tea things onto the tray and, with the dogs at her heels, crossed the hall to the kitchen, Nest wheeling more slowly behind her.

. . .

Lyddie made a final note on the typescript, fastened the sheets of the chapter into a paperclip and leaned both arms on the desk, hunching her narrow shoulders. Black silky hair, layered into a shiny mop, curved and flicked around her small, sweet face: ivory-skinned with a delicately pointed chin. Dressed warmly in a cloudy-soft mohair tunic, which reached almost to the knees of her moleskin jeans, nevertheless she was chilly. Her tiny study, the back bedroom, was cold, the light dying away, and she was longing for exercise. The large dog, crammed into the space between her desk and the door, raised his head to look at her.

"Your moment just might have come," she told him. "You just *might* get a walk. A quick one."

The Bosun—a Bernese Mountain dog—stood up, tail waving expectantly, and Lyddie inched round her desk and bent to kiss him on the nose. He had been named, after consultation with her Aunt Mina, for Byron's favourite dog, Boatswain, whose inscription on the monument to him at Newstead—*"beauty without vanity, strength without insolence, courage without ferocity, and all the virtues of Man without his vices"*—was particularly apt for his namesake, at least so Lyddie believed.

"You are very beautiful," she told him, "and good. Come on, then, and careful on the stairs. You nearly had us both down yesterday."

They descended together and he waited patiently whilst she collected a long, warm, wool jacket and thrust her feet into suede ankle boots. As they walked through the narrow alleys and streets that led into the lanes behind Truro, Lyddie's attention was concentrated on keeping the Bosun under restraint until, freed at last from the restrictions of the town, he was released from the lead. She watched him dash ahead, smiling to herself at his exuberance, remembering the adorable fluffy puppy that had been waiting downstairs for her on the morning of her first wedding anniversary: a present from Liam.

"You need company," he'd said, watching her ecstatic reaction with amusement. "Working away up there, alone all day while I'm at the wine bar."

It was just over two years since she'd given up her job as an editor with a major publishing house in London, married Liam, and moved to Truro, to live in his small terraced house not far from the wine bar that he ran with his partner, Joe Carey. It was a trendy bar, near the cathedral, not sufficiently prosperous to employ enough staff to enable her and Liam to spend many evenings alone together. Usually he was at home for what he called the "graveyard watch"—the dead hours between three o'clock and seven—but this week one of the staff was away on holiday and Liam was taking his shift. It made a very long day.

"Come in as soon as you've finished," he'd said, "otherwise

I'll see nothing of you. Sorry, love, but it can't be helped."

Oddly, she didn't object to going to The Place; sitting at the table reserved for staff in the little snug, watching the clients and joking with Joe; eating some supper and snatching moments with Liam.

"No fertilizer like the farmer's boots," Liam would say. "We have to be around for most of the time. The punters like it and the staff know where they are. It's the secret of its success even if it means irregular hours."

She never minded, though. After the silence and concentration of a day's copy-editing she found the buzz in The Place just what she needed. Liam's passionate courtship had come as a delightful, confidence-boosting shock after a three-year relationship with a man who'd suddenly decided that he simply couldn't commit to the extent of he and Lyddie buying a house together or having children, and certainly not to marriage. James had accepted the offer of a job in New York and Lyddie had continued to live alone for nearly a year, until she'd met Liam, after which her life had begun to change very rapidly. She'd missed her job and her friends, and the move had been a frightening rupture from all that she'd known, but she loved Liam far too much to question her decision—and her darling old aunts were not much more than two hours away, over on Exmoor.

Aunt Mina's call had caught her within ten minutes of finishing work but she'd let her believe that she was all done for the day. They were such a pair of sweeties, Mina and Nest, and so very dear to her, especially since the terrible car accident: her own parents killed outright and Aunt Nest crippled. Even now, ten years later, Lyddie felt the wrench of pain. She'd just celebrated her twenty-first birthday and been offered her first job in publishing. Struggling to learn the work, rushing down to Oxford to see Aunt Nest in the Radcliffe, dealing with the agony of loss and misery: none of it would have been possible without Aunt Mina.

Lyddie hunched into her jacket, pulling the collar about her chin, remembering. At weekends she'd stayed at the family home in Iffley with her older brother, Roger; but she

and Roger had never been particularly close and it had
needed Aunt Mina to supply the healing adhesive mix of
love, sympathy, and strength that bound them all together. In
her own grief, Lyddie had sometimes forgotten that Aunt
Mina was suffering too: her sister Henrietta dead, another
sister crippled. How heavily she and Roger had leaned upon
her: sunk too deeply in their own sorrow to consider hers.
The small, pretty house had been left to them jointly and it
was agreed that Roger, an academic like his father, should
continue to live there until he could afford to buy Lyddie out.
Until she'd met Liam, Lyddie had used the house as a retreat
but, when Roger married Teresa, it was agreed that between
them they could afford to raise a mortgage which, once it
was in place, would give Lyddie the sum of one hundred and
fifty thousand pounds.

Running the wine bar meant that she and Liam rarely
managed to visit Oxford but Roger and Teresa had been to
Truro for a brief holiday and, for the rest of the time, the four
of them maintained a reasonable level of communication.
Nevertheless, Lyddie felt faintly guilty that she and Liam had
more fun with Joe and his girlfriend, Rosie—who worked at
The Place—than they did with her brother and his wife.

"It's all that brain," Liam had said cheerfully. "Far too serious, poor loves. Difficult to have a really good laugh with a
couple who take size nine in headgear. Roger's not too bad
but dear old Teresa isn't exactly overburdened with a sense
of humour, is she?"

Lyddie had been obliged to agree that she wasn't but felt
the need to defend her brother.

"Roger can be a bit insensitive," she'd said. "He's generally a serious person but there's nothing prissy about him. At
least he's not patronizing about other people having a good
time." She'd added quickly, "Not that I'm implying that
Teresa . . ." and then paused, frowning, trying to be truthful
without criticizing her sister-in-law.

Liam had watched her appreciatively. "Careful, love,"
he'd warned. "You might just have to say something really
unkind if you're not careful."

She'd been embarrassed by his implication but Joe had intervened. They'd been sitting together in the snug and Joe, seeing her confusion, had aimed a cuff at Liam's head.

"Leave her alone," he'd said, "and get the girl a drink. Just because you can't understand true nobility of spirit when you see it . . ." and Liam, still grinning, had stood up and gone off to the bar, leaving Lyddie and Joe alone together.

As she paused to lean on a five-bar gate, watching the lights of the city pricking into the deepening twilight, Lyddie attempted to analyse her feelings for Joe. He was always very chivalrous towards her, unlike Liam's rough-and-tumble way of carrying on, and his evident admiration boosted her confidence which, because of Liam's popularity, could be slightly fragile. She'd been taken aback by the hostility she'd encountered from some of Liam's ex-girlfriends and it was clear that a few of them did not consider his marriage to be particularly significant. Two or three women continued to behave as if he were still their property: they obviously had no intention of changing their proprietorial habits and treated Lyddie as an intruder. Liam tended to shrug it off and she quickly learned not to expect any particular public support from him: they were married and, having made this statement, he expected her to be able to deal with these women sensibly. This was not quite as easy as it sounded. Apart from the fact that her confidence had been seriously damaged by James's departure, her husband was extraordinarily attractive—hair nearly as black as her own silky mop, knowing brown eyes, lean, and tough—and he knew it. Without his presence The Place was a little less exciting, the atmosphere less intimate. He had an indefinable magic that embraced both sexes, so that men called him a "great guy" whilst their women flirted with him. There was a sense of triumph at a table if he spent longer than usual talking and joking: the male would have a faintly self-congratulatory air—Liam didn't waste too much time on dullards—and the woman would preen a little, a small, secret smile on her lips, conscious of the other females' envious stares.

Joe's quiet, appreciative glance, his protectiveness, helped

Lyddie to deal with the competition and she rather liked to
hear Liam protesting against Joe's attentions. Of course,
there was Rosie to consider. Lyddie had hoped that she and
Rosie might become more intimate but, although she was
friendly, Rosie had a touchy disposition, and a searching, cal-
culating gaze that held Lyddie at arm's length. There might
be several reasons for this: perhaps Rosie felt less secure in
her relationship with Joe because of Lyddie's married status;
maybe she slightly resented the special treatment that Joe,
Liam and the other members of staff accorded Lyddie. At
The Place, Rosie was one of the waitresses and that was all.
Lyddie was careful never to respond too flirtatiously to Joe
when Rosie was around but it was often hard, when Liam was
chatting up an attractive female punter, not to restore her own
self-esteem by behaving in a similar manner with Joe.

Lyddie turned away from the gate, called to the Bosun—
who gazed reproachfully at her, as he always did, amazed
and aggrieved that his fun should be cut short—and headed
back towards the town, thinking about the Aunts. It seemed
rather unfair of Helena to ask Aunt Mina to cope with her
older sister for so long.

"Two months?" she'd repeated anxiously. "It's an awfully
long time, Aunt Mina, especially if she's being a bit dotty. I
wish I could help but I'm booked up for the next six
weeks . . ."

She could hear that Aunt Mina was battling with several
emotions and so she'd tried to be practical, pointing out the
obvious problems of dealing with an elderly and strong-
minded woman—who was probably in the grips of dementia
or Alzheimer's—with no help except limited assistance
from another sister who was confined to a wheelchair. At the
same time, Lyddie was able to identify with Aunt Mina's
need to help Georgie.

"She is our sister," she'd said—and once again, Lyddie
had remembered how, ten years before, Mina had had the
strength to bear the horror not only of Nest's injuries but
also of the death of their sister Henrietta.

Lyddie had swallowed down an onrush of sadness.

"You must do what you think is right," she'd said, "but do tell me if it gets tricky. Perhaps we could all club together for you to have some help if Helena and Rupert don't suggest it themselves. Or I could work at Ottercombe if necessary, you know."

"I'm sure you could, my darling," Mina had answered warmly, "but we'll probably manage and it will be a change for us. Now, tell me about you. Is everything all right . . .?"

"I'm fine," she'd answered, "absolutely fine. And Liam too . . ."

By the time they'd finished talking she'd had the feeling that Aunt Mina had already made up her mind about Georgie, and suspected that the telephone call had actually been to make certain that all was well with her niece in Truro rather than to seek advice. Lyddie was filled with a warm affection for her aunts; there was a toughness, an invincibility about them both. Nevertheless, a trip to Exmoor would put her mind at rest. Lyddie put the Bosun on his lead as they made their way back through the narrow streets, thinking now of the evening ahead, her spirits rising at the contemplation of supper at The Place with Liam and Joe.

LATER, IN the scullery at Ottercombe, Mina was clearing up after supper. The routine was generally the same each evening: Mina prepared to wash up whilst Nest, sitting beside the draining-board, would wait, cloth in hand. Once dried, each item would be placed on the trolley next to her chair and, when it was all done, Mina would push the trolley into the kitchen whilst Nest went away to prepare for the remainder of the evening's entertainment: a game of Scrabble or backgammon at the gate-legged table, a favourite television programme, or a video of one of Mina's much-loved musicals. She had never lost her talent for reading aloud and books were another mainstay of their amusement. Their simple diet included not only the well-loved classics—Austen, Dickens, Trollope—but also included Byatt, Gardam, Keane, and Godden and was interleaved with travelogues, a thriller, or *The Wind in the Willows,* depending on their mood. Lyddie

occasionally brought along a current best-seller or the latest
Carol Ann Duffy volume to liven up their appetites.

Mina dried her hands on the roller towel behind the
scullery door and wheeled the trolley into the kitchen whilst
the dogs continued to lick at their empty, well-polished bowls.

"You've finished it all," she told them. "Every last scrap."

Polly Garter and Captain Cat pattered after her into the
kitchen but Nogood Boyo remained, quartering the floor,
just in case some morsel had been mislaid.

As she put the plates back on the dresser and slid knives
and forks into the drawer, Mina was making plans for
Georgie's arrival. Although she'd known almost immediately
that this visit couldn't be avoided—how could she deny her
own sister?—nevertheless, she was deeply unsettled by the
thought of it. Her own anxieties about whether she could
cope had been overshadowed by Nest's formless premoni-
tions. Or were they formless? Every family had skeletons of
one shape or another—and Georgie had always loved secrets.
She'd used them as weapons over her siblings, to shore up
her position as eldest, to make herself important.

"I know a secret"—a little singsong chant. Mina could
hear it quite clearly. Her heart speeded and her hands were
clumsy as she arranged the after-supper tray, lifted the boiling kettle from the hotplate of the Esse, made the tea. Was it
possible that Georgie knew Nest's secret?

"Don't be more of an old fool than you can help." She
spoke aloud, to reassure herself, and the dogs pricked their
ears, heads tilted hopefully.

If Georgie had suspected anything she would have spoken up long since. And, if she'd kept silent for more than
thirty years, why should she speak now? Mina shook her
head, shrugging away her foolish forebodings. It was Nest's
fear that had infected her, bringing the past into the present.
There was no need for all this silly panic. Yet, as she refilled
the kettle, her heart ached suddenly with a strange, poignant
longing for the past and she thought she heard her mother's
voice reading from *A Shropshire Lad:* Housman's "blue remembered hills."

Mina stood quite still, her head bowed, still holding the kettle. The land of lost content: those happy, laughter-filled years. The tears had come much later . . . Presently she placed the kettle on the back of the stove and bent to caress the dogs, murmuring love-words to them until the moment passed and she was in command again. Picking up the tray, willing herself into calm, Mina went to find Nest.